Five hundred years they have searched—
for a man of love and courage,
a hero who defies death.
Now, in the Bronx, they have found him.

THE
SECOND
SON

The Miracle: High above Manhattan's Fifth Avenue
a young construction worker falls from the twenty-
fourth floor of a skyscraper. But what might become
a tragedy, instead provokes the most extraordinary
chain of events to occur in almost 2,000 years.

The Lover: And it comes to pass that world leaders
from Washington to the Vatican hail Joseph Turner
as a savior. But Joseph wants no part of it. He
wants the love of Maggie Dillon, the beautiful
woman whose past could destroy him. And he wants
to be a workingman again—to soar on massive
iron girders above the glittering New York City sky.

The Man: Millions will revere him. Two women will
love him. All will be stunned by his immense mercy
and power. He is the hero the world has been waiting for—in the most electrifying thriller of the year!

THE SECOND SON

CHARLES SAILOR

AVON
PUBLISHERS OF BARD, CAMELOT AND DISCUS BOOKS

THE SECOND SON is an original publication of Avon Books. This work has never before appeared in book form.

AVON BOOKS
A division of
The Hearst Corporation
959 Eighth Avenue
New York, New York 10019

First Avon Printing, October, 1979

AVON TRADEMARK REG. U.S. PAT. OFF. AND IN
OTHER COUNTRIES, MARCA REGISTRADA, HECHO EN
U.S.A.

Printed in the U.S.A.

ACKNOWLEDGMENTS

The birth of *The Second Son* would not have been possible without the assistance of Ms. Barbara George and Dr. Cheri Adrian. I also want to thank Matt Mattavich of the Ironworkers Local 433 for his help; and Joe Santos and John Krzemien for being there when I needed them.

DEDICATION

To my friends and family, whose love
and understanding helped me get past
the fear and realize a dream.

PART I

ONE

On Devon Street in the Bronx, the decayed brownstones, abused by time, weather, and their occupants, released their residents to another frigid winter morning. The clouds pressed down and stubbornly refused to crack for even the smallest patch of sun or blue sky, a sullen reminder that this was Monday.

Joseph Turner, lunch pail in hand, stepped into the hallway, turned, and took a quick last look around his one-room apartment. Lights, space heater, burner—all off. He keyed the deadbolt lock on the front door and turned to head down the stairs. But then he turned back, unlocked the door, and checked the apartment a second time; he felt strangely as if he had forgotten something, or as if something were missing. He'd felt this in waves for the last week—ever since his birthday, he realized now—but couldn't connect the feeling to anything in particular. A second look around the room told him everything was in order, and he locked up again and walked quietly down the rickety stairs.

At the second-floor landing he stopped in front of apartment 2B to check on Mrs. Wilkerson. The muffled sounds of the television set told him she was, as usual, up and watching "The Morning Miracle Hour." He tapped on the door.

"It's open, Joseph," she piped.

The wiry little old lady sat wrapped in a blanket on the couch. She was absorbed in her program. Without taking her eyes from the set she lifted a hand in a gesture partly of greeting, partly to say "Wait a moment."

"Thank you, Lord," a woman's voice was saying. "Praise sweet Jesus," Mrs. Wilkerson answered, then sighed and turned to Joseph with a smile. "Good morning, Joseph. How high up you going today?"

She asked him every morning, following the rising of the building with a wistful enthusiasm, regarding the ironworker with a mixture of excitement and concern.

"Should be at twenty-four."

"Ah . . . almost halfway. You'll be finished before spring." She frowned slightly, and Joseph watched her glance out the window, wishing the confining cold away. Her arthritis grew so painful with the onset of winter that she could only walk supported by two canes; she rarely went out.

"Can I do anything for you today? Bring you anything?"

She shook her head, smiling up at him again. "No, no, thanks. Don't know what I'm frowning about. I've got the handsomest young man in the city taking care of me. And Brother Bridger to comfort me. He healed some blind people this morning. Someday . . . I'm really going to go there."

"You know I'll take you anytime."

"I'd love that . . . maybe when the weather gets warmer."

Joseph knew she would never go; that would mean really testing the power of miracles. He didn't believe in miracles himself and would have hated to see her disappointed. Returning to her program, she seemed peaceful and happy. "See you tonight," he said as he turned to go.

"Today," the television envangelist was saying, "God is going to give you something that will make you completely different from this day forward. God is going to give you something greater than you have ever had . . ."

Joseph closed the door quietly behind him and headed down the stairs. As long as she kept her evangelist on the other side of the television set, she could have hope, he thought. Maybe there are times when people are happier with beliefs than with realities. The thought surprised him and made him a little uncomfortable; he had long believed that people were better off facing the truth, whatever it was. Mrs. Wilkerson's faith seemed an exception . . . it would be so cruel to take her hope away.

He zipped up his jacket, pausing a moment to let his body adjust to the shock of the subzero air. He felt his lungs contract and his nostrils begin to ache. He liked the cold, though, because it smothered all the odors. Not even the garbage piled high in front of the stoops, can on top of can, or the refuse regurgitated onto the sidewalk from the poorly fastened giant green plastic bags could cut through the clean, cold air. Even Mother Nature sometimes hides the truth, he mused. A city snowplow went by, groaning against the winter and pushing its brown-and-white waste to the curbs. Joseph breathed deeply and turned up the collar on his freshly cleaned beige coat. He took the ten front steps of his brownstone in two jumps and began an easy jog down the street.

His high-boned cheeks reddened in the cold. He had a handsome face, with an almost negligible nose squarely situated above full lips, now partially opened to draw in the frigid air across perfectly straight, ivory-white teeth.

It was his mahogany eyes people noticed as he passed, eyes that held an odd, disquieting strength and what seemed the seed of a phosphorescent flame that danced in them as he ran.

As he anticipated being far above the city, suspended in air and space, balancing on high iron, he felt a surge of excitement. After twelve years he still felt the thrill most ironworkers lose after one or two years on the job. It was the only kind of work he'd ever wanted to do.

When he was eight he often sneaked away from the orphanage to the nearest construction site. They always found him there, staring up open-mouthed at the ballet of the big men at the top. Through high school he worked hard to get his body in shape, working out at the gym, swimming, playing football. And at eighteen he joined the Sea Bees to learn his trade. When he finally made it back to the city, his first stop was the Union Hall, Local 40. In two weeks he was climbing iron, first as a welder, finally, now, as a connector, the most demanding, most exhilarating—and most risky—of high-iron jobs. It had all paid off. For the last twelve years he had been exactly where he wanted to be: swinging and fastening mammoth erector sets in the sky above New York City.

Now his well-trained muscles carried him effortlessly down the snow-covered sidewalks. The only thing he loved as much as his buildings were the streets of the neighborhood where he'd grown up and the people who lived on them. The kids from the orphanage who'd made it beyond the Bronx got as far away from the city as they could. Joseph had come back to share his life with the kind of people who had given him a home when he had had none. They had been generous despite their own poverty and given him hope in the face of their own despair. He'd made a life for himself and had more money than he needed. He knew no other way to pay them back than by understanding their struggle and lightening it whenever he could.

Down the street, Joseph spotted a familiar figure in a bright blue coat. Teresa Rodriguez, who lived with her four children in a three-room apartment in his building, trudged resolutely down the sidewalk with her youngest, Miguel, in tow. The screaming and crying four-year-old, bundled in a coat two sizes too small, alternated between dragging his heels and running to keep up with her. Joseph's steps quickened. Miguel was pleading to be carried, and his mother, without turning around or loosening her grip on his tiny hand, replied angrily, "No, Miguel! You too big. Now hurry up, hurry up!"

"Morning, Teresa."

She turned, startled. Her grip loosened and Miguel broke free and flung himself around Joseph's legs.

"Hey, Miguel, why all the tears?" Joseph gently pried the little hands free and boosted the child to his shoulders.

"He fuss all the morning." Her heavy Spanish accent was thickened by her exasperation and she looked close to tears herself. "We go to clinic yesterday and wait all day. They say come back this morning. We maybe wait again all day."

They headed down the street together. Teresa pulled her frayed blue coat closer around her pregnant body. She wore the coat all year round, trying to resist the grayness of her world with bright colors. She'd had to work much harder to keep her family together since Antonio had gone. She looked tired.

Miguel giggled atop his perch. "Gitty up, gitty up!" he yelled, tugging on Joseph's ears and shaggy brown hair. Joseph whinnied and Miguel laughed delightedly. Teresa smiled, her anger dissolving. "I too busy, I forget. Miguel need to play."

At the corner, Joseph brought the boy down to his feet, then bent over and scooped up a small handful of snow. "So do you, Teresa," he said, tossing it at her.

She laughed and for a moment her eyes sparkled, like those of an excited child.

Joseph turned back to Miguel. "And as for you, you're getting so big that right now you're too heavy for your mommy, and I gotta go to work, so you're gonna have to use your own legs and help her out, *sí?*"

"*Sí,*" Miguel nodded as he took his mother's hand.

Mrs. Rodriguez looked gratefully at Joseph. "*Gracias.*" She smiled down at Miguel, who tugged impatiently on her hand, and the two headed across the street. Joseph watched them. Her shoulders slumped for a moment and then straightened with determination. People like Teresa Rodriguez carried their poverty with a special kind of dignity. There was no attempt at pretense, no attempt to hide. They were poor, and that was the way they lived their lives. Dreams were made up of being less poor; with God's help the grocery money would last out the week and the kids wouldn't grow out of their clothes before a new hand-me-down was found.

As he watched her, Joseph felt more deeply than he had in months how difficult it was for these people to hold on to hope; and he felt once again that odd sensation of something missing, something he couldn't quite grasp. He felt frustrated by the enormity of the suffering around him. He could comfort and help Mrs. Wilkerson, Teresa and the kids. This morning, though, none of it seemed enough. Why do they have to live like this? He thought he'd stopped asking the question a long time ago. He'd do what he could, but there's a limit to what you can do for people! he told himself angrily.

OK, Turner, he ordered, shaking off the feeling and heading for the bus stop. So get up top and see how the world looks from there. There's a clearer perspective at twenty stories up.

From up there, life looks simple.

TWO

JOSEPH GOT OFF the bus at Madison Avenue and walked a few blocks toward the construction site. The twenty-four-story superstructure of steel beams reached into the cold winter sky. He crossed the street, cutting through traffic and ignoring the honking cars. Through the open gates of the high-boarded site, Frieda Zellar stood beside her open coffee wagon. Her bony frame was nearly engulfed by an oversized faded green parka. Wrinkled hands barely extended to the ends of its sleeves, and her weathered face was half hidden by the hood and its worn fur lining. She poked a loose strand of gray hair back inside the hood, turned to her truck, pressed the coffee spigot, and filled a styrofoam cup.

"Black coffee and a bearclaw coming up . . . and this morning it's on me."

Joseph reached in his pocket and pulled out a dollar bill.

"Put it away 'fore I crack you 'cross the knuckles."

He pushed the bill toward her. "Come on, Frieda. You're a businesswoman."

"And don't forget it, putz. I've been running this since the moyle visited you in the hospital. Now, if you want your coffee?" She held the coffee back from him.

Frieda was hard-nosed and Joseph liked her. He put the money back in his pocket and she handed him his breakfast. "You don't get anything for nothing in this world," Joseph said.

With satisfaction she watched him down the coffee and roll. "There's a hassle going on in the trailer between Corollo and Reynolds. Not a big hassle, mind you, but it's not a little hassle either. It's kind of an in-the-middle hassle."

"And you want me to check on it?"

"You're a very smart boy for a goy."

8

Joseph smiled at her. "Frieda watches over her boys."

"You oughtta talk. You take care of your friends better'n most people take care of their frickin' family."

"They are my frickin' family. I'll see what I can do."

Joseph finished his coffee and roll and walked toward the construction supervisor's trailer. He heard angry voices inside. He opened the door to see Don Tate, the welding-gang pusher, standing uncomfortably by, while the general foreman, Frankie Corollo, bellowed at Bart Reynolds. Corollo, whose solid low-built frame and flattened nose gave him the appearance of a pit bull, leaned far over his desk, as if only his white-knuckled grip kept him from springing over the top at the taller, slighter man standing in front of him.

"Goddammit, the inspector Magnafluxed those welds and the work's crap! Now I gotta have twenty of 'em cut out! That means I gotta have two guys washing that shit out. And two more rewelding. And I don't have time for that shit!"

Reynolds bent over until he was almost nose-to-nose with Corollo. "You son-of-a-bitch! I ain't the only one who worked twelve and I ain't takin' the rap! I'm the best damn welder you got. And I *just quit!*"

"No, you didn't! You just got fired. Pick up your time!" Corollo raged, then turned to Tate. "Notify the Union. I don't want to see his face within a hundred yards of this place!"

"Don't worry, you won't," Reynolds called over his shoulder as he stormed across the trailer and out the door, pushing Joseph aside as he went.

Tate wiped his hand over his balding head, then spoke hesitantly. "He's a bridgeman, Frankie. You sure you want to do this?"

"I don't care how good he is! I warned him twice and I won't have a boozer working for me even if I have to get out there and do it myself."

Joseph watched Corollo push a few papers around on his desk, then said evenly, "Morning."

Corollo looked up. "Turner. When'd you come in? Don't answer that. Look," Frankie said, pointing at him with a finger the size of a sausage, "I know Reynolds is your friend, but I don't want to hear any shit about how it's just a shooter in his coffee on cold mornings, or how good he is at his job

. . . or that all those bad welds couldn't be his. I'm five weeks
behind schedule, the manlift fell three weeks ago, and this
fuckin' buildin' is fuckin' jinxed. I don't want to hear any of
that shit. Understand?"

Joseph nodded. "Yeah."

Corollo sighed heavily, dropped down, and leaned back in
his chair. "OK. Shit, you may be right about Reynolds. But
he walked in just after the inspector dumped all over me,
and the booze on his breath . . ." Corollo crumpled a piece
of paper angrily and threw it on the floor. "Well, fuck it."
He looked disgusted and a little embarrassed, and the harsh-
ness left his voice. "Ya need somethin'?"

"No. Just stopped in to say good morning. Guess I'll go
on up. You seen Sweet?"

"In the heater shack."

Corollo went back to his papers and Joseph stepped out
of the trailer. So far this morning the yard didn't feel much
better than the street. When some people have got problems,
he thought, they'll always find a way to make them bigger.
Bart was stomping toward the gate. "Hey, Bart!" he yelled.

Reynolds stopped and hesitated for a moment before turning around. Rather sheepishly he walked back to meet Joseph. "Joey, sorry I pushed you. Corollo just gets to me."

"I know. It's OK." Joseph paused for a moment and
looked at his friend, who averted his gaze.

"Those welds weren't mine, dammit."

"I know that, but the booze is."

"Oh, shit, man, all I had was a taste in my coffee this
morning."

"That's not the point. You know the pressure that
Corollo's under. He's scared to death of another accident."

"Yeah, well he didn't have to lay into me like that." His
chin jutted out resentfully.

"You asked for it, Bart. You smell like a day-old bar rag.
Do you really want to quit?" Joseph asked.

"Nah, but he canned me, so what fuckin' difference does
it make?"

"A lot, I think—if you're willing to go in and talk to him
straight."

Bart grimaced. "Oh, fuck."

"What've you got to lose? If he doesn't listen—"

"I'll bash his face in," finished Reynolds. But it was too belligerent and both men burst out laughing. Reynolds gave Joseph a friendly punch on his arm and returned to the trailer.

After a few minutes Bart came out with a big puzzled grin on his face. "I can't believe it. Corollo apologized to me." He squinted suspiciously at Joseph. "What'd you say to him?"

"Nothin'; just lay off the shooters, huh?"

"Yeah, you got it. See ya later and . . . thanks, ya know?"

The construction yard was coming alive with activity, trucks moving into place and men, emerging from the construction trailers surrounding the site, crisscrossing the yard and beginning to climb up into the building like ants. Joseph crossed the yard and stopped outside a makeshift plywood shack, its small tin chimney belching a thin stream of gray smoke.

"Sammy?" Joseph called through the closed door. "You wanna work today or not?"

The door opened and a curly-headed giant came out, put on a hard hat, and thrust one at Joseph. "Hell, no, I don't wanna work today. It's gonna be *cold* up there."

"So what's new?"

Sammy threw his arm around Joseph's broad shoulders and they headed toward the silver-painted manlift on the building's west wall. Sammy Sweet had been his partner since Joseph began working as a connector. Sweet had taken him under his wing and taught him the finer skills of the job. A huge, playful sheepdog on the ground, Sammy moved with uncanny grace and skill at the top. Joseph learned quickly. From the mutual respect and trust so important in such a team, a deep friendship had grown.

They entered the manlift and Sammy nodded to the one-armed operator at the lifting-system controls. "Mornin', Quince. Drop us at twenty-two—gently!"

As the cage rose, Quince turned from the controls. "You want in on the football pool?" he asked eagerly. "It's only a fin."

Sammy quickly produced a five-dollar bill and Quince handed him a sheet from a box on the floor.

"What about you, Joey?"

"No, but thanks."

"Don't tell me ya can't afford it. You're gettin' a guaranteed forty, aren'tcha?"

"Sure, but you know I'm not a gambler, Quince. I never do anything risky."

The manlift operator shook his head and they chuckled.

The lift passed seven, where a work gang prepared to pour concrete onto the steel decking. As the lift continued to rise, the sounds of the city were lost in the pounding and clanging of metal. At twelve Joseph saw the inspectors supervising the cutouts of the bad welds. The sound of the carbon-air arcs was deafening as the compressed air was forced through the carbon arc to wash out the metal. The cage stopped at fourteen to pick up two welders, and stopped again at sixteen to drop the two workers off. Most of the welding gang were already on their four-by-six plywood floats, suspended from the perimeter beams over the city. As the cage neared the top, the popping of the automatic welders was drowned out by the rifle-shot blasts of the bolt-up gang's impact wrenches. The manlift whined and jerked to a stop at twenty-two, and Turner and Sweet exited onto the derrick floor. The giant derrick crane sat in the middle of the steel flooring, its eighty-foot arms stretching up through the opening on the floors above. Jack Soukup, the crane's operating engineer, waved to Joseph and Sammy from inside the cab as they headed to the gang ladder.

A young long-haired worker made his way past them toward the life. "Hey, Redriver," Sammy called, "if you gotta take a leak, do it from here. People down there'll just think it's yellow snow."

The young man looked serious. "Goin' down. Gettin' off. Had my cards read last night. The lady said somethin' bad would happen if the wind got over ten knots. It's almost that now."

He scooted past Sammy, who called after him. "Hey, man, what's her name? Ya ain't shinin' us on. I know ya got some dolly stashed down the street."

"I ain't got no dolly, Sweet, and I ain't goin' down the hard way like my old man did."

Joseph looked thoughtfully after Redriver as he disappeared down the lift, and then turned to Sammy as they began climbing the gang ladder. "His wife had a new baby last week. He's probably feeling extra careful."

Though any of them could leave the top whenever they felt like it, no questions asked, Joseph himself had done so only once: during his first year as a connector, the day after he'd seen his first man fall. He'd never been superstitious like Redriver and many of the others, but like all ironworkers he respected their unwillingness to work on top if they felt the least bit apprehensive.

"Well," Sammy said as they reached twenty-four, "I'm still tryin' to get that Indian to laugh. He always looks like he's in the middle of Wounded Knee."

"Hey, c'mon, you guys!" Casey Shaw bellowed. The two men turned and walked across the temporary steel decking toward their foreman. The gang pusher was a thin, angular man in his late thirties. While he perused the shop plans laid out on a perimeter beam, the tag-line man swung an eight-pound hammer down on the beams laid out on the floor, to dislodge the ice that had formed during the night.

The bellman stood by with a speaker mike in his hand, while the hook-on man climbed the crane's mast. Joseph and Sammy strapped on their work belts with two full bolt bags, then added the rest of the forty pounds of hardware: sleever bar, twelve-inch crescent, bull pin, and spud wrench. The hook-on man was at the top. They watched while he knocked the crane's choker loose, kicked out the boom arm, and scrambled back down the fifty feet to the deck.

"We're ready to go," the foreman yelled.

"Right," the bellman replied, bringing the mike to his mouth. "Okay, Soukup, run the choker and headache a couple of times."

The crane's engine turned over and the crew stood by while Soukup tested the lifting system on an empty load. It ran smoothly.

Joseph and Sammy pulled on their work gloves and turned to Shaw. "What's first, Casey?" Joseph asked.

The gang pusher pointed to two column beams sticking high into the air, thirty feet apart, on the east wall. "I need goalposts. We'll billboard that way out."

"You got it," replied Sammy. He and Joseph each headed for a column beam and monkeyed up to the first flange, twenty-five feet above the deck. The hook-on man had hooked the choker to the center of one of the three-ton perimeter beams, and when the tag line was secured to one end, the crane lifted the beam toward the two connectors. The tag-line man paid out only enough rope for the beam to rise without swinging as Soukup, two floors below them, followed the bellman's commands. "Up . . . up . . . high . . . boom down . . . swing left easy . . . easy on the boom . . . boom down . . . swing down . . . high." On the last stop command of "high," the beam was almost parallel to its column placement. The two connectors swiftly and silently went to work. Joseph hung on to his column and began rocking the new beam in with his feet while Sammy guided the other end, giving Joseph the slack until the piece of iron was aligned. Joseph straddled it, wedged his sleever bar between the column beam and the perimeter, and slipped his bull pin in. Sammy did the same and they simultaneously inserted two high-strength bolts into the steel. Joseph unhooked the tag line and dropped it to the deck. Sammy slid out to the choker, pulled the pin out of the safety to release the iron from the crane, and slid back to the end of the beam to wait for the next piece of iron to come up.

Joseph stood on the opposite end of the newly placed perimeter beam. Fiftieth Street and St. Patrick's Cathedral were just below them. He looked across the cathedral spires and out over the clouded city, expecting the vast expanse of space to bring him his usual sense of peace. But this morning it wouldn't come.

"Hey, Joey, what's up?" Sammy called to him.

"Nothing. I dunno."

"Ya look like ya lost your best friend."

Joseph made binoculars out of his hands and looked toward Sammy. "Nope—still there."

"Ya got that right."

Joseph smiled and looked down to see the raising gang complete the hook-up of another beam. He turned back to see Sammy sitting with his legs dangling over the side of the beam and his head tilted back, trying to catch snowflakes with his tongue.

"You're crazy."

"I know," said Sammy, laughing, "but if I don't keep busy I'll freeze solid."

"They're about ready."

Sammy nodded and the two men scaled their individual columns fifteen feet up to the final flange. In position, Joseph signaled to the bellman, who verbally maneuvered the dangling piece of iron up the forty feet to them.

"Up . . . up . . . up . . . up . . . high." When the second perimeter beam reached eye level, Joseph and Sammy saw a thin layer of frost covering it. They glanced at each other and Joseph grimaced good-naturedly. It would be his turn to slide to the choker. "Guess it's just my lucky day."

Sammy shrugged, smiling. "Sorry, old buddy."

The beam began to move again. "Swing left, easy . . . boom down . . . high." The crane stopped but Joseph had to duck quickly. The beam swung in, clanging loudly against the column he stood on. The bellman yelled into the speaker. "Up easy! Boom left . . . it's on order . . . high." Now it was just above the two connectors, but at a slight angle with Joseph's end too far out for him to reach. The tag-line man pulled the line, bringing Sammy's end in closer. Sammy held on to his column with one huge gloved hand and reached up with the other, getting a grip on the outside webbing of the center-hooked beam. After taking a firm hold, he let go of the column, grabbed the inside of the beam with his other hand, and stretched up to guide in the iron.

The bellman directed for Joseph's end while Sammy held his. "Boom . . . right . . . down easy . . . high."

It didn't stop.

Instead, the beam dropped several feet, so fast that Sammy had no choice but to hang on. Joseph watched horrified as Sammy was yanked off the eighteen-inch platform and out of the superstructure. The crane arm went out, jerking the line from the tag-line man's grip. The beam was now off balance, tipping with Sammy's weight, and it swung out erratically, carrying Sammy over the city, desperately hanging on to the end of the slippery piece of cold steel.

"My God!" Joseph yelled.

"What the hell is going on?" the bellman screamed into the speaker.

"I missed the dog!" Soukup screamed frantically.

"Get up on it!!" the bellman bellowed, hitting the emergency bell on the speaker box.

"I can't. It's stuck, I can't get it back!" cried the crane operator over the ringing of the emergency bell.

Sammy screamed. "Joey, help me! Oh, God, get me in!"

"Hang on!" Joseph anxiously watched his end of the beam come slowly in. His column was in its path. "Come on . . . come on," he whispered urgently. He could save Sammy *if* the beam reached him. A few passing seconds seemed like forever. Then it was close enough. He grabbed it, looked over to see Casey Shaw scrambling up Sammy's column, and looked out at Sammy.

The wind whipped around him while he hung twenty feet from the wall of the building, perpendicular to the spires of St. Patrick's and about three hundred feet above the gathering crowd below. His face was contorted with fear and the struggle to hang on. "Don't let me fall, Joey. Don't let me fall." His hands slipped another inch down the beam.

"Hang on, Sammy! I'm gonna get you! Just hang on!" Joseph's mind raced. Sammy couldn't hold on much longer. Even if there was time for him to climb out on the beam, his weight would increase the tilt, endangering Sammy further. There had to be a way. Then Joseph saw it. He quickly unbuckled his work belt, dropped it to the deck, and wrapped his powerful arms around the beam.

"What the hell you doing, Turner?" Shaw screamed.

"I've got to pinwheel it. Get ready to grab him!" His lungs sent the cold air streaming in a white mist around his face as he drew his legs up and took a couple of deep breaths. Holding the beam, he exerted all his strength and pushed off against the column.

"I'm gonna fall!" Sammy screamed hopelessly.

"No, you're not!" Shaw commanded. He watched in stark terror as Joseph's powerful thrust sent him swinging into space, bringing Sammy back into the superstructure. Shaw grabbed him, supporting him as he let go, and helped settle him onto the flange as the beam swung past them. Sammy clutched the column beam, unaware that Joseph had traded places with him.

With Sammy off the beam, Joseph's end began to drop as it continued to swing, slower now. Then it stopped. Its momentum was lost, and it had not come full circle. The wind tore his hard hat off. His eyes were fixed on the axis of the beam, and he didn't hear the screams from the crowd below. He heard nothing except the single thought pounding in his head: get to the choker. As numbness crept through his fingers and arms, he tried to claw his way up the steeply tilted length of iron.

The beam was like a teeter-totter with no counterbalance. His strength waned and he felt himself slipping. Desperately he tried to pull his legs up and wrap them around the beam, but it was hopeless. Suddenly his arms and legs were empty. He heard a scream of terror—"NO-O-OOOO!!!!" He didn't know it was his own voice.

A kaleidoscope of earth and sky swam around him as he clawed the emptiness, tumbling end over end. Fear rushed through him. There was a loud buzzing in his ears, and pressure filled his chest.

Then quiet, peaceful surrender and blackness engulfed him. Joseph Turner hit the street.

THREE

MEN STOPPED WORKING and listened as the alarm bell rang ominously through the steel building. Then came the cry:

"Man in the hole!"

It was passed down through the twenty-four floors. As it reached each man he laid down his tools, picked up his lunch bucket, and headed solemnly down from the building. They looked at each other with eyes filled with anger and pain.

"Who is it?"

"I don't know."

"They said Turner."

"Oh, shit . . . not Joey," came the voice of the shop steward when Quince made the obligatory call to his office.

On twenty-four, Shaw and the others pried Sammy loose from the column beam and helped the shocked ironworker to the deck. Tears streamed down his face. "Joey . . . Joey . . . Joey . . ." he murmured as the crew led him into the manlift. When the lift reached twenty-two, Sammy looked through the wire-mesh door and saw Soukup standing beside the crane cab, his head buried in his hands. Sammy's pain turned to rage. "I'm gonna kill that s.o.b.!" he screamed hysterically. "Let me outta here!" He grabbed the manlift operator, pulling him away from the controls.

Shaw grabbed Sammy as the lift stopped and the door opened. Reynolds came toward them and entered the lift, and the operator took them on down.

"I know, Sammy," Reynolds said, holding him by the shoulders as Sammy fought persistently. "But there wasn't anything he could do."

On the ground the door opened. Sammy broke from them and ran across the yard. Reynolds followed and caught him by the arm before he reached the gate.

"He needs me!" Sammy cried, twisting away.

"No, Sammy. There's nothing you can do for him."

"It woulda been me, it coulda . . ." Sammy slumped onto Reynolds. His body was racked with painful sobs.

"I know, I know," said Reynolds gently.

Sammy stepped back and wiped his hand across his face. "I'm OK. I'm goin' to him." The big man walked slowly out the gate.

When Officer Jack Donovan, the Fiftieth Street beat cop, heard a woman's voice cry out, "He's gonna fall!" he had looked up to see a small figure swinging on a beam, dangling over the city. By the time he crossed the street a crowd had gathered and traffic had begun to snarl, cars screeched, bumper rear-ending bumper as gawking drivers craned their necks trying to see the cause of the excitement. He pushed at the pedestrians. "Get out of here! Somebody's gonna get hurt!" But they moved only inches and their numbers continued to grow, spilling over the sidewalk. A man yelled, "He's going to make it!" and Donovan gave up and joined the excited onlookers, who were urging the tiny figure on as the dangling beam moved into the superstructure. As he neared the building and was grabbed by another figure a cheer went up. But it was broken off by a gasp followed by a curious hush.

"He's still on it!"

"No . . . it's someone else!"

They watched and pointed, wondering aloud if this was some daredevil game. "What's going on up there?"

"Are those guys crazy?"

"LOOK OUT!" A speck hurtled toward them, growing until it smashed into the street behind them, sending fiberglass splinters into the crowd.

"His hat!"

Not until the tiny figure separated from the beam did terror strike. The yelling, screaming crowd ran frantically, scattering in all directions to escape the falling body.

The crowd returned slowly, then more quietly, toward the spot where the body had landed. They pushed and shoved, trying to get a look; even Officer Donovan's incessant yelling and whistle-blowing didn't budge them. He tried to reach the body, then decided it was fruitless and raced to his callbox. There was nothing he could do for the poor bastard anyway.

Across the street inside St. Patrick's, a well-dressed businessman ran up the center aisle. His voice pierced the morning Mass. "Father, come quickly! A man is dead!"

Without hesitation the young priest hastily genuflected and hurried from the altar past the sparsely populated pews. He raced down the church steps and around the corner into the street. Following the businessman, the priest pushed his way into the crowd. "What happened?" he asked.

"He fell," the man said, pointing up. "He fell from the top."

Two young street toughs elbowed their way in front of him. "You lost, dammit!" the one behind demanded. "He fell! Now gimme my five bucks!"

"You'll get it. I just wanna see!" He made his way to the front of the crowd.

Then, his eyes wide, his jaw hanging open, he pushed his way back to his friend. "Jesus, Jimmy. Jesus . . . he's sitting up!"

The priest heard it at the same time he heard the first alarmed cry: "Oh, my God. He's alive!"

The crowd recoiled in shock, stepping back and opening a space around the man on the ground. A woman grabbed at her chest and fainted, slumping into the crowd packed around her. A bespectacled little man ran for the phone booth on the corner.

The priest charged through the retreating spectators. Then suddenly he stopped, staring.

Joseph sat on the ground, looking around him. His head tilted back and his eyes stared glassily up at the iron tower from which he had fallen.

"Are you . . . hurt?" The priest knelt beside him, waiting.

Joseph looked down and moved his hands over his body. His pants and coat were torn and soaking wet from the snow. He felt his legs, chest, arms, then his face and head. Nothing, he found nothing. No breaks, no cuts . . . no pain. Nothing.

The beat cop came rushing toward him and stood over him. "You've got to be dead!" he bellowed in bewilderment.

"I guess so," said Joseph numbly.

"Joey!" Sammy's voice came through the crowd and he appeared next to the cop, then fell to his knees beside Joseph. "You're alive . . ." he whispered.

"I . . . guess . . ." Joseph started.

"Lay down, Joey," ordered Sammy, pulling off his coat and laying it behind Joseph. "You shouldn't move."

"He's right," said the priest. "Lie down and wait for the ambulance."

Joseph stared at Sammy. Suddenly his body began shaking uncontrollably. And then he felt Sammy's arms around him and this time he floated, much more slowly, to the earth.

FOUR

"N.B.C. MAY I HELP YOU?" The switchboard operator answered.

The excited little man had finally gotten through the busy line. "Yes, oh, my God, I see a man, he falls off a building on Fiftieth Street."

"One moment, please. I'll transfer you to the newsroom."

"Newsroom, Ferris."

"Hello, hello, this is Jacob Rubin. I just see something I don't believe. I just see a man he fall off a building, here on Fiftieth Street across from St. Patrick's Cathedral."

"Ahh, yes, Mr., ah, Rubin, we're aware that a man fell and we're sending someone out. Thanks for your call."

"Wait, you don't understand. I see him sit up!"

"You saw . . . wait a minute. Hold the line." Ferris's voice boomed across the newsroom. "Carson, I think you better take this one. It's about the fall at Fiftieth."

"I can't even find anyone to get out on it! Can't you handle . . ."

"You better take it. Guy's name is Rubin."

"Jack Carson here. Mister Rubin, is it?"

"Yes, yes, Jacob Rubin. I tell you I see the strangest thing I ever see in my life, a man he fall maybe three hundred feet off a building, to the middle of the street. My God, I don't believe what I see! The man, the man, gets up and he just brushes himself off. He's not hurt, there's nothing wrong with him."

Carson hesitated. "I see, Mr. Rubin. We'll check it out."

"I'm the first one to call, right?"

"Yes, and thank you for thinking of us," said Carson, as he started to hang up the phone.

"Wait! I own Rubin's Jewelry Store on Fifty-Fourth Street. You maybe use my store's name on the news?"

"Well, Mr. Rubin, I'll see what we can do. Rubin's Jewelry Store on Fifty-Fourth . . ."

"Yes, yes, that's right. Don't forget."

The receiver clicked in his ear and the senior news editor of NBC slammed the phone down and scanned the busy newsroom. He'd been trying to get someone out on this story since the police radio call, but everyone was on something else. Now the crank calls were starting; he had to get someone to find out what was going on.

He grimaced as his eyes fell on the newest member of the NBC news team and the biggest bumbler Carson had ever seen make it to New York. Jerry Matthews's performance since he'd arrived made it almost impossible to believe he was the same man who came from Philly with a record of five remarkable scoops in as many months. Someone's idea of a bad joke, maybe. Well, he had to send someone.

"Matthews!"

The young reporter was reading the final rewrite on his latest story while unconsciously bolting down breakfast, a peanut-butter sandwich. At the sound of Carson's voice he jumped to his feet, swallowed too quickly, and tried desperately to appear nonchalant as his voice choked out, "Yes, sir. Yes, sir, Mr. Carson."

"I want to talk to you!"

The editor turned on his heels and headed back into his glass-enclosed office.

Matthews scurried after him. He stepped into Carson's office and closed the door behind him, feeling like a little kid about to be punished by his father. He looked at the tall gray-haired man seated behind the desk and hoped he wouldn't notice the nervous twitch above his left eye.

"Mr. Carson, I can understand you're being upset, but I can explain—" Oh, shit, even his voice quivered.

"Matthews! I don't want explanations! You're batting five out of six and the only reason you got one right is because you didn't have to leave the office. So don't remind me with explanations. I want you to cover the fall on Fiftieth."

Matthews grinned excitedly. "Yes, sir, thank you, Chief. I'm on my way."

"Hold it . . . *Hold it!* Sit down, Matthews, rest your brain."

Matthews half-heartedly smiled, turned back and eased into the chair.

"We're going to take this one slow and easy. A construction worker fell twenty-four stories off the building going up on Fiftieth. Get some crowd reaction."

"Yes, sir."

"And this time remember to take a camera crew. This is TV, remember? It's a little box with pictures in it."

"Yes, sir." Matthews's twitch had become almost spasmodic. He put a finger on it as he stood and inched slowly toward the door.

"With *sound.*"

"Yes, sir. I won't forget the sound man again."

"Press pass?"

"In my wallet, sir." Matthews patted his back pocket and hoped Carson wouldn't notice it was empty.

"I want this ready for the six o'clock."

Matthews nodded. "You've got nothing to worry about." He stepped out of the office.

"And, Matthews, doublecheck this. A call just came in that the guy is alive. Sounds crazy, but find out. *If* he's alive, follow him to the hospital. And if he's talking, get an interview."

"And if he's dead, sir?"

"Then the interview's off." Carson scowled and pointed a finger at Matthews, who was one step ahead of him.

"I know, sir. Get this one right or—"

"Or you can use your typewriter as a suppository."

The ambulance from Bellevue Hospital ran red light and siren, but progressed slowly through traffic. The paunchy driver was leaning out the window, leering at a female motorist. His partner was biting at a hangnail that had been bothering him for days.

"Ernie, for Chrissake, at this point it's gonna take two days."

"Yeah, well I ain't breakin' my neck to pick up a corpse."

"Guess you're right. If they got a guy who fell twenty-four stories all they need's a shovel."

"I can't figure why they just don't call the street cleaners. I was holdin' three aces when this run came. First good hand I've had in a week."

The ambulance wheeled around the corner onto Fiftieth Street and headed toward the crowd of people blocking the sidewalk and street.

"This one really drew the sightseers," the attendant remarked.

"And some of them are going with us if they don't move," sneered his partner.

At the edge of the crowd several police officers prodded the spectators back, giving the ambulance clear access. The vehicle ran up over the curb and jerked to a stop. Both men climbed out and went around to the back. As they pulled a folding stretcher out they were joined by an officer.

"He's over here," directed the cop.

A big dark-haired construction worker looked up from the group and waved urgently to the attendants. "Hurry, you guys! Hurry!"

As they wheeled the stretcher up behind a priest they looked at each other quizzically. The guy on the ground was in one piece. His eyes were open, looking around at the people bending over him. He looked like he was resting comfortably. The driver turned to the cop. "Hey, where's the body?"

"That's him, the guy layin' on the ground."

The two attendants looked down at Joseph then back to the officer. "I don't think you understand. We're here to pick up a guy who fell off a building," the driver retorted.

"He did. Twenty-four stories."

"Hey, c'mon, man. I didn't ride in here on a wagonload of pumpkins. I've picked up people who've fallen off buildings before. Who's kiddin' who?"

The cop took a menacing step toward him. "Pick him up. Put him in the ambulance and take him to the hospital. Now!"

"Right, General," the driver answered, throwing a mock salute in his direction. "We'll take him, but he'll end up in the psycho ward."

Joseph watched them from far away. He saw them come toward him. There were hands under his shoulders and hands on his legs, lifting him upward, but it wasn't his body, because he felt no pain.

"Be careful, you bastards," Sammy's voice said near him, and then Sammy's mouth moved again. "Corollo and I'll meet you at the hospital, Joey. It'll be OK. Just take it easy." And the mouth kept moving but the words drifted off.

Then there was metal around him and white sheets. The slam of the doors shot through his head. He closed his eyes and felt himself rolling backward, and blackness and blue sky swirled like oil in water to the wailing, wailing. Sounds of breathing above him mixed with grating voices.

"Goddamn traffic."

"Remember the one we scraped off the pavement on Fifth Avenue?"

"Looked like a strawberry malt. Sixteen stories they said."

"That was nothing."

The breathing got closer. "Hey, fella."

Joseph tried to turn his head away but he felt numb. He opened his eyes, and the blurred face shrank away. Then he closed them again and the black oil swallowed up the blue sky and the wailing as the voices disappeared.

FIVE

JOSEPH WAS RUSHED into the overcrowded emergency room at Bellevue. The examining intern was puzzled at first, then angry. He shook his head over the torn shirt and pants.

"OK, no injury, you say you feel fine, just shaken. Now what the hell really happened?"

Joseph just looked at him. "I told you what happened."

"Well, I've got people dying in here. I don't have time to discuss your delusions. I'll send you to X-ray and see what they can find."

Joseph saw the Union's business agent, Greg Palmer, coming toward them. "Just a minute; we want this man checked out *thoroughly*. He fell twenty-four stories and the insurance company wants every test you've got for internal injuries."

The intern's face filled with rage. "I don't know whose farce this is, but you're paying. Nurse!" he yelled. "Get this guy out of here. Take him to X-ray and see if Dr. Blumenthal will see him afterward." The intern looked at Palmer with disdain. "Blumenthal's a neurology resident on call. It's my guess if there's a problem it's in this guy's brain."

Palmer was quiet but firm. "I want Dr. Weisman to see him. Is he here?"

"You expect a lot. Yeah, he's here."

"This isn't an ordinary fall. I'll talk to Weisman myself." Palmer stormed off.

For the next four hours Joseph was X-rayed, tested, and probed, shoved from machine to technician to hallway where, lying uncomfortably on the examining table, he waited, exhausted, for someone to make sense of what had happened—or not happened—to his body. Finally an orderly wheeled him into another examining room and pulled a curtain around him, making a small cubicle. It was a quiet, private place, and he found himself drifting gratefully into sleep.

"Mr. Turner." He awoke to see a tall gray-haired man in his late forties enter and draw up a chair close to the examining table. Joseph slowly sat up, reached for his shirt, and began putting it on. "OK if I get dressed?"

"Well, not just yet."

Joseph lay back down. "Well?"

The doctor cleared his throat and fiddled nervously with his stethoscope. "Mr. Turner, I'm James Weisman. Greg Palmer's a friend of mine and he asked me to see you."

"Thank you."

"I've checked and doublechecked all of your X-rays and tests." He sighed. "You are a very lucky man. I can't seem to find any problem. No internal injuries. I do recommend strongly that you stay here overnight for observation." He paused. "But the best tests we've got say there's nothing, nothing at all—physically."

"You're sure?"

Weisman looked straight at him and Joseph trusted his directness. "As sure as I've ever been—and as I can be, under the circumstances."

The tone in Weisman's voice told Joseph that the doctor was trying to say something more. He decided to help them both out. "What you haven't said, Doctor, is that you're worried about how this will affect me mentally."

Weisman looked down. "Exactly." He moved uncomfortably in his chair. "I have no way to help you understand what happened to you. I don't understand it myself. So . . ."

"So what would you do if you were me?"

"If I were you, I'd treat what happened as an—" He paused to gather his thoughts. "—as an elongated nightmare."

"A what?"

"An elongated nightmare," repeated Weisman. "This isn't medical advice. It's personal advice. As a doctor, I have nothing more I can say. But what I would do if I were you is just forget this ever happened. Ignore it as you would a bad dream."

Joseph slowly shook his head. "I'm afraid I can't do that." He paused a moment and thought. "Don't you think, Doctor, that it would be better for me to accept what's happened as fact, as reality, and deal with whatever happens with it the best way I can?"

Weisman nodded. "Of course, normally that would be the best way to handle it. But you don't seem to understand." He stood up, and his voice grew more intense. "Mr. Turner, you didn't have so much as a small cut, not a single bruise. Don't you see? This is not natural."

Joseph felt anger rising in him. He sat up on the table. "Natural? What's natural? Is it any more natural for me to forget all about it?"

"No." Weisman looked down and shook his head slowly, raised his head, and met Joseph's eyes. "You're not going to take my advice."

"That's right, sir, I'm not. I appreciate your concern, but I don't see how I can."

"Will you stay overnight?"

"I don't see any point. You said you gave me all your best tests." Joseph reached for his shirt and began to get dressed.

"Well, take it easy for a while, very easy." Weisman got up. At the entrance of the cubicle he turned back to Joseph. "I've been a doctor for over twenty years. I've seen almost every medical problem your mind can conjure up. I've seen unaccountable survivals and unaccountable deaths. But nothing like this. What happened—what *didn't* happen—to your body in that fall has me totally baffled."

"I appreciate your honesty, Doctor. Perhaps," Joseph said smiling, as he finished dressing, "it would be best if you tried to forget all about it. Or just consider what's happened to you as an elongated nightmare."

Weisman's face broke into a grin. "What excellent—useless—advice! Go on, then. Your friends are waiting for you. Take care."

He opened the curtains for Joseph and followed him into the corridor. As Turner made his way down the hall, the doctor took a last look, frowned, then turned and headed in the opposite direction.

In the crowded hospital waiting room Sammy paced nervously back and forth, stopping every once in a while in front of Frankie Corollo, who sat below a "No Smoking" sign tensely chomping on the end of one of his infamous huge green cigars. Next to Frankie a small baby girl, still bundled against the subzero weather, sat sucking a plastic pacifier in her worried mother's lap.

"Hi, sweetheart," Sammy said to her, bending down, but the baby started to cry and Sammy embarrassedly resumed his pacing.

A young man across the room anxiously tapped his wing-tips in rhythm with the grocery-store music piped through the intercom, and kept tapping even when the music was interrupted by a doctor's page.

"Do you have to do that? It makes me nervous," Sammy said to him.

"You're pacin'. You make me nervous," the young man answered.

Sammy shrugged and dropped into a chair, but after forty-five seconds he was up and walking again. Then he heard Joseph's voice.

"Let's get out of here, Sam. The place smells like shots."

Sammy stepped quickly to Joseph, put his bearlike hands on his shoulders, and looked hard into his eyes. "Joey, you're okay?"

"So far as anyone can tell," Joseph said, answering his eyes.

Corollo got up and raced to Joseph, slapping him on the back. "Hey, you're okay!" Corollo's voice was loud; he looked scared.

Joseph pulled back. "Yeah, nothing broken—yet."

"Uh, sorry," Corollo said, looking around embarrassed. "I'm, uh, just so glad you're all right, ya know?"

"Sure," Joseph answered. "Come on. I want to go home."

"Course you do," Corollo answered, pushing him toward the door. "Maybe on the way you'd like to stop and have a shooter. Some of the boys are waitin' at the little place on Thirty-Fourth Street. They'd like to see the famous . . ."

Sammy interrupted him. "Joey, your name's all over the radio."

Joseph rubbed his hand over his forehead. "Look, I hope you guys don't take this wrong, but I think I'd like to just go to my place and be by myself awhile. I really don't want to have to talk to anybody right now."

"Right," said Sammy turning to Corollo. "He needs some rest."

Corollo's voice jumped again. "You betcha, right to your place, no problems."

Sammy took Joseph by the arm and headed him down the corridor toward the exit. "We're parked real close, we'll have you home in no time." They buttoned their coats and Sammy pushed through the double doors.

A crowd of reporters rushed at them, thrusting microphones into Joseph's face. They all talked at once, while cameras whirred and flashbulbs popped.

"Mr. Turner!" A voice rose over the rest. "I'm Louise Ryan, the *Times*. How does it feel to be alive?"

Before he could answer, a young man had pushed his way in front of her. "Jerry Matthews, NBC. Would you explain the accident to us, Mr. Turner?"

"How did it happen?"

"How'd you feel while falling?"

Other voices slapped at him. Joseph recoiled from their blasts, stepped back, paused a moment, then regained his orientation. "I want to be left alone, if you don't mind."

Matthews shoved his microphone closer. "You must understand, Mr. Turner, our viewers want to know what happened up there. How it felt falling twenty-four stories, what the doctor said, so if *you* don't mind . . ."

Sammy started for him, growling, "I'm gonna straighten out your face, you little turd!" But Joseph caught him midstride, grabbing his arm.

"No, you're not," Joseph said. "We're gettin' out of here, now!"

"Whatever you say," grumbled Sammy. He looked from Joseph to Matthews and back, then headed down the steps, elbowing his way past the reporters. Joseph and Corollo pushed their way through the crowd. As they headed towards Sammy's car, they heard Matthews shouting behind them. "You won't get away that easy! The public's got a right to know!"

The crowd of reporters followed the ironworkers to their

car and were still shooting questions as the blue Chevy pulled away.

Matthews turned to his two-man crew. "C'mon, we'll follow them. Carson wants a story and I'm going to get it."

SIX

SAMMY'S CHEVY SPED along the East River. The windshield wipers slapped an ominous beat. Snow fell heavily now. Joseph sighed and leaned his head back.

"Hey," Corollo said. "There's an NBC station wagon back there."

"Can you lose them, Sam?" Joseph asked.

"I'll give it a try."

The three rode in tense silence as Sammy accelerated and made a left turn onto a side street. He then made a series of right and left turns, eventually returning them to the arterial. The news car was no longer in sight and Sammy spoke quietly to his friend. "It's OK, Joey, I think I lost them."

Joseph nodded appreciatively, leaned back in the seat again, and closed his eys.

Frankie's voice boomed from the back seat. "Joey— what happened? I mean, we saw you fall, and . . ."

"I'm really tired, Frankie. And I don't know."

"He fell and he's OK. So that's all that matters," Sammy said.

"Yeah, but, Jesus . . ." The fear in Corollo's voice began to sound like panic.

"Frankie, lay off. Later," Sammy said angrily. He searched for something else to talk about. "You hear about Redriver's new kid?"

"Another one? Busy guy," laughed Corollo. "Hey, Joey, you maybe want a good woman tonight? Or maybe after fallin' you don't feel much like gettin' it *up?*"

"Hey . . ." Sammy's voice threatened as he turned his head toward the back seat.

"Just jokin', just jokin'. Keep your eyes on the road."

"Look at that excuse for a church," Sammy said, groping

for a neutral subject. "They tore down my church and put a glass house up. Can't even recognize the Virgin Mary—looks like something outta the Museum of Modern Art. Whole religion's changing, not the same anymore. When they started the masses in English, Rosa and I left. We go to church on the East Side now. Damn, everything's falling apart these days." Sammy shook his head and his voice trailed off, "Uh . . . sorry."

Joseph opened his eyes and looked across at his friend. "It's okay. Thanks for trying." He turned and looked out the window. The snow thickened as they turned onto Southern Boulevard.

"How about some music?" Frankie said, not waiting for an answer, reaching between the bucket seats to snap on the radio. He caught a newsman in midsentence. ". . . and though our corrsespondent, Dick Buckles, was at Bellevue when Turner was released, the ironworker was too shaken to give an interview. As all of you WHIM listeners know, Johnny Hicks' Hotline show is comin' up next, and he'll be tryin' to get Joseph Turner *live* on the air."

Joseph reached out and flipped off the radio. Was it just this morning that he'd jogged down this street? Everything here looks just the same, he thought. But I'm not.

"Sorry, Joey," Corollo was saying, "didn't know they'd uh . . ."

"Relax, Frankie, it's all right. I'm just not sure how to handle all this yet. I need some time to myself."

"Well, you're gonna get it. You're home," Sammy said as he jerked the car into the curb in front of the Devon Street brownstone. They got out of the car and entered the building.

Outside, the WNBC station wagon reappeared, slowed, and parked. Matthews jumped out, threw the press parking card onto the dashboard and ordered the others, "Get the equipment out. Hurry." Two men hustled the camera and sound recorder out of the back.

Joseph unlocked the door to his third-floor apartment and turned to Sammy.

"You want me to stay here for a while? I can call Rosa."

"I'll be all right. You go on home, Sam."

"You take as much time as you need, Joey," Corollo said. "Don't even think about coming back until you feel like it."

"Sure. Thanks." Joseph entered his apartment and closed the door behind him. The single room was chilly; the windows had never sealed. Joseph turned on the small space heater in the corner and lay down on the bed.

Corollo and Sweet headed back toward the stairs. "Couldn't you leave him alone?" Sweet asked angrily. "He didn't want to talk about it, but you kept pressing him."

"Well, I wanted to know," retorted Corollo. "It's only human to have a little curiosity. Besides, you didn't do so hot. Get off my case."

Sammy was about to argue when they saw Matthews and his news crew coming down the hall. "What the hell are you doing here?" Sammy shouted, as he and Corollo confronted the newsmen and blocked their access.

"Freedom of the press, the First Amendment. Now if you don't mind," said Matthews, trying to squeeze past them.

"We do mind," retorted Frankie.

"Yeah, turn your little college ass around and get out of here," added Sweet, doubling up his fist, "before I make your dentist bill look like the national debt."

"I'm going to talk to Turner and you're not going to stop me," Matthews blustered, but he looked scared. He turned to his cameraman. "Turn it on. If they start anything, I want it on film."

The cameraman hit the lights and began filming as Sammy hit Matthews in the mouth with enough force to send him sprawling some ten feet backward into the soundman. They fell to the floor in a heap. Then, with a snort, Frankie went for the camera, throwing one hand over the lens and the other over the operator's face, shoving the man half way down the narrow hallway. The door to 3A opened when the cameraman fell and Allen Cochran, a wiry, half-strung-out hype, stuck his head outside his door to see Sammy yank Matthews from the floor with one hand and slam him against the wall, sending a white mist of plaster falling from the aging ceiling and a red mist of blood spurting from the stunned reporter's nose. Cochran decided his services were not needed and slammed the door shut as Joseph emerged in full stride from his apartment.

Sammy was about to deliver another bone-crushing blow

when Joseph grabbed his arm angrily. "Stop it! All of you stop it, right now!"

Frankie got off the cameraman, but not before pushing his camera further down the hall. When Joseph pulled Sammy away from Matthews, the reporter slid down the wall to a sitting position on the floor.

Joseph's angry eyes darted from Sammy and Corollo to the reporters. "What the hell? This is stupid. Who are you?"

"Jerry Matthews, Mr. Turner. NBC—"

Sammy nervously shifted his weight. "He was gonna bother you. I . . . I told him to leave—"

Joseph cut him off in disbelief. "And you had to hit him? Why? You don't need to protect me. I could have handled it. You didn't have to beat him up."

Bracing himself against the wall, Matthews struggled to his feet, wiping the blood from his nose. "I'm going to sue you for everything you've got!"

Joseph pointed at him. "No, you're not. Now be quiet. I'll talk to you in a minute."

Matthews looked up, surprised, suddenly forgetting his anger and the painful bruises on his body. He was going to get his story.

"Have your dentist send me the bill," Sammy said.

"Forget it. I've got insurance."

The building's superintendent, Abe Curlin, came up the stairs and made his way past Frankie, who was helping the cameraman to his feet. Curlin carried a wrench in one hand. "What the hell is going on here? I can hear the commotion all the way in the basement."

"Just a little misunderstanding, Abe. It's over." Joseph turned to Frankie. "Why don't you help the boys carry their equipment down to their car."

"Yeah, sure, Joey."

Frankie picked up the camera. The cameraman and sound-man followed him down the stairs.

Curlin started away, then turned back to Joseph. "By the way, Rodriguez's rent is due again."

"I'll pay," said Joseph.

Curlin raised his right hand in acceptance and began his journey back to the basement.

Joseph looked at Sammy and motioned at Matthews. "Help

him to my room so I can fix him up." Joseph headed back to his apartment. Sammy guided Matthews behind him.

"Who's Rodriguez?" Matthews asked.

"A lady with four kids and one in the cooker. Joseph helps her out every now and again."

"You mean Turner pays her rent?"

"Yep."

"Where's Mr. Rodriguez?"

"Where he always is—in jail."

Matthews grinned knowingly. "Oh, so Turner and Mrs. Rodriguez have a thing going."

Sammy stopped and glared at him. "Are you kidding? Joseph? That's ridiculous."

"Why does he do it then?"

"Because they're poor, and he's a generous guy. He likes to help people."

Now this, Matthews thought, is turning into a hell of a human-interest story. He entered the apartment and looked around the room, making mental notes: a bed, a nightstand, a chair, a table, a small stove and refrigerator, a lamp, a heater, a ten-inch television set, and a radio. A bulletin board was covered with scraps of paper, several pictures of kids, and a basketball was just under the bed. Matthews walked over to a three-shelf bookcase in a corner and glanced over the titles. Classics mostly, and several worn volumes of philosophy filled the shelves. Joseph emerged from the bathroom carrying a wet cloth and a bottle of hydrogen peroxide. "You interested in philosophy?" Matthews said.

"Interested. Sit down." Joseph began cleaning the blood from Matthews's face.

"Anything in particular?"

"No."

"You don't live very high for an ironworker. You must make nearly thirty thousand a year. Where's it go?"

"Hold still," said Turner, applying the cloth to the reporter's nose.

Matthews was frustrated. This guy wasn't your ordinary ironworker. He decided to try directness. "I want an exclusive from you."

"What!" exclaimed Joseph, drawing back.

"An exclusive. You know, you tell me your story and nobody else."

Joseph looked over at Sammy for a moment and shook his head. "No, you don't understand," he said, setting the brown glass bottle on the nightstand. "I'm not telling anybody anything. I want my privacy."

"Well, that's all fine and good," said Matthews, "but the press isn't going to let you alone and, well, I'm already here, and I really need this story. It will mean a lot to me."

Turner walked to the sink and washed his hands. "I want you to understand this. No story. I'm hoping that in a day or two people will forget what happened. Then I can go back to work. Your publicity won't make it easy for people to forget. It'll only intensify their curiosity and complicate my life. So I'd appreciate it if you'd just let me get back to living." He pulled the towel from the rack, dried his hands, turned back, and looked directly into Matthews's eyes. "The fall should have killed me. I know that. I've got to deal with it and it isn't easy. You'll do what you want. But I won't help you."

Jerry felt confused. It wasn't an order or a demand, and it wasn't a plea. It was a simple, direct fact. However much he needed this story, he didn't want to hurt this man. There was something very special about Joseph Turner. "Okay," he answered finally. His voice was quiet. "Then I warn you. You want to protect your privacy? Get the hell out of your apartment. Stay with friends. Check into a hotel. Do something, but don't stay here. If they haven't already got your address, every station and newspaper in town will within the next few hours, and they'll bird-dog you till they get a story." He was telling himself that this was only a strategic withdrawal and that he'd be back, but deep down he didn't feel sure. He really wanted to let this guy off. How he'd cope with Carson he didn't know. He stood and moved toward Joseph, holding out his hand. "I wish you luck."

Now Joseph was surprised. He took Matthews's hand. "Thanks. Good luck to you, too."

"Yeah." Matthews nodded a goodbye to Sammy and left. When he reached the entry hall he saw Frankie standing inside the windowed front door by the half-jimmied mailboxes.

"You get your story?"

Matthews shook his head. "Nope. But it's okay. So long." He opened the door, cautiously negotiated the icy steps, and made his way through the flurries of snow to the network's double-parked station wagon.

In the apartment Sammy got up to go. "Sorry about the fight."

"Forget it, Sam."

"Joey," the big man began earnestly, "you saved my life. I'll never forget that."

"No more than you've done for me hundreds of times up there."

"But never like that."

Joseph nodded solemnly, accepting it. Then he smiled. "Let's just say I love you. Now get out of here. Go home and see Rosa. Have a good dinner and relax. We both have a lot to be thankful for; we're alive."

"I'm worried. I think you should do what the reporter said, you know, about staying with friends. I want you to come home with me at least for the night."

"Nope. I'll stay here. I'll be fine, Sammy. Get some rest, and don't worry."

"You can't ask me to do that, Joey." Sammy looked down, then back up at him, this time more intensely. "I'm confused and scared. What the hell happened up there? Why weren't you hurt, for Chrissake?" Sammy slammed his hand against the door. "I'm sorry, dammit, I'm as bad as Corollo."

Joseph moved to him and put his arms around his burly friend. "I don't know, Sam. Luck, God, freak accident, I just don't know. But," he said as he gently loosened his embrace, "I do know it happened and I'm alive and I've got to get past this thing."

"You're always so damn sensible," said Sammy, shrugging his shoulders. "But what if it doesn't work? What if that newsman was right and the papers and TV do hound you? Then what?"

"Then," said Joseph scratching his head, "then I'll have to deal with it when it happens. Go home." He put his arm around Sweet's shoulder and showed him to the door. "Go on!"

"If you need me you'll call, right?"

"In a flash," Joseph answered.

"I don't know how to thank you for getting me in up there."

"You already have," said Joseph. "Now go home, Sammy, go home to Rosa."

Sammy nodded and walked into the hallway. He turned back toward Joseph to find the door closing quietly. A look of pain crossed his face; he bit at his lower lip and headed slowly for the stairs.

Less then ten minutes after Sammy left, Joseph got his first phone call requesting an interview. The story had been carried on the AP and UPI wire services, and it seemed that the more insistent he was about htis privacy the more persistent the media became. While the man from the *National Enquirer* was on the phone, the first annoying knock came at the door. He explained to the writer on the phone that he wasn't interested in their money and hung up. Then he got off the bed, walked to the door, and opened it. Louise Ryan, the reporter from the *Times,* stood there with a photographer who began snapping pictures. Joseph started to close the door, but she wedged her foot inside. He opened it and faced her. Her appraiser's eyes looked him over.

"Look, lady, I'm exhausted. I know you're only doing your job, but I'm going to get some sleep so you'll have to do it someplace else."

"My story's with you, Mr. Turner. I have only two questions."

Joseph sighed heavily. "Hurry up. Two."

Ryan removed her foot and waited a moment. Then: "One: how did you stage that fall? Two: why?"

Joseph felt a rush of fury come over him and he worked to steady his voice. "I wore a flight jacket and I got bored waiting for the elevator. Now goodbye."

The reporter laughed. "Surely you don't want me to print that?"

Joseph controlled himself and spoke calmly, but his eyes bored into her. "You said two questions. You just asked them. I don't give a damn what you print. But it *was* an accident. Good night." He slammed the door.

He stood listening to the departing footsteps, then walked

over to his small refrigerator, retrieved a beer, and sat down on the bed.

It was all happening too fast. It was too much to deal with all at once. He should be dead right now—

He looked around the room. Maybe he was, he kidded himself ironically—if so, he hadn't made it to heaven. He felt bewildered, a little frightened. He'd never resisted change, never resented the unexpected, but this came out of nowhere and led nowhere. A chill washed over him. He shook it off. There's nothing to do but take things as they come, but please, let them slow down.

The phone rang again and he picked it up. "Yes?"

"Mr. Turner, Jerry Matthews. Mr. Turner, I'm sorry to bother you, but I wanted you to know. When I got back to the network my boss laid into me about the story. I haven't been doing too well around here, and this was the last straw. Either I put together a story on you for the ten o'clock news, or I lose my job."

"I see," Joseph said. "You're in a tough spot."

"So I'm doing a story, Mr. Turner. But I'll be as careful as I can. I'm sorry."

"Well," Joseph said gently, "do whatever you have to do. And Jerry . . ."

"Yes?"

"Thanks for your call."

"Right."

Joseph lay back down on the bed. He stared out the window into a snowy sky. The short winter days brought an ominous early darkness to the Bronx.

It's going further than I expected, but maybe people will forget. Maybe it won't last, he thought.

The phone began to ring again. Joseph stared at it, wishing the incessant ringing would stop.

It didn't.

SEVEN

By 9:15 PEOPLE FROM CBS and NBC as well as two more newspapers had come by the apartment. Whenever they gave him a moment's peace his own mind wouldn't; it spun with questions he couldn't answer, refusing to let him rest. He couldn't think and he couldn't stop thinking. He had to get out. Whoever was pounding at the door would have to get their story elsewhere. Joseph opened his window, silently stepped out into the darkness, and slipped down the fire escape.

He walked down Devon Street, feeling insulated by the freezing cold that kept most of the neighborhood inside their warmly lit apartments. He began to relax, breathing easier as he continued to walk, passing strangers who paid him no more attention than they ever had. He smiled to himself; the apartment had been a trap, making him feel like the whole world was closing in on him, while in reality there were millions of people out there who'd never heard of Joseph Turner and probably never would.

He found himself wandering into the infected porno district of the Bronx. It was like traveling in a neon box. The garishly lit buildings jutted up forming impenetrable walls, their blinking lights reflected off the low hanging gray lid of sky. Out of the mass of clouds the snow began to fall again, not in peaceful flakes, but in a torrential rush that seemed like fluttering white curtains.

A month ago the streets had been alive with commerce. Tonight the business of displaying, hawking, and selling flesh was conducted indoors. An occasional patrol car cruised the area, but here they were the enemy, shut out in the cold.

A thin tangle-haired man stepped from the shadows.

"You're looking kind of cold, friend. I got just the remedy for you."

Joseph shook his head. "No thanks."

The seedy intruder didn't give up. He grabbed Joseph's arm and pointed toward a lighted uncurtained window. "You didn't even see what I had to offer, friend. Now don't be ungrateful. Just let your imagination run wild."

Through the window he watched an overfed prostitute give him a well-practiced half smile and jut out her heavy breasts. "Thanks, but no thanks," he said kindly.

The stout hooker blew Joseph an affectionate kiss and then, when he turned his back and headed down the sidewalk, gave him the finger. The tangle-haired pimp yelled and laughed after him, "You don't know what you're missing!"

"Yes, I do, friend," mumbled Joseph sadly, feeling a twinge of loneliness that brought with it an image of steel-blue eyes beautifully framed by dark chestnut hair. He could almost feel the closeness of her body; the memory hurt. Stop torturing yourself, he told himself firmly, and quickly turned his attention back to the street.

He stopped at the lighted doorway of a candy store. Through the glass he could see stacks of newspapers and magazines on display. Curious, he stepped in and stared at the picture centered on numerous front pages. IRONWORKER LIVES AFTER FALL! the headlines said. IRONWORKER DEFIES ODDS! NEW YORKER FALLS AND LIVES! CONSTRUCTION WORKER PLUNGES TO LIFE! Endless mirrors . . .

He put a quarter on the counter, picked up a copy of the *Times,* and went back out to the street.

A drunk black man, humming an ancient soul tune through his cracked lips, stumbled and tripped his way up to Joseph. He reached out with his chapped hands, grasping the front of Joseph's jacket.

"You gotta, you gotta," said the hummer.

"I gotta what?" Joseph asked quizzically.

"You just gotta have some spare change. I needs me one more shot of red dog so's I can go to sleep." He smiled a wide toothless grin for his would-be benefactor.

"I understand," said Joseph, gently easing the derelict's grip on his jacket. "But I'm not giving you money for booze."

He reached into his pocket and pulled out a half-dollar. "Here, this will get you some soup."

"You betcha, boy."

Boy . . . boy . . . he hadn't heard that for a long time. He looked into the maze of broken blood vessels that surrounded the aged man's dark, lonely eyes. The face reminded him of Willie Johnson, once Head of Maintenance at the South Bronx Home for Boys, whose services had been terminated when Joseph was only twelve. He'd been a hero to the boys where heroes were few, a former professional boxer who delighted them with stories, especially about the fight with Graziano. "There is winners and there is losers in this world," he'd said to Joseph more than once, "and you is one of the winners. I know it don't seem like it now, boy, but one day you is gonna see your name in lights."

I don't think this is what you had in mind, Willie, he thought, smiling at the picture on the *Times* after the old man had gone, but the smile disappeared as he began to read. He stuffed the paper into the nearest trash can.

He walked until the cold hurt, then headed back home, sure that he would be left alone the rest of the night. On Devon Street a yellow Datsun station wagon was pulling up in front of his brownstone. Lettered on the sides and rear of the car was "WABC—Eyewitness News." A tall black man wearing a camel coat got out, checked a piece of paper and the street numbers on the front of the brownstone. Joseph ducked into the alley next to the building and tried to quiet his heavy breathing while he surreptitiously watched the newsman mount the front steps and enter. "Dammit," he said angrily, heading back in the opposite direction.

He spent the night in the first hotel he found, a two-dollar-a-night flophouse.

Early the next afternoon he woke up, got himself some food, and looked around for a theater where he could sit out the rest of the day. He'd picked up a morning paper and found himself on page two. The article made him a "mystery man," with more details about his background and personal information on what he did with his money and how he lived. Joseph felt angry and exposed, and he wanted to be somewhere where he would be invisible.

A double-feature rerun of *Superman* and *Oh, God!*

seemed irresistibly appropriate and he sat spellbound in the musty, overheated, rundown theater for the rest of the afternoon. He found himself laughing more at the foolishness of his being there than at the movies themselves. By the time he walked out into the evening he felt drained.

He also felt smelly, and his reflection in a café window told him he looked as bad as he smelled. Ironic, he thought: yesterday on the front page, today on skid row. He needed a shower, a shave, clean clothes. Not home, though, not yet. Not ready for that. And not the Boys' Club . . . that would be a circus. He stopped in at Woolworth's, picked up an inexpensive shirt, underwear, and razor, and went to Casey's Gym off the Grand Concourse. He exercised for an hour, finding anger and frustration in his body and working them out, then sat in a sauna until the beefy proprietor insisted he leave. He took a shower and decided not to shave. He might be less easily recognized.

After leaving the gym he headed for Augie's Bar and Grill, a neighborhood joint likely to be empty for another hour or so. When he arrived Augie was listlessly wiping down the worn oak bar with a dirty towel. There were only five other patrons. At the bar, a man who looked like a trucker was hustling a black girl in an orange dress; beside the pool table two street toughs were arguing angrily over whose shot was next. Their companion, a pock-marked girl wearing worn levis and a dirty sweatshirt, leaned against the wall next to the half-empty rack of cue sticks, her index finger imbedded half way up her left nostril. She was obviously enjoying the rift.

Joseph sat at the bar and ordered a draft and what he was sure would end up a Crisco-burger. No one paid special attention to him, and he began to relax. As he sipped his beer he listened to the conversation between the girl and the man, who was trying to con her into believing he played left tackle for the Jets. She wasn't who she claimed to be, either. Joseph recognized her as the girl Sammy had pointed out to him when they were in Augie's last week. She passed herself off as a dancer at a midtown disco joint, but she was in fact an undercover narcotics cop out of Fort Apache. Probably she was working a discreet surveillance on the customers.

Wonder what would happen if everyone dropped their

lies? Laid their cards on the table—just for one day? The kids playing pool, street kids who never allowed anyone to know how scared they were; the trucker who wanted to make himself more exciting for a girl he found attractive; the narcotics agent, spending her life spying on other people. Everybody's hiding, he thought—at the moment, even me.

Augie delivered the hamburger and turned away, impulsively switching on the television set mounted high on the wall behind the bar. The old Zenith illuminated the dimly lit corner of the tavern as the Knicks game blared through the weak picture.

"Hey, Augie," the trucker yelled. "How much you got on this one?"

"Fifty. The way my luck's runnin', the bastards'll blow another game. I was tryin' not to watch."

A few minutes later the boys from the Commonwealth finished off Augie's hopes with a fast breaking lay-up just as Joseph finished his dinner. He watched the cardigan-clad loser open the register and check the cash; there wasn't anywhere near fifty dollars yet. As he slammed the cash drawer closed with a loud clunk, the ten o'clock wrap-up edition of Eyewitness News emerged in living fade-in on the screen.

Joseph looked up. "Hey, Augie, game's over. How 'bout turning it off?" It was too late. A copy of his union identification photo stared out from behind the newsman. Joseph sickened.

". . . and a follow-up on Joseph Turner, the construction worker who miraculously survived a twenty-four-story fall yesterday without a scratch . . . while saving the life of a fellow worker."

"Hey," Augie said, his head snapping around. "My God, that's you!"

Joseph didn't respond. His eyes, like everyone else's in the bar, were fixed on the screen. He wanted to get up, get out, but he couldn't. What was the point? He felt as though he was a part of the immobile stool on which he sat. He saw photos of the superstructure on Fiftieth and shots of Sammy and himself at the hospital. The TV cast a soft light on Joseph's face as he wiped the nervous perspiration from his forehead with a wet left palm.

The network showed filmed interviews with the ambulance

driver, now dressed in a gaudy sport coat and tie. He vehemently denounced the fall as a trick or publicity stunt. A field commentator questioned Dr. Weisman, who said simply that he was unable to medically explain the freak accident. He asked that he be left alone and stated that the same courtesy should be extended his patient.

Joseph unconsciously nodded. The trucker looked at him from beneath knitted brows. The policewoman stared in amazement, her head swiveling back and forth between Joseph and the television.

The priest from St. Patrick's explained that God had interceded.

When Sammy's middle-class pitched-roof house appeared, Joseph leaned forward closer to the set. He watched his friend, seated by Rosa on the worn living-room sofa, fumble for words to explain how grateful he was for Joseph's saving his life. Then Sammy described the fall, playing it down; he seemed to be trying to protect Joseph from the onslaught of more publicity. When the broadcast invasion ended, Joseph sighed heavily, resigned to the fact that it wasn't over yet. He stood up, fished into his pocket, and laid a five on the oak bar.

"No way, man!" bellowed Augie, waving off the money. "It's on the house. You're the most important person that's ever been in my place. Lemme buy ya another drink. We got a hero with us, folks!"

Joseph shook his head. "Thanks anyway, but I've got to go," he said, turning from the bar. As he left he felt six sets of eyes burrowing into his back.

It was late, cold, and dark. Feeling tired and raw, Joseph headed home on the icy sidewalks of the Bronx. The snow had stopped again but it felt as if more hung in the sky, waiting, giving the city a respite before a new storm hit and dumped another load onto the streets. As Joseph entered the brownstone, a snowplow, its yellow rooflights flashing, was taking advantage of the hiatus to scoop away another layer of winter.

Inside the doorway Joseph removed his boots. Mrs. Wilkerson, the Rodriguez children, and most of the other tenants would have long been asleep. Not wanting to wake anyone, he quietly negotiated the three flights of well-worn stairs and the hallway to his apartment.

Pinned to his door was a note from a CBS newsman requesting an interview "at his earliest convenience." Resentment welled up through his exhaustion as he crumpled the note and entered the apartment. Scattered on the floor were more papers and business cards. He leafed through them quickly and threw out all but the personal notes from neighbors and friends.

As he began to undress he heard Allen Cochran pacing the floor of the apartment next door. That nervous pacing was familiar; he hoped Cochran hadn't been waiting for him to come home. But he heard the door open and the knock at his own; he finished pulling his shirt off and opened the door to see a strung-out Cochran puffing furiously on a joint.

"Hi, Allen." Joseph waited for Cochran to speak, but he just stood there, his eyes dilated and glazed, his feet shuffling uncomfortably.

"Allen," said Joseph pointedly, "what can I do for you?"

"Uh," he stammered, reaching into the pocket of his patched surplus service khakis and producing three crumpled pieces of paper. "I've got these for you." He handed them to Joseph.

"What's this?"

"Notes from reporters."

"How'd you end up with them?"

"Everybody who came to your door found a note there already, and tore it off, and threw it down the hall." Ailen's tone became ingratiating. "Then after they'd leave I'd go get it. I saved them for you."

"Thanks, Allen, I appreciate that."

Joseph started to close the door but Cochran stopped him.

"I'm in a bad way, Joey."

"No," Joseph said, shaking his head.

"Please, I need a loan, just till Friday. I get paid then."

"I said no, and what do you mean you get paid on Friday, Allen?"

He stared blankly.

"Allen?" repeated Turner. "You don't even have a job."

"I'll get one. I promise. I'll pay you your money back, really."

"That's not the point. Look," said Turner strongly, "if I give you some money you'll be on the streets trying to score in fifteen minutes, and you'll be back tripping on the junk tonight." Turner reached out and touched Cochran's arm. "I'm not going to help you kill yourself."

"Please, Joey, I got people coming by. Please loan me some bread." He was frantic.

"I won't do it."

"What do you mean?" whined Cochran.

"Which word didn't you understand? I-won't-do-it! Good night, Allen."

He closed the door and walked over to draw the curtains to his only window, flipped on the space heater, and finished undressing. The phone rang. He put it in the ice box, silencing the menacing instrument. He switched off the wire-hung bulb in the middle of the room and crawled into the crisp, clean sheets.

When his eyes closed, his mind flooded with the events of the last two days. At the moment of the fall it all stood still; he was shocked to realize that while falling he had felt not terror but some other strange fear, and not fear alone but also a warm sensation of safety. He wondered how other men felt in such moments. Some had lived. He remembered reading about a woman in California who'd fallen eight stories and walked away without a scratch. It happens.

But twenty-four stories? There was no human explanation for the accident to have ended the way it did. For the first time in a long time, Joseph found himself thinking about God. He hadn't dealt with that notion in years.

As he reached out more and more for sleep, his mind drifted backward, backward farther than he wanted it to go. But he couldn't stop it . . . screeching tires, horns, shattered glass, and twisted steel and a three-year-old boy calling, "Mommy!" and then the stillness of death. He felt tears come again for the first time in such a long time. Maybe time would fade the memory of the fall as it had the nightmare of the collision.

At the edge of sleep he saw himself standing once more on the twenty-fourth story. He watched himself slip off the girder and fall through endless space.

Before he hit the ground, Joseph Turner was asleep.

EIGHT

THE SOUND OF CRASHING and breaking wood jolted him awake. It sounded as if Cochran's door were being torn off its hinges. As he grabbed for his jeans he heard a man's voice bellow through the thin walls: "Police! Freeze, motherfucker, or you're dead where you stand!" Then came a gunshot and an icy chill ran through Joseph's veins. He jumped for the door and pulled it open. Inside Cochran's doorway stood the black woman in the orange dress and two men, a tall grim-looking man in a rumpled suit and a younger bearded one in faded jeans—all three with guns leveled at Cochran and the pool-playing trio from Augie's. One of the kids lay on his back in the middle of Cochran's apartment, blood spreading from his belly. His knife lay on the floor three feet across the room. He writhed with pain, screaming, "Oh, God, oh, God, Jesus, help me."

The two men spun Allen, the girl, and her companion around and up against the wall and began to frisk them. The girl snapped her head around angrily. "You killed him, you bastards, you killed Carlos!"

"Hook her up!" yelled the tallest member of the narcotics team.

The young bearded officer pulled his cuffs out and hooked the girl's hands behind her back, then closed them so tight that she screamed in pain as blood trickled down her wrists, between her fingers, and onto the floor.

Joseph went unnoticed standing in the doorway. The cops quickly cuffed Allen and the dark-haired suspect. The team leader turned to his female partner. "Call it in. Have them send out an ambulance and a shooting team."

"Right, Sarge." She turned and almost bumped into Joseph. "You!? Get back. Everything's under control. We're

50

police officers." She flashed her tin at Joseph and pushed past him through the hallway, now filled with pajama-and-bathrobe-clad tenants shoving their way into better vantage points to see the drama and gore.

Carlos continued to roll on the floor in agony while the bearded officer read the suspects their rights and the team leader searched the apartment for drugs. Finding nothing in the bureau, the sergeant crossed the room and checked under the mattress. The pusher continued to scream in pain.

"Do something for him," pleaded Joseph from the doorway.

The cop finished searching the bed and said, "We're cops, not doctors."

Joseph moved to the wounded man, got on one knee, and pressed the palm of his hand over the open wound.

"What the hell are you doing? This is a crime scene!" yelled the infuriated undercover cop.

"He needs help," Joseph said, looking directly into the angry officer's eyes.

"Get out of here, or you'll end up just like him!" The cop pulled his gun, pointing it at Joseph and easing back the trigger.

"If he does, it'll be headline news by morning!"

Joseph knew the woman's voice, and he slowly turned his head to see her.

"Who are you?" demanded the officer.

"Louise Ryan, the *Times*." She flashed her press pass in the irate officer's face.

"He interfered with a police officer in the line of duty. That's a felony!"

"No, he didn't," snapped the reporter. "He kept an asshole sadist from letting this kid die. Now if you don't want my paper all over you like that cheap suit you're wearing, I'd suggest you put that gun away!"

Reluctantly the officer complied, glaring at Joseph. "You're luckier than shit, man. Now get out of my sight."

"I'll stay with him until the ambulance arrives—OK?" said Joseph.

"Sure it's OK," Ryan answered.

The officer snapped his head around and frowned furiously at her.

"What's going on here, Don?" The female cop had returned and stood in the doorway, her eyes darting from the reporter to Joseph and then back to her boss.

"Nothing," said the team leader. "Toss the place and see what you can find. I came up empty."

"Right," she said, moving to the open closet, where she expertly patted down each garment. After a few seconds she withdrew Cochran's shooting kit from the pocket of an old Army field jacket.

"Uncle Sam wants you now," she said, smiling triumphantly at Cochran and waving the shooting kit. He was frightened and hyperventilating as he pressed his face tightly to the flaking plaster wall.

The bleeding suspect seemed to have become more tranquil since Joseph had begun applying pressure to the wound. He had grown still and his breathing was easy and regular. Joseph watched the muscles in his forehead relax. Then he looked up at Louise Ryan. "What are you doing here?" he asked.

"Saving your neck, apparently."

"I'll get to that. I meant: why did you come back?"

"I have something for you."

Joseph shook his head and sighed heavily. "This is a strange time for presents."

The sounds of sirens rose from the street below.

"What have we got, Bob?" asked the tall narcotics officer from across the room. His partner looked out the window to the street below. "Looks like the lieutenant, two backup units, the shooting team, a wagon, and the ambulance."

Soon the tiny apartment filled with more officers, and two paramedics wheeled a gurney into the room. As they moved in next to the wounded youth, Joseph got up and moved over to the door next to Louise Ryan. His right hand was covered with drying blood.

One of the attendants opened a first-aid kit and extracted a large white compress. The other tore open the youth's shirt. Shock filled his face. "What the hell," he said as he examined the abdomen. Finally he looked up at the arresting officers. "When did you shoot this guy?"

"About fifteen minutes ago."

"Looks more like three days. This wound's nearly closed up. There's not even any infection."

"What?" exclaimed the officer. "We all saw him shot! And there's still blood all over the floor."

"I see the blood, officer. But this body's healing."

The cops looked at one another and then moved in for a closer look at Carlos's stomach. A large purple bruise spread across the skin, but the wound was closed.

"See?" said the examining paramedic. "Nothing."

The team leader looked at Joseph, who stared blankly at Carlos. "You saw it! Tell them!"

"Yes, it was there when I . . ." Joseph stopped and the officer finished the sentence for him.

"When you put your hand on it." The officer looked scared. He stepped back from Joseph and asked, slowly, "What'd you do anyway? What are you—some kind of magician?"

Joseph was looking down at his hand. The others stared at him in silence, waiting expectantly for an answer.

"He doesn't know. He was just trying to help." Louise Ryan took Joseph by the arm, turned him around, and led him into the hallway, past the onlookers, and through his open door back into his apartment. "You better sit down," she said, dropping her hand and turning to close the door behind her. In the hall the gurney was pulled out and the police officers led the suspects through the clearing crowd. She closed the door and leaned against it, standing quietly, watching Joseph. He sat on the edge of the bed, his head lowered, his tense arms clutching the side. His body began to shake. "You're scared," she said softly. "And you don't scare easily. So this is tough. I'm sorry." She said it calmly and openly, without fear and without pity.

He looked at her and she seemed more solid than anyone or anything he'd seen all day. His body stopped shaking. "I'm scared shitless. I don't understand any of this. I think I'm going crazy."

"No," she answered firmly and evenly, "you're not. It's the facts that are crazy."

He pushed himself up and went to the basin to wash his hands. She stood quietly watching for a moment, then pulled the chair out from the table and sat.

"If I'm not crazy now, I'm going to be," he said, drying his hands and turning back to her.

"Well," she answered, "that's a possibility. But it may not be necessary." A smile played at her eyes. It was a challenge.

He shook his head and smiled back at her. "You are a tough lady," he said, sitting again on the bed and studying her. She was dressed severely in a charcoal pinstriped suit, but her body was relaxed. She had a square face, a set, determined jaw, and large, deepset brown eyes that looked like they took in every detail—like a camera, he thought, that doesn't miss a thing.

She smiled, acknowledging, then the smile faded. "About yesterday . . ."

"Forget it. Don't apologize. It was centuries ago."

"I wasn't going to apologize. I was doing my job. But I was wrong, and I want to tell you that."

He nodded.

"You had me baffled, because I believed you. So after I left I started at the beginning. I talked to the men working up there with you, I questioned witnesses on the ground, I even managed—God knows why he did—to get Weisman to talk to me. I've questioned fourteen people. They all confirm your story."

"I'm sorry to hear that. It would be easier to think I'm nuts."

"I know." There was sadness in her eyes now. She looked down quickly and opened her purse, pulling out what looked like a shred of metal. "A kid who saw you fall gave this to me. He pulled it out of the pavement."

Joseph took it, feeling sick to his stomach as he turned it over. "My watch."

"Yeah, what's left."

The crystal was gone and the dial was twisted, but the hands clearly showed the time of impact: 9:23.

"Facts," she said.

As he looked at it she saw his hands tremble and tears well up in his eyes. "I'm so tired," he said. "I don't know what's happening to me. And that kid in there . . ." Panic crept back into his voice.

"Look," she said. "There's some explanation. There always is." She paused. "I want you to let me help you."

"Help me?"

"Yes. Help you find the answer."

"Thanks, but—"

"I know, Joseph Turner doesn't need help. Joseph Turner helps other people. But this time he could use someone. Use me."

He looked at her suspiciously. "What do you get out of it?"

"Eventually—a story. What kind I'm not sure. But I'm not in a hurry. I won't push you, and I won't write the story until I've discussed it with you. Until then, you can go off the record anytime you want. But I want to know all about you, and all you can remember about the fall and about that kid."

"I don't know where to start for the answers."

"Tonight, neither do I . . ." Her voice trailed off. She walked to the door. "Wait a minute." She turned back. "I have an idea, somebody who might be able to tell us something. It's a little crazy, but . . ."

"Well?" he asked impatiently.

"Have you ever heard of a man by the name of Bridger? An evangelist—a faith healer?"

"Yes. But what's that got to do with—?"

"He has a network show and I personally think he's a schmuck. But a few months ago I met him in connection with a story, and he has a good deal of experience with what people call 'miracles.' I know it sounds stupid, but he might give us a clue."

Joseph got up and walked to the door. "Miss Ryan, I'm not a religious person."

"I'm not either. It doesn't matter. What have we got to lose?"

He shrugged. "Why would he talk to us?"

"You seem to be forgetting who you've become. Besides, he owes me a favor. I'll call him first thing tomorrow and set up an appointment. OK?"

"I guess so."

"I'll talk to you in the morning. Don't forget to take your phone out of the deep freeze."

He smiled and opened the door for her. "I'll do that. And Miss Ryan—"

"Louise."

"Thanks."

She stepped out and the door closed behind her. Louise Ryan, she said to herself, there is more in this for you than a story. Confess. You are fascinated by Joseph Turner. Of course I am, another voice answered. Miracles or not, Joseph Turner is no ordinary man.

NINE

JOSEPH SAT in an almost empty subway car on his way into
Manhattan at 10:30 Wednesday morning. He'd awakened
early, unable to sleep past 7:00, and had worked himself into jumbled confusion since. In his first waking moments he
felt with relieved certainty that the events of last night had
been only a crazy nightmare, but he had turned over to see
the twisted piece of metal staring insistently at him from the
nightstand. Facts, Louise Ryan had said. She had called to
confirm the appointment for 11:30 and he had felt ridiculously impatient to go—and get it over with. A few minutes
later he picked up the phone to call her back to cancel, then
realized he didn't know where to call.

This has nothing to do with me! he thought as the subway
car rumbled toward his meeting. I live on Devon Street in
the Bronx and I put up buildings, and whoever it is who
miraculously survives falls and shows up on the front page
and has gunshot wounds change under his hand is some
Joseph Turner I'm not at all familiar with . . .

Suddenly he felt uncomfortable and looked around. He
was being watched. A chubby little black boy with an oversized natural hairstyle coolly observed him from across the
aisle. The child turned his head away, but Joseph saw the
enormous brown-black eyes glide slowly back in his direction, and the head followed.

"Who is you?"

"Good question . . ." Joseph said to himself, barely audibly.

"Is you famous, mister?"

"Why?"

" 'Cause I seen your picture on the front page of the paper, so you must be famous. You gots to be either a movie star, a politician, or wanted by the pigs. Now which is it?"

"Didn't you read what the paper wrote?" asked Joseph, fighting back a smile.

"I don't reads. But I figure you ain't no movie star"—he looked Joseph up and down—" 'cause you don't dress like one. And you probably ain't no politician 'cause you ain't travelin' in no limousine . . . So what's the pigs after you for?"

"Nothing."

A look of disbelief crossed the boy's face. "Ah, c'mon, you can tell me . . . maybe I can help you. You runnin'? It won't cost you much . . ." he whispered conspiratorially.

"Thanks, but no, really. I fell off a building and . . ."

"Hey, man, you's that guy they's been talkin' 'bout on the radio. Geez, was you lucky. You's Joseph . . ."

"Yeah, what's your name, hustler?"

"Abdul Mohammed," retorted the boy proudly, staring straight ahead. When Joseph didn't respond he turned to him. "Well, this week anyway. My real name's Leroy."

This kid was having some problems with who he was, too. "How old are you, Abdul?"

"All right!" bellowed the boy enthusiastically. "Gimme five." He held out his small hand palm up and Joseph slapped it. "I'm thirteen," he lied.

"Really?"

His eyebrows knit. "Well, would you believe twelve?"

"No."

"Eleven, then. That's almost the straight and skinny, 'cause I'll be eleven in January."

"That, Abdul, I'll believe. How come you don't know how to read? You go to school?"

"Now and then, now and then. But why learns? I don' needs it, man, for what I's goin' to be when I grows up."

"What's that?"

"I's gonna be a revolutionary like Mohammed," he answered matter-of-factly.

"Oh, I don't think so," Joseph said, shaking his head.

"What you mean you don't think so, man? I knows it!"

" 'Cause Mohammed knew how to read."

"No shit!" replied Leroy, stunned. "You jivin'?"

"Nope."

"Damn!" he pounded his fist into his thigh. "Now what the fuck am I gonna do? I's too old to learn! Well, I ain't changin' my plans. I got it all worked out."

"Yeah. I had it all worked out when I was your age too. I never changed my plans, either." Joseph thought quietly for a moment. "But look," he said casually, "about the reading. If you change your mind about that part—you aren't too old —you go talk to a friend of mine. Leon Asher. You know the Boys' Club just off the Grand Concourse? He teaches basketball there, and he's an English teacher. Tell Leon that Joseph Turner said he'd teach you how to read."

"Leon Asher? Ah, I don't know. That Club's for faggots and queers. You *sure* Mohammed knew how to read?"

"Far as I know. And anyway, what could it hurt? You never know what you're going to need to know. I mean, with you going to be a famous man, and all."

Leroy stifled a proud grin. "Hey," he said, "you like bein' famous?"

"Hate it. But then it wasn't in my plans."

The subway slowed and stopped. Leroy jumped up.

"Good luck, Abdul."

"You too, mister," he answered as he backed through the open doors and onto the platform. The train pulled away.

Shortly after 11:00 Joseph climbed the stone subway stairs to Fifty-Ninth and Lexington. At street level he was met by the frigid November wind. It cut through his clothes and penetrated his bones, but he hardly noticed. He walked briskly across Fifty-Ninth toward Fifth Avenue, oblivious to the prematurely Christmas-decorated store windows. His mind was on the meeting.

Perhaps it was stupid to go but—like he'd said—what could it hurt? And maybe he could get just a clue to what this was all about.

He reached Central Park and headed up Fifth Avenue. His pace had quickened to a jog, and he fought running. Half a block up the street he saw the address-embossed sides of the forest-green canopy in front of the building. The canopy flapped in the winter gusts. Beneath it shivered a tall, lanky doorman wearing a red uniform, accented with gold braids. He reflexively jerked open the door for Joseph. "Morning, sir," he grumbled.

Joseph nodded a thank you and quickly entered the lobby. Louise waited for him. She smiled warmly. "I wasn't sure you'd actually go through with it."

"Neither was I."

She asked the security guard at the reception desk to announce them to Mr. Bridger, then guided Joseph into an elevator and pressed a floor button. The door closed and the high-speed elevator began its smooth ascent to the fifty-fifth floor.

"This guy sure lives in style."

"And he's very protective of it, Joseph . . . That's one of the things I wanted to warn you about. Paul's skeptical of miracles he hasn't witnessed, especially by someone he's never heard of. I don't know for sure if he's protecting God or his own gold mine and I don't care. He's knowledgeable and might be helpful."

The elevator stopped and Joseph and Louise exited.

Paul Bridger, dressed in cords and a cashmere sweater, greeted them effusively in the foyer of the penthouse. "Louise, my dear, your loveliness brightens the cloudiest day. And you must be Joseph Turner."

Joseph caught a wink from Louise as he grasped Bridger's outstretched hand. "Yes, I am. Thank you for seeing me."

"I've been looking forward to it," answered Bridger.

A maid appeared and took the visitors' coats. Bridger motioned them into an enormous study, which seemed more a showcase for the movie stars and politicians photographed with the man whom many believed to be the world's greatest healer. Bridger showed off a picture of himself and the President with the childish pride of a man thoroughly impressed by his own renown. Then they sat on a sofa and chair situated near a wall to wall window that framed a breathtaking view of the city. The maid came in with a sterling tea-and-coffee service and set it on the table nearest Louise.

"I'll do the honors," Louise said. "Tea or coffee, Joseph?"

"Coffee, black, please."

"And I'll have tea." Bridger turned to Joseph. "I've read the newspapers and spoken briefly with Louise but I'd prefer to hear the story from you."

"I'm not sure where to start."

"The beginning is usually a good place," he chuckled. "I'm sure, though, that this experience is very unusual for you and must be confusing. Take your time."

Joseph sat quietly for a moment, not certain he wanted to tell Paul Bridger his story. He didn't like the feeling he got from this man. Bridger was too slick. But like Louise said, it was information he wanted. Nobody said he had to like Bridger. "It started Monday. I was working on a high-rise, fell twenty-four stories, and wasn't injured. That was confirmed by the doctors at Bellevue. I finally accepted it as a freak accident."

"That was all in the papers. What I'm really interested in is how you felt."

"It scared the hell out of me. I was scared to death."

"Not quite." Bridger sipped his tea. "What sensations did you have other than fear?"

"It all happened so fast . . . I remember being scared, my ears were ringing—buzzing would be more correct—then all of a sudden there was this strange fear that was also peaceful. I felt kind of warm and safe. Then I blacked out."

"Warmth, you say?"

"Yes."

"That's most interesting, Mr. Turner, most interesting . . ." he mused.

"What?"

"The feeling of warmth or heat. Many healers, myself included, feel a rush of heat through their bodies at the moment of healing. But don't take me wrong. That doesn't mean you're a healer."

Joseph took a deep breath and sighed. "Good, because I don't want to be."

A wry smile crossed Bridger's lips. "Of course you don't. Now. Let's continue. What happened next?"

"Last night my next-door neighbor was busted by some narcs."

"Was he the one shot?"

"No. One of his friends—a pusher, I think."

"Go on."

"Well, one thing led to another and I ended up applying pressure to his wound and . . ." Joseph's voice faltered.

"And?"

"And when the paramedics arrived the hole was gone, just gone." The fear and confusion Joseph had felt the night before returned.

"Not gone."

"Oh?"

"You mean healed, don't you?"

"Yes, I guess so. In fifteen minutes."

"Did you feel warmth in your hand when you put it on him?"

"No."

Bridger sat back, looking relieved. "Ah, well then."

"Paul," Louise interrupted, "for Chrissake. In healings sometimes the warmth's there and sometimes it's not."

"My, my, you do complete research. How impressive."

"You bet I do. So cut the crap. Look, Paul, Mr. Turner is not one of the little boys from the tents after your job. He could care less. He just wants some answers."

Bridger appraised them for a moment. Joseph watched him discard a layer of polish. "What do you want to know?" Bridger asked.

Joseph leaned toward him, his voice intense. "I want to know why I wasn't killed in that fall. I want to know what's happened—or happening—to me. I want to know when it's going to stop."

Bridger nodded. "Well, yes. Of course we can't know for sure."

"Give me some suggestions."

"It is possible that when you fell, the power, the warmth, was running through your entire body, and maybe, just maybe it acted like a shield, protecting you from injury."

"That's hard to believe."

"I can imagine."

"It's just not reality."

"Let me tell you a story. There are two men in the Philippines who perform operations on people without surgical instruments. They just use their fingers. I've seen them remove organs—kidneys, appendices, and thyroids—by just reaching in and pulling them out. Then, when they're finished, they simply wipe their hands over the wound and the bleeding stops, the skin heals, and there is no scar. The network that airs my show had a documentary on it showing everything I've told you and more. It went on the air, and it was ignored. The American Medical Association was silent. Because it 'wasn't reality.' It seems obvious to me that you have the healing power. You've told me that yourself. The fall—some fluke, maybe. The wound—unlikely, highly unlikely that there's any natural explanation."

Louise moved impatiently in her chair. "What about something like hypnosis, Paul, some psychological change? Bleeding can stop, wounds can heal."

"Not in fifteen minutes, Louise."

"OK," Joseph said, "so assume that's what it is. Healing. Account for it. Give me a way to understand it."

"I'm afraid I can only tell you what I believe, and surely you already know that from my television program."

"I don't watch your program."

Bridger didn't move but his mouth tightened slightly. "Oh. I see. Well. There are four explanations for the phenomenon of healing. Some healers believe that what they do is a natural phenomenon we don't understand yet. Some healers explain it as an extrasensory psychic phenomenon. I attribute my own gift to God, to the immense inconceivable power of the Holy Ghost and the spirit of the blessed Christ Jesus, who—"

"And the fourth?" Joseph interrupted the blossoming sermon, to Bridger's obvious displeasure.

He spoke sharply. "Illusion, of course."

"This is no illusion."

"I agree with you."

"But a healer? I'm not the type."

"I agree with you on that, also." He looked straight at Joseph. Bridger didn't like him, but he hadn't quite finished measuring this man yet. If Joseph Turner were in fact a healer he might just fade into the woodwork. But then again he might not. Perhaps there was some way he could be useful. "I tell you what, Mr. Turner. Would you like to be certain about this?"

"Of course."

"Right now?"

Joseph looked over at Louise; she shrugged. "Yes, right now."

"Then I have a way of proving this one way or the other." He rose. "Excuse me for a moment. I'll be right back."

"I told you he was a little strange," Louise said, as she re-filled Joseph's cup for him.

"I can't tell you how much I hope this test fails," murmured Joseph. When Bridger returned he had a single-edged razor blade in his hand. He placed it on the table.

"What are you going to do with that?" Joseph asked.

"Nothing. You are. Do you believe you can heal, Joseph?"

"No."

"Good. Do you trust that I'm a healer?"

"I don't know. Maybe you are."

"Well, do you think that as a man of the cloth I would let you hurt yourself?"

"I'm not sure. I guess not."

"Fine, then. I want you to pick up the razor blade and slit your left wrist."

"What!" exclaimed Ryan.

"Slit it hard."

Joseph gaped at him. "You're crazy!"

"You said you wanted to know."

"Very dramatic, Bridger, and very stupid. At worst I'd need a few stitches. I'm not here for your fucking show."

Not very tractable, Bridger thought. "Mr. Turner, I have a reason for wanting to know myself. You see, if you do in fact have the healing power, I'm in a position to make you an offer."

"An . . . offer?"

"If you can heal, and if you accept Jesus as your personal savior this very day, you can be making ten thousand dollars a week, guaranteed, starting tomorrow."

Joseph was speechless with anger; he couldn't believe what he was hearing.

"You see, I've got more healings scheduled than I can handle. I've got one in Memphis on Monday you can have. I'll introduce you on the show tomorrow, you can do some of your stuff, and they'll be lining up to see you by the time you get to Tennessee. Fifteen, maybe twenty thousand people."

Bridger saw that something was wrong, that he wasn't reaching Turner. "There are people who need you. People who can't see, can't hear, can't walk. People who are dying.

And the children, Joseph, the children. You can help them too. Now what do you say? Are you with me?"

Joseph held himself tight and took a deep breath. "What do these people have to pay to see you?"

"Depends on the city. Usually about seven-fifty a head."

Joseph stood up and shook his head slowly, then he stared hard at the man seated before him and emitted the anger bit by bit. "Jesus, Bridger, you disgust me. You make those people pay. As if they hadn't paid enough already! And you use their suffering to hook me into your plushy scheme! 'And the children, Joseph, the children!' You make me wanna puke . . . *Reverend.*"

Joseph stormed out of the study, through the hallway, and out the front door, slamming it behind him.

"He won't be able to do it by himself! Who does he think he is anyway?" snapped Bridger at Louise as she took Joseph's coat from the maid and headed for the front door.

Before opening it she whirled to meet the evangelist, eye to angry eye. "Who? Who does he think he is? Just the man who's obviously got your number." As she turned and left the penthouse, Bridger stomped back into the study.

Louise watched the floors tick away as the elevator descended to the lobby. Joseph's anger had jarred her for a moment. It was unexpected, exciting. She'd suddenly found herself acutely aware of his body. Somewhere she had been hearing him tell Bridger off, but most of her was appreciating the sensuality of his taut, muscular frame and the perfect combination of gentleness and strength in a man.

The elevator stopped and she came back to the ground with it.

Joseph was pacing the lobby floor like an angry bull, his hands jammed into his pockets. He spun around as Louise approached. She couldn't contain a big smile.

"You found that amusing?" he said, irritated.

"No. Delightful. You were terrific."

"Thanks a lot. Listen, I just wanted to say goodbye and really, thank you for—"

Louise held up her hand. "Hold it. You're not getting away that easy. I get one more hour. Come on, I'll buy you lunch."

She took him to an exclusive, quiet rooftop restaurant where she was known and they wouldn't be disturbed.

They spoke no more than ten words during the meal. He finally pushed his plate away and sat staring out the window. Clouds were returning from the north. There would be a new storm.

Suddenly he turned to her; he'd almost forgotten she was there.

"I know it was awful," she said, "but did it help?"

Joseph nodded. "I found out I might be a healer." The word sounded ugly to him.

"What are you going to do?"

"I'm not going to do anything."

"Then it was a waste of time?"

"Not at all. That guy did me two favors. I came here hoping he'd have answers to what's been happening to me. All he had to offer was a multiple choice from which you can choose any one because nobody really knows. That's the same as saying there is no answer, so I can quit looking. And he did something else. He made it clear to me that I don't want any part of it—if I've still got it. I've decided to forget it."

"Can you do that?"

"I've got to. I want my life back to normal. Oh, hell."

"What's the matter?"

"Last night. Can you find out if the police have told anybody about last night?"

"You mean the healing?"

Joseph nodded.

"If you're worried about publicity, don't be. I took care of it."

"What do you mean?"

"I went by the precinct last night after I left your place."

"And?"

"Let's just say the captain and I came to a mutual understanding."

"Louise, now it's your turn to can the crap. What did you really tell him?"

"You really want to know my trade secrets?"

"I asked, didn't I?"

"Okay . . . I told him that if there was any leak to the press, I'd personally see to it that the *Times*'s next headline read COP THREATENS TO MURDER GOOD SAMARITAN. And that if he didn't want the entire Sunday *New York Times* crammed up his ass sideways, he'd better do as I asked."

Joseph laughed. "And he went for it? You're amazing."

"I can't take all the credit. I got the distinct feeling that they wanted it kept quiet as much as I did."

"What if your boss finds out?"

"He knows me. He'll figure I'm onto something and have good reason for keeping the lid on it."

He sipped his coffee and then set it down, fingering the rim of the cup. "You've made this easy. You know, I could understand this whole thing a little better if I felt different, but I don't. I feel the same now as I've always felt."

"Just a regular old normal human, huh, Joseph?"

"Yeah."

Her eyes narrowed. "I don't think you've ever been normal."

"What's that supposed to mean?"

"You're too nice. You're too innocent. You're too straight. When somebody offers you fame and fortune you tell him to get lost. You're too honest. You're too generous. And—you've got supernatural powers that you want to forget about. You're too naïve."

"Are you finished?"

"You wanna cop to the naïveté charge?"

"No."

"You really think you can forget it?"

"I've forgotten worse."

"Joseph, what are you going to do if you find out you really can heal?"

"For now, nothing."

"Would you like to use it?"

She watched him mull it over. "Yes, if I could find a way to give it away, and if it didn't turn into a freak show."

"I think you'll solve that problem. That kid's wound—"

"I don't want to hear about it. Jesus, I wish none of this had ever happened."

"I don't think wishing is going to help."

"Sounds like one of my lines. But I think I'm changing my philosophical position."

"To?"

"What I don't know won't hurt me."

"But you do know."

"Not yet. Not really. And I'm going to stop this before I find out for sure."

TEN

By THURSDAY THE ACCIDENT was old news. The sensation of the fall had been replaced in the headlines and on television by the storm that had crippled the city. Eighteen inches of snow had fallen Wednesday, and by Thursday afternoon the official weather-bureau count had the figures at thirty-six inches. The storm had literally buried the city, as well as its occupants' memory of Joseph Turner. The phone calls to his tiny apartment diminished, then stopped.

His decision to put the experiences of the last few days behind him gave Joseph an enormous sense of freedom. For the first time since the fall, he had time to register the fact of his survival and to experience the joy of being alive and unhurt. Tomorrow he would be back up in the sky connecting beams, and life would blessedly return to normal. There was only one problem he hadn't yet taken care of, but he'd work that one out with Sammy tonight. This afternoon he wanted to play.

He made his way through the snow to the Boys' Club and found Leon Asher supervising a young crew of snow-shovelers pressed into duty on the sidewalk.

"Joey!" one of them yelled when they spotted him. Dropped shovels flew so fast that Asher had to dodge out of the way. "Joey!" "Joey!" The boys mobbed him, punching at his arms and dragging him by the sleeves into the building.

"Hey, you guys, cool it!" he said, laughing.

"You OK, Joey?"

"Tell us what happened!"

"Wait a minute!" Joseph extricated himself and tousled a few heads. "OK, OK. I fell and I'm OK. Lucky Turner."

"Well, what was it like?" A freckle-faced ten-year-old pressed in closer.

"Come on, you guys, give me a break. I'll tell you about it later."

There was a chorus of "Aaw, Joey—" but he broke it off. "Anybody want to go skating?"

"Yeah, me!"

"I've got to go home."

"Not today."

"I want to go!"

"Me, too!"

"OK, kids, come on." On the way out, Joseph stopped at the door where Leon Asher waited.

"You all right, Joey?"

"Yeah, terrific. Thanks. Did a new kid come by yesterday or today? Name's Leroy."

"You mean Abdul. Came in this morning. Stood around awhile and then edged up to the subject of reading. He's coming again tomorrow. Funny kid. Special kid, I think."

"They're all special. See you."

The boys tugged him out and they all hopped a bus into Manhattan.

Uptown the signs of the coming holiday season were everywhere. The streets were lined with festoons of pine boughs accented by brightly winking red and green lights. On many corners Salvation Army Santas rang their bells, hoping that the busy shoppers would pause long enough to drop a few coins in their buckets. The gaily decorated store windows tempted the passing throng with unaffordable treasures.

At Rockefeller Center they rented skates and the boys raced onto the ice. Joseph chased them around amid shouts and giggles and then sat on the sidelines to watch.

It had been almost a year since he'd been here. The memory still hurt, less frequently now but no less intensely. A slender figure floating gracefully across the ice, laughing blue eyes peeking but from beneath the caramel knit cap. There was so much joy in you, Maggie Dillon, and so much pain.

He didn't want this today and tried to let the chestnut-haired woman float into the past, then pushed her away roughly by heading back to the kids on the ice. "Grrrrr!" he roared after them.

After a few falls in the next hour, mittens and pants grew

wet, and sooner than they wanted he herded them out of the rink, up the steps to the street, and toward the subway.

The cloudy sky was almost dark by the time he deposited the boys and headed for Queens. Soon he was trudging up the stairs to the front porch of Sammy's modest brick two-story home. Long heavy icicles hung from the eaves and gutters of the steeply pitched roof, and he ran his gloved hand over one as he waited for someone to answer the doorbell. Suddenly the door flew open and he found himself smothered in one of Sammy's bear hugs.

"Damn, I been worried about you!" he bellowed. "Are you all right?"

"Sure, I'm fine, except if I hear that question one more time I'm gonna throw up," Joseph answered through the hug.

"I ought to punch you out," Sammy groused as he danced Joseph down the front steps and tumbled him into the knee-deep snow covering the front yard. "I've been trying to call you for days, ya fuck!"

"Samuel!" Rosa yelled as she stood in the doorway, hands on her hips, laughing at the sight of the two grown men trying to bury each other in the snow. "Get in here, both of you, before you catch pneumonia."

They both sat up and Sammy laughed. "Us? You got to be kidding. Nothing can hurt us, right, Joey?"

"Right!"

"Wrong. In the house, or you'll be wearing the lasagna."

As they reached the door Rosa put her hands on Joseph's shoulders, stopping him. Tears shone in her eyes above her smile and she spoke very softly. "Joey. What you did—"

He pulled her close and hugged her.

"Go, wash up for dinner, you two," she said, pulling away and shoving them into the house.

Sammy's place felt more like a home to Joseph than anywhere he'd ever lived. It was the home he didn't remember from childhood, warm, comfortable, always smelling of something good in the kitchen. He felt especially grateful for it tonight, and when he'd finished washing up he settled himself into the living room. Sammy found him sitting before the fireplace in his favorite old brown-Naugahyde chair. The chair wrapped itself around him and he was nestled into it as if he'd grown there.

Sammy was quiet now. He walked to the fire and stirred it, then stood against the white mantel, which held knick-knacks and memorabilia collected over the twenty years of his marriage.

"Well, Joey," he said, "what's been happening? I've been worried. I called and called."

"Sorry, Sam. I had to stop answering the phone. Too many reporters. And then a lot of other weird things've been happening, and I've been trying to sort them all out."

"Anything you want to talk about?"

"No. What I want is to forget it all. And get back to work. You been back up?" It was a question that held much more than his casual voice betrayed, and both men knew it.

"How about if we talk about it after dinner?" Sammy said, heading for the kitchen. "Rosa!"

"Come on, both of you, dinner's ready."

Joseph followed Sammy into the kitchen to the small table clothed in blue and white checks and laden with pasta, bread, salad, and wine. Rosa piled the food on their plates and Sammy poured the Chianti, taking immense pleasure in the simple, comfortable normalcy of their routine.

"Everybody's been by since the accident," Sammy said, setting the bottle down. "All the guys. They went to your place too but didn't find you. Soukup came by twice. He feels shitty."

"I'm sorry he does. Did they ever find out what happened?"

"Oil was gone. Oil pan had a hole ripped in it the size of a quarter. They figure it must have happened when they jumped the crane up Saturday."

They ate in silence for a while, the memory of the accident making them somber.

"Rosa, this is delicious," Joseph said, pulling them out of their gloom and back to the present. "Hey, I saw you guys on TV. Did they bother you much?"

"Rosa finally locked the door on them."

"You bet I did. They come around here poking and snooping."

"They didn't want to tangle with Rosa, I bet," Joseph winked at her. He stopped eating and looked at them more seriously. "I saw what you were trying to do on TV . . . to keep them off of me. Thanks."

"We'd have done more if we could," Rosa answered.

Sammy refilled their glasses. He was still solemn. "I've been thinking a lot since the accident."

"Yeah," Joseph nodded.

"I been asking myself a lot of questions, questions I'd never thought much about before. In all those years up top, Joey, I never came so close to dying. Oh, I came near losing an arm a time or two, but nothing worse than that. Monday I really thought I was gonna be dead. And for a while I thought you were dead. Since then, things have seemed a lot more important to me." He reached over to Rosa, who sat picking her food, and touched her hair. "I love this woman."

Rosa looked at him lovingly and then turned her gentle dark eyes to Joseph. "Sammy's been going to church every morning, Joey. He lights candles and prays for you."

There was something in what they were saying beyond the words, but Joseph didn't want to press. They were building up to it and it would come out soon enough. He stood up and cleaned the plates from the table, then sat back down and waited.

"Joey," Sammy finally said, "I can't risk leaving Rosa alone. I can't work up there with you anymore."

Joseph felt his stomach begin churning and his breath shorten. "Sammy—are you sure?"

"What would Rosa do without me, Joey? And how can she live worrying now every day? Besides," he said, more firmly now, "it's time. I'm too old for it. You know most guys stop long before my age. I'm dangerous to work with."

"That part's not true, Sammy. You're still better than any of us."

"No. It's not fair to either of you. I'm through. So that's that. It's over." He stood up and headed out of the kitchen.

Joseph sat still watching Rosa, whose eyes followed Sammy out of the room. She turned back and lowered her head.

"Rosa?" he said, his voice a whisper. "What's this about?"

Her voice came back quiet and very sad. "It's not me, Joey. It's him. He's afraid. He's had nightmares every night, about the building, about the fall, about dying. He doesn't want me to know. But he doesn't think he can go back up. He's afraid to try. He's scared, Joey, really scared."

"So am I."

"But you're going back up?"

"I have to. It's my life. But I'm not sure I can do it alone."

"Joey, take him with you. Make him go. It's his life too. He's fooling himself, thinking he wants to quit. But he can't fool me. I'm his wife. I know him. If he doesn't go back up there, he'll never be the same. No good for himself and no good for me. Take him. Show him he can still do it."

"If I do, it'll be as much for me as for him, Rosa."

She smiled sadly and reached her hand to him, touching his as he rose.

In the living room Sammy sat in his chair watching the fire devour the wood. Joseph threw a new log onto the fire. The crackling orange and yellow flames swept over it. He sat on the couch and the two men silently watched the fire consume the log. Joseph turned to Sammy.

"Sam, I once met a man, an old man, in the Bronx. He lives on my block. A few years ago while he was crossing the street he got hit by a taxi. He wasn't hurt. But he never tried to cross any street ever again. Now he walks round and round that one measly block, a prisoner of his own fear."

Sammy turned and looked at him, but said nothing.

"I don't want to end up like that old man, Sam."

"Why would you?" Sammy asked, puzzled.

"Because I'm scared. I don't know if I'll ever have the nerve to go back up."

"Oh, sure you will, Joey. I know you."

"That's funny."

"What?"

"I believe the same about you, Sam."

"I can't go up there again because of why I told you. Rosa—"

"Sam, I want my old life back. Up there. With you. I want it more than anything. I came here tonight to ask you to help me go back up there and get it."

Sammy didn't answer but instead bit at the skin on his upper lip and turned back toward the fire.

Rosa leaned against the kitchen door jamb watching the

two men she loved. Then she walked to Sammy and knelt by his chair and put her hand on his. "Whatever you do, I'm with you, Sam. But Joey needs you now. I hope you go."

Sammy got up and turned to Joseph. "If I'm going to do it, I've got to do it right now. So get your coat."

ELEVEN

It was ten after nine when Sammy parked his Chevy just past the gates to the construction site. The building's upper floors lit the night like a lodestar. The small night crew worked under the illumination of giant klieg lights, jumping the giant derrick crane. The manlift had been raised to the twenty-fourth floor.

Joseph and Sammy picked up hard hats and silently walked toward the wire-mesh cage elevator. Sweet looked as if he was going to throw up; then it passed. But he appeared ashen. "Maybe we ought to wait till tomorrow. They're busy up there tonight."

"It'll be OK, Sam," Joseph said. "We're going to do it together."

"I know."

They reached the outer cage door and waited for its descent. The elevator reached ground level with a clunk. Sammy recoiled from it. The cage doors slid open and the operator looked at them curiously. "You on the crew? I don't remember seeing either of you before."

"Day crew," said Joseph, surprised at the calm in his own voice. "My name's Turner and this is Sweet."

The operator's mouth dropped for just a second as he stared wide-eyed at the two men. "You're the guys who . . . ?"

"Yeah, that's us," Sammy said, glowering at him.

Joseph touched Sammy on the shoulder and spoke to the operator. "We'd like to go up top."

"Sure . . . sure."

Joseph stepped into the cage. Sammy followed, crossed himself, and closed the doors.

They rode past twenty floors in strained silence. The operator's eyes darted nervously from one man to the other, and his hand rested on the control buttons as if he expected them to change their minds.

"How you doing, Sam?" Joseph's voice was shaky now. He had knots in the back of his neck and his fingernails cut half-moons in the palms of his hands.

Afraid to look out through the snow flurries at the city, Sammy had faced into the building, staring, ever since they left the ground. "I don't know if I can do it."

"Me either, Sam."

Sweet whirled around and glared at his partner; his eyes were hostile. "I don't believe you! I think you're lying to me!"

Joseph grabbed Sammy's shoulders and looked him square in the face. "I've never lied to you and I don't plan to start now. I am scared!"

Sammy shrugged and swallowed hard. "Sorry."

"It's all right. We're going to do it together, or not at all. Which is it?"

There was a long silence. Finally Sammy said, "Together."

The elevator passed the twentieth floor and continued to twenty-two. The floor was flooded with light; the crane was gone. A man from the jumping crew was waiting for the lift. It stopped. The operator opened the door and whispered something to the man. He nodded and waved them on. Twenty-three . . . they heard the shouts of the men working with the crane. Twenty-four. The lift slowed and stopped. Joseph reached past Sammy and slid the door open. Sammy once again made the sign of the cross and they stepped onto the steel decking. The men surrounding the derrick had grown quiet, watchful. They'd gotten the word.

Joseph spoke to Sammy out of the corner of his mouth. "Let's go up one."

Sammy nodded. They walked to the gang ladder and climbed to twenty-five. As they neared the side of the building facing Fiftieth Street, Sammy suddenly stopped. "Joey, I can't do it."

Joseph had been thinking the same thing. His knees felt weak. He turned and looked at Sammy, now trembling with fear. "Sammy," said Joseph sternly. "This is no time to freeze on me." The words were as much for him as Sammy.

"I can't help it, Joey."

"You can help it! Breathe! Deep! That's better. Now concentrate on what you're doing. We're going up the columns."

The giant curly-headed man wiped the nervous sweat from his forehead. "OK, Joey. I'm OK. I'll take this one." Sammy walked determinedly toward the corner H beam.

Joseph stood motionless, watched him monkey slowly up the first few feet of the beam, then walked to the column thirty feet across from Sammy's and began his own ascent, stopping every few feet to calm his jittery nerves. His confidence began to return, and by the time he'd settled onto the first flange the fear was gone. He looked over at Sammy, who waved and yelled, "Hey, what took you so long?"

Joseph laughed then looked out over the city. It was a beautiful sight. Tears stung his eyes. Everything was going to be okay. Life was back to normal. He brushed away the tears and called back to his friend. "Tell 'em, Sam!"

"Right!" Sammy cupped his hands over his mouth yelling, "We're Sweet and Turner! The best damn connectors in the world!"

"Let's go home, Sam!"

"Right!"

As they stepped off the gang ladder onto twenty-four the night crew greeted them with applause. After much back-slapping and congratulations, Joseph and Sammy finally extricated themselves from their well-wishers and headed down from the building. The night-crew supervisor was standing in the open door to the construction trailer when the duo passed. Sammy turned to him and smiled. "Will ya leave a message for Frankie Corollo that Turner and Sweet'll be to work in the morning?"

"You bet I will!" The supervisor smiled as they headed out the gates.

"We did it, huh, Joey?"

"We sure did, Sam."

When they reached the car Joseph looked across the roof at Sammy. "Drop me at my place?"

"Why don't you stay with us tonight?" Sammy slid onto the seat, closed the door, and slipped the key into the ignition.

"Nope, you spend the rest of the evening with Rosa," Joseph said, getting in. "I need a good night's sleep."

"OK, suit yourself! Boy, Joey, do I feel great," said Sammy, pulling from the curb. The Chevy cut through the traffic on Madison Avenue. Sammy slapped Joseph's knee. "I feel like I did when I was ten years old and found my first *Playboy*."

"I know what you mean. I'm so ready to get back up there I can hardly wait for tomorrow."

"There's no going back, Joey. Only forward. From now on."

"You said it . . . Hey, what's that?"

They had turned onto 106th Street. In front of them was a police barricade. In the middle of the next block a five-story building was engulfed in flames.

"Damn, will ya look at that!" exclaimed Sammy as he slowed to turn left at the barricade.

Joseph didn't answer. He had opened his door and was getting out of the moving car.

"Hey! Where the hell ya goin'?" Sammy said.

Joseph was already around the barricade and pushing his way through a crowd the police were having a difficult time controlling.

Sammy wheeled to the curb, slammed the Chevy into park, and bolted after his friend. "What the hell—" he said to no one in particular. Turner was pushing his way up to a television news crew that was intently watching eight fire companies, including two hook-and-ladder units, battle the holocaust.

Sammy maneuvered next to Joseph. "What the hell are you doin', Joey? Ya scared the hell outta me when ya jumped from the car that way."

Joseph took his gaze from the fire long enough to say, "I don't know, I don't know yet." His eyes returned immediately to the building. The fire leaped up the outside walls through windows blown out by the intense heat.

Beside them, a TV newsman stepped out in front of his camera. The black reporter was tall and slender with a high-boned face capped with a short-cropped natural. "OK, Johnny, tell me when we have speed." The cameraman nodded while the newsman gently patted down the right side of his windblown hair. When the camera operator cued him, the reporter cleared his throat twice, brought the microphone up, and began: "This is Jackson Bullock, Eyewitness News in Manhattan. We've spoken with Fire Captain Michael Munroe, who's informed us that this tragic blaze was accidentally started by a grease fire on the second floor. But the cause is not the real story here tonight. At this moment two heroic members of the New York City Fire Department are somewhere inside that inferno trying desperately to bring two children trapped on the fourth floor out to safety. They're battling the clock; during the evacuation the fire department discovered a cache of weapons and explosives hidden in the basement of the building. With the fire raging out of control there is little doubt that the building will explode. The only question is . . . when?"

Behind the reporter, a weary-looking fire captain motioned to a young police lieutenant. "Get those people back." He indicated the crowds at either end of the street. The lieutenant headed off, while Munroe spoke into his bullhorn. "All units, except pumper 751, pull out to the ends of the street." He lowered the bullhorn and stared at the building. "Damn! Where are those guys?" he wondered aloud. "They've got to get out soon!"

Six uniformed policemen moved toward the crowd where Joseph and Sammy stood. "All right, move it back," yelled an officer as the crowd reluctantly inched backward.

"We're staying here a little longer," said Jackson Bullock. "No, you're not."

Joseph saw two policemen escorting a young couple through the crowd. Tears streamed down the man's face, and the woman screamed hysterically. "My babies, my babies! Please save my babies!"

She tried to wrench away from an officer's viselike grip. He tried in vain to calm her. "They're doin' all they can to save them, lady."

Bullock frantically pointed toward the front door of the brownstone. His cameraman zoomed in and caught two firemen dressed in white asbestos suits and wearing oxygen units stumble through the wall of flames and down the front steps. Joseph saw the smoke rising from their suits as a fireman altered the flow of his hose and turned it on them. He also saw that they weren't carrying the children. The fire captain and several other firemen grabbed the rescue team, abandoned the pumper, and the group headed down the street toward the crowd where Joseph and Sammy stood.

"Damn," said Sammy, looking from the holocaust to Joseph, who stood as if in a daze, eyes riveted on the burning brownstone.

"Captain Munroe," said Bullock as the group of firemen approached. The fire captain stopped in front of the camera next to the reporter and removed his helmet. "My men couldn't reach the fourth floor. The heat was much too intense." He wiped his face and continued. "They were running out of oxygen; it was too damn hot! Those kids wouldn't be able to breathe in there."

The distraught mother screamed and crumpled to the ground. Joseph heard them but stared straight ahead, feeling oddly apart from the people clustered around him. He felt alone in an invisible tunnel connecting him with the burning building.

Suddenly he bolted forward past a policeman, running full out toward the burning inferno.

"Stop that man!" screamed Munroe, and two firemen took up the chase.

"Stay on him, Johnny!" yelled Bullock to his cameraman. A scream went up in the crowd as Joseph beat the two pursuing firemen to the building and ran up the steps, disappearing through a wall of flames.

"Oh, Joey!" Sammy screamed, and buried his head in his hands.

"Do you know him?" asked a braided-haired teenage girl standing next to Sweet.

Bullock saw Sammy lift his head and nod, "Yes." The reporter grabbed the ironworker and pulled him out of the crowd in front of the camera.

"What's his name?" asked the interviewer eagerly.

Stunned, Sammy mumbled softly, "Joseph, Joseph Turner." The big man began to break down and cry.

"I know that name! I know that name!" exclaimed Bullock, straining to remember. "He fell off a building Monday, didn't he?"

Sammy nodded. Suddenly there was a loud crash; the left

side of the burning roof collapsed one floor. "Oh, my God . . . Oh, my God!"

Captain Munroe shook his head and turned away from the building and lives he couldn't save.

"Is there any chance?" Bullock asked of Munroe.

The captain shook his head. "None! It's got to be at least three thousand degrees in there."

Inside the building a strange cool wind swirled around Joseph as he ran up the burning third-floor stairs. The fire crackled and raged everywhere around him. The railing collapsed as he reached the fourth floor. The walls lining the hallway were buckled under the weight of the fallen roof and the intense heat. Joseph screamed out, "Where are you?" There was no answer and he ran down the hall, kicking open apartment doors as he went, met by flames that reached out but couldn't touch Joseph Turner. Finally he found the right door.

The two unconscious children, separated from him by a wall of flames, were huddled together on the floor next to a broken window. The wall of flames parted as Joseph walked to them and snatched one in each arm. Both were severely burned. Whirling around, he ran from the room.

Outside, Jackson Bullock spoke into the camera. "It's a tragic scene indeed. Three lives lost. Two children, tenants unable to get out of the building, and a crazed onlooker, Joseph Turner, who ran into that burning deathtrap, and who only three days ago fell twenty-four stories and miraculously survived." Suddenly an astonished Bullock gasped, "My God, there he is!"

A cry went up in the crowd as they saw Joseph, holding the two children, emerge from the flaming doorway and run down the front steps.

Munroe was lost in amazement. "I don't believe it! It's impossible!"

Joseph reached the sidewalk as the first thunderous explosion erupted behind him, severing the front wall. The ironworker dashed into the street as an orange mushroom flame reached high into the night's darkness, and the five-story wall crashed down onto parked cars and pumper 751. The vehicles were demolished.

Joseph ran as behind him erupted three more deafening explosions. Shielding the unconscious children from the flying debris, he finally reached two firemen and handed over the children. A cheer rose behind Sammy as he stood, shocked, eyes wide and mouth open.

"It's a miracle!" cried the braided-haired teenager.

When Bullock had gotten a close look at the children and Joseph, he loudly pronounced, "They're not burned. None of them are burned. It's impossible!"

Joseph's head snapped around and looked at the children. The burns had disappeared.

Afraid and confused, he bolted past the police, firemen, Bullock, and Sammy and waded into the throng of curious onlookers. The crowd reached out to touch him as he ran. Sammy ran after him and caught his arm. Joseph turned, his face distorted in fear. "I've got to get away, Sammy! Away! Let me go!" He broke from Sammy's grasp and disappeared around the corner into the night.

Oh, God, oh, God, help me . . . the words screamed through Joseph's mind as he ran. His body ached, his lungs begged him to stop and rest, but he couldn't. Escape . . . escape. Like a hunted animal he pumped the cold night air in and out of his body as he darted through the streets. People stared as he raced by, and the more they looked, the faster he ran.

At the corner of Forty-First Street and Eighth Avenue he felt his legs buckle and he stopped, leaning against a building, trying to catch his heaving breath. He was wet with sweat and he felt sick. What had made him run into that building? Why did he do it? The crowd, the television cameras, the flames swam in front of him. How could he let himself slip back into this horror? He knew: the children, Joseph, the children.

So now there was no more question. No mistake. No illusion. It was real, it was happening, this was it.

When he raised his head he was looking at a world of chrome and glass. Still shaking, he walked slowly into the Port Authority Bus Terminal.

At 11:00 Jackson Bullock could hear the Eyewitness News anchorman's rundown of the day's top stories over the

PA in the network's hallway. Clutching two metal cans under his arm, he darted down a connecting corridor, skidded to a stop in front of a door marked "Telecine," and pounded loudly.

A large-busted, bespectacled, red-haired girl snapped open the door. "Not so loud!"

Bullock shoved the two cylindrical cans into her reluctant arms. "I want this on a chain right now! I'll cue you to roll it!"

"Yes, sir," said the projectionist, as the harried reporter ran off in the direction of Studio Four.

When fatherly Harry Crane saw Bullock rush through the padded studio door, weave his way between cameras continuously giving the emergency cut signal, and sit at the field commentator's desk still wearing his overcoat, the anchorman figured that the President had been shot. The balding veteran newsman quickly wrapped up the story on the Middle East peace initiative and turned the program over to his colleague.

The red light on camera three came on. It stared directly at the reporter. "Good evening, ladies and gentlemen, I'm Jackson Bullock. As you recall, a New Yorker named Joseph Turner fell twenty-four stories from a building he was working on Monday morning, and not only survived, but miraculously was unhurt. This evening I saw Joseph Turner perform a second miracle as he rescued two children from a fiery holocaust. You can draw your own conclusions from the film."

The footage ran. Jackson Bullock had nothing to say.

By the time the film had ended, phones began ringing all over the city. People couldn't wait to tell their friends about "The Iron Man of Manhattan," a phrase proudly coined by Jackson Bullock on Eyewitness News.

TWELVE

On Greenwich Villages' Christopher Street in his Art-Deco adorned duplex, Jerry Matthews looked at his pregnant wife's belly mounding under the blanket. She had had a rough day and he was glad to see her sleeping so peacefully. The phone rang and he grabbed for it before the second ring. "Yes, who is it?" he whispered.

His eyes widened as he heard Carson's voice blare over the line. "Are you asleep?"

"Me? No, no, no. I, uh, never sleep, chief."

"Well, wake up, 'cause we've been scooped!"

"By who?"

"Whom."

"Whom."

"ABC."

"On what?"

"On your friend Turner."

"What are you talking about?" asked the bewildered young reporter.

"The fire tonight!" yelled the news editor loud enough to cause Sherry to stir. "Your friend ran into a fire tonight, saved two kids, wasn't burned, and ABC, those farts, got it on film! It's the hottest story since Watergate! I'll bet the phones haven't stopped ringing at ABC! They'll win an Emmy!!"

"Yes, sir."

"What?"

"I mean, no, sir. I mean, what do you want me to do?"

"Find him! And get the one thing those bastards at Eyewitness didn't get."

"What's that?" he said, afraid to hear the answer.

"An interview, an exclusive interview!"

85

"Well, I don't know. Joseph's kind of a funny guy. You know what I mean?" In his mind Jerry saw Carson's face flushed with anger. He knew from the tone in the chief's voice that he was holding him responsible. He looked at Sherry, then, reluctantly, "Yes, sir, I'll get right on it."

"Fine," exclaimed Carson's voice over the line. The loud click reverberated in Jerry's ear as his boss hung up.

Jerry slammed the receiver into its cradle, then stared at the phone. He hated this job, he hated Carson, he hated himself for what he was going to do. After a few seething moments he yelled, "Damn you" at all three, and stormed out of bed into the adjoining bathroom.

When he flicked on the light, Sherry eased herself out of the bed. "Honey?"

"It's Carson and he wants me on a story about Joseph Turner."

"You like him."

"Yeah." He pulled her as close as he could get her.

"You'd better get going." She gently moved him away.

"Aw, honey . . ."

"OK, then. Shall I call Carson and tell him you'll be late?"

"See you later," he said.

Uptown, Louise Ryan sat engulfed in the finale of a 1950s musical revival. A young usherette stopped next to her aisle seat and whispered in the reporter's ear. Louise quietly made her way to the lobby and called her office. In a moment she hung up and hailed a taxi. "Take me to Four-Thirty-Three Devon Street in the Bronx."

For the fourth time since he'd gone to bed, Abe Curlin was awakened to insistent pounding on his door. "Who's there?" yelled the irate superintendent as he swung out of bed, grabbing the Ernie Banks–autographed Louisville Slugger that rested against the wall. There was no response, just more knocking. "I said who's there? I got a baseball bat in here!"

"It's me, Abe, it's Sammy Sweet. Open up," boomed the heavy voice.

"OK, OK, I'm comin'." Curlin clumsily unfastened the four safety locks and removed the iron bar that braced the door closed. "Dammit," he said, jostling the loosely hinged door open. "What's going on, Sweet?"

"Have you seen Joey?"

"What's everybody lookin' for Turner for? There's been newspeople all over the place again. What'd he do now? Fall off another building? Dammit, I need to get some sleep."

"Have you seen him?" asked Sweet more insistently.

"No. Are you gonna tell me what's goin' on?"

"It's a long story, Abe. Listen, you got a passkey, right?" The burly pajama-clad man nodded.

"I want you to let me inside Joey's. I'm going to wait for him there."

"Shit," whined Curlin. "I don't want to go back up those stairs tonight, Sweet." Curlin reached into the pocket of the gray work pants hanging on the footpost of the bed, fished out a set of keys, and tossed them to Sweet. "Please, you go, bring the keys back in the mornin'."

"Thanks," Sweet said, crossing the room and heading out the door.

Sweet sat in Joseph's apartment in front of the television, pretending to himself he was watching. He had called Rosa but she had heard nothing. Where would Joey go? Sammy racked his brain but hadn't a clue.

When Jerry Matthews reached Joseph's brownstone, he hurried up the stairs and knocked lightly on the door of 3B. Sammy flung the door open. Matthews's heart sank.

"What do you want?" Sweet demanded loudly.

"Oh, well, uh, is Mr. Turner here? I thought maybe I, uh, could talk to him for a minute?"

"You can't," said Sweet. His eyes burrowed deep into the scared reporter.

"Why don't you let him decide?"

"He ain't here."

"You know where he is?"

"You think I'd tell you if I did? He don't need no reporters."

"Listen Mr.—"

"Sweet. Sammy Sweet."

"Mr. Sweet, it's true I'm here for a story, but it's my asshole boss. I want to get the story, but I want to help Turner, too. You've got to believe that, because it's the truth." The ironworker's glaring eyes looked calmer. "You don't know where he is?"

"No. I'm lookin' myself."

"Maybe I can help you find him."

Sammy sighed heavily in resignation. This guy wasn't gonna let go. "Come in," he muttered, stepping aside.

Matthews crossed the room and sat on the edge of the bed as Sweet closed the door and leaned against it. "Do you have any idea where he might be?"

Sammy shook his head.

"You know he rescued two kids in a fire tonight?"

Sweet nodded, but remained silent.

"Talk to me, dammit," Matthews said quietly. "I'm not going to print it. It's off the record!"

Sweet licked his lips and ran a massive hand through his hair. Pacing the floor, he said, "I was there. . . . The last time I saw him he came out of the fire and started runnin' through the streets. I tried to keep up with him but . . ."

A knock at the door interrupted him. They looked at each other, and Sammy walked over and opened it.

"Oh, Jesus," Matthews said.

"Is Joseph here?" the woman asked.

"Who are you?" questioned Sweet.

"I'm Louise Ryan, a friend of Joseph's, Mr. Sweet," she said, trying to put him at ease.

Matthews jumped to his feet. "And she works for the *New York Times*."

"Hello, Jerry," she said, clearly not happy to see him.

"What can I do for you, lady?" asked Sweet harshly.

"First, you can get that tone out of your voice. Then you can tell me where the hell Joseph is—if you know. You want to protect him and I can understand why. So do I."

"I don't believe you," said Sweet.

"Then give me a minute to convince you. Joseph spent yesterday with me. We had a meeting with a friend of mine. And I was here," she pointed at the apartment with authority, "two nights ago when his next door neighbor got busted and a pusher got shot."

Sammy wrinkled his brow quizzically. "I don't know what the hell you're talking about, lady."

"Why don't you ask Joseph?"

Sammy didn't answer but stood shifting his weight from side to side.

"So you don't know where he is," she said, watching for a sign of contradiction. "Then ask the super—what's his name, Curlin? He saw me with Joseph. After you've satisfied yourself we can go about the work we've got ahead of us."

"What work's that, Ryan?" Matthews queried, hands on hips.

"The business of finding him, and helping him if he needs it. Now are you going to let me come in or not?"

"I think it's OK, Mr. Sweet," said Matthews, never taking his eyes off Louise. "I know her. She's a tough reporter, but she doesn't lie."

Sammy looked at Matthews and gave a slight shrug.

"Thank you," Louise said. "May I come in now?"

She walked past him and sat down at the kitchen table. "Now, do you have any idea where he might be?"

Before Sammy could answer, Matthews blurted, "Wait a minute. Before we say anything why don't you tell us what Joseph was doing spending the day with you?"

Louise debated with herself for a few moments but finally gave in. She wouldn't get their help any other way. She told them all that had happened with the pusher and with Bridger. When she had finished they were stunned.

Sweet paced back and forth the five strides from wall to wall. Finally he stopped. "This is all crazy. Joseph's got to be scared to death."

The phone rang and all three stared at it, no one making a move to answer.

Finally Louise picked it up. "Hello." There was a long pause as she listened to the voice of Jackson Bullock apologizing for calling so late, and requesting to speak to Turner. "One moment, please," said Louise, capping her right hand over the mouthpiece. "It's the reporter from ABC who shot the footage tonight. He wants to talk to Joseph."

"What are we going to do?" asked Sammy.

"We're going to get these guys off him. Jerry, you tell him you're his doctor, that you're checking him into a hospital for some rest, some peace and quiet, and refuse to give him the name of the hospital," said Louise, holding out the receiver to her reluctant conspirator.

"What name should I use?"

"Make one up, and be convincing!"

Matthews drew a deep breath, took the phone, and said loudly, "Thank you, nurse . . . Hello." There was a short pause. "No, this isn't Mr. Turner. I'm Mr. Turner's doctor. Doctor Robert Dean Carruthers. No, I'm not issuing any statements at this time. I'm having Mr. Turner admitted to a hospital for tests and recuperation. This has been a great strain on my patient."

Sammy and Louise smiled broadly at the authority in the young reporter's voice.

"No, I'm not going to issue the name of the hospital. My patient needs rest. In a few days, if he so desires, he'll hold a press conference. But I believe he'll probably speak with two of his dearest friends first, Louise Ryan of the *Times* and Jerry Matthews of WNBC. No, I'm terribly sorry, I've got to go now. The ambulance is ready to leave. Good night, Mr.—what's your name? Yes, that's right, Bullock." Jerry abruptly hung up. "Gotcha!" he said, staring at the phone.

They all laughed. Louise got up from the chair, walked to the window, and turned back to Sweet. "Do you have any idea where he might have gone? A friend's place, maybe?"

"Nope. He yelled at me that he had to get away."

"From the city?"

"I don't know."

"Well, then we've got our work cut out for us."

"How the hell are we going to find him?" asked Matthews.

"Same way you and I work every day, Jerry," she said authoritatively. "You've got sources and so do I, and we're going to use 'em. We'll check Kennedy, La Guardia, Grand Central, Port Authority, the cab companies. We'll find him; someone has to have seen him. I've got some stills of Joseph in the car; we can show those."

"What about me?" Sammy asked. Somehow he had to keep these reporters from getting to Joey first.

"Check with his friends . . . any place you think he might go. Then go home. Maybe he'll call you there. He'd surely never think of trying to get you here. We'll leave a note for him and we'll use your place as a command post. Both Jerry and I'll keep checking in with you."

"Give me your word you'll call me first if you find anything."

"You'll be the first to know," Matthews said. "Where do you want me to start, Lou?"

"Wherever you like. I can take the airports; I've got access at both Kennedy and La Guardia. I can use their computers, records, anything."

"OK, I'll take Yellow and Checker cabs, and Port Authority."

"Fine. Then I'll cover Grand Central. Let's get going."

Sammy gave the reporters his phone number and within five minutes the trio left the Devon Street apartment. As his car moved through the now-quiet streets, Sammy found himself half hoping Matthews and Ryan would strike out. If anyone was going to find Joseph, he should be the one. If only he could know his friend was at least safe. Who would Joseph go to in trouble? He strained for a name and got a face: Maggie Dillon. No, Joseph wouldn't go to her; he wouldn't even know how to find her. She was probably in Miami this time of year, but Joseph hadn't been in touch with her for months and she never stayed anywhere for long. His eyes searched the sidewalks as he drove, wishing his friend would magically appear. He didn't, and Sammy headed home to Queens.

When Louise arrived at Kennedy she was surprised to find no one in the airport public relations office—until she remembered that it was 2:00 A.M. At a pay phone she called the head of the department at his home. His objections to coming to the airport at that hour were overcome by a reminder of an old favor he owed her. Calling in favors for Joseph Turner was getting to be a habit, she thought. When the department head arrived she quickly obtained access to the airline computers and within half an hour was able to verify that Joseph Turner hadn't flown out of Kennedy that night. Ten minutes later she was driving through heavily falling snow toward La Guardia.

Jerry Matthews had put his contacts at the cab companies

to work with press photos of Turner and left them to check out his description with the drivers, starting with those who had been in the neighborhood where Sweet said he lost him. By 3:30 Matthews was showing Turner's picture to a ticket agent at Port Authority.

"Maybe, maybe not. It could be but I just can't be sure," the young man said without interest.

"Take a good look. It's really important," Jerry said, holding the photo out again.

The agent looked at it and shook his head. "Man, I don't know. I sold a ticket to a guy at the beginning of my shift who looked a little bit like this, but . . ." He tapped the picture lightly with his index finger, pressed his lips tightly together, and shook his head once again. "Nope, just can't be sure."

"Where'd the guy buy a ticket to?" asked Matthews.

"Oh, I'm sorry, but we've got regulations. We're not allowed to give that information out. It's against company policy." He smiled at Matthews. "Sorry."

Matthews reached into his pocket and produced a ten-dollar bill which he slid across the caged counter. "Where?"

The agent inched his fingers toward the bill while looking around to see if his supervisor had witnessed the move. "Boston."

"Thank you," Matthews said, snapping back the bill, to the astonishment of the ticket agent, and rushing to a phone booth.

When Matthews's call came, Sammy and Rosa were sitting in the kitchen silently drinking their third pot of coffee. Sammy jumped for the phone. "Maybe it's Joey! Hello . . . Oh, Matthews. What? It can't be. Just a minute . . ." He covered the receiver and looked at Rosa. "Rosa, this reporter says a ticket agent at Port Authority thinks Joseph went out on a bus to Boston tonight."

"Boston?"

"I don't want this guy following Joseph all over the place. I've gotta tell him something."

He turned back and spoke into the phone. "No, Matthews, he was wrong. Joseph just called us a few minutes ago . . . Yeah, he's in New York . . . No, he doesn't want anyone to know. Some hotel . . . Okay. Keep in touch." Sammy hung up the phone.

"Sammy . . ." Rosa began accusingly.

"We gotta protect him from those vultures, Rosa." He smiled slightly. "That kid'll be busy for weeks checking every hotel in New York."

"I guess you're right. Sammy, does Joseph know anyone in Boston?"

"I don't think so. Wait. Not in Boston, but you've gotta go there to get to Provincetown."

"John Stanton!"

"Sure—why didn't we think of him? I'll call him, Rosa, tell him we think Joseph's coming there and ask him just to call us when he gets there safe. Then let's get some sleep."

When Louise Ryan called the Sweets from Grand Central she listened very carefully to Sammy's story. He wasn't telling the truth. He obviously knew something, and she obviously wouldn't get it out of him. She tried anyway.

"Sammy, I haven't spent the night looking for Joseph for a story. He's going to need some help."

"He says he's fine. Joey can take care of himself."

"You really don't understand. Before tonight, Joseph Turner was a curiosity; his news value dropped to zero in two days. That won't happen again. What's happening to him is too big. A lot of people are going to be after him for a lot of things. You can't imagine the kind of exploitation he's going to be up against. He—"

"I don't know where he is."

"You don't know what you're doing." She slammed the phone down hard. These ironworkers were the most stubbornly naïve men she had ever met.

THIRTEEN

FROM THE WINDOW table of a second-floor restaurant in the center of Munich, Emil Rothstein stared out the thick curved glass at the sleet that unmercifully attacked the Königsplatz. The bespectacled bulldog of a man looked at his watch and sighed. Two o'clock. She should be here by now, Rothstein thought. I'm positive we said the Hotel Königshof.

He began to pick nervously at the loose button on the coatsleeve of his gray pinstripe suit, and his mind inched back to this morning's conference in East Berlin. The communists would probably take his findings with their usual little regard. So often these days his efforts had led to disappointments.

"Papa?"

He turned to the young woman who stood beside him, rose, embraced her, held out her chair. "You look lovely."

"You look tired."

He ordered her a cocktail and sat silently, waiting.

"You leave tomorrow for London."

He nodded.

"I wanted one more chance to try to persuade you."

He smiled. "I thought so."

"Papa, stay here with us."

"And disrupt your family! You, Karl, the children are settled together, happy. You do not need an old man to interfere in your lives."

"You would not disrupt, not interfere!"

"Darling, my home is in Rome, now."

"Rome! You're never there! You traipse around the world —we get cards from Greece, Canada, Australia, the Philippines. You need a rest! You haven't stopped working since you closed your law practice in New York. It's been almost ten years! Since then it's been one investigation after another."

"I like it. It is often exciting. My work is my life now."

"Papa," she said intensely after a moment. "Have you accomplished what you wanted?"

He sighed. "Almost. Certainly all I could reasonably have hoped for."

"Ah. It is the 'almost' that makes you tired."

"Yes. More often lately, I have felt some . . . disappointment."

"There. You see? You need some time off, time to yourself."

He nodded. "Well, perhaps you are right. A week or two might do me good. They could find someone else to—"

A dark-haired, fine-boned man had approached their table. He looked nervous.

"Luici? Hello," Rothstein said to him. "You remember my daughter—Kristina, Luici Bermano."

"I'm sorry, Emil, but I must interrupt," the black-suited man said, nodding to the woman and then quickly turning back to Rothstein. "Emil, they want you in New York tonight. Something's come up. Thomas is packing your bags and the plane is being readied."

"New York? And so quickly?"

"Emil," Luici said intensely, his voice lowering, "the code name is Nicholas—do you hear? Nicholas!" The excitement in Bermano's dark eyes was suddenly mirrored in Rothstein's.

"The dossier and profile?" Emil asked hastily.

"On their way by plane."

"You have a name?"

Bermano handed Emil a folded piece of white paper. He flipped it open and read: JOSEPH TURNER.

Rothstein closed his tired eyes as if in silent prayer. Then he opened them and spoke quickly to Luici. "I'll meet you both in the lobby in fifteen minutes. Call New York and make them aware of my arrival."

Luici wheeled on the heels of his black loafers and half-marched from the restaurant. Rothstein watched him exit then turned back to his daughter, who looked exasperated. "Papa, you're going off somewhere else?"

"I must."

"But we have just agreed—a rest for you now is so important."

"Believe me, Kristina, there is nothing so important as this."

FOURTEEN

THE BUS RUMBLED from Interstate 95 into Boston. Wearily Joseph got off and crossed through the terminal lounge to the coffee shop to wait for the connecting bus. He fought to keep his mind clear, bringing himself back again and again to one thought: Get to Provincetown. Get to John. John would help him think.

A young uniformed Army private slipped onto the stool next to him. The curly-haired youth looked at him closely. "I'd say you need about three more days," he said.

Joseph turned. "What?" he asked, confused.

"For your beard to grow out. Then nobody'll be able to recognize you."

Dammit, thought Joseph. He tried to keep his voice easy. "Do I look like someone you know?"

"It's OK. I was watching the tube in the station when you walked past in the lounge. Morning news. My name's Andy, Andy Wood." The soldier awkwardly held out his hand and Joseph shook it.

From across the counter a middle-aged woman with a road map of a face leaned over and stared at them. "Hey!" she said, pointing at Joseph, "aren't you that guy from New York? The one they been talkin' about on the TV? Sure, I seen you."

Joseph winced, but before he could answer he heard Andy Wood's voice. "No, lady, this is my brother, Bobby. He only looks like the guy on TV. People been confusin' him with that guy all morning."

The woman looked at them suspiciously and mumbled something, then finally turned her attention to her movie magazine. When he was sure she wouldn't hear he whispered, "Thanks."

Andy Wood smiled conspiratorially. "You bet, Bobby."

Joseph waited for the questions to begin, but they didn't come. Wood seemed entirely uninterested in what had happened in New York. "You catching a bus to somewhere?" was all he asked.

"To Provincetown."

"Me too, but my girl is meetin' me in Hyannis and we're driving down. Hey, you want to ride with us? It'll keep you away from your fans."

He started to say no, but he felt so tired of feeling the need to hide. "You sure?"

"It's no trouble, really."

"Let me pay the gas?"

"If you want to."

"I don't know why you're doing this. And I guess I'm feeling suspicious."

"Do I need a reason to help someone out? It doesn't look like you do."

Fifteen minutes after the bus arrived at Hyannis, Joseph was in the back seat of a 1967 Mustang behind Andy and his girl cruising toward the tip of Cape Cod.

He had never seen the Cape in the clutches of winter. There was peace for him in the old, lonely-looking frame houses of Yarmouth and Harwich, surviving winter upon winter with strength and grace. Attached to the snow-laden branches of the trees he spotted a few remaining yellow-brown leaves, small bastions of Indian summer weakening in the battle against undesired change.

No tourists enjoyed the great dunes of Eastham, the sandy coves of Wellfleet, the pine woods of Truro. The coast was locked in winter, unmercifully buried in snow.

He had let his mind drift, but nearing Provincetown he found himself rehearsing explanations to John and Bonnie. No matter how he tried it, it sounded crazy.

The sea was throwing eight-foot thunder-busters against the Provincetown shoals when the car pulled through the split-rail gates onto John Stanton's cabin-studded beach property. Most of the structures' rock chimneys stood smokeless against the gray November sky. The snow fell peacefully on him as Joseph got out of the car in front of the main house.

He thanked Andy Wood and his girl for their help and waved the young couple off.

Behind him the front door to the aged wood two-story house opened and Amy Stanton yelled at the top of her lungs. "Uncle Joseph, Uncle Joseph's here!" She raced down the stone steps as fast as her five-year-old legs could carry her.

He spun around in time to catch his snowsuited godchild in a midair leap from the third step. "How's my girl?" he said, spinning the wispy-haired angelic-faced child around.

"I saw you on TV!"

The spinning stopped. "You did?" Well, he thought, one problem solved. John already knew.

"Uh-huh. Are you going to be on again?"

"I hope not."

The massive front door opened wide as her father emerged wearing a yellow cardigan sweater and brown slacks.

"Your daddy looks more like a golfer than a minister," Joseph said, setting Amy to the ground as John took the steps two at a time to get to his friend.

"Yeah, I'm the Arnold Palmer of religion," smiled Stanton, grabbing Joseph by the shoulders. "Man, am I glad to see you."

"I guess I should have called."

"You know you didn't need to. Anyway, Sammy Sweet telephoned about an hour ago, said he was pretty sure you were headed this way. How do you feel?"

"I don't know. Numb. Where's Bonnie?"

"In town buying groceries." Stanton motioned to the lodge. "Come on, let's go in. I've got some tea on, and I'll get you some fresh clothes."

"Uncle Joseph, what's that on your face?" Amy asked, tugging at his pant leg.

He ran his hand over his face and looked at the soot on his fingers. "Dirt."

"You got whiskers, too. Don't kiss me again, OK? It hurts. You need a whisker buzzer."

"I need more than that."

"C'mon," she said, leading him by the hand into the house. "I'll show you where Daddy hides his. He'll let you use it."

He took a long time showering, letting the warm water soothe his body. Then he got out, wrapped a towel around him, and stood in front of the foggy mirror. The first clear spot opened on the glass and he watched his face emerge. He couldn't take his eyes off it. Past the black stubble and circles under his eyes, it was still Joseph Turner. Worried. Intense. But still the same man. No. Not the same. Nothing would ever be the same. The pain in acknowledging what he knew to be true rushed through him as if he'd just uncapped a pressure cooker. He pressed his hands into the mirror to stop the tears.

He heard the front door open and John's voice telling Bonnie he was here.

"Is he all right?"

"I think so. He looks exhausted. He's in the bathroom cleaning up," Stanton said in a soft voice.

"I'll heat up something to eat."

Quickly Joseph splashed some warm water on his face and toweled it dry. A knock came at the door.

"I've got some clothes. Can I come in?"

"Sure."

John handed him a shirt, slacks, and sweater. "Bonnie's home. She's whipping up some food."

"I'm just about finished. I'll be out in a minute."

Joseph had tried to keep his voice light but John saw the pain. "Joey."

His eyes blurred as he met John's look. It was full of compassion and understanding and strength. The need for his own strength melted away, and he slumped into his friend's arms.

"You're going to be all right. You're going to find your way through this."

Joseph stood back and nodded. He wanted to believe it, but the gnawing in the pit of his stomach told him he didn't.

"We'll be in the kitchen."

"Johnny . . . thanks," Joseph said as the door closed.

He shaved, slipped on the clothes, and walked from the bathroom down the hallway. He could hear voices in the kitchen, but he wasn't quite ready and he walked away from them and into the oak-paneled living room. Fire blazed in the enormous hearth. It seemed to reach out and draw him closer. He felt a sudden chill as he watched the flames feed off the giant logs. He turned away and walked to the picture windows that looked out over the Atlantic.

The normally sandy beach was buried by three feet of fresh snow. Only a few of the taller shoots of beach grass remained visible, poking their dried tops toward an invisible sun that could only lighten the thick gray mass of clouds stretching unbroken from the horizon. Serenity . . . if I stay here long enough, maybe some of it will rub off. Lost in thought, he didn't notice Amy's presence next to him until she slipped her tiny hand in his. She stood quietly by him, looking out. Silently, hand in hand, they watched the snow fall into the Atlantic and become the sea.

It was late afternoon before Joseph, John, and Bonnie sat down to talk. By then Joseph felt a million miles from New York and was already settling into the cozy warmth of his friends' family. A few hours' playing with Amy in the snow left his body tired and his mind fresh, and sitting now at the glass-topped table in the enormous kitchen sipping hot coffee, he wondered why he hadn't come here days ago.

"Amy asleep?" he asked Bonnie.

"Uh huh. You wore her out—she'll nap for another hour."

"She doesn't know it yet, but she's going to be gorgeous like her Mom."

"Oh, she knows it," John said. "They both do." He smiled at his wife, who had a model's sharp, classic features and tall, lithe body. Her dark brown eyes looked innocently back at him through unfashionably mussed strands of shiny blond hair.

"You spoil us."

"You spoil me too," Joseph said. "Both of you. You know, all the way here, I wondered how you'd take this—how you'd react to me. I should've known. You've made it so easy."

"We saw the news. We don't need to know any more, Joey, unless you want to talk about it," John said.

"That's right. We can make the whole subject taboo if you like," Bonnie added.

"It's tempting. It sure is tempting. But no. I'm at a point where I really need to talk about it." He felt his stomach tighten. "Is that OK with you?"

"Of course."

"When I walked away from that fall," he started slowly, "I felt like I had no choice but to accept the fact that it happened and go on from there. I wondered why the hell I was being given a rematch with life, but OK, I could live without knowing. The reporters were a pain in the ass but after two days I was old news. I really thought it was over."

They waited quietly for him to continue.

"Only then something happened, something else that didn't get into the papers. A kid was shot in my building. Some stupid cop did it. I heard the commotion and went in and no one was doing anything for him. His stomach was ripped up badly and I put my hand on it to stop the bleeding. Well, it stopped, all right." He hesitated. "I don't know how to put this. It stopped, and the wound closed up completely. The kid was lying there bleeding to death; five minutes later he was healed."

John and Bonnie looked at each other. "Are you sure that's what happened?" John asked.

"I wish I wasn't."

"Go on."

"I wanted some answers. A friend set up a meeting with a guy named Paul Bridger."

"The evangelist?" Bonnie asked.

"Yeah. Well, I didn't get any answers. He seemed to think it was a fair bet that I have some special healing power."

"Uh-huh."

"But he's such a showman that by the time I left I didn't want anything to do with it. All I wanted was to get back to normal."

John shook his head slowly. "And then the fire?"

"Yes. And this is where it all comes apart for me. The fire was more than strange. It was inconceivable. First I found myself getting out of Sammy's car. I didn't know why. I didn't have the slightest idea why. Next I found myself running into that building. It wasn't me—I swear to you, it wasn't me. My mind was totally independent of my body. My brain said no and my body said yes. I mean, normally when you tell yourself to do something, you do it, right? I mean if your mind tells your hand to pick up a spoon, you pick up a spoon. If your mind tells you to sit down, you sit down. Right? Well, not mine. Not this time. Oh no, I go running into a burning inferno and suddenly I just know that I'm commiting suicide. But I don't know why."

"Good grief," John murmured.

"And then I'm running through the fire surrounded by— I don't know how to explain it, but it was like cold air. Like I was in a bubble or something. The air was cold enough to give me goose bumps."

"It's giving me goose bumps right now," Bonnie said, taking John's hand.

"OK," Joseph continued. "I run up four flights of stairs and finally find these two little kids, about the same size as Amy, and they're burned, really burned. It made me sick." Joseph winced at the memory. "I grabbed them up, one in each arm, and headed back to the stairs. But there weren't any stairs anymore. They were gone—caved in, burned away, gone. Oh, shit, this is so crazy. I swear to you they *weren't there*. I remember thinking, my first thought was to try the fire escape. But that's not what I did. My body went ahead and took the first step anyway. And guess what: I felt the step under my foot. I could see all the way to the first floor. Not a stair in sight. But suddenly I was running down those nonexistent flights of stairs. Then the next thing I knew, I was out of the building."

He was breathing heavily and he took a moment to let his heart slow down. "When I got to the street, I was so freaked out about the fire I just stood there. But when I looked at the two kids and saw that their burns had healed, I really went crazy. I only remember running and running and running."

"I'm glad you ran here," John said after a moment.

"It was all I could think to do. John, I need you to help me with this. I don't understand any of it, let alone how to deal with it. I keep thinking that if I tell you enough, you'll see something I've missed. And right now I feel afraid to ask you what you think."

"You know what I think."

"That there is no human explanation."

"Joseph," Bonnie said gently, "did you at any time have a sense that there was some special power working in you?"

"I don't have any words for it that make sense to me. But

yes, certainly at the fire. And before that, maybe—energy, something—I don't know."

"You're special, Joseph," Bonnie said.

"That scares hell out of me. Bonnie, I want to know I'm still *human*. And I'm beginning to feel like I'm not."

John looked straight at him and spoke with utter confidence. "You're perfectly human. *And* you apparently have an unusual power."

"Joseph," Bonnie asked, "have you had anything like this happen before?"

"No."

"Anything when you were younger? Think."

"Nothing. Ask John. He knew me all the time I was in the orphanage. So why now, so suddenly?"

Bonnie found herself staring at Joseph's hands. She looked up and met his eyes.

"And there's another question that I can't get out of my mind: why me?"

"A better question is why a schmuck like Paul Bridger," John said, getting up.

"I don't know how to handle this, John."

"You don't have to know right now. Stay here, think, feel, we'll talk. You need some time."

Joseph sighed. "There's a lot you haven't said, for a preacher."

"Like what?"

"Like God has given me a gift and I should be grateful for it and—"

"You don't need me to say it. Besides, you can hardly be grateful for something you don't want."

"It's making a mess out of my life!"

John put his hand on Joseph's shoulder. "At least of your plans. And your assumptions. But what it will do to your life is still an open question."

FIFTEEN

POOR WEATHER DELAYED National Airlines flight 801 from Miami to Kennedy for two hours. Disgruntled passengers crowded around the baggage carousel grumbling at the unmoving conveyor belt.

One passenger, a tall, chestnut-haired woman in a soft blue-gray wool suit and sable coat, stood coolly off to one side, scanning the crowd, her impatience betrayed only by her frequent glances at her diamond watch. When people saw her they stared at her deep-set steel-blue eyes, tanned skin, and wide sensuous mouth. She looked back at them uninterestedly, obviously accustomed to such attention and for the moment bored by it.

When the belt finally started to move luggage down the ramp, she pointed to two tan leather suitcases with brass nameplates: M. Dillon. The skycap quickly retrieved them and led her through the baggage security check to the Eastern Airlines counter.

"You want I should wait, Miss Dillon?" he asked.

"Please." Her smile and her voice were unexpectedly warm.

The line moved slowly and Maggie Dillon found herself checking her watch again. She had been on the beach when she heard the radio report of his fall and the rescue of the children; she had finally given up trying to reach him by phone and caught the first available flight to New York. She was glad she'd thought to call the Sweets when she couldn't get Joseph on the phone—though it was hard getting anything out of Sammy. Thank God for Rosa, she thought. She moved to the pixie-faced young woman across the counter. "A ticket on your next flight to Boston," Maggie said to her.

"I'm sorry, but all flights to Logan International have been canceled. They're snowed in; the airport's been closed since this morning."

"Damn," Maggie said, the frustration of the last few hours showing now. "Do you know when they expect to open it up?"

"Probably tomorrow morning."

Maggie hesitated. "I've got to get there tonight."

"I am sorry, ma'am. You could go into the city and catch a bus or train, or you could rent a car. We have special rates with Budget."

"No, thanks anyway." She walked back to the skycap. "I need a taxi."

"Yes, ma'am."

"One that will take me to Provincetown, Massachusetts."

The lanky porter's eyes widened as he set the bags down and hurried out to the cab stand. She watched him speak to three cabbies before he came back through the glass doors. "I found one that will make the trip. But he wants $270 plus gas and a guaranteed twenty-percent tip."

"He's got it. Let's go."

While the cabbie stowed her suitcases in the trunk of the taxi she tipped the porter ten dollars. Appreciatively he doffed his scarlet cap and opened the rear door. Gracefully she slid onto the seat. The porter closed the door with care as the driver climbed in behind the wheel and closed his. The young cabbie craned his head around.

"You got cash, lady?" he said in a thick Russian accent. "I can't take check."

"I've got it."

"You show me, please? You understand, I hope? No offense."

She withdrew four hundred-dollar bills from her purse, handed two to the driver, and held the other two up for him to see. "When we get there. No offense."

He stuffed the bills into his dirty blue shirt pocket. "You been around, lady," he said, smiling at her in the rearview mirror as he put the cab in gear and pulled out.

Staring straight ahead, Maggie settled back for the ride. For the first time all day she noticed that she felt nervous. She had come without hesitation and had spent the flight in memories and in worrying how Joseph was taking all of this. It wasn't until she'd reached Sammy and Rosa and found out he was in Provincetown and all right—physically, at least— that she'd been able to stop worrying about him and come face to face with her own decision to come back.

She forced herself to consider the fact that it was more than possible he wouldn't want her. He'd made that clear enough when she'd left. Still, in all of the last eleven months she had assumed that one day she would be with him again. It had not occurred to her that he could die in the meantime, and she had been shocked that he had come so close to death.

But there was more to it than that. That he had lived could hurt her more; no one gets that close to death without changing, even stubborn people like Joseph Turner. She still loved him in a way she'd never felt about another man, and she knew him well enough to know that loving her wasn't something he'd taken lightly. But how would he feel now? The damn news stories were probably exaggerated, but whatever the facts, Joseph had been through a lot. She had told herself that he needed her, but she knew, clearly, that much of her motive for coming was to check out her ground. She wasn't ready to let go of him, and she needed to know that her connection, however extended, was still intact. Rosa had said that he wasn't with another woman, but still, she wondered. She had considered calling the Stantons before she left the airport but had not. She had been afraid that Joseph would tell her not to come. He might have decided he no longer loved her—and if so, she wanted a chance to change his mind.

With anyone but Joseph Turner, she thought as the cab moved up the turnpike, she would be utterly confident of her ability to do that.

SIXTEEN

A PRIVATE 747 taxied to a stop in front of a large hangar at the Teterboro, New Jersey, Airport. The ground crew quickly rolled the portable stairs up to the door on the port side of the massive fuselage. The hatch seal broke on the white door as it gently swung open. Emil Rothstein, followed by Luici Bermano and Thomas Fletcher, walked down the steps to a waiting airport courtesy bus.

The bus quickly pulled out and headed toward the north end of the freshly snowplowed field to a heliport. A uniformed Customs officer watched the bus approach and walked to meet Rothstein, who stepped off first and handed him three passports. Quickly the officer doublechecked the diplomatic seal, stamped the documents, and handed them back with a crisp salute. "Welcome to America, Mr. Rothstein. Our office will notify the State Department of your arrival."

"Thank you, Officer, but I contacted State from the plane when we entered U.S. airspace."

"Matter of formality, sir. We'll still have to notify them."

"Suit yourself," said Rothstein as he moved off toward a waiting helicopter.

Bermano and Fletcher, a stout Scotsman ruddy-faced from the cold, handed the luggage over to a member of the ground crew, who quickly put them into the double-bladed transport. Rothstein and his aides entered the chopper. The stairs were folded in behind them and the door locked closed. Gracefully the aircraft tilted forward, lifted its tail, and ascended into the evening sky.

As the shuttle made its way to the city, Rothstein reviewed his plans for the investigation. He found himself wondering whether it would end as all Nicholas investigations had ended in the past—with no positive proof—and ordered his mind back to the details of the business.

Through the window he could see the lights of the city come into view. New York had always been good to him; he hoped it would be good to him now, give him the information he needed to make the right decision. Joseph Turner. What would he be like? If he turned out to be a fraud it would be evident soon enough.

He hadn't noticed the approach to the East River Heliport near the Queensboro Bridge, and was startled to be descending. There was a slight jolt as the helicopter wheels settled onto the landing pad.

Shortly Rothstein and his aides were met by a limousine. Rothstein greeted the driver with a broad smile. "Hugo, I'm glad to see you."

"I too am happy," the driver answered in a heavy Eastern European accent. "You stay at Waldorf?"

"Yes."

At the hotel the doorman opened the rear door of the car. "Welcome back, Mr. Rothstein."

"Thank you, Richard." Emil looked up at the ceiling of the porte-cochère and spotted several burnt-out bulbs. "You really should get those replaced, Richard."

"Yes, sir." The doorman smiled. "You never miss a thing, Mr. Rothstein, do you?"

"Not usually," remarked Emil, smiling as he walked through the glass doors into the lobby.

At the desk the hotel manager, hearing Rothstein's name, came quickly out from his adjoining office. "Mr. Rothstein! How wonderful of you to stay with us again. We are honored."

"You are most kind. Now, if you'll excuse me."

"If there is anything we can do—" The manager gestured with open, upturned hands. "Captain! Show Mr. Rothstein to the Presidential Suite. His aides have the one adjoining."

"Right this way, sir," the captain answered, showing them to the elevator.

As the elevator rose, Rothstein turned to his two aides. "We'll meet in my sitting room in fifteen minutes. We're going to work, gentlemen." The elevator doors opened on the twenty-eighth floor, and Bermano and Fletcher watched Rothstein move hurriedly to his suite.

"What's with Emil, Luici? Why the hurry?" asked Fletcher as they entered their room.

"He's getting old, Fletch."

"He's been old before."

"Yes, but now he realizes it."

"That could be very bad for us. When we work too fast the chance of error is much greater."

"He won't make a mistake. Not with this one. It's too important."

Fletcher sat squarely on the cushion of the wing chair. "You worked on a Nicholas file once before, didn't you?"

"Once, in Greece, almost ten years ago now."

"What happened?" asked Thomas.

When Bermano answered his voice was low and far away. "He died."

Rothstein stood shirtless in front of the gold-framed bathroom mirror. He flushed his face with repeated handfuls of cold water and then toweled it dry. He took a closer look at his face. A few more lines, and the circles are deeper around my bloodshot eyes. Ah well, he thought, the age of my body is not important. What is important is my mind, my thoughts, my energy.

There was a light rap at the door. He grabbed his shirt and hastily put it on.

The sitting room of the Presidential Suite was lavishly appointed in the style of Louis XIV. Its heavy deep gold draperies hung from a sixteen-foot ceiling. Flowered Persian carpets graced the floor. Two bouquets of fresh yellow roses had been placed on the end tables.

Emil sat in a tapestry-upholstered chair next to the exquisitely carved coffee table. His two aides sat on an adjacent matching couch. He began solemnly. "My friends, around this table, affairs of the world have been discussed by presidents and heads of state. Make no mistake. Our mission is of as great an importance as any of theirs. We must make every effort to complete our job quickly and precisely."

Bermano and Fletcher nodded.

"Don't be tempted to draw premature conclusions from the dossier information that Joseph Turner is three years older than the man we're seeking. *Everything* must be examined. There are no means beyond our grasp, and the only restriction is secrecy, especially where the media is concerned. Do I make myself clear?"

"Yes, sir."

"Fine. At six tomorrow morning you will meet a man named Gumbali at the coffee shop on the southeast corner of Twenty-Eighth and Park. He'll give you a packet." Rothstein paused long enough to pull an envelope from the black leather briefcase at the side of his chair. He handed it to Bermano. "Give him this. It contains five thousand in small bills. Don't lose it. And be extremely careful with the packet he gives you. It contains all the identification I need to conduct the investigation undercover."

"Is he Mafia?" asked Bermano.

"That's ridiculous, Luici. There is no such thing as the Mafia . . . at least not since *The Godfather* came out. Let's just say he is a devout Catholic."

Luici smiled. "How will I know this Gumbali?"

"He has only one ear. As soon as you get me the ID's, Luici, I'll need you to go to the Bureau of Vital Statistics for copies of three birth certificates—Joseph Charles Turner, Susan Burton Turner, his mother, and William Ryder Turner, his father—and the death certificates of his parents. I need the name of the doctor who pronounced them dead."

"Tomorrow's Saturday, Emil. They'll be closed."

"Not for you, they won't. A woman named Morales will meet you there. I was once her son's attorney. She'll give you photostats of the documents. As soon as I've got everything in my hands, no door will be closed to us."

"And me?" asked Fletcher, laying his hand over the spot in his stomach that kept grumbling.

"I want you to begin surveillance. Go to Turner's apartment in the Bronx, 433 Devon Street. Follow him, get some pictures for me. And keep a record of everybody he talks to. Beginning at six o'clock tomorrow morning, Joseph Turner is never to be out of our sight."

SEVENTEEN

THE CRUNCH OF SNOW beneath their boots was the only sound heard as Joseph and John walked along the dark Provincetown beach. The storm had passed, the sky was clear, and the ocean barely lapped against the shore. Their frozen exhalations streamed silently into the night.

Dinner had been quiet, Bonnie and John absorbing what Joseph had told them and no one really knowing what to say. Joseph had grown increasingly gloomy, and a couple of drinks after dinner did not help. Finally John had suggested a walk, and now, a mile down the beach, the liquor caught up with them.

Suddenly John stumbled and caught himself. "Pass the flowerrrs, good buddy," he said, slightly slurring his words.

Joseph handed him the bottle of Four Roses, and he took a long pull. "Ahhhh," he said, like a dying lion. "Are you there yet?" he asked, trying to blink his eyes alert.

"I'm getting there."

"Well, I'm approaching the summit quickly. Here."

John handed the bottle back and Joseph drank.

"If I fall down face first, roll me over, will you?"

"Of course I will, Johnny."

"You know, one thing you told me has me totally buffaloed. I can't figure it out . . ." He turned to Joseph. "No stairs, huh?"

"Nope," said Joseph, shaking his head, and then tilting it back to look at the sky. "Will you look at those stars?"

"What stars? Give me the bottle." John crooked his index finger at Joseph, who passed the bottle back. It slipped from the minister's hand and landed upright in the deep snow. "Praise the Lord," said John, stooping to retrieve it. "You know, Joey, Jesus drank."

"Scotch?"

"Noooo, wine . . . I would have shit, you know that?"

"When?"

"When there weren't any stairs."

"Wouldn't you've prayed?"

"Oh, yeah, sure. But I bet I would've still been afraid. And just last week I preached about fear."

"Really?"

"Yeah." John tilted up the empty bottle. He brought the mouth of it to his eye and stared at the stars. It made him dizzy; he threw the bottle into the ocean. "I talked about the fear that can be gen . . . can be generated by a few spoken words on television and ra . . . dio . . . the kind of crazy violence in the world today."

"What'd you say about it?"

"I was hoping you'd ask. I said, 'We don't need to fear anything.' What do you think about that?"

"Profound. Really profound!" Joseph said, nodding drunkenly.

"I said that inside all of us is the power to meet and solve any problem. I've got to take a leak."

"So what are you waiting for?" said Joseph, pointing at the water.

"Right," replied John, unzipping his fly and turning toward the ocean. He continued talking, looking at Joseph over his shoulder. "Where was I?"

"Solving problems."

"Oh, yeah. I quoted John, Chapter Fourteen, Verse Twenty-seven, where Jesus," he exhaled loudly, "admon . . . admonished his followers. He said, 'Let not your hearts be troubled, neither let them be afraid.' " He zipped his pants shut and turned to Joseph. "Are you following me?"

"I think so."

"Good. 'Cause here I am," he spread his arms wide, "in my favorite place in the world, with my best friend, who I've just found out can perform miracles, and instead of being happy, I'm very, very scared."

"You?"

"I don't know what the hell the answers are."

"You don't?"

"Nope. I don't have the foggiest idea what to tell you to do. I'm a failure," John said, starting to cry drunkenly.

Joseph reached out and put his arms around his friend. "Johnny, relax, will you please? You're not a failure."

"I'm not?"

"No."

"Good," Stanton said, his composure returning. "Have you got any ideas?"

"Yeah. I'm going to let the whole thing die down. Then go back to New York and live an ordinary life."

"Oh, sure. And then someday one of the boys at the club'll break an arm playing basketball and you'll just stand there and do nothing. Oh, yeah."

"I'll take him to a doctor."

"Oh, yeah. And when you pick him up, his arm'll heal. And the whole damn thing'll start all over again." Stanton slipped in the snow and then caught himself. "Man, your life has changed. Face it!"

"I've been facing it since last night. It doesn't help."

"You know, Joey, I heard a story once about a man who was crossing the street and got hit by a taxi. He wasn't hurt but he never tried to cross another—"

"I told you that story."

"You did?"

"Yes."

"Well, thanks. I use it in all my 'fear' sermons."

Joseph thought quietly for a moment. "You know, Johnny, I have to start looking at this positively. What's really so bad about what happened?"

"Everything," John said, shaking his head slowly.

"No, not everything. I lived through the fall and the fire, didn't I? I saved four people's lives. That's all positive stuff, right?"

"Yeah."

"Well, look. I can go back to New York and live and I'll use what power I've got when I have to."

"Yeah, Joey. I know you. You need to use it. But, Joey, people won't leave you alone when they know."

"Oh, right. I'll have to figure out a story for the press when they find me. And they will find me."

"What can you tell 'em? You don't know anything," Stanton said.

"You know what I told one reporter?" Joseph said, beginning to laugh.

"What?"

"She asked me how and why I staged the fall. I told her I wore a flight jacket and was tired of waiting for the elevator." They both burst into hysterical laughter. Joseph fell back in the snow.

"A flight jacket! That's terrific! I love it," John said, reaching out and pulling Joseph to his feet. "You know, if you were Jesus it would explain everything."

"It would?"

"Yep. Why don't you see if you can walk on the water?"

"OK," Joseph said, walking toward the waterline. "Don't let me drown."

"You can count on me."

"OK, here goes." Joseph took two giant steps into the icy water, then, knee-deep, turned back to John. "Well, that rules that out!"

The two laughed again.

"Come on, old buddy, let's go home," Stanton said.

Joseph stomped out of the water, and arm in arm, wet, cold, and very drunk, they stumbled up the beach.

When they neared the well-lit house a taxi was pulling out of the drive. "You expecting anybody, Reverend?" Joseph mumbled, straining his drunken eyes to distinguish the figure on the porch.

"No, I don't think we are."

"Well, they got suitcases."

"Oh, shit."

Then she moved, and Joseph knew. "Maggie!" he whispered. John reached for him but he was running.

"Maggie!"

She turned toward the sound and he raced up the front steps into her arms, tears streaming down his face.

"Oh, Maggie," he said, holding her tightly.

"I was afraid I'd lost you, Joey," she said, burrowing her face into his neck.

He breathed the scent of her in deeply. "How did you know where?"

"Rosa." She lifted her head and looked into his eyes. "I've missed you so much."

"You don't know—" he started, but John was beside them and Bonnie at the door.

Maggie broke from him to give the minister a hug. "Thanks for taking care of him, John . . . I hope I'm not an intrusion?"

"Of course not. But let's get inside; I'm freezing my buns off," slurred Stanton, grabbing Joseph with his free arm and heading them into the house past Bonnie, who held the door open.

"Hello, Maggie," Bonnie said with a slight chill in her normally warm voice. "I didn't expect to . . ."

"See me here?"

"Well, no."

"I hope I'm not a bother," Maggie said, looking from Bonnie to Joseph.

"No," Bonnie said stiffly. "Not at all. I'll be in the kitchen. I think the boys could use some coffee. Hey, Joey, your pants are frozen. How'd you get so wet?"

"Don't ask," Joseph said, looking at John and holding a finger across his lips to silence him.

John arched his eyebrows and blurted out, "He was trying to walk on water."

"John!" exclaimed Bonnie.

"Well, he was," said Stanton sheepishly. "We were experimenting."

Bonnie turned to Maggie and pointed down the hall. "I put Joey in the guest room. I'll bring a dry pair of pants."

"Right." Maggie looped her arm in Joseph's and led him off. John yelled after them, "Don't let her take your pants! It's the last stronghold we've got!"

"John, quiet, you'll wake Amy!" Bonnie said angrily.

Joseph looked over his shoulder at his scolded friend with laughing eyes before departing into the den.

When Maggie answered Bonnie's knock at the door she was handed a clean pair of pants and a yellow terrycloth bathrobe.

"The robe will be easier," Bonnie said, shaking her head at Joseph, who now sat on the edge of the tweed hide-a-bed wrapped only in a blanket.

"I think you're right." Bonnie closed the door, and Maggie moved to Joseph and put her arm around his waist. "C'mon, lover, stand up."

"I'm sorry, baby."

"Sorry about what?"

"Getting so drunk."

"It's all right, Joey. Everything's all right now." She unwrapped the blanket, helped him get his arms into the bathrobe, pulled it tight around his waist, and tied the sash. "Come on, let's get you some coffee."

He tried to get up but couldn't. "I think I better call it a night."

"I'll tell Bonnie."

When Maggie returned to the bedroom he was curled up on the bed and fighting to keep his eyes open.

She sat next to him, placing his head in her lap. "Close your eyes, drift away, baby," she whispered softly. "Just sleep. Sleep."

What hadn't fully registered the night before hit him with the force of a blow when he awoke. Maggie was there. He smelled her perfume, felt the touch of her hair and the warmth of her naked body next to his. She purred like a kitten in the crook of his arm.

He spent an hour watching her sleep. With each passing minute he grew more angry. Why did she show up now—after eleven months? As much of the previous night as he could remember, she had acted as if nothing had happened between them, and he had gone along with it. Finally he could stand her touch no more, and he inched away from her, slid his legs out of bed, slowly got to his feet, and began dressing Angrily he shoved his legs into the clean trousers and pulled on the Irish knit sweater. He was sitting on the edge of the bed putting on his socks when Maggie stirred and opened her eyes.

"Morning," she said, reaching out and touching his back. It stiffened.

"You're angry," Maggie said, rising on her elbow and using the sheet to cover her firm, round well-tanned breasts. "OK, Joey, let's talk."

Her voice wasn't loud but he snapped at her anyway. "Quiet, before you wake everybody up!"

"Sorry," she whispered.

"Why the hell did you come back, Maggie? Business slow?" He meant his words to hurt.

"No. I came because I love you."

"Bullshit!" he snapped.

"I do. If you'd died, I'd have . . ."

"You'd have what?" Joseph said, jumping to his feet and storming over to the built-in bookcase. He turned back slowly. "Gone crazy if anything happened to me?"

"Yes."

"I don't believe you, Maggie! You aren't the type."

"Can't you just accept the fact that I care about you, that I was worried?"

"Not for a minute. Look, I've been through a lot lately. I'm just not up to any more right now. I don't want to be hurt by you again. Not now or ever," he said, turning away.

"Tell me what you've been through, Joey."

"You can read it in the newspapers," he said bitterly.

"Joey."

Finally he turned back to her. "OK," he said, sighing heavily, and he told the story once more. "Now you know the facts. What's hard is living with them. I'm going back to New York to face all of it—how, I'm not sure."

"Do you have to go back?"

"What the hell else am I supposed to do? Take off for the mountains and live in a cave? This is my life, Maggie."

She knew she had to be careful, but he could read her well. She might as well say it now. "Come back with me, Joseph."

"What?"

"Come back with me to Miami. I have enough money that we can live very well, well enough for you to hire someone to keep the press off. You can do anything you want to. Be a healer or nothing at all—for a while. Just live and rest. In a year or so—" she stopped, searching his face. He was still angry, but something was reaching him.

"Wait a minute, Maggie." He didn't want to listen to her, but the idea of it was so easy. It would be so simple to be away from all of it, to be with Maggie . . . No. It was impossible.

Maggie rose from the bed, wrapping the sheet loosely around her, and moved behind him. "What if I tell you that I want a life with you? I didn't come here for that. I didn't know that's what I wanted until I saw you again. But it is. What if I tell you that I'll do anything you ask? I couldn't do it before. I'm willing to try again, if you'll let me. Joey, I'll stop."

Joseph turned slowly back, the flame in his eyes burning wildly. "You'll never stop. You can't. You need whatever it gives you. Whatever *that* is."

"You're wrong, Joey! I can, and I will. All you have to do is ask."

"What am I? Your knight in shining armor?" His words had the edge of a finely ground blade.

"Maybe," she said quietly, intensely, reaching up to touch his face.

"Maybe's not good enough! Don't you understand?" Joseph drew away from her touch and paced to the window. He pushed open the white drapes and stared at the ocean. "Once I was your knight in shining armor, but I didn't have a castle. I didn't want one then, and I don't want one now. It was OK with you for a while. You didn't need it either, so you said. But after a time what I could give you wasn't enough. That's when you left. You went back to fucking for money."

She met his glare evenly and said nothing.

"It hurt, Maggie. It still hurts." Joseph turned, ran his eyes over her and spoke with hushed anger. "You like the money it gives you, the freedom, the power, and probably the revenge. No, you'll never get it out of your blood."

"You can't be sure."

"Yes, I can. Maggie, once there were two blind men, one blind from birth, one blind for a day. The one newly blinded was the one who missed his sight. I've never had money or power and don't miss it. You don't miss it now, but you will."

"Joey, I'm not a blind man in a parable. I'm a woman." She allowed the sheet to fall to the floor around her feet. "And I want a second chance to love you, a second chance to see again. I've been blind. I'm not now."

She moved closer to him and he resisted his desire. He turned his head away as she stepped close to him.

"I want to be trusted again. I want your love." Her voice was thick and sweet. "I need you, and I think you need me. Don't you?"

He tried to think of anything but the vision of her standing in front of him. His mind fastened on the thick carpet beneath his feet, the volumes in the bookcase, the feel of the sweater against his nervously perspiring sides. Nothing helped. "Maggie, of course I—"

She stopped his words, pressing her full lips to his and moving him to the bed. "Try it, try it for a week," she murmured softly, pulling the sweater over his head. His hair spilled wildly around his face and she stroked it from his eyes, moving his head down so he could watch her undress him. He felt unable to move, unable to resist. His heart beat rapidly. His breath became short and labored. Gently she began to kiss his face, his neck, his ears. He felt a shuddering surge of warmth as she softly stroked the hair of his chest. His hands lay paralyzed at his side as feelings mixed with memories.

Gently she took his hand, held it next to her full lips, and began to kiss and suck his fingers. His eyes slid closed. He tried to reopen them but couldn't. He felt her firm breast under his hand, the erect nipple sending a chill through him. If he had wanted to speak, he would not have been able to, for the muscles in his jaw shook violently. Ever so slowly she moved her body against his, her smooth skin sliding down his as she kissed it with warm, moist lips. Finally he reached out and buried his fingers in the silkiness of her long chestnut hair.

Why am I doing everything I promised myself I never would again? he thought, but his question went unanswered as her warm lips touched his loins. Pain and pleasure exploded in multicolored lights behind Joseph's eyes as he drifted away in ecstasy.

In the Country French–furnished master bedroom at the opposite end of the house, Bonnie paced, smoking nervously. Fury welled in her dark-circled eyes. She kept wishing that John would wake up, stir, snore, do anything! Finally unable to bear the silent torment another second, she shook him. "Wake up, John, wake up!"

She watched his eyes flutter open. A look of shock crossed his face. "What's the matter? Why are you smoking?" He sat up, resting his back against the cold brass of the headboard. "Sweetheart? What's wrong?"

"Her, her downstairs!" Bonnie said, resuming her pacing and puffing.

"Bonnie," John said with soft deliberation. "It's not our place to pass judgment on Maggie. Only God can do that."

"It's our house, John!"

"And she's a hooker . . . so what? She's not going to hurt us. What are you really upset about?"

She turned away from him. "What she's going to do to Joey."

Stanton swung out of bed and walked around to face her. "Bonnie, Maggie came here because she knew Joey needed her. She was willing to put herself wide open to ridicule to help him. She knows you don't like her. She's known it for years, ever since she found out you know. She came anyway, to help him."

"I don't believe that, John, and I can't believe you do. She's here because she knows he's vulnerable right now and she wants him back—at least for the time being."

He considered it. "Maybe you're right. But we're not his parents."

There were tears of frustration in her eyes. "John, you're his best friend. Joseph has a gift, a very special gift, and Maggie knows nothing about what that means. She'll see it as something to exploit or to ignore. Either way, if he's with her he gets hurt, badly hurt."

John pulled his wife close. "You're awfully hard on her, Bonnie, and I think you're underestimating him. Believe me, Joey can take care of himself. Nothing's going to happen that he doesn't want to happen."

It was noon before they saw Joseph again and learned that he was considering going to Miami.

EIGHTEEN

As President of ABC News, David Brooks knew that he would be held accountable if anything was amiss in the sensational story Jackson Bullock had broadcast on Thursday night. It was such coverage that kept them number one; still, sitting now, preparing for the visit of the FCC investigator, he wondered if it was worth it. His call to the head of the FCC had produced no additional information, only the "suggestion" that he cooperate fully. He looked across his conference table desk at Bullock. "I have no reason to doubt your integrity, Jack. Your work is high-caliber and I like you personally—"

"Excuse me, Mr. Brooks, but I've worked for you for six years, and until today the most contact we've had is a handshake at an affiliates dinner! So don't give me any crap about liking me."

"OK, OK, take it easy. All I want is your word that the footage we ran coincided in every detail with what you witnessed."

"It did."

"And there's no way it could have been, ah . . . prearranged?"

"Are you kidding?"

"Sorry, Jack, I had to ask. If the FCC says they're coming in to investigate a story, I've got to cover all angles. Any luck with the Turner fellow?"

Bullock shook his head. "We're still looking."

"Well, if he's a phony, that's their problem. Damn. Never known those guys to work on Saturday. I was looking forward to the Texas game."

Bullock remained silent.

The intercom buzzed and the two men froze for a split

122

second before Brooks pressed the buzzer and answered. "Yes."

"Mr. Schreiber is here." Her well-modulated voice was a little higher-pitched than usual. Everybody was on edge.

"Thank you, Kathy. Please show him in." Brooks rose from his chair as the secretary ushered the man into his office. Brooks met him with a broad smile and outstretched hand. "Good afternoon. David Brooks."

"Fred Schreiber, FCC," said Emil Rothstein. He took Brooks's hand but did not return the smile.

"It's a pleasure," Brooks continued. "And this is our distinguished field correspondent, Jackson Bullock."

"Mr. Bullock," Rothstein nodded.

"Would you like some coffee?" Brooks asked.

"No, thank you." Rothstein took a seat and reached inside his suitcoat for his wallet. "My credentials."

"No need, Mr. Schreiber, really," said Brooks smiling. "Do I detect a German accent?"

"You do."

"How is it that you are working for the government?"

"Henry," replied Rothstein matter-of-factly.

"Oh, yes, of course. I believe I remember his mentioning your name when I was with the White House. I was press secretary for four years, you know."

Brooks's small talk gave Rothstein time to sum up both men. Brooks was too friendly. Bullock seethed with frustrated anger. Both were afraid. Bermano did a good job setting this up, he thought. "Shall we get down to business?" he said sternly.

"Of course."

"As you know, I'm here concerning your filmed account of a rescue of two children from a fire. I believe the rescuer's name was Joseph Turner. The commission received a phone call yesterday from a very reliable source who stated that your network was involved in an attempt to deceive the public about the nature of the incident. I'm here to investigate the allegation."

"It's utterly preposterous," Brooks answered calmly.

"That's what the person who complained to us thought."

"I mean," said Brooks, controlling his irritation, "that the allegation is preposterous."

Bullock was unable to contain his anger. "The call had to have come from one of our competitors. I shot and commentated that story accurately."

"No, Mr. Bullock. The call came from inside your own organization."

Bullock looked to Brooks who looked to Rothstein. "Who placed the call?"

"I'm not at liberty to divulge that information."

"This is insane," Brooks said angrily, getting to his feet.

"Maybe, but I'm here to make a determination. Shall we start with the film?"

Brooks wiped at his brow with a clean white handkerchief. "I wouldn't let you leave without seeing it!"

Emil relaxed a little; this was proceeding nicely. "I'm sure I don't have to tell you about the seriousness of the matter. You realize that if I should find a shred of evidence that you have indeed misled the public with sensational journalism, it could end in a Senate investigation—and your license."

"I'm certain that the matter can be cleared up today," Brooks said, obviously shaken but trying to hide it. "You may judge our confidence by the fact that, as you see"—he gestured toward the empty chairs—"our attorneys are not present. Now," he said, standing, "will you accompany us to the screening room?"

Shortly Rothstein was seated between Brooks and Bullock watching Turner run through the flame-engulfed doorway of the tenement. The sight of him returning from the flames carrying a child in each arm, and none of them burned, made Rothstein's hand tighten its grip on the arm of his chair. The camera followed the frightened ironworker as he ran through the crowd and out of sight. The lights came on as the film flickered to an end.

"There," said Brooks. "Truth or fiction, Mr. Schreiber, which is it?"

Emil looked at Brooks intently, knowing the executive was hanging on his words, then stood without answering, walked to the aisle, and turned back. "Very impressive film. Now, what editing has been done?"

"None of significance, Mr. Schreiber. Are you suggesting—?"

"It cannot be discounted."

Brooks withdrew several documents from a folder in front of him. "I have here several affidavits, notarized of course, from witnesses at the scene." Bullock stared, startled. "I thought such confirmations from the fire chief, the childrens' parents, and others might clear up the matter quickly."

Rothstein took the affidavits. "You have saved me considerable work, Mr. Brooks."

"In our own interest."

"I would like a copy of the film to have it checked. Assuming that the film and these affidavits are in order, we may consider the matter closed."

Brooks and Bullock sighed audibly.

"Thank you for your time, gentlemen. I'll show myself out."

This much verified, Rothstein thought as he left the office and entered the elevator: Joseph Turner, one; Rothstein, zero.

The elevator descended and at the first floor he stepped out, nodded to the security guard, and walked through the heavy glass doors onto the Avenue of the Americas. Hugo was waiting by the open door of the limousine.

"I trust all went well?" he asked.

"Very well indeed, Hugo," Rothstein answered as he got in. "To the Tea Room now."

Rothstein entered the Russian Tea Room on West Fifty-Seventh and quickly scanned the long narrow restaurant, overflowing with holiday customers. He raised his eyebrows at the sight of the Christmas decorations on the walls. Thanksgiving was still five days away. Luici was waving to him from a table along the near wall. He made his way down the busy aisle.

"How'd it go?" Bermano asked as Rothstein sat down.

"You did splendidly setting it up, Luici, splendidly. You put the fear of God in them. As an old DA friend of mine used to say, it was a walk in the park.' "

"And?" asked Bermano.

"And so far, Mr. Turner appears to be worth our continued interest."

Bermano let out a low whistle.

"Was there any trouble at BVS?" Rothstein asked.

"None. I got the photostats; the medical examiner who signed his parents' death certificates is Dr. Theodore Carpenter, retired. He now lives up in Rye." Luici handed a manila envelope across the table to his boss. "The address is in the packet. Dr. Carpenter will see the 'City Attorney' Monday at six." He looked past Emil toward the door. Emil saw him start with surprise.

"What is it?"

"It's Fletch."

Rothstein turned to see Fletcher approaching them. He stopped at the table. "He's not there, hasn't been since Thursday. The superintendent of the building thinks he's left town."

"Sit down, Fletch."

"I've spent the morning arranging with the superintendent to notify us if he returns. And I've spoken with the neighbors —very low-key, of course. I explained that the parents of the children wanted to speak with Turner. Several of the neighbors referred me to his friend Sweet."

"Were you able to contact Sweet?"

"He lives in Queens. I telephoned and told him a representative of the mayor's office would like to stop by, that it concerned a medal for Turner's heroism. He was very receptive. I set it up for five o'clock tonight, his home."

"Fine," said Emil turning to Bermano. "What about the orphanage?"

"I called. A Suzy Vickerman ran the home while Turner was there. She retired some years ago."

"Is she still in the city?"

"Yes, and I have her address and phone number."

"Set up an appointment for me—I mean for the City Attorney—sometime tomorrow."

"Certainly."

"And the reports on the fall?"

"They appear completely verifiable so far."

Rothstein saw Bermano's tension. "We must remember, Luici, that we have been this close before. I know it is difficult, but we must proceed with method and great care. Let's take some time to relax and enjoy our meal."

When Rothstein left the Tea Room, the limousine headed directly for Queens. His meeting with Sweet went well enough. Turner's friend was more than pleased that the city was going to recognize Joseph with a medal for saving the two children as well as Sweet himself. However, when Rothstein questioned him about the possibility that Turner had staged either of the events, the ironworker became enraged and threatened to throw the city's representative through the front door.

"Surely you understand, Mr. Sweet," Rothstein said, trying to calm him. "The Mayor's office must be positive. Such inquiries must be made."

"I was there!" Sammy yelled, pounding his fist on the kitchen table. "Both times! Even if he wasn't my friend—I saw it!"

The testimony of the only eyewitness to both events was important to Rothstein. He was able to obtain some new information as well. Under the guise that they should be officially invited to the presentation ceremony, Sweet provided a list of Turner's friends. But the ironworker had insisted he did not know where Turner presently was.

About that, Emil thought as the long black car pulled away from Sweet's home, Sweet had lied; perhaps something had made him a bit uneasy. So the list would have to be checked carefully as well. More than likely there were important names missing.

A phone call to one name on the list confirmed Emil's suspicions. Frank Corollo mentioned that Turner had once been "very close" to a woman, a Maggie Dillon. Emil put Bermano to work on her.

Late Sunday morning Bermano brought him the report. Margaret Elaine Dillon had been born and reared in Shaker Heights, Ohio, in a well-to-do family. Her father had been a prominent banker in that city until accused of embezzlement four years ago. His daughter had graduated with honors from Vassar, but the beginnings of a successful career in New York came to a quick halt when her father's notoriety made front page news. She entered a different career: police records obtained through the District Attorney's office indicated that she had been arrested twice by the NYPD for prostitution. But she was no ordinary hooker; she was an extremely high-priced call girl who received no less than a thousand dollars a night compensation for her services. Her connection with Turner was unclear, but the last notation in the report suggested that it was not finished. Having found that she wintered in Florida, Bermano traced her to Miami and discovered that she had left for New York on Friday. It was an unlikely coincidence—and so very possible that finding Dillon would lead them to Turner. Besides, Fletcher had turned up nothing on his whereabouts; it was the best lead they had, and he put Fletcher on it.

Rothstein had more important business, for it was still not certain that they would want Joseph Turner when they found him. A check of his years with the Navy, his activities at the Boys' Club, his relations with his friends turned up little of interest. Turner was unusually well liked and unusually generous, it appeared, but that could be accounted for in any number of ways. There were the remaining witnesses to the fall and fire to check, the doctor who examined him at Bellevue, and the reporters who had done independent investigations. Bermano should have that information by Monday morning.

Yet whatever they turned up, Rothstein reminded himself as he drove to his meeting with Suzy Vickerman, there would still be one discrepancy that must be reconciled. Only those who knew about Turner's early years could possibly provide the crucial information.

When he arrived at the simply furnished apartment of Suzy Vickerman, a pensioner whose seventy-some years had not totally destroyed her beauty, Emil repeated to her the story he had given Sweet. Before presentation, he said, the Mayor's office wanted to ascertain that no embarrassing incidents from the past might arise to mar the honor of the award to be bestowed on the valiant ironworker.

She was more than gracious and happily recounted the story of how Joseph came to be placed in the home for orphans after the accidental death of his parents when the state investigators had found no surviving relatives. She also told him all she could remember about Turner through childhood and adolescence. There were only two possibly embarrassing incidents which she knew of, but she was sure they were not at all serious.

All children, she said, go through a period of lying. For several months when Joseph was six, he had begun to insist that his father was going to come and take him away. He knew it to be true, he said, because he had spoken with him. Many times she had reprimanded young Joseph about the lie because it upset the other orphans, and she had been afraid for a time that he was slipping from reality into a fantasy world; but after a few months he had stopped telling his story.

The only other incident occurred when he was twelve. Joseph and another boy had been captured in an attempt to pilfer model-airplane kits from a local toy store. They were turned over to the Home instead of the police. Punishment for the crime had been worked out between herself and the store's proprietor. The boys were required to sweep the store each afternoon for a month. That was the last of their stealing.

The other child, Rothstein learned to his great interest, was John Stanton, now a minister in Provincetown, Massachusetts, and to this day Turner's best friend. Miss Vickerman told him that both men still sent Christmas gifts each year to the boys living in the Home.

When Fletcher called late that night, Rothstein dispatched him to Provincetown.

Monday morning Bermano arrived early with his final report. The witnesses, a Dr. Weisman, the reporters, all confirmed their information. Bermano had had some difficulty with the reporter from the *Times,* whose suspicions had been so aroused that Bermano was quite certain she would be investigating them. Rothstein was considering the best means of putting her off the track when the phone rang.

"Yes?"

"Fletcher. I've found him."

"And?"

"And he appears to be staying for a while."

"Stay with him. I'm sending Bermano to join you. You tell him where to meet you. I have one more appointment this morning. Call me back no later than one o'clock."

He put Bermano on the phone and got ready to leave the hotel. The *Times* reporter would have to wait.

At five minutes to eleven, the Monday before Thanksgiving, Hugo pulled the spotless limousine into the snow-packed horseshoe drive of the white-pillared Carpenter mansion in Rye.

Rothstein let himself out. "If you want to come back for me . . ."

"No, sir, I wait on you."

Emil, briefcase in hand, rang the bell of the red-brick colonial. A black-uniformed maid answered the door and guided him through the Early American–furnished home to a connecting hothouse where an energetic old man in gardening clothes and a fishing hat was busily tending an abundant collection of orchids.

"Doctor, the man from the City Attorney's office is here," said the maid loudly. She turned to Rothstein as Carpenter approached. "He's hard of hearing."

"Thank you," said Emil, extending his hand to the aged practitioner. The maid reentered the house.

"Theo Carpenter," said the wrinkle-faced man.

"Harold Jacobs, City Attorney's office," Emil said loudly. Carpenter motioned with his hand. "You can lower your voice," he whispered. "Being hard of hearing is, shall we say, convenient. Especially when Annie," he pointed in the direction which the maid exited, "tries to get me to do something I don't want to. You understand?"

Emil smiled. "Yes, I think I do."

"What can I do for you, Mr.—?"

"Jacobs, Harold Jacobs."

"That's right, I remember now," said the old doctor, going back to pruning his flowers. "Do you mind?"

"No, of course not. I'd like to ask you about a traffic accident which occurred thirty-one years ago."

"That's a long time . . ."

"It involved a young couple named Turner, and a child, a boy about three."

The doctor stopped clipping, turned, and fixed his eyes on Rothstein. "Turner. Yes, I remember. What about it?"

"I was hoping you'd tell me. You signed the death certificates."

"What'd you say your name was?"

"Jacobs."

"You work for whom?"

"The New York City Attorney's office."

"Hogwash!"

"I beg your pardon?"

"You heard me. It's the same as bullshit!"

"I have identification."

"So what? It's probably phony. Now, you want to tell me the truth about who you are and why you're here?"

Momentarily nonplussed, Rothstein stalled. "What makes you think I'm lying?"

"Mr. Whoever-you-are, I was in practice for a very long time, learned it was more important to read patients than to listen to them. Patients often lie—for drugs, for sympathy, to get into the hospital, to get away from husbands, wives, bill collectors, whomever. If you're going to treat a person successfully, you learn to tell if he's lying. And you are."

This never would have happened ten years ago, Emil thought. Watch yourself. "I'll make you a deal," he said softly. "You tell me what you know, and I'll tell you who I really am, and who I really work for." Rothstein could hear the sincerity in his own words and a part of him despised it.

"You've got a deal," Carpenter said, resting against the raised bed of flowers. "What do you want to know about the Turners? Both parents were dead on arrival. With the recent publicity, I presume your real interest is in the boy, Joseph, isn't it?"

"Yes."

"Let me see . . . It was April, I think. Yes, it had to be, the trees were starting to bud. I'd been appointed Medical Examiner that year, taken office in January."

"Exactly what happened, Doctor?"

"Automobile accident—head-on—happened at night in Manhattan somewhere." Dr. Carpenter looked first to Emil then off through the glass wall of the hothouse. "You'd have to check with the police for the facts of the accident itself. But they brought the bodies to the morgue. You know the attendants aren't allowed to pronounce them dead at the scene?"

"Yes, I know."

"Well," exhaled the old man, "they brought the three bodies in—"

Emil cut him off sharply. "Three?"

"Yes, that's why I remember it so well. The boy was dead too."

Rothstein successfully swallowed the gasp that tried to escape from his chest. He took a deep breath. "What do you mean—dead?"

"Technically. His heart was stopped. There was not a mark on his body, but he was dead. No respiration, no pulse. I was curious, because usually there's some visible sign of the cause of death in an accident fatality, but not with the boy. So I rechecked him. I used my stethoscope—no heartbeat. I had turned away and my assistant was about to move the body when he called to me. He'd thought he felt a pulse. I checked again. Sure enough, the heartbeat was there. Only took us about five minutes to have that child screaming and crying."

"And you're certain there was no heartbeat the first time?"

"Certain."

"And no injuries?"

"None. They kept him in the hospital for a few days. We never told anyone; there seemed no reason to, and of course he was too young to understand any of it. Then the courts placed him at the South Bronx Home for Boys. I thought of him now and then over the years, but didn't hear of him again until he was in the papers. Kind of spooky, huh?"

Emil was extremely agitated but tried not to show it. "These things happen, doctor. I'm sure you've seen many miracles. Well, thank you for your time," he said, turning to leave.

"Wait," the doctor stopped him. "Your part of the bargain."

Emil turned back. "Oh, yes. I'm an investigator for Military Intelligence. We're doing an in-depth background investigation for a Top Secret Crypto clearance. Please don't mention that I was here."

He didn't wait for Carpenter's response.

Rothstein maintained his outward control until he was inside the limousine. There he sank back into the seat and allowed the excitement and fear to rush through his body.

"You go back to hotel now?" Hugo asked, his face and voice reflecting concern. Rothstein looked ill.

"I'm all right, Hugo. Just give me a few minutes to relax."

This could really be it, he thought. This really could be it. The idea was overwhelming. A lifetime of searching, hoping, being afraid of hope, and now just a few more days . . . He stopped himself. There were indeed a few more days; his work was not finished. And to carry out the final step, he needed to clear his head—and his conscience. He had told so many lies, and he was about to do worse.

"Hugo, we passed a church on the way here, just down the road. Take me back there."

"Yes, sir," Hugo said, putting the car in gear and pulling out of the drive.

At Saint Francis's Catholic Church, Emil Rothstein entered the confessional, knelt, and crossed himself. "Forgive me, Father, for I have sinned . . ."

Rothstein returned to his suite at the Waldorf feeling drained but at peace. It was fifteen minutes before Fletcher was to call. He could only wait. Finally the phone rang.

"Fletcher?"

"Yes?"

Rothstein felt a new surge of energy as he once again took charge. "I'm finished here. We're taking him with us tonight. Handle him carefully. Nothing must go wrong. The plane will be at Logan, ready to leave at two in the morning. We're going home."

NINETEEN

By monday morning Joseph was making plans to go to Miami. He and Maggie spent most of Saturday alone talking, surprised at how little difference the eleven-month separation had made. The lives they had built apart from each other dissolved in the prospect of living together again; it felt more like a continuation than a renewal of their intimacy. In some moments Joseph found himself feeling suspicious of how easy it was, but she teased him out of it and he let her. He was aware that there would be barriers enough to cross in the months ahead, and he was content to meet them as they came. He had stopped trying to understand much that had given him fear and pain in the last week and found himself more than willing to suspend judgment on what now gave him pleasure.

On Sunday after attending morning service in John's small chapel, they had lunched alone at a cozy restaurant overlooking Provincetown Harbor and trudged through deep snow to Monument Hill. From a vantage point shared only by a monument to the Pilgrims who had also begun a new life here by the sea, they savored the winter beauty of the Cape and the small city below. Beneath a clear winter sky now lonesome for the company of a cloud, they held each other and looked beyond the land to the old stone lighthouse a quarter-mile offshore which clung to an island no bigger than its base. The lighthouse appeared very small but very solid against the angry assault of the sea.

Maggie shivered and snuggled closer to him. "I'm getting cold. I'm not used to this refrigerated world."

"Well, my snow princess," he said, pulling her fur hood closer around her face, "in a few days you'll be back digging your toes into warm sand. Do you know," he said, pointing to the beach, "that pirates used to lure ships onto the Cape to loot them? Then they'd rape the women right there on the beach."

"In the snow?"

"Of course. Want me to show you how they did it?"

"Wouldn't you like to rape me somewhere more comfortable?"

He picked her up and headed down the hill. "You soft modern women," he complained, as they drove back to their cabin, "have no appreciation of passion."

The cabin John had given them was sparely furnished, but they had little need of furniture. They spread blankets by the fireplace, cooked their supper in the flames, and made love by firelight far into the night.

On Monday morning they walked up to the house to borrow John's station wagon. Relations between them and the Stantons had been strained since Saturday afternoon, so Joseph was surprised when Bonnie greeted them warmly and pulled Maggie off into the kitchen. "John's in the study; we'll join you in a few minutes."

When he entered the study John motioned him into a leather chair across the desk and looked at him silently for a moment. "You look happy," he said finally.

"I am. Happier than I've been for a long time."

"I'm glad. And your plans?"

"We're going to Miami for a while—long enough for me to pull myself together. I've got a lot of years ahead of me to use this power, John. I want some time to myself first. Eventually we'll go back to New York. I know my real life's there."

"I'd be surprised if you weren't back in the Bronx within a month," he smiled.

Joseph chuckled. "Yeah. Well, one day at a time. I just hope nobody decides to drown on the beach in Miami. Is it still OK if we take the car today?"

"Sure. Be back for supper? We were thinking of the Charlie Tar. You're welcome to join us."

Joseph looked at him questioningly. "Bonnie?"

"Bonnie's fine." He handed him the keys.

"We're going down to Eastham. We'll stop back by the restaurant and make reservations—eight o'clock?"

"Sounds good."

The women were coming down the hall as they stepped out of the study, and the four friends went to the front door together.

"See you tonight," Bonnie said, squeezing Maggie's hand.

Maggie leaned to her and kissed her on the cheek. "Thanks."

"What was that all about?" Joseph asked her as he started the car and let it warm up before backing out the gates.

"Bonnie's wonderful!" Maggie answered. She turned to him, her face glowing. "How much do you know about her?"

"That she's a marvelous woman, a good friend, thoroughly in love with John, who adores her, and a terrific mother. Of course she's wonderful."

"No, I mean, how much do you know about her past?"

"Only that she was a very successful model. John fell in love with her when she was on the cover of *Glamour*, as I remember. He married her the month after her last cover for *Vogue*."

"Yes, well. She told me something else—something she said she told John only last night . . ."

"Can you tell me?"

"Yes. You know how cold she was, how angry, when I came here. The other few times we've met it's been really hard for me. She said that she told herself, told John, it was because she hated the way I've lived and didn't want to be around a woman like that or have her around Amy." Maggie sighed a little. "And also that she didn't want me around you. She thought I'd hurt you, which I did." She reached over and ran her fingers over his hand. "But there was something else. It's tough for a model getting started in New York. Bonnie was very young. A few times, at the beginning of her career, there seemed to be only one way to get a job."

Joseph looked at her. She was looking past him out the window to the sea, her mouth slightly open. She looked very innocent and very young. "And now," he said gently, "when you come into her life, you remind her of that girl back there."

"Yes."

"But she came to terms with that last night?"

"Yes. It was very brave of her, Joey. I remember what

it was like when I told you, after the second time we met ice skating at Rockefeller Center."

He reached his arm around her and pulled her next to him. "It was a long time ago, Maggie. And a long time for Bonnie and John, too. I'm glad it's out, and over, and that you two can be friends." He brushed a tear from her cheek. "Now, let's have our day."

They spent their morning tobogganing on the great snow-covered dunes of Eastham, playing in the snow like children until they were bumped and bruised and out of breath. On the way back they stopped to make dinner reservations, then drove into the center of town and stopped at Gosnold Street.

"Here!" he shouted, jumping out of the car and running around to her side to pull her out. "I want to show you something!" He led her into the park to an outdoor band-stand and stood her facing the stage. "Now, my dear, stand right here—it's the best seat in the house."

"Joseph—what are you doing?"

He grabbed a branch from the ground, stripped its twigs, and stood on the stage with his back to her. "Now listen to this! Tum, tum ta tum tum," he hummed, conducting his make-believe concert band in what was apparently a rousing march, waving his arms wildly and finally turning to her with a deep bow. Maggie laughed and clapped and he reached down and picked an imaginary flower and threw it to her. She caught it and put it in her hair. "Oh, play another one!" she giggled.

"Of course, Miss," he said, bowing again. "A love song."

Since Fletcher had been in Provincetown he had discreetly followed Joseph. When the couple drove off after a brief stop at the Charlie Tar he hurried inside, learned of their dinner reservations, and took a few minutes to survey the restaurant. "It's perfect," he told Bermano by phone. "I'll make your reservation. You pick up the tools and parts and I'll meet you at the hospital."

When Fletcher arrived at the Provincetown Community Hospital, Bermano had already cased the parking lot and located the hospital's two yellow and white ambulances. Fletcher waited until darkness had settled in and then pulled the rented Ford into the lot beside one of the emergency vehicles. Quickly he got out, lifted the hood of the ambulance, and unclamped the distributor cap. Retrieving a pencil from his shirt pocket, he coated the inside terminals with lead and replaced the cap. He slammed the hood shut. A chill of excitement raced through his body; everything was falling into place nicely—that ambulance would be unavailable for anyone's use that night.

As they drove back to wait on the road near Stanton's property, Fletcher described the restaurant in detail to Bermano, and they carefully reviewed their timetable.

"What name is the reservation under?" Bermano asked.

"Dr. Fermi. I mentioned that he was a distinguished surgeon, visiting the hospital here. Are we to contact Emil?"

"No, he's not due in Boston until later. If something should happen, go wrong—"

"It won't."

"No, but if you need to, you can reach him after eleven at the Bello and Sons Funeral Home."

It was just after seven when Joseph and Maggie stepped from the shower and toweled each other dry. Maggie put on a peach-colored satin robe that clung seductively to her moist skin. Joseph loosened the towel from her hair and pulled her next to him. "I want you."

"Ummm, that's nice to hear. But we don't have time."

"We've got fifty years at least."

"Which includes an occasional time out for a meal," she said, kissing him on the nose and spinning from his grasp to enter the bedroom. "Now get ready. Bonnie and John will be waiting."

He followed her and sat on the bed, watching her move around the room.

"Are you going to get dressed or not?" she said.

"Are you going to live with me from now on or not?" he asked.

"If that's the only way I can get you dressed, yes."

"I'm not playing. Maggie. I want to know."

She stopped buttoning her blouse and looked at him. "What is it that you really want to know?"

"If you're going back to New York with me when I go."

He wasn't demanding. He looked very open, very vulnerable, and she sat by him and hugged him against her. "You sure picked a peculiar woman to give you guarantees, Joey. And that's what you're asking for right now. Well, I know not to make forever promises. Both of us have been let down and left alone too many times for that. But for as far as I can see, lover—yes. I don't want to live without you anymore either. Wherever you go, as long as I can have you to be with, to play with, to make love with, I'll be there."

He raised his head and kissed her eyes. "I don't know why," he said to her, "since you're right about forever promises, but right now I'm feeling more secure than I've felt for years."

"Good," she said, getting up and finishing her buttoning, "then we can go to dinner, and you won't be left alone because your lover starved to death."

When the Stantons' station wagon pulled into the parking lot of the Charlie Tar Restaurant, halfway between Provincetown and Eastham, the Ford lagged just far enough behind to allow the four time to enter the building. Then the dark-eyed Italian parked next to the Stantons' car. From the glove compartment Fletcher removed a hammer and screwdriver and handed them to Bermano, who got out and knelt next to the rear of the station wagon. Expertly he punctured the gas tank, then handed the tools through the open window to his accomplice. Fletcher slid behind the wheel and started up the Ford. As the ruptured tank drained its contents into the frozen gravel and the rented Ford disappeared down the highway, Bermano entered the restaurant.

Dr. Fermi requested a table directly across the room from Turner and his party. The lights were low and the room was filled with hanging ferns and potted benjamina figs, which made it difficult to see, but as his eyes adjusted he could see Turner's face reflected in the mirrored walls. He checked his watch. It was 8:20. He had exactly fifty minutes to wait, then ten minutes to accomplish his mission before Fletcher returned.

The fifty minutes passed slowly. Bermano found it hard to keep his eyes off his target. This Turner looked quite ordinary, except . . . except that he looked so happy. It was the brightness of his eyes, perhaps . . . or the broad easiness of his smile. Bermano forced his eyes away.

At exactly 9:10 Dr. Fermi rose, walked into the anteroom of the restaurant and entered one of two adjoining wooden phone booths. The light came on as he closed the door and pretended to dial. A couple passed through the anteroom; he waited until they had gone. Keeping an eye on the cashier, whose back was to him, he removed a small suction cup from his pocket, licked it, and placed it on the adjoining glass panel between the two booths. Then he took out a glass cutter, cut a hole the size of a softball in the pane, and pulled the severed glass away with the suction cup, placing both in his pocket. That done, he dropped a dime in the pay phone and dialed.

The phone in the next booth rang and the cashier left the register and came to answer it. "The Charlie Tar. May I help you?"

"Yes, I'm trying to reach a customer of yours, Joseph Turner."

"I'll see if he's here."

"Wait," said Bermano urgently. "Tell him it's Sammy Sweet."

"Yes, Mr. Sweet."

Bermano's heart beat wildly as he pulled a tubular CO_2-operated styrette from his pocket and twisted the cap at the end. He ordered his hand to stop shaking and his fingers stilled as he watched Turner cross the busy dining room and enter the booth.

Turner picked up the phone. "Hello, Sammy?"

In that moment Bermano thrust the styrette through the opening and against Turner's back. The CO_2 forced the drug into his body. Bermano watched as Joseph reeled in the booth and stared in shock at his assailant. Turner could not speak. Within several seconds his eyes rolled back in his head and he fell from the booth onto the anteroom floor.

The cashier heard the crash and shrieked when she turned but Bermano was the first to get to him. He checked his pulse and was listening to the heartbeat when the Stantons and Maggie rushed from their table.

"My God, what's happened?" Maggie screamed, as she knelt next to Joseph.

"I'm a doctor," Bermano said authoritatively. "He grabbed his head and then collapsed. I'll call the hospital."

Bonnie knelt next to Maggie, and John stood near them keeping curious onlookers from gathering. Maggie cradled Joseph's head in her lap; he looked pale and his breath was short and shallow. When Bermano left the phone booth, she was rocking back and forth and wailing softly, "Joey, oh no, please be OK . . ."

"Miss," said Bermano, "he mustn't be moved. The ambulance will be here in a moment."

The manager stepped toward them. "What is it, doctor?" he asked, with the deep concern of a lawsuit in his voice.

"I can't be sure, but it looks like a cerebral hemorrhage. Has he had a bad fall lately?"

Stanton nodded dazedly. "Yes."

They all heard the ominous sound of the approaching ambulance. Bermano knew Fletcher would need his assistance with the gurney but waited until the siren had stopped in front of the restaurant before running out the door. In a moment he reappeared with Fletcher, who was now wearing what appeared to be hospital whites, and between them they wheeled the gurney up next to Turner.

"Lift him evenly," said Luici.

The manager and John helped to lift Joseph's body onto the stretcher. Together the four men raced the gurney out the door to the ambulance.

Maggie followed them out. "Doctor, can I ride with him?"

"I'd rather you didn't. Follow us in your car." Stanton took Maggie by the shoulders and led her to the station wagon.

Bermano climbed in and closed the massive rear door to the ambulance. "Let's get out of here," he said as Fletcher threw the vehicle into gear, reactivated the siren, and swung the ambulance out of the parking lot and onto the highway. The station wagon had just enough gas to follow the ambulance for a mile. Then John's car chugged to a stop at the side of the road. Maggie, now hysterical, clutched frantically to Bonnie as the ambulance disappeared from sight.

Inside the hospital vehicle Fletcher craned his neck around. "The car's up ahead, off the road."

Bermano braced himself as Fletcher pulled off Highway 6 onto a secondary road leading to the beach. Behind a small stand of pines they transferred Joseph to the back seat of the

Ford and covered him with a blanket. Fletcher changed into his suit, and the two men headed onto the highway toward Boston.

Before the Provincetown police found the stolen hospital vehicle, Bermano had wheeled the Ford into the rear entrance of the Bello and Sons Funeral Home on Boyleston Street in Boston.

Emil waited inside. "You're late. It's well after one."

"Sorry. We didn't want to speed, couldn't take the chance," replied Luici.

"Where is he?" asked Rothstein.

"In the back seat."

Antonio Bello approached from down the hallway. "Mr. Rothstein, we're ready."

"Thank you, Antonio. He's in the back seat of the Ford."

"We will take great care. Tino!"

Bello's son answered his father's call and together the two men headed out the back door.

"What about the airport, Emil?" Luici said with concern.

"It's taken care of. Customs is expecting us to leave with a body. A dear, departed colleague. The crew is waiting for us now."

"I'll bet they can't wait to get out of U.S. airspace," Fletcher said, smiling.

"That, my young friend, is an understatement!"

Within fifteen minutes Joseph lay inside a bronze coffin in the back of the funeral home's finest hearse. Emil rode in front with Bello, while Fletcher, Bermano, and Tino followed in the Ford.

At Logan International, the two-car convoy entered the complex through the south gate. As the two vehicles drove across the apron toward the waiting 747, a U.S. Customs car, its blue lights flashing, pulled from its space in front of the office and rolled across the taxiway. All three cars stopped next to the in-flight truck that had been requested by Rothstein to lift the casket into the plane.

The Head of Customs at Logan stepped from his car and approached the arriving group.

"Mr. Rothstein, please?" he requested officiously in his thick Bostonian accent.

"I'm Rothstein," Emil said, smiling and extending a hand.

The customs officer returned the handshake but not the smile. "Gerald Endicott, U.S. Customs. I'll need to see your passports and a death certificate." His speech was quick and curt.

"I have them right here," Emil answered, reaching inside his overcoat to his suitcoat pocket and handing the documents to the official.

"There are four of you leaving, including the body?"

"That's correct."

"I'll hold on to these until I see the deceased." Endicott slapped the passports and death certificate against his right thigh and walked past Rothstein to the rear of the hearse. Luici shot Emil a look of apprehension.

Rothstein raised his thick brows and paced after the head of Customs. "This is highly irregular, isn't it?"

"Is there some reason you'd rather I didn't view the body?" asked Endicott suspiciously.

"No, of course not; it's just that we're usually extended immunity from search."

"I understand that, Mr. Rothstein, but you must remember that your delegation is not an official diplomatic one, but instead one to which we extend certain diplomatic courtesies."

"Are you a religious man, Mr. Endicott?"

"Only off duty. The body, please?"

Rothstein nodded and turned his attention to his aides and the Bellos. "Place the casket on the truck lift and open it, please." The four men rolled the casket to the back of the hearse and carried it the five yards to the front of the inflight truck, placing it on the lift. Antonio Bello unscrewed the lid and then turned to Endicott.

"I'll let you open it," he said, grimacing.

Endicott walked to the side of the bronze coffin and lifted the viewing lid. The smell of death permeated his nostrils as he gazed at the waxen corpse of a man in his sixties. Quickly he shut the lid.

"Damn," exclaimed Endicott, shuddering. The Customs official quickly stamped the passports and handed them back to Rothstein with the death certificate. "Have a pleasant journey," he said sardonically.

Rothstein nodded his reply, then watched the obviously nauseated man return to his car and drive away.

Bello had resealed the coffin. "If ever I can be of assistance again . . ." he said to Rothstein.

"Antonio, you will be remembered," Rothstein said, shaking the man's hand and stepping onto the truck's platform with Bermano and Fletcher. "Assure your wife that her uncle will receive a proper burial."

"She knows that. Have a safe journey. God be with you."

Rothstein motioned to the driver, who immediately activated the lifting system. At the jetway the co-pilot and engineer assisted Bermano and Fletcher with the casket. With everybody safely aboard, Emil closed and sealed the door.

At exactly 2:34 A.M. on November 23, the flight controller of Logan International gave the Rothstein jet clearance for departure. As soon as the mammoth jet reached cruising altitude, Rothstein watched Bermano and Fletcher extricate Joseph from the bottom of the casket. They checked his pulse and, satisfied that he was all right, carried him to the bedroom at the rear of the plane. They laid him gently on top of the purple velvet bedspread and covered him with a similarly colored down comforter.

The kidnapping had been successful.

TWENTY

JOSEPH SLOWLY OPENED his eyes, struggling to see through the blurred darkness. His throat was dry and his mouth tasted bitter. "Maggie?" he whispered, reaching across the soft bed to find emptiness. No one there. The room vibrated to a low-pitched roar, but in his grogginess he made no sense of the sensation. Then the room pitched slightly and leveled; his body moved instinctively with the motion. An airplane? He made out the curvature of the cabin walls. He raised himself up on his elbow, swallowed to unplug his ears, and struggled to sharpen his vision. The memory of the restaurant, the phone booth, a fuzzy picture of a man's face, and then the sensation of losing consciousness returned to him as his eyes began to adjust to the small amount of light that filtered in around the windowshade and seeped from beneath a doorway across the cabin.

He started to call out, stopped himself. Whoever had knocked him out or drugged him in the restaurant must be on the other side of that door. He strained to hear, cocking his head toward the muffled sounds of movement.

He sat up, aware of heaviness and stiffness in his body but no pain. He pushed off the blankets covering him and reached out to lift the windowshade halfway up. Sunlight poured into the cabin. He had no idea what time it was, or even what day. He leaned to look out the window, to see only clouds below. He turned back to a room alive now with color, the rich purples of the rug and curtains, fabric-covered chairs, blankets; golden reflections off the lacquered wood of the walls and small table and the polished brass of ornate fixtures. Whoever owned this airplane lived in great luxury. He felt bewildered by contradiction: how could someone living in a room such as this be capable of the violence that had

145

brought him here? And what could they want *him* for? And only him? Or were Maggie and the Stantons here too?

Slowly shifting his body, he placed his bare feet on the thickly carpeted floor, stood, and moved cautiously toward the door. He caught faint whispers of men talking. He reached out and firmly closed his hand around the brightly polished brass door handle. Slowly, calmly, gently, he pressed the handle until he felt the latch release. Silently he eased the door open an inch.

Through the opening he surveyed the larger cabin. A vaguely familiar dark-haired man sat at a desk. A red-haired man slouched while eating in one of the velvet chairs. There was a quick movement from the couch. Joseph's eyes shifted to see an older man look up from his sheaf of papers and over the top of his glasses toward the door.

Their eyes locked. Joseph felt a surge of anticipation. The man on the couch stiffened, then, raising himself to a sitting position, never changing his focus, he called out, "Fletcher, he's awake."

The red-haired man swirled around, his mouth full of food. He stared wide-eyed at the tall, trim figure partly visible in the slightly opened doorway. The man at the desk stopped writing and looked up, and Joseph recognized him as the man in the phone booth.

He pushed the door open slowly, his hand still grasping the doorknob, his knuckles white from his grip. The men stared at him; it seemed a long time before anyone spoke.

"Hello, Mr. Turner," came the abrupt address from the man on the couch.

"Who are you?" Joseph asked, his voice level but obviously angry.

"My name is Emil Rothstein. Please come in."

"Who are your friends?"

"These are my associates, Thomas Fletcher," he said, pointing to the man with red hair, "and this is Luici Bermano."

"We've met," Joseph said icily. "You didn't answer my question, Mr. Rothstein."

"What do you mean?" There was an odd mixture of assurance and respect in Rothstein's voice. Was it to put him at ease or to keep him calm? He was aware that his own physical presence dominated the room: he was a large, muscular man, and none of the three was any match for him, nor did they appear to have weapons. He kept his back to the door.

"I said, who are you?" His eyes riveted on Emil Rothstein. Rothstein did not speak.

Joseph strode quickly into the room to the small table in front of Fletcher. In a flash he leaned over, picked up a small paring knife from Fletcher's plate, and, still facing the other two men, placed the point of the knife sharply against Fletcher's neck. Bermano started to get up but Rothstein put up his hand. He continued to watch Joseph calmly.

"Oh, my God!" Fletcher moaned.

"I don't give a damn what your names are," Joseph said. "Who are you? What am I doing here? Where are you taking me?" Joseph nudged the point of the knife into Fletcher's neck.

"Emil!" blurted Fletcher in a wailing tone.

"Be quiet, Thomas. He won't hurt you."

"Are you certain of that?" retorted Joseph.

"Quite certain, Mr. Turner," Rothstein replied. "You are not a man who kills. You are a man who heals. You'll not harm Thomas. So please sit down. This is not necessary."

"How do you know about me?"

"Well, the whole world knows certain things about you, Mr. Turner. Your healing is common knowledge. You're a famous person."

"What do you want?"

"It is necessary for you to accompany us. I am sorry that I cannot yet tell you why."

"But you've kidnapped me! Why?" Joseph demanded, pressing the knife a little harder against Fletcher's throat.

"Because it was necessary that you come safely and immediately, without conflict or a public scene. I have reason to believe you would not accompany us voluntarily."

"You're right about that. And my friends? Are they here too?"

"No. Only yourself. But your friends have been contacted and notified that you are safe and that you will be away for a time."

"Away where? Where are we?"

Rothstein glanced at his watch. "It's seven A.M., that puts us about twenty-six hundred miles from Boston."

"Which direction?"

"Over the Atlantic."

"Where are you taking me?"

"To see a man who can explain what has been happening to you: why you lived through your fall, what happened in the fire, and why you're able to heal."

"Who is this man?"

"I'm not at liberty to answer that question," Emil said, shaking his head.

"Why not?"

"I'm sorry. I know this is very confusing, but I cannot answer your questions. We will do everything else in our power to make you comfortable. Now. please put the knife down. You can't hurt him. Your body will heal him as soon as you cut him, and I'm sure he's very uncomfortable in that position. No one is going to harm you, believe me."

"Why should I believe you?"

"Because nothing will be gained by not believing me. I couldn't fly you back to Boston even if I wanted to, you see; we're past the halfway point. Please put the knife down. Come and join me here on the couch, and I will explain all that I can about what has happened. Would you like some coffee?" He turned to Bermano. "Luici, bring Mr. Turner some coffee."

Joseph relaxed his grip momentarily on the knife and watched the younger man at the desk rise slowly and move to a small table on the opposite side of the room. Luici poured two cups of coffee and placed two rolls on a plate.

Joseph pulled his hand away from Fletcher's neck, keeping a firm grip on the handle of the knife. He stepped cautiously over to the couch and sat in a position where he could see all three men and both doors.

Rothstein spoke again. "You're in a Boeing 747, about thirty-six thousand feet above the Atlantic, heading east. But I cannot tell you where we will be landing."

"Thanks a lot."

"Please be patient, Joseph. Forgive me," he said, hesitantly. "May I call you Joseph? I really don't like formalities. You may call me Emil."

"No."

Rothstein did not hesitate. "As I was saying, Mr. Turner, please be patient with us."

"I'm not."

"We are on a very important mission representing an international, or, better yet, a *universal* organization which has a great interest in your gift."

"What organization?"

"I know my vagueness is surely bewildering and confusing to you but you'll discover our intentions and motivations soon enough. For now, we must wait."

Joseph knew he had very little choice in the matter. He took a sip of coffee and washed the last taste of sleep from his mouth, put the cup down and picked up a roll. Was this food drugged too? He looked down and noticed that his left hand was still gripping the paring knife. "You won't mind if I hold this, will you, Mr. Rothstein?"

"If it makes you feel more comfortable, Mr. Turner. We'll be having breakfast in a short time and you can use it then, if you like." Rothstein half-smiled as he spoke. Joseph did not return the smile.

Rothstein watched him intensely.

"Will you stop staring at me like that? I'm not going to do anything."

Rothstein broke his stare. "No, of course not. Sorry. I'm simply interested in you, Mr. Turner."

"In the way I eat?"

Rothstein laughed. "No." He threw up his hands. "This must seem so strange." He shook his head, smiling.

His smile was disarming and this time Joseph returned it in spite of himself. "Strange is an understatement."

Joseph pondered the possibilities. The plane was headed for Europe. Rothstein had an accent, German or East European. Who would he be working for? Obviously someone very wealthy. They went to a lot of effort and expense to get him. Was this some kind of political act? Rothstein had the elegance of a diplomat but was obviously capable of violence. Perhaps some Eastern European country? He had read about the great interest of the Russians and East Germans in psychic phenomena. Perhaps they were interested in him as a potential subject in some kind of research? Was this what Rothstein meant about answers? But then why not simply ask him to go? Besides, he couldn't be that important.

Well, if not a political act, then what? It could be some very wealthy individual, maybe someone terminally ill—and also a little crazy—who hoped Joseph could cure him and devised this incredible kidnapping scenario. Rothstein would make a good rich-man's emissary—but would he work for some lunatic?

Joseph studied his captors. Unlikely-looking kidnappers —none of them fit the part they seemed to have played in his abduction, least of all Rothstein.

But then I'm not right for my part, either, he thought. A kidnap victim in some international conspiracy? A healer so famous that someone wants him in Europe—and so badly that they force him there?

Was it only yesterday he'd told Maggie how secure he felt? He sat back, trying not to think, telling himself simply to wait.

Rothstein seemed to have read his thoughts. "We have a long ride ahead of us. Then, you will have all of your answers." He hesitated a moment before continuing. "And we shall have ours."

TWENTY-ONE

WHEN THE AIRPLANE finally began its descent, Joseph felt his body tighten with excitement. The waiting had seemed interminable. He would know soon.

He watched Bermano walk across the cabin and pull the windowshades down; they did not want him to see the city below. Soon he felt the wheels lock, and within minutes there was the jar of the touchdown and the roar of reversed engines. The plane slowed smoothly, turned, taxied, stopped.

"Shall we go?" said Rothstein, standing.

They walked quickly to the cabin door, and as it opened Joseph looked out into an enclosed walkway. He looked for signs but there were none, and the walkway ended in a covered portico over the open doors of a waiting limousine. It came to him suddenly that they were as much concerned about his being seen as about his seeing.

Rothstein followed him into the car, closed the door, and the vehicle moved off. The windows had been blackened and a curtained heavy glass window was drawn between them and the driver. Rothstein pushed a button and exchanged a few words with the driver, in German. Joseph listened for a place, a name, but heard none.

"No customs check?" he asked Rothstein.

"That has all been taken care of, Mr. Turner. We have about an hour's trip ahead of us, and you may want to get some rest."

"I've rested so long I'm exhausted."

Emil smiled kindly, nodding respectfully, but remained silent, impenetrable.

Joseph looked down, tracing his finger over the brown stripes on his shirtsleeve. They looked like roads, endless roads, ending nowhere but in empty space. Suddenly he slammed his fist into the seat, wishing it was the window. He wanted to break out, get space, get free; well, a broken window wouldn't get it for him. He looked over at Rothstein, who seemed calm. He'd have to wait, stay alert, keep himself together.

Once more he directed his thoughts to his captors, letting his mind sift through what he knew. No customs check upon arrival. A private plane and a limousine meeting it right on the runway. Money, power, connections. They clearly had it all.

But why was his presence such a secret? Now that he was in their territory, country, whatever, what the hell could he do, anyway? He had no passport, no money; all his identification had been packed away in Fletcher's briefcase. It had to be that they didn't want him to be seen. Why? Were they afraid he'd be recognized? That thought seemed ridiculous. He wasn't *that* famous. Maybe his captors were. If the plane or Rothstein, or the car and the driver, were easily identifiable, then anyone looking for him would know where Joseph had gone. But would anyone be looking?

Rothstein had said that the man he was going to see was someone with answers. At the moment, that possibility was all the future Joseph had to hold on to.

It was certainly a different future than what he'd been planning. He thought of Maggie, hoping she wasn't afraid, knowing she must be. Or did they tell her more than they told him?

Rothstein stared ahead but was acutely aware of the man beside him. He had watched Joseph closely. Despite the small outbursts, Turner was remarkably calm. Rothstein was glad. Such inner strength would be much needed in the hours ahead.

The car finally came to a stop and the doors opened. Joseph stepped out into the cold night; they were inside a courtyard, surrounded by buildings whose sixty-foot walls rose ominously in the damp, moonless night.

"This way, please," said Rothstein, taking Joseph's arm. He was hurried over stone steps into the well-lit, seemingly deserted structure, then taken through long halls and up two different broad staircases to a suite of rooms hung with tapestries. He entered and Rothstein stood at the door. "Please be comfortable for a few minutes. Then I shall return and we shall talk. If you need anything at all, push that button there." A young dark-haired man dressed in a dark-blue suit appeared next to Rothstein in the doorway. "Carlo will bring you whatever you need." Before Joseph could answer, the door closed and he was alone.

Like a newly caged cat he explored his surroundings. The small windows were barred from the outside, and all he could see through them was black nothingness. Inside his two high-ceilinged rooms the furnishings, though elegant, provided no information, as they were a conglomeration of antiques from several European countries. There were no magazines or books, no printed material of any kind. The patterned tapestries on the walls filled the rooms with greens and golds. Here was wealth—old, old wealth. He began to explore again, looking for some clue to where he was being held.

In a small room one floor below, Rothstein stood with Bermano in front of a television monitor watching Joseph move about his rooms. Behind them an elderly white-haired man with a hooked nose, dressed in a white robe and satin slippers, sat in an elaborately worked high-backed chair, also watching. They spoke in Italian.

"He is young and strong," the old man said, "and impatient. Go now, have your talk. You have one hour. Then we must make the examination."

When the door to Joseph's room opened, he was startled to see a much subdued Emil Rothstein. The older man looked very tired and very sad.

"Are you all right? Is something wrong?"

Rothstein composed himself quickly. "Everything is fine, Mr. Turner."

"For you maybe. But what about me?"

"Let's talk, and eat," he said as Carlo wheeled a service cart into the room. Rothstein motioned for Joseph to sit at the small oak dining table. Reluctantly, he sat across from the bespectacled man and waited until Carlo had placed steak dinners in front of them, poured wine from a crystal decanter, and left the room.

"Doesn't he ever say anything?" asked Joseph, eyeing the door as it closed quietly.

"He can neither speak nor hear. He reads and writes four languages fluently, including English, and can understand it from your lips."

"This place gives me the creeps!"

"I'm sorry," Rothstein said as he cut into the filet.

"When do I get to meet the man?"

"I'm afraid it won't be until tomorrow morning."

"Damn you, Rothstein! You said—"

"I know, please forgive me. It is not up to me."

"This is ridiculous. I'm sitting here eating dinner with a man who kidnapped me! Why?" Joseph asked loudly, slamming his fork to the plate.

"So we can talk informally," answered Emil.

"For the purpose of?"

"Knowing you better." And letting him know you, Emil didn't say.

"Well?"

"You have learned in the last few weeks that you have acquired a remarkable power."

Joseph said nothing. He finally gave in to his hunger and began to eat.

"How do you feel about it?"

"I don't know. Different ways at different times. I'm not even sure I have it. It's just happened a couple of times. So if what you want is for me to heal someone, don't count on it."

"No. It's not that. But I am certain you could. What if you were certain?"

"Look. If I can heal people, at will, I'll do it. But in my own time and on my own terms. I already had one offer and turned it down."

"I know."

"You know what? How do you know?"

"I have conducted a thorough investigation of you. It was a man named Bridger, I believe."

"I want to know why."

"Soon. Mr. Turner, how do you explain your power to yourself?"

"I haven't."

"Have you considered it as a gift from God?"

"I've never been religious."

"You read philosophy."

"For practical purposes, practical wisdom. I guess it's been my substitute. I'm interested in how people should live. They don't live very happily, as a rule."

"Those who know you tell us you expend much effort to make others' lives happier."

Joseph shrugged. 'When I can."

"You're a good man, Mr. Turner. You care a great deal about people."

"Yes."

"Have you always?"

"I guess."

"When you were very young, your family was taken from you. Have you felt alone since then?"

"I can't explain it to you, but, no." Joseph's speech began to slur as he continued. "I've been lonely, of course, but I haven't felt the kind of aloneness you'd expect a child like that to feel." Joseph grabbed the sides of the table with both hands as the walls began to swirl around his head. "I feel dizzy," he mumbled as he tried to stand. "What have you done?" Rothstein came around the table and supported Joseph while he fought to keep his eyes open. He finally collapsed, unconscious.

The door opened and the elderly white-haired gentleman, walking with the aid of a gold-headed cane, entered the suite, followed by Rothstein's aides. Silently he studied the unconscious man for a moment, then, clutching the pendant hanging around his neck, he instructed quietly in Italian. "It is time to proceed. Look for the mark."

Bermano and Fletcher moved Joseph to the bed and began to undress him, carefully and systematically checking every inch of his body as they removed his clothing. Finally Bermano turned to the old man and bowed. "There is nothing."

"Good," the old man acknowledged, then turned to Emil. "There is nothing more to be done until morning."

Emil walked with him to the door, speaking for his ears alone. "Is it necessary to do the test that way?"

"Yes, Emil." There was much gentleness in the old man's voice.

"But if he is not—"

"Then he will die. But the knowledge of it will not leave these walls."

"Forgive me, but is there no other way?"

The old man was angry now. "Emil," he exclaimed, "you know this decision is not mine alone."

Emil nodded solemnly and opened the door. His superior left without another word, and Rothstein turned back to Joseph, naked and still unconscious. "Cover him!" he said angrily. Bermano and Fletcher did as ordered and quickly left the room. Rothstein looked down at the sleeping man. "May God be with you, Joseph Turner," he said softly. Then he too left the suite.

Early the next morning, sunlight from Joseph's window inched slowly across the floor, up the side of the bed, and touched his head. But it was the sound of the door opening that caused his eyes to flicker open. It was Rothstein; he looked ten years older. He carried a tray containing cups and a coffeepot to the bedside table and pulled up a chair.

"How do you feel?" Emil asked.

"Angry." Joseph fluffed the heavy down pillow, then sat up, resting it between his back and the headboard. "You look terrible, like you haven't slept."

"I haven't," Emil answered, pouring a cup of coffee and holding it out to Joseph.

"You first," Joseph said. Rothstein smiled, took a sip, then offered the cup again.

Joseph took it. "Why did you drug me again?"

"It was necessary."

Rothstein looked worried. "What's the matter?" Joseph joked, half-hopefully. "Find out you got the wrong guy?"

"I sincerely hope not, Joseph." The intensity with which Rothstein spoke carried a meaning much deeper than his words, and Joseph's smile disappeared.

"What happens now?"

"In a few minutes you will get dressed and accompany me to another room for a meeting with my superior."

"Finally. Then what?"

Rothstein shook his head. "I don't know. It's best we take this one step at a time. I took the liberty of having your clothes cleaned last night. They're in the armoire."

Emil pointed at the large antique mirrored cabinet across the room, then stood. "Drink your coffee. I'll be back for you in half an hour. Please be dressed, Mr. Turner." Joseph nodded and watched him cross the room and leave the apartment.

In the next thirty minutes Joseph grew increasingly anxious. As he dressed, Rothstein's words—"I sincerely hope not"—turned over and over in his mind. No matter how much he drank, his mouth felt dry. His heartbeat seemed to reverberate off the walls of the room. Something had gone wrong; Rothstein was extremely upset. Joseph felt woozy, sick to his stomach, and scared. He paced the room until the door opened again. His head reflexively snapped around as Rothstein entered.

"It's time."

"Good. Let's get this over with," Joseph said, following Rothstein out the door.

Once in the elaborately decorated hallway, Rothstein pointed toward two twenty-foot wood-and-brass doors at the far end. "That's the room," he said, taking Joseph by the arm. Together, they made what seemed to Joseph an endless walk down the deserted corridor. Finally they stood in front of the massive doors. Emil raised his right hand and knocked. The mighty doors swung inward.

They were at the foot of the red-carpeted center aisle of an immense medieval chapel. The pillared walls rose fifty feet above them to stained-glass windows. The room was filled with shafts of colored light. At the other end of the aisle, steps led up to an ornate altar. Before it an old man in white-and-gold satin robes and a white skullcap sat on an elaborate gilt throne. On each side of the aisle, dark wood pews were occupied by about thirty standing men, attired in red, purple, blue, brown, and yellow robes. Emil guided Joseph between them down the aisle toward the throne.

Joseph stopped suddenly and pulled back. "What the—"

Rothstein cut him off. "An Ecumenical Tribunal, Mr. Turner. Please." Emil motioned down the aisle to the white-haired hook-nosed man sitting on the golden throne.

"Mr. Rothstein, bring him to me," commanded the old man in heavily accented English.

"That's your superior?" Joseph said, looking at Rothstein. Emil moved him forward again. "Yes," he said quietly.

Stunned, Joseph pointed to the man seated on the throne. "But isn't he the—"

"Yes."

"My God!" exclaimed Joseph. A murmur arose from the robed men in the pews on each side of him. "Oh—I'm sorry," he said. The men stared at him. He stared back, utterly bewildered.

Finally Emil and Joseph stood directly at the base of the three stairs looking up to the throne. On each side stood an elaborately costumed man holding a double-edged sword. On the immediate left was a man in a long red robe.

"What am I supposed to do?" Joseph whispered nervously to Emil. But Rothstein had stepped aside.

"You are Joseph Turner?" the man on the throne said to him.

Joseph nodded.

"I am the Servant of the Servants of God, Pope Alexander IX."

Joseph looked at him, fumbling through his mind for some behavior that seemed appropriate. "Sir—" he stopped.

Rothstein's voice came softly behind him. "You address him as Your Holiness."

"Oh, Your Holiness." He nodded a small bow and looked up questioningly. "You brought me here?"

"That is correct."

"But why? Surely there's some mistake."

"We do not think so."

Joseph felt suddenly more composed, and somewhere mixed with his awe there was anger. Was all this secrecy and the kidnapping set up by the Pope? A religious leader? "Then may I ask, respectfully request, some explanation?"

"You must not be angry with us," said the Pontiff evenly, "for your presence here could be the culmination of a search that began five hundred and thirty-one years ago."

"That's a long time, Your Holiness. But I don't understand what it has to do with me."

"Let His Eminence explain, Mr. Turner." Rothstein's voice was soft and reassuring.

"Mr. Turner," said the Pontiff, "Mr. Rothstein is the Legate a Latere of Miracles for the Holy See."

"I don't know what that means."

"It means he investigates miracles for the Vatican, for me. He has investigated yours."

"Miracles? What—"

The Pope held up his hand to silence Joseph. Then with voice raised, he began a rhythmic chanting proclamation. "In the Year of Our Lord, fourteen hundred and forty-seven, the Blessed Pope Nicholas V was visited by the Archangel Uriel. That messenger of our Holy Father delivered unto Nicholas the greatest of all gifts, a Prophecy: He said unto Nicholas that one day our Heavenly Father, the Lord Almighty, would send to His children on earth a man who would die and be reborn, who in his thirty-second year could fall from the highest mountain and be unscathed; could walk through the fires of Hell and be unburned of flesh; whose heart would be so pure that it could not be stopped until after Good Friday of his thirty-second year. In his time on Earth he will deliver a message of life to the world. Every Pope since Nicholas V has had the duty to continue the search for such a man."

Pope Alexander paused and looked over the room. It was filled with tense, excited silence.

"The Archangel warned Pope Nicholas to beware of the imposters of darkness, for another man would come upon the earth to oppose the will of God and try to destroy His Word. That man would carry the mark of Satan, the sign of 666." The Pontiff's aged eyes looked directly into Joseph's. "Last night an examination was made. Your body is free of the mark.

"We believe that you have been sent by God. We believe that you are the man God has sent in fulfillment of the prophecy."

Joseph's head was spinning, trying to grasp what he heard. "What?" His voice echoed loudly through the chapel. "I'm Joseph Turner, an ordinary person. Why do you think—"

"We have several reasons for believing so."

"Your Holiness, pardon me, but you're wrong." And you're all crazy, Joseph said to himself.

"And," continued the Pontiff evenly, "we must be certain."

"Wait just a minute," Joseph said, holding up his hand in desperation. "You are wrong, mistaken. I'm thirty-four."

"No, Mr. Turner, you are thirty-one—this is your thirty-second year."

"I mean no disrespect, Your Holiness. But I ought to know how old I am! I was born thirty-four years ago."

"Yes, the first time. But you died at the age of three in the accident that took your parents, and were given new life. You were reborn a short time later."

"No," said Joseph, shaking his head and looking to Rothstein for support.

"Yes, Mr. Turner," Emil said.

"Wait, you don't understand," pleaded Joseph. "I didn't fall off a mountain."

"The modern buildings of today are like mountains," said the Pontiff, stroking the head of his gold cane.

"Please, listen, I don't know why you're doing this, but—"

The Pope cut him off. "The apartment-house fire symbolizes the fires of Hell. A damnation no ordinary man could have endured."

"Wait." He needed time to think and had none. "What about the last part of your prophecy: a heart that can't be stopped? You see, I—" But the memory of the fall and the fire overwhelmed him and he stopped. He turned to look at the gathering.

Then the Pope's voice filled the silence. "We have not forgotten. That is what we must now test," the Pontiff ordered.

"What? Wait a minute!" Joseph said, turning back to see the Pope signal the guard on his right.

The guard quickly produced a .45 caliber automatic and leveled it at Joseph's chest.

Joseph sucked in his breath in horror as the bullet exploded from the gun. For a second he thought he could see the projectile racing at him. Then he felt something hit his chest and he was knocked backward into the men behind him.

Several seconds later, Joseph opened his eyes and stood looking down at the bullet that lay on the floor where he'd been standing. Totally dismayed, he looked up at the Pope.

The Pope moved from his throne to Joseph, went to his knees, bowed to kiss Joseph's feet. The priests, bishops, and cardinals knelt and prayed aloud.

The guard who had fired dropped the pistol, fell to his knees, and buried his head in his hands. "Please forgive me!" he said. Rothstein, also kneeling, wept.

Wide-eyed, Joseph stared at the kneeling men. He felt something on his shoulders and looked around to see a cardinal placing a golden robe around him. Then the Pope raised his head and over the clamoring of bells that now filled the chapel, Joseph heard the Pope's voice.

"Blessed be the Father, the Son, and the Holy Ghost! *Gloria in excelsis Deo!* We have found the Second Son of God!"

PART II

TWENTY-TWO

HAZY LATE MORNING SUNLIGHT filtered through the high arched windows of the Pope's private apartment. Joseph Turner, the woven-gold robe still draped over his shoulders, sat on an elevated white satin armchair, watching dust float in the shafts of light. Lesser, distant bells had joined the clamor of those at St. Peter's, their rhythmic orchestration carrying him far beyond the rustle of robed figures and drone of muted voices around him inside the room.

Every few moments a near, familiar voice reached him as though from a distance. "His Excellency Angelo Cardinal Pacelli, Director General of the Administrative and Economic Services of the Holy See," Emil Rothstein murmured quietly beside him, as a procession of aged scarlet-clad figures continued to drift before him in and out of his awareness.

Joseph saw them as if from far away, feeling, as he had since the Pope's pronouncement, like an unwitting participant in some strange Renaissance pageant. The rest of the ceremony—the chanting, the music, the praying and weeping—had melted together for him. When it was over, he let them move him out of the chapel, through halls lined with cassocked priests and bishops bowing deeply as the assemblage passed, and into these rooms. He had resisted nothing, volunteered nothing. It was as if his world had slipped a final gear. Outside was a delirium he could neither understand nor control. Inside all was quiet.

"His Excellency Giulio Cardinal Mendetti, Secretary of the Congregation of Extraordinary Ecclesiastical Affairs," the familiar voice continued, as another scarlet-robed, solemn-faced man approached, kneeled, rose, and retreated to join

165

the other members of the Sacred College surrounding the
Pope on the other side of the room.

Pope Alexander, suddenly wearied by the tension that had
been with him for the past twenty-four hours, looked up from
his desk with its stack of reports and documents and allowed
himself a moment to escape some of the burden of his responsibility. He was acutely aware of how much the anxiety
and excitement of the last days had drained his energies, yet
he felt stronger now than he had in months. It was nearly a
year since he'd suffered a mild heart attack, and until the
recent pains in his chest had forewarned of a possible second
attack, he'd steadfastly ignored the subtle hints aimed at per-
suading him to retire. Even in moments of private contempla-
tion, when he had sometimes imagined what it would be to
be a private citizen, retired and living his remaining months
in peace and solitude, a strong feeling that his work was not
yet finished and an even stronger belief that God would
retire him when he was ready, had kept him in office, determined to continue as much as possible to fulfill his responsibilities. He was grateful now for his decision and for the
secrecy he had imposed on the few who knew of his present
condition. He would be taxed heavily to bear the increased
load on his already heavy schedule, but none of that mat-
tered now.

For the last hour a steady stream of bishops from the various departments of the Roman Curia had been coming in
and out of the apartment carrying documents, whispering
messages, and casting sideways glances toward their Holy
Guest. Now his own eyes were drawn again to the Blessed
Son, and he felt once more a wave of benevolence and grati-
tude and love. The Holy Joseph's expression, so full of youthful innocence and ageless 'wisdom, had not once lost its
serenity since their return from the chapel. The Pope said
a silent prayer of thanksgiving for the opportunity of his own
service, and then abruptly pulled himself back to his work.
Now, with whatever time remained to him, taking care of
administrative details was how he could best serve the Second Son of God.

When he had finished approving the immediate documents, ascertained that priority actions had been set into mo-

tion, and watched all but the six-member Commission for Service to the Second Son of God leave the room, he turned to his Secretary of State. "Dominic, we mustn't keep the Holy Son waiting longer."

Dominic Cardinal Belazzi pursed his thin lips slightly and glanced through the papers in his hand. "Just a few more items, Your Holiness. A call from the U.S. Embassy. Mr. Sackheim feels that under the circumstances a special liaison should be established to keep the U.S. State Department informed of any new developments."

Pope Alexander nodded. "It would be most undiplomatic of us to refuse. What else, now?"

"We have already had two calls from our ministers at the World Bank. They are most concerned about the immediate potential for large fluctuations."

"We will take up the matter at our meeting later this afternoon. Until then, keep me closely informed of all political and economic dislocations, however insignificant they may appear. Now, my brothers, is there anything else?" He looked around the silent circle of cardinals. "We are ready then. And please, I wish only *English* spoken in the Holy Son's presence."

Alexander rose, leaned heavily on his gold-headed cane, and walked slowly toward Joseph as the others moved in behind him.

When Joseph felt Emil's hand on his arm he looked around to see the Pope's white head bowing in front of him. "Holy Son of God," the Pope was saying, "please forgive us for the delay. Will You be pleased to talk with us for a moment?"

Jarred by the touch and the question that demanded response, Joseph recoiled, struggling not to come back to the alien world around him. Wait, he wanted to say to them. Wait. Don't push me.

But the words wouldn't come, and he only rubbed his hand over his eyes. They took this for assent; more white satin chairs were drawn up, and once the Pope was seated the other men took places on either side of him.

"We offer ourselves most humbly to Your service," Pope Alexander began in a voice of joyous solemnity, "and we

ask Your indulgence so that we may inform You of the
preparations that have been made to ready the world for
Your work here on Earth."

Joseph stared at them. Unaware of his withdrawal, they
looked at him expectantly.

Finally he sighed heavily, resigned to the victory of that
part of him that shunned escape even into his own mind and
demanded his return to reality, however difficult. He decided
to listen, to try to let their words make sense, absorbing the
contradiction between the self that he knew and the person
they behaved as if he was. He forced himself to nod.

"Naturally we have considered the consequences of this
most holy event in the most careful detail," the Pope continued. "We have attempted to determine a course of events
that we hope You will find appropriate."

Joseph's voice came in a whisper. "What do you want me
to do?"

Pope Alexander answered quickly. "Oh, nothing, nothing,
Holy Son, assuredly! It is we who are here to serve You!"
His eyes sparkled with excitement. "Because there is so much
to be done," he continued, "we have taken the liberty of
composing a schedule. The tailors, cobblers, and photographers will be here within the hour. The jeweler is at work
on the designs for Your ring and pectoral cross. The press
office is preparing information packets for general release.
While those are being readied we have scheduled private
meetings to acquaint You with the congregations, tribunals,
and commissions of the Holy See."

Joseph listened, but the details were swept away by his
total incredulity at what he was hearing. His body was numb;
only his eyes moved, vainly searching the faces in front of
him for some sign of understanding.

"We have prepared briefs on the world's moral and spiritual problems," the staccato voice continued, "with special attention to those in crisis. The princes of the Church will be
arriving this evening and tomorrow to receive Your counsel
on these matters. A press conference is scheduled for Friday."

Joseph's breathing became heavier, his heart quickened.
His muscles tensed and he started to speak. No one noticed.

"Because millions of people will want to make the pilgrimage to Rome," the Pontiff continued, "we have carefully detailed a schedule of audiences, public and private. On Saturday we will appear before the people together. Then—"

"No," Joseph said softly.

Pope Alexander stopped short. "What? I'm sorry, Holy Son, did you say something?"

Joseph rose from his chair, the robe falling from his shoulders. He looked directly into the old man's eyes. "No!" he said, more desperately now. "Stop it! All of you, stop!"

The room froze, staring. Slowly, without taking his eyes from Joseph, the Pope nodded toward Rothstein, who stood and put a hand on Joseph's shoulder. "It's all right, Mr. Turner. You don't have to be afraid."

Joseph wheeled at him. "Afraid! I've got every right to be afraid! Mr. Rothstein, in the last forty-eight hours you've kidnapped me, drugged me, shot at me, and then told me I'm the Second Son of God. From in here, it feels like either I'm crazy, or I'm surrounded by a castle full of misguided lunatics!"

He turned back to the men seated before him. "Look, I'm struggling to hold on to whatever sanity I've got left. I want you to listen to me. I don't believe any of this. I don't even know what it means."

For the first time, Pope Alexander looked confused. "What?"

"I don't believe," Joseph said slowly and deliberately, "that I'm any 'Son of God.' "

One cardinal gasped audibly and two others crossed themselves. The Pope touched the gold cross hanging from his neck as if in need of reassurance and studied him intently now, obviously troubled. The others averted their eyes, looking down or at each other.

"I guess you didn't expect this," Joseph said, "but that's it, gentlemen. I just don't believe it."

The man called Belazzi, a slight, dark, wiry man who seemed less startled than the others, stroked his chin thoughtfully. When he looked up, his small piercing black eyes bored directly into the man in front of him. "Are you telling us," he asked quietly, "that you're prepared to deny it?"

For a moment Joseph felt confused again; it was not a question he had confronted so directly. "No. Uh . . . I don't know. I don't even know what I'd be denying. I don't understand; can't you see that? This is all too fast and so different from anything I've ever understood."

"Holy Son—" the Pope began.

"Don't call me that!"

Alexander nodded acquiescence then spoke calmly, even sympathetically now. "Forgive us, Mr. Turner. We have evidently proceeded too quickly. We did not anticipate that God would send You to us without this knowledge."

Joseph relaxed slightly.

"Naturally, You will require time to accustom Yourself to the idea. Meanwhile, we shall continue the preparations."

Joseph's eyes widened in astonishment. "Didn't you hear anything I said? I don't need time. I want this stopped." He looked around the circle, sensing something like fear. Suddenly he had a sinking feeling that there was more behind their discomfort than his own words. But what?

They were all looking at Pope Alexander. When he finally spoke he seemed to be weighing his words carefully. "Mr. Turner, we are faced with a difficulty here. You see, the world has already received the blessed news."

Joseph felt the blood rushing to his head; he felt dizzy and the room began to spin. He stepped back, leaning on the chair for support. "Would you mind repeating that?" His voice trembled.

"We have announced that You have been revealed to us as the Second Son of God. A private announcement early this morning to the princes of the Church, a public announcement about an hour ago."

"But you couldn't have done that!" He turned to Rothstein. "This isn't real, is it? I mean, no one asked me."

"It's real, Mr. Turner."

He turned back to the others, searching for some way to make them understand. "But if I'm the Son of God, don't you think I should've had some say in it? Don't you know what this could do to my life?"

Pope Alexander spoke mildly, but with full certainty. "Your destiny has been shaped by God, Mr. Turner. We have only played our part."

Their faces looked up at him implacably; he felt utterly unseen, unheard. They did not see a man before them; they saw only their own conception. He knew no words with which he could reach them.

Joseph's jaw tightened. His eyes steeled as he pulled himself up, using his anger to control the fear that sent tremors through his body. He faced them squarely, and willed himself to speak with authority.

"Gentlemen, there's no point in talking any more right now. Contrary to everything you may wish to believe, standing before you is a very human being, with a very human body, and it's been through a lot since yesterday. So if you don't mind, I'm going back to my room to get some rest."

Something in his tone or manner apparently reached them. Even the Pontiff had the grace to look flustered. Joseph breathed easier.

"Of course, of course, Holy Son—Mr. Turner," the old man said. "We will defer discussion of the rest of our plans until You have rested. Please forgive us our discourtesy. We want only to do all in our power to help You. Mr. Rothstein, would you kindly escort Mr. Turner to his rooms."

They stood respectfully while Emil guided Joseph into the Pope's private elevator. All remained anxiously silent long after it had disappeared. Then Alexander tapped his cane briskly on the marble floor. "Come, come. Let's continue with our schedule. There is much to be done." He turned and walked back to sit at his desk.

Cardinal Pacelli's round face reddened with alarm. "But, Holiness, what about the audiences this evening and tomorrow, the press conference? Everything has to be canceled immediately!"

"Slow down, Your Eminence. We will postpone today's schedule, and determine tomorrow's tomorrow."

"And in the event He continues to deny—?"

"He will not." Pope Alexander's response was curt. Then he paused and looked thoughtfully at the distressed men in front of him. He had not anticipated their need for reassurance. "My brothers, do not be alarmed by the Holy Son's confusion. Certainly this is the one state of affairs that we had not anticipated. But it will not continue. This morning He is exhausted, disoriented. He needs time, and we can use some ourselves for further preparations."

There was a strained silence. Cardinal Mendetti pushed

his thick gold-framed glasses high onto the bridge of his Roman nose and spoke brusquely. "Evidently we were premature in making our announcement."

Several heads nodded.

"My brothers," Alexander answered, irritated now that he must contend with their anxieties, "we have been guided in this matter by God. We trust He has some purpose for this circumstance as well."

Although aware that the Pontiff expected this to end the issue, Belazzi, finding an opportunity open, was unwilling to let the matter drop. "I appreciate what you are saying, Holiness, but I, like Mendetti, fear we have placed the Holy Mother Church in grave danger by proceeding with such haste. The normal procedures—"

Pope Alexander stopped him. "It's interesting, isn't it, gentlemen, that this disagreement among us was settled and all doubts clearly alleviated just a short while ago—only to reemerge at the first unexpected difficulty? But nothing can convince me that we would have better served God or the Holy Mother Church by our normal procedures—collecting more documents and more evidence on Joseph Turner, spending years and years to investigate Him only to reach the same conclusion we reached this morning—perhaps fifty years after His death?"

"There are good reasons for the established methods of the Church," Belazzi objected.

"Of course there are. They shield us from the necessity of taking risks." He smiled at the shocked expressions his remark elicited, then spoke more somberly, resuming the official "we" of his authority. "Brother bishops, we appreciate your concern and counsel. But the fact remains that the Holy Son has been revealed to us and, through us, to the world. Had we rejected him, rejected our duty out of fear, He would have found another way, while the Church retreated behind procedure and ritual. In this matter there is no precedent upon which we can fall. There is only the guidance of the Holy Ghost."

The gentle ring of the Pope's private telephone cut off any response to the Pope's words. He let it ring one more time before lifting the gold receiver from its cradle and turning his attention to his caller. It was Emil Rothstein.

"No, Mr. Rothstein. I expected your call. Is He comfortable in his new rooms?"

"As much as can be expected, Your Holiness. He created quite a stir when he dismissed the staff assigned to him. He has agreed to allow Carlo Lambessi to remain. He is not one to be impressed with or very interested in luxurious accommodations. However, I have found something that did pique his interest—our evidence. The Nicholas Prophecy, the reports and documents on him. He wants to examine it all."

"We will instruct the Holy Office to send them over immediately."

"Have them include the original Latin and the English translation of the prophecy, and a Latin-English dictionary. He may want to do some doublechecking."

"As He wishes. Thank you, Mr. Rothstein."

After hanging up the phone, Alexander responded to the unspoken questions on the faces in front of him.

"The Holy Son has begun His work. He wishes solitude in His search for truth. Let us also return to our work and meet at eight this evening for a review of ceremonial arrangements and assignment of duties."

One by one the cardinals bowed, kissed the Papal ring, and left the room. Only Belazzi remained.

"Holiness, may I speak freely?"

"Dominic, my friend, I sensed you were still troubled. Please."

Belazzi's hesitation was unusual in their private conversations. He seemed to need encouragement.

"Dominic, you have been my confidant for many years. Much has passed between us that we would share with no other."

"Thank you, Holiness. What is on my mind is difficult to express. It seems impossible to me that this ironworker could be . . ."

His voice trailed off as the Pontiff's eyes widened in alarm. "Dominic, I have wanted you to speak freely, yet my position is an awkward one. As Supreme Pontiff I must ask you to exercise caution in your words when you speak of Him."

Dominic nodded. "Yes, Holiness. But the *man* Joseph Turner. Is it not possible that we have been misled? Given too much credence to reports made by a layman and a series of as-yet-unexplained phenomena? And there are many other irregularities . . ."

"You have already heard me speak on this, Dominic."

"But, Holiness, have you contemplated at any length the cost to Holy Mother Church should we be proven wrong?"

Alexander bridled. "And you, Eminence—have you contemplated at any length that the Holy Spirit has abandoned the See of Peter?"

"Of course not," Belazzi said, sighing.

Pope Alexander remained quiet for a moment, looking for the words with which to help his doubting friend. "My brother," he said gently, "you expressed similar doubts before this morning's final test, the final proof to us all. We all bore witness to the Holy Son's reticence to accept His holy state, but we also all bore witness to those things that made Him known to us. The Holy Spirit has guided us in making Him known to the world, has given us the courage to do that which we feared. We cannot now turn our backs on what we know, have witnessed with our own eyes, simply because the Chosen One appears to be in doubt. His doubts offer a great temptation to all of us. Our act of faith is being tested. We will offer a special Mass for strength to overcome this temptation and meet the test."

Belazzi could not explain to the Pontiff—could not even explain to himself—why the final test had not been proof to him. But even if he could explain, he knew this man well enough to know that there was nothing to be gained in pressing the issue further. There was no bridging the gap that now separated the two old friends.

They had had many differences over the years, even before Marco Vasari had become Pope. Belazzi had often objected to Vasari's liberal views and impulsive ways, but Belazzi's opinions had always been valued by the older man. The fact that Belazzi had Papal patronage had not gone unnoticed among his colleagues, and he had exercised his privileges with skilled diplomacy, aimed at maintaining high visibility and unquestionable integrity. When he had learned the state of the old man's health he had felt genuinely alarmed, but he had not hidden from himself the sensation of anticipation that had accompanied the news that Vasari was considering

retirement. Dominic Belazzi wanted to be the next Pope, had harbored a secret ambition to become Pope for as long as he could remember. He had even been considered by many members of the last conclave, only to lose out in favor of the older man. He had waited and worked hard. Age was now on his side. At the moment his ambition appeared realizable, the Nicholas Investigation had provided the Pontiff with one more excuse to delay his decision. Now Vasari had placed the Church, and with it the Papacy, in the gravest danger. Belazzi resented the old man's blindness to the impossible position in which he had placed them all. For of what use was an elected Vicar if a proclaimed Son was here to guide His people? None, excepting perhaps administrative duties. Belazzi told himself that he would accept such a situation if a true Son had come—but this Joseph Turner? It was inconceivable that the guidance and leadership of mankind should be turned over to a man who hadn't the spirituality of the lowest parish priest. Somehow this ghastly mistake would have to be rectified before the Church suffered irreparable harm.

The Pope had taken his cane and walked to the arched windows overlooking the courtyard. "You know, Dominic," he said, "I have a confession of my own to make. There have been many times, in moments of despair, when even I doubted and feared that the Nicholas Prophecy was not a true prophecy. It sometimes seemed to me that our Blessed Pope Nicholas may have had too many glasses of wine on that night in 1447 and had simply—how shall I put it?— 'imagined' the visit. But now we have living proof within these walls!

"We have been given the blessing of living in the most important moment of history since the Resurrection. It is truly remarkable, isn't it?" The old man's face glowed with happiness.

"Yes, Your Holiness."

There was something like regret in Belazzi's voice, and Pope Alexander wished the younger man could share his own certainty. Well, he thought, God will reveal the truth to you in his own time as well. "This is such a blessing for our Church, Dominic. Certainly the final proof to the world of the sovereignty of Catholicism is that God has sent His Son to us."

He paused, reminding himself of the difficulty. "Of course, we must assume that many will not believe. Especially since Joseph Turner is not exactly what we were expecting. One of our own—some mendicant priest, perhaps—would have been simpler, certainly. That this Joseph Turner is not a Catholic, not a religious man even—this was a possibility for which God did not prepare me."

TWENTY-THREE

THE WORLD BEYOND Rome coped with the first shock of the Vatican's news as well as could be expected.

Moments after the bells began ringing from St. Peter's at seven that morning, Rome time, Gerard Cardinal Baudry, Dean of the College of Cardinals, swiftly and quietly left the chapel for his offices, where his staff waited with two sealed messages. The first, a coded message, he ordered sent immediately via Vatican Radio to every archbishop, bishop, papal ambassador, delegate, and cardinal of the Sacred College not presently in Rome:

> THE PROPHECY OF THE BLESSED POPE NICHOLAS HAS BEEN FULFILLED. WITH GREAT URGENCY AND THE MOST SUPREME JOY, THE HOLY FATHER REQUESTS YOUR PRESENCE OR THAT OF A DELEGATE IN ROME IMMEDIATELY.
>
> WE WILL SHARE THE BLESSED NEWS WITH THE WORLD TWO HOURS FROM YOUR RECEIPT OF THIS MESSAGE. FULL INFORMATION AND INSTRUCTIONS FOR ADMINISTRATION OF PUBLIC RESPONSE FOLLOW.

By 7:45, the stream toward Vatican City had begun.

At 9:07, the international wire services received the second message via the Vatican Press Office and—after numerous calls for verification—flashed the news to the world:

> ROME, ITALY. THE VATICAN . . . POPE ALEXANDER IX PROCLAIMED THIS MORNING THE PRESENCE ON EARTH OF A "MOST HOLY AND BLESSED SECOND SON OF GOD, THE NEW KING OF KINGS." THE PONTIFF IDENTIFIED THE "NEW MESSIAH" AS AN AMERICAN IRONWORKER, JOSEPH TURNER OF NEW YORK.

A special notation to all subscribers followed:

> SOURCE IS THE POPE. ONLY DETAILS AVAILABLE ARE
> FROM THIS MORNING'S DELAYED EDITION OF L'OSSER-
> VATORE ROMANO; SEE COPY REPRINTED IN FULL BE-
> LOW. NO FURTHER INFORMATION WILL BE RELEASED
> UNTIL THE PRESS CONFERENCE ANNOUNCED. NEW YORK
> WILL SEND ALL AVAILABLE INFORMATION ON TURNER.

The three American television networks interrupted normal programming with news bulletins of the announcement
in the middle of the night. The calm, cleverly self-protective
wording of the broadcasts belied the confusion and battling
behind the camera.

At NBC in New York, the assistant news director who was
first handed the wire copy grimaced impatiently and handed
it back.

"What is this, some kind of hoax?"

"Not as far as we can tell."

"Check it with the other services."

"I did."

"Call Crowder. Isn't he still on assignment for us in
Rome?"

"Yes, and I did. He gives me the same story."

The assistant news director thought for a moment. He
didn't want this one on his head. "Call Carson."

"Johnny?"

"This is no time for jokes. Get me Jack."

When the assistant director read the wire story to a sleepy
Jack Carson, the director's voice boomed back. "Get the
damn story on the air!"

"But we can't run it straight!"

"We have to. It's the Pope, for Chrissake."

"The Pope's gone bananas."

"Maybe, but it's a damned important story either way."

The assistant director squirmed in his chair. "Let's wait
for morning. That'll give us time to check it out."

"Are you kidding? And let ABC and CBS scoop us?"

"We could make awful fools of ourselves."

"No. Just be careful how you word it—'Highly reliable
sources reported tonight that the Pope has announced, et

cetera. However, we are still checking the details of the highly unlikely story'—you know, the usual stuff."

"Want a full story?"

"No, just a bulletin, but be cool. We don't want anyone to take it too seriously."

"What else?"

"Get a team on Turner. We may need a mini-documentary. Then alert Franklin; if there *is* a press conference, he'll want it. And see if you can reach Boyd in London. Get him on his way to Rome now to see what the hell's going on. Damn, I wish we still had Walters for this. And, oh, get Matthews."

"Who's Matthews?"

"You know—the guy from Philly. He's gotten pretty friendly with Turner. He could be helpful. Arrange a conference for the top group two hours from now. I'll meet you upstairs. Otherwise keep this as quiet as you can."

Jerry Matthews was awakened in the middle of the night. This time the friend of the possible Second Son of God was told a limousine would pick him up in half an hour to take him to a meeting with the President of News.

At the conference Matthews was informed of his new status—NBC's Special Correspondent to Joseph Turner—and told to be ready to accompany Franklin to Rome. While the men around him argued over the story, Matthews reflexively checked for his press pass; this time he had not forgotten his wallet. He sat back, basking in the knowledge of his special relationship with the Second Son of God. For him there were no doubts; he knew Joseph Turner.

When Louise Ryan heard the news in a 4:00 A.M. call from the Senior Editor of the *Times,* she exploded in anger. "What the hell are they doing to him?" she asked. "What are the bastards up to?"

"It's the Catholic Church, Louise," her editor told her. "Get on a plane and find out."

"I'm on my way."

At dawn, Sammy and Rosa Sweet sat at the breakfast table staring at a newspaper. For the first few moments they had read quickly, Rosa leaning over Sammy's shoulder. Then they looked at each other numbly.

"Sammy, do you believe this?"

"I dunno. Joey is my best friend, but he's not what you would call Jesus material. I mean he's a terrific guy and all that, but—"

"But the Pope—"

"Yeah. The Pope."

"How long since you been to confession, Sammy?"

"Too long."

"Wanna go to church?"

"Yeah."

John Stanton was up early finishing the final draft of his Thanksgiving sermon when the classical music from his radio was interrupted by a bulletin. He put down his pen and sat for a long time, thinking, remembering. Then he went in to wake Bonnie. When she pulled herself out of her little-girl sleep and finally heard him, she got up quickly and pulled on her robe. "What do you believe, John?"

"I believe it's true."

"We've got to tell Maggie."

Bonnie wakened her, handed her her robe.

"What's wrong?" Maggie said, startled out of sleep and frightened. Then her stomach turned. "Is it Joey?"

Bonnie nodded and quickly added, "It's OK. But it's something we didn't expect."

"He's all right!"

"I think so, yes. But you need to hear something."

Bonnie led her to John's study. The radio was on an all-news station and Bonnie nodded to Maggie to sit down and listen.

When the bulletin was repeated a few minutes later, Maggie responded in a way they had not anticipated: she laughed.

When she noticed that they were not laughing with her, she stopped. "But—surely you aren't taking this seriously! Joey?!" She looked at them astonished.

"Yes, we are, Maggie," John said to her tenderly.

And then she began to tremble uncontrollably with fear. It started in her chest and moved through her until she couldn't stop shaking. "What's going to happen to him? What are they going to do to him? What's Joey—"

John stopped her growing panic. "We don't know, Maggie. He's apparently all right. You're afraid for him?"

Her mouth tightened, her eyes narrowed in pain, she lifted her head to them. "For both of us."

Paul Bridger did not find out until later that morning. He was so angry that he hurled a four-thousand-dollar museum-quality Tang Dynasty terra-cotta war horse against his bedroom wall. He spent the next hour examining his insurance policy to determine whether it was covered against accidental breakage. It was, but somehow he didn't feel any better.

TWENTY-FOUR

IN THE FIRST MOMENTS of awakening in the morning light, Joseph found his eyes fixed on the gilded crucifix nailed to the wall facing his bed. The man's body hung down distorted in pain; his neck twisted upward and his eyes and mouth opened to the blue emptiness above him.

"Oh, God," Joseph murmured painfully, closing his eyes again and turning his body away. He lay there for a few more minutes, listening to the chimes of bells and the singing of a choir somewhere far away, reminding himself that this was Thursday and his second day at the Vatican. He sighed heavily and opened his eyes again, pulling himself out of the four-poster bed, deliberately avoiding looking at the opposite wall. He had crossed to the marble bathroom when he heard a sound at the door off to the left. Carlo came in quietly, carrying a blue satin dressing gown.

Joseph's eyebrows lifted but he donned the gown and headed once more toward the bathroom. Carlo was ahead of him, kneeling beside the tub, drawing the bathwater and testing it with his elbow. He reached for soap and a cloth. Joseph's eyes widened as he took a step backward. "Forget it! Get it out of your mind!"

Carlo smiled and nodded.

"No!" He took Carlo by the elbow, raised him to his feet, and gently but firmly pushed him out of the room.

When Joseph emerged from the bathroom a few minutes later, he found his clothes gone, replaced by gold-embroidered silk robes. Carlo stood by the bed, ready to help him dress. "What the—! Carlo, where are my clothes?"

Carlo picked up the robe.

Joseph shook his head. "I want my *own* clothes, Carlo."

The silent young valet looked a little frightened, but he

nodded his understanding and hurried out of the room. A few minutes later he returned with Joseph's clothes. Emil Rothstein came in behind him.

"Thanks, Carlo. Good morning, Mr. Rothstein."

"Please, just Emil. You didn't like your robes?"

"I just want my own clothes."

Emil smiled. "No one expected the Son of God to arrive in jeans. I suggested that you would probably prefer them, but they were convinced you would wish clothes that befit your station."

"Tell them my Levi's befit me just fine, thanks." He took the jeans and shirt and began to dress. "I guess I might need a change or two."

"We'll take care of it. How are you this morning? I brought the documents last night, but you were already asleep."

"I was exhausted. I'm still a little weak, a little shaky, but much better. I'm anxious to get started on your papers."

They moved into the sitting room. While Carlo brought breakfast they prepared to work. Three large bound volumes waited on the table in front of the couch. Joseph sat down and faced them. His stomach churned.

With Rothstein at his side, he opened the first of the volumes and pored over the documents. He felt the hours of the morning pass with turned pages and shifting sunlight, and he read slowly, feeling his calmness grow as curiosity replaced his fear.

The illuminated manuscript of the prophecy itself looked authentic enough. Emil translated the Latin for him; it was exactly as he had been told. It could have been faked, of course, but there would be others who could examine its authenticity and Pope Alexander couldn't refuse to let them.

The reports on himself included interview transcripts, newspaper reports, and copies of legal documents, even medical records. For a while he felt as if he were reading the story of someone else's life, a perfectly ordinary life, except for a string of bizarre events linked only by their improbability. Two events in particular seized his attention. The first was the doctor's report of his "death" at the age of three. He struggled to recapture memories of what had followed the accident, but between the terrifying crash and vague images of awakening later in the cold whiteness of the hospital, there was nothing.

The second was a reiteration of the final words of the prophecy: *"According to the prophecy of the Archangel Uriel, the Second Son of God cannot die until after Good Friday of his thirty-second year."*

"Emil . . . when's Good Friday?"

"April fourth."

A chill ran through his body. That was less than five months from now. A sudden sense of urgency told him that some part of him believed what he read, believed that in some way he had very little time. He closed the second volume quickly and turned to the last, a series of reports of previous "Nicholas" investigations. The reports proved one thing: the Vatican was very, very thorough; none of the eleven men who had been investigated over the last five centuries had fit the prophecy as completely as he did. None of them, it appeared, had been subjected to a final test.

Turning the last page, he reached up and flipped on the table lamp and sat back in the darkening evening, deep in thought. Their "explanation" was as preposterous as the events themselves. Yet he'd found no holes; if this was some kind of hoax, it was incredibly elaborate. He let that possibility go; if they were mistaken, they were sincerely mistaken. He looked at Rothstein.

"You sure covered all the bases."

"Shall I take that as a compliment to our thoroughness, Mr. Turner?"

"Joseph. If you want. Actually, I should hate you for prying into my life like this, but I don't. It doesn't seem to matter now."

Rothstein nodded. "Did you learn anything?"

"No—I don't know. Seeing it all in black and white makes me feel a hell of a lot more solid and sane."

"Do you wish anything else?"

"Yes, but I don't know what it is."

Emil studied him. "You're not convinced, then?"

He shook his head. "No. Mountains and flames of hell leave a lot of room for interpretation. There must be plenty of people whose lives could be made to fit this, people you haven't even looked at." As he said it, he felt how weak an objection it was. These men were not likely to have missed a possibility.

Emil hesitated, then asked intensely, "And the bullet?"

A wave of dizziness washed over him; he tried vainly to throw it off. "I don't know. How am I supposed to know that wasn't some kind of setup? Kidnappings, shootings—you guys are pretty bizarre."

Emil spoke sadly, kindly. "Joseph, these are pious men, honorable men, devoted to their faith. They did not do these things capriciously, without much thought, much prayer, and much agony."

Something in Rothstein's manner, his calm certainty, made it impossible not to believe him. Joseph's voice came back almost a whisper. "I know. And honestly, the bullet. I can't explain it away. It's just—" His mind searched. "It seems like if anyone should know I'm some special person, chosen by a God, I should. But no God has spoken to me about it. Doesn't that seem damn peculiar to you?"

Emil smiled. "Well, yes, frankly, it does. But God does not always work in understandable ways. I have no doubt He will speak to you in time."

"I'm not sure I'd know He was talking if He did. I've never been religious. Doesn't that bother anyone?"

Emil looked slightly uncomfortable. "Some of us, yes, it does. But it doesn't bother me. Naturally, I've always assumed that a spiritual teacher must be a person of faith. But watching you has made me think that your doubt may be a very important part of God's plan. We're living in an age of doubts and confusions. In your doubt, you're like so many people in the world today. Perhaps the person to take them toward a better life must be a person like themselves. For whatever He has chosen you to do, God will give you the knowledge you need."

Joseph got up and walked across the room. He turned back, leaning against the windowsill. "You're unshakable, aren't you?"

"Our faith is unshakable."

What he felt right now, as he listened to this man, was envy, envy of his sureness. "But how are you so certain? How can you know for sure? How can I know? How can I believe it?"

"What is it that would make you believe it? What is it that you're waiting for?"

"I don't know. A visit from angels, I guess," he said impatiently, gesturing toward the smiling white-winged creatures looking down at him from the ceiling fresco. "A visit from angels, a voice from a whirlwind."

"Ah, yes. That would make it easier. But it doesn't always happen that way, not for any of us. I understand even Papa Vasari had great difficulty accepting his election as Pope. He secluded himself in prayer and meditation for several days.

"Joseph, even when everything around us is pushing us in a particular direction, even when the path before us is the inevitable choice—sometimes stepping forward requires the courage of an enormous risk. And then sometimes, all it takes is for us to stop resisting in order to be able to make the leap."

It makes sense, Joseph thought. But he felt the resistance in him still strong, the great fear returning. His legs began to shake under him and the image he'd awakened to this morning filled his vision. *"But I don't want to make the leap!"* he said loudly. Angrily he turned and went into the bedroom, reached out and jerked the crucifix from the wall. He strode back and stood before Rothstein, clutching the gilded cross with its awful burden, holding it out in front of him. "I don't *want* it. All of you act like this is some great gift you're giving me. But look at this, Emil, look at it! This is what *I* see— no gift, but a horror! Even if it's true, I can't want it!" He raised his arm, flung the crucifix across the room, and watched it crash against the floor.

Emil was visibly shaken, but his clear gray eyes held only infinite sadness. "I'm sorry, Joseph, truly sorry." He got up, crossed the room, reverently picked up the crucifix, and stood looking back at Joseph. "Is there anything else I can do for you now?"

"Yeah—get that thing out of here." Joseph felt the tightness leave his body, his shoulders sag, his voice soften. "Emil, I'm sorry. Thank you for your help today and for what you said. It's just so *hard* to think it's true. And it's getting harder to think it's not. I'm running out of objections."

"Do you want me to stay with you this evening?"

"No, I need to think. Hey—" he said, suddenly looking

at his watch. "That announcement the Pope said you made. When would it reach the United States?"

"Why, yesterday morning, early, their time."

Joseph lurched for the telephone. "I've got to call them! My friends in Provincetown—"

"Pronto," came a voice.

He looked at the receiver helplessly; Emil stepped over and took it from his hand. "I'll ask the operator to put through a call." He spoke into the receiver and hung it up. "It will ring when they're on the line."

"Thanks," he said as Emil crossed the room, nodded his goodbye, and closed the door behind him.

Please, John, be home. Joseph closed his eyes, wishing, please, Maggie.

It was almost an hour before the phone rang. He grabbed the receiver. "Hello! John? Bonnie? Hello?"

The sound of John's voice crackled across the transatlantic connection. "Joey! Are you all right?"

"Johnny, it's good to hear your voice. I'm in Italy. Have you heard?"

"What? This connection is awful."

"I said, what have you heard?"

"An announcement—did you tell them to make it?"

"Are you kidding? They didn't even tell me about it till after they'd made it. They're so sure I fit their prophecy, John. It's crazy, isn't it?" Tell me it's crazy, he thought. "What? I can't hear you."

"I didn't say anything. They're so sure you fit, and you're so sure they're wrong?"

"I *think* so, I *hope* so. I've been beating my brains out trying to find some hole, something not right, but I can't find anything. Wait a minute; aren't you?"

"What?"

"I said aren't *you* positive they're wrong?"

There was a long silence, then "No."

Joseph felt the weight of his body sink down onto the couch. "Oh, John, not you, too."

"Now listen," John said gently, comfortably, "I just meant that it's not totally inconceivable to me. Not at all. It does surprise me that you're there. I mean, the Catholic Church is the last place I'd expect to find you. But there must be a reason." John's voice disappeared into the static and reappeared again. "Joey, I know how incredible this all must seem to you, and as long as you have doubts, you have to check them out." It was the voice of the brother Joseph remembered. "If God is involved, if he's chosen you for a special purpose, you'll come to know it. If He's not, you'll know that too."

Joseph shook his head. "Johnny, I don't want to know. I don't know how to know. I don't know where to start. I can't even grasp what it would mean to be the 'Second Son of God.'"

John's voice lightened. "Well, there's a book about the first one."

"Yeah, I understand it has an unhappy ending."

"Well, not necessarily—depends on how you look at it."

Even through their half-joking, he felt the panic return. "Johnny, I don't want to wait to find out."

"What?"

"I said I want out of here."

"I'm sorry it's so tough on you, kid. At least it's a safe place to stay right now. I hope you'll give yourself some time."

I may not have much time, he heard a voice inside him answer. But "I miss you guys" was what he said, vainly trying to fight back tears.

"Joey, you wanna talk to Maggie?"

"Yes, yes. Please, wait—John, thanks for being there. I needed to talk to you."

"Any time you need it, I'm here. I'll put Maggie on."

"Thanks."

When Maggie's voice came through the crackling on the line it was soft. "Hello, Joey."

"Baby, are you OK?"

"No. When are you coming home?"

"Soon, as soon as I can. I wish I could hold you right now."

"I've got to know something. Do you believe what they're saying is true?" Her voice sounded very tired, dulled with pain.

"No . . ." The word didn't come out easily.

"I can't hear you."

"I don't want it to be true."

"That's different."

"Nothing has happened to make me feel, deep inside, that it's true."

"I don't believe it either." Her voice hardened. "But what we believe doesn't seem to matter anymore. Joey, the life we planned—it's over, isn't it?"

"Babe, don't say that. We can't know that yet. I'll be back. None of this changes how I feel about you."

"But it changes everything else. You don't know what it's like here, Joey. Reporters pounding on the door, phone calls, people driving by the house. It's mad here, Joey. There's no way for us to live. And . . . and"—he heard her tears—"for me, Joey. I don't know how to conduct a love affair with a man half the world believes is the Second Son of God. I'm not the right material. I wouldn't know how to play the part."

He felt himself sinking again, stunned by the havoc wreaked in his world, reeling from another hope lost, one more place he could no longer turn. He wanted desperately to tell her that it didn't all have to change, that everything would work out for them, that they could escape, go somewhere else, just as they had planned—but he knew that he could not make it true. "Maggie, Maggie," he moaned.

"Joey, I think I've got to get away for a while."

"What are you going to do? Where will you be?"

"I don't know, sweetheart."

"But I'll be coming back. When I do, whatever I do, I'll want you with me."

"Perhaps." He heard only the utter lack of hope in her voice. "If you do come back, when you have this worked out, when you know for sure what you want, what's possible, maybe then."

There was nothing he could do now, nothing he could say to hold her. "I love you, Maggie."

"I love you, too. Take care of yourself. Goodbye, my love."

"For now."

When the phone went dead Joseph held it for a long time, wanting to keep her with him as long as he could.

He felt his loneliness fully now, his isolation, the complete loss of the life he had hoped for. It was even more than Maggie's leaving. The announcement had trapped all of them into behaving as if it were true. The way things were working out, it might as well be true. Damn these men, damn this church, he thought. They've even robbed me of my dreams . . .

But he knew that those dreams had been lost irretrievably long before he got to Rome, lost in the moment his hand had slipped from an icy girder and left him falling into a world that would never be the same for him again.

TWENTY-FIVE

WHEN EMIL ROTHSTEIN left Joseph's suite he walked slowly down the hallway toward the Borgia rooms, where the late night meeting of the Commission for Service to the Second Son of God was in session. He felt troubled. They had asked him to join them in order to learn about Joseph Turner's state of mind, or spirit, but he would not be able to give them the clear answer they wanted to hear, and they would want from him his best judgment of how quickly Joseph would be ready to assume his role. He had made many judgments of men in his time, but in this case he felt it an impossible task. Joseph Turner would be ready when Joseph Turner was ready.

The pressures upon all of them were tremendous now that the announcement had been made, and he knew, though he had not told Joseph, that while they had been able to contain public reaction so far by promising further news at the press conference still scheduled for tomorrow, to delay much longer would be virtually impossible. Many decisions in many people's lives had been suspended in the uncertainty created by the Second Son of God's silence. Should the silence last too long, uncertainty would turn to fear or anger or could even solidify into opposition.

He did not envy the men who had to cope with the enormous practical difficulties created by the Holy Son's confusion, but his personal sympathies lay entirely with Joseph's spiritual struggle. Since returning to the Vatican this time he had found himself increasingly resenting the single-minded self-assurance of these men who acted with so little concern for individual human problems. He found himself feeling alien among men whose vision of their Church was so wide, but whose vision of the individual human soul was so narrow. The absolute devotion to a spiritual cause which had drawn him to them originally many years ago he now questioned, for it created a kind of blindness to people's human needs. He had seen that blindness operate in the matter of the test and of the announcement, had argued in vain that Joseph's own well-being and wishes should be of primary concern. But their decision had already been made and they had met his arguments with their usual dogmatic faith in the rightness of their own way. He was not entirely sorry about the difficulties their way had created for them.

He had not wanted to trouble Joseph with the pressures they faced nor with the problems arising from the sheer numbers of people who were arriving in Rome. The hotels were already full to capacity and the police had been forced to allow nearly fifty thousand people to set up camp in St. Peter's Square. By the next night, they estimated another thirty thousand. At the moment the only thing limiting arrivals at all was that trains, planes, and roads were so clogged it was becoming virtually impossible to get into the city.

The guard at the door of the Borgia rooms greeted him and opened the door for him to enter. Inside, the members of the Commission sat around the conference table deep in conversation; Emil bowed toward Pope Alexander, then slipped quietly into an empty chair.

The Commander of the Swiss Guard was again revising estimates of the expected crowds upward. ". . . and therefore it is essential that we rely upon civilian police to assure security within the City. We simply do not have the men."

"Proceed with your arrangements, then," Pope Alexander answered with obvious irritation, "what is necessary is necessary. But return responsibility to our own people as quickly as possible." He turned toward the large, dark-haired man at the end of the table. "Cardinal Monteverdi, you have been waiting to speak."

"Thank you, yes. In our earlier discussion of world response, Your Holiness, we failed to take up the point raised concerning the fears that have been generated by our announcement. I do not believe we have yet done enough to reassure those who mistakenly regard the Holy Son's coming as the end."

"If you will excuse me, Cardinal Monteverdi," Cardinal Mendetti interjected, "the Press Office has issued several statements daily designed specifically to allay that fear, and the reports already received from the bishops indicate that what fear remains will subside in a reasonable time. The consensus of the Commission from the beginning has been that in general the shock of the news would be felt most strongly for a week to ten days. And nothing has happened to change that estimate."

Nothing so far, Emil thought. But if Joseph should not appear soon?

"Two weeks from now," Mendetti was continuing, "most of the people will have resumed their lives very much as before—"

"Except," Pope Alexander interrupted, "that they will devote considerably more attention to their relationship to God, His Sons, and the Church."

"Of course." Several around the table nodded, pleased.

"My brothers," Pope Alexander continued, "I fear that I must bring us back to the more difficult issue facing us. Our most immediate question is how we are to proceed regarding the Holy Son Himself—with the delay in His own acceptance of His spiritual authority. Several of you have alluded this evening to the added confusion His public silence is already beginning to cause among the people, the suspicions of political intrigue being generated among the world powers, the potential for extended dislocations in world economy."

"All of which," Secretary of State Belazzi interjected, "are thus far well under control in my office."

"Yes, fine, thank you, Cardinal. But what I wish us to attend to now is what alternatives we might consider for further action. Specifically, with what we must do about the press conference still on schedule for tomorrow. Emil," Pope Alexander said, turning to him at last, "what can you tell us about progress in the Holy Son's own mind and heart? We pray that He may have moved closer in these last few hours to the realization of His divine mission."

Emil felt all eyes turn to him. Some of them, he knew, were jealous eyes that resented his privileged closeness to the Holy Son. With the partial exception of Pope Alexander, he had no confidence that any of these men would grasp the depth of the inner struggle of Joseph Turner, and he felt himself Joseph's only real advocate among men who, however ready they were to serve the Holy Son, could feel only impatient incomprehension toward the human Joseph.

"The Holy Son has read the documents, Your Holiness, and he is considering the implications most carefully."

"And is He feeling differently? Is it your judgment that we may proceed with our arrangements on schedule?"

Emil weighed his words carefully. "Your Holiness, he is still in much personal confusion. I judge that he is much closer to acceptance of his spiritual destiny"—he was careful not to say "of his divinity"—"but he is by no means at peace. He struggles still with his spiritual dilemma."

The Pope sat back, considering. "You believe that He needs more time?"

"I do."

"Can you venture to say how much more?"

"I regret to say that I do not feel competent to judge in such an extraordinary case."

Belazzi leaned forward. "Pardon me, Your Holiness, but it is now impossible to delay the press conference."

"But if the Holy Son is not ready to appear, Cardinal," Pope Alexander said coolly, "what alternative do we have?"

"We have the alternative of assisting him to become ready."

The Pope's eyebrows lifted in question. "And how is that to be done?"

"For two days now," the Secretary of State said, "on the respected advice of Mr. Rothstein, we have kept the Holy Son completely uninformed of what has been occurring. It seems to me that this policy leaves him to attempt decisions without being in possession of all the facts, and leaves us to make decisions without the benefit of his direction. It is my strong recommendation, therefore, that we lay before him our dilemma, and learn his wishes. We can present the reports of the Commission on world reaction, the tentative schedule of events, and the resources we are prepared to place at his disposal. It is unfortunate that circumstances force us to move so swiftly, but on the other hand, a full account of what needs to be done may provide a welcome opportunity to put aside his subjective confusion and grasp the responsibilities of authority. Given a full understanding of how much is being offered to him here, surely he will not refuse."

Emil watched the other Cardinals add their assent to a point of view they shared and were relieved to have Belazzi express for them.

"Mr. Rothstein?" Pope Alexander asked him, "you do not appear to agree with the other members of the Commission."

"Truly, Your Holiness, gentlemen, I do not. We cannot fail to be conscious of how unprepared our Holy Guest is to confront the kinds of decisions you wish to put before him. By background, by education, he is not accustomed to dealing with such issues, or with the details of the temporal functions of the Church."

"Well, of course he is not," Belazzi answered. "That is why God has put us in his service. But surely he is entitled to full knowledge, and to full opportunity to guide us. And," Belazzi added, "we have already learned the unfortunate consequences of proceeding with action without the benefit of his approval."

"I thought that what we had learned," Emil replied, "were the consequences of assuming that he was more prepared to face the tasks before him than he was."

Pope Alexander listened to his aides thoughtfully. Cardinal Belazzi, he knew, was in part motivated by his lingering disbelief in Joseph Turner and a desire to see this young ironworker challenged. Should He fail to take authority, that would confirm the validity of Belazzi's own lack of faith. Still, there was much in Belazzi's argument that was persuasive. He knew personally the dangers of too much solitude, too much time for inner confusion and doubt to feed on itself, as he knew the healing power of external responsibility. And they had taken a questionable step in withholding information from Him Whom it most concerned. In truth he had been feeling increasing discomfort about making decisions without the Holy Son's full knowledge and choice. Emil's argument that this young man was not prepared for His responsibility ignored the obvious fact that it was God who sent a simple man. They could not presume Joseph incapable of directing the affairs of His own Church. Undoubtedly He had a special wisdom in such matters. Finally, he recalled the conviction that had come to him so strongly last night in his chapel, that since God sent him a man without knowledge of His own divinity, it was evidently the role of Christ's Vicar to help Him understand and accept His responsibility to humankind. Thus far he had granted little assistance.

Much of the logic, then, was on Belazzi's side.

And yet he had learned over many years to have the deepest confidence in Emil Rothstein's judgment of men, and Emil was firmly opposed to any action that created additional pressure on Joseph Turner. Without voicing the threat directly. Emil had made it quite clear that should they push too hard or too fast, they might very possibly lose Joseph Turner altogether and alienate Him from the Church that was His temporal home. Surely it was his duty to carry the scepter until the Holy Son was ready to take it from his hands.

"My brothers," he said finally, "we have reached a decision. The press conference tomorrow will be cancelled; we will issue a simple statement that the Holy Son is in seclusion. Cardinal Baudry, proceed with the plans for the coronation but do not issue invitations or announcements. Cardinal Pacelli, you may strike the first set of new coins, but we will withhold distribution. Cardinal Belazzi, we shall lay the information you spoke of before the Holy Son at the earliest sign of His acceptance; please see that it is ready and easily available. And from you, Mr. Rothstein," he said to the relieved friend of Joseph Turner, "we shall eagerly await the news for which we all pray. We know you are well aware of how little time remains—for all of us."

TWENTY-SIX

Carlo Lambessi was concerned. Across the table the Holy Son listlessly picked at His breakfast. He seemed more depressed this morning than ever, and Carlo wished there was something he could do.

He was grateful for being chosen as the Holy Son's valet, such an honor for one so young with only three years of Vatican service. Being chosen had given him a new understanding of God's purpose in giving him his affliction. Though he had long ceased questioning God's will, he felt clearly for the first time that not being able to speak or to hear had been not merely a punishment or a test, but a gift of God's incalculable goodness.

He was troubled, however, by how little service he had been to the Holy Son. Almost everything he offered to do was rejected. The Holy Son was very kind, of course, and he understood that He simply preferred to do most things for Himself, but it left Carlo searching for ways to be more helpful.

As he had watched the Holy Joseph grow increasingly sad, he could not help thinking that what He needed was not someone to bathe or dress or shave Him, but someone to help Him find a way to relieve His inner suffering. He dared not think he himself should be that person. But now, as he saw the Holy Son even more sad on this third morning, he could not help searching his own mind and heart for some small contribution he might make.

He wrote on his pad and shyly handed the note across to the Holy Son: "Beautiful place here. You wish to see beautiful rooms, great art in palace? I call someone to guide?"

Joseph read the note and smiled sadly. "No, Carlo, thank you, I'm just not in the mood."

Carlo wrote again. "Forgive Carlo, but maybe You stay sad sitting in room? Maybe looking beautiful things help?"

Joseph put down his fork and looked at the pale, shy young man across from him, understanding how hard he was trying to help. Until now, he had seen Carlo as just one more strange Vatican being who treated him as a nonhuman God, but as he looked into the clear blue eyes watching him he felt Carlo's understanding of his very human sadness. "Thank you, Carlo," he said. "And you're probably right— I do need to get out of here and do something else for a while. Would you come with me, show me around here a little?"

Carlo looked embarrassed but pleased. "You honor Carlo, Holy Son," he wrote. "Of course, yes. You wish special places?"

"No, just show me your world here. Let's just walk."

They left together and spent two hours exploring long hallways leading to rooms leading to hallways and to more rooms. The high-ceilinged corridors were spacious and airy, and all of them were decorated with brilliantly colored frescoes. Joseph was surprised to see on these walls and ceilings not only Biblical scenes, but also the fabulous creatures of pagan mythology, satyrs and fawns and nymphs playing in vine-filled forests. Other halls were decorated in patterned marble and carved stone, the huge figures on the ceiling engaged in heroic battles, with golden angels watching. The vastness of the palace and the richness of colors, of marble, stone, and gilded wood, made him lightheaded. He felt the energy of a body used to physical exertion returning and he began to enjoy the feeling of movement.

"Hey, Carlo," he called after a while, careful to turn his face toward the young man at his side, "all these angels are getting to me. Let's run back."

To Carlo's surprise, the Holy Second Son of God took off jogging down the corridor. There was nothing for him to do but run to keep up so he could point out the complicated turns of the way back. He saw doors open and angry, grave-faced men, their work interrupted by the unceremonious clomp-clomp of running feet down their stately halls, emerge and then stand open-mouthed staring after the Holy Son and his valet.

By the time they reached Joseph's suite both of them were laughing.

"You feel better now?" Carlo scribbled quickly when they were back inside and had caught their breath.

"Yes, yes, Carlo, I do," said Joseph, still laughing. "And maybe I've found my mission, too. Maybe God brought me here to liven this place up."

In Suite 402 of the Rome Hilton, Louise Ryan glanced away from the telephone she had stared at for the last twenty minutes to look again at her watch: 1:40. Let's see, she thought, that's fifty-one hours since I heard, twenty-three hours since I've slept, plus an extra night for jet lag, thirteen hours since I've had anything to eat, and two hours I've been waiting for this call. Jesus, if we ran the newspaper at the speed Albert runs his Embassy, the morning edition would be out every night at eight. How long can it take to telephone a simple demand to the Vatican?

The phone rang and she grabbed it. "Ryan."

"Lou? Albert. Well, it wasn't easy but I think I've got you in. When I told them, they said if all we wanted was face-to-face verification that Joseph Turner was alive and well, the Ambassador was welcome to visit."

"What did you say?"

"I told them you didn't trust *him*, either."

"Correct."

"And I assured them of your security clearance, and put my own neck on the line if anything went wrong."

"You're a pal, Albert."

"Uh-huh. So they put a call through to the Holy Son, as they referred to him, and asked him if he wanted to see you, and he said 'Hell yes, I do'—direct quote courtesy of an operator who knows no English and simply repeated the Holy Son's words verbatim. You're to go to the Holy Office at two-fifteen where you will be met by a Monsignor O'Rourke. He'll take you into the Vatican to meet with Mr. Turner in the Vatican Gardens. You're invited for a late lunch."

She felt a slight leap in her stomach, dismissed it as hunger, and hastily made a joke. "In this rain we're having a picnic?"

"Who am I to know? Maybe he'll make the rain stop."

"Jesus, Albert . . . Well, I need the food anyway. Did you OK Jerry too?"

"Oh, yes, it's fine."

"Good. Call him for me, will you? I've got to run." She slammed the phone down, grabbed her briefcase and dark blue raincoat, and headed out to find a taxi.

As the taxi inched its way through the rain-snarled traffic, Louise clicked open her briefcase and fingered through her collection. It was all there: the notes she'd made from her conversations that morning, the obviously hurriedly printed statement distributed at the noon non-news conference at the Vatican Press Office, the items she'd picked up from the shops around St. Peter's Square, the little white box and contract bid copy Albert's friend's friend had gotten from someone else's friend's friend inside the Vatican.

She closed the briefcase and sat back, for the first time letting herself notice that she was excited. She had been trying to find him since the night of the fire, and when he turned up here it had been an impossible struggle to get through to see him. But all the pressure had worked and now, in only a few minutes, she would be there. Since she landed in Rome she had not thought about how he was taking it all. She knew he was not fully resolved. There had been no statement, no news conference. She had no idea what to expect from him. She asked herself whether she would have gone to such lengths for an interview if this were only a news story. The answer was obvious.

The taxi stopped before the Holy Office. Soon she was seated in a limousine beside a dark-robed, rosy-cheeked elderly man whose icy formality she thought came from the sin of envy. They passed through barricades, under arches, through the nearly deserted streets past yellow buildings and neatly manicured lawns and stopped, finally, before the entrance to the Gardens. Father O'Rourke stepped out and opened an umbrella for her, then led her along winding paths toward a two-story building. "The cottage of Pius IV," he said, pointing.

Joseph saw her coming from far down the walk at a characteristically determined pace that left behind the man walking beside her. As she climbed the stone steps to the entrance she pulled off her rain-drenched raincoat, shaking water onto the lifelessly solemn guard standing at attention in the doorway. When he looked down to brush off the drops she moved past him into the building, leaving both Monsignor O'Rourke and the guard with nothing to do but watch.

"Please leave us now," Joseph said without taking his eyes from her. He reached an arm around her and led her out onto the covered porch to a chair. "You don't know how glad I am to see you," he said.

Louise's smile broadened. "You look a wreck, Joseph. Does that go with the job?"

As he sat down across from her he ran his hand over his three-day stubble and remembered the dark circles he'd seen under his eyes in the mirror this morning. "I haven't accepted the job," he shrugged.

"Offers not high enough?"

He laughed. "I'd forgotten what it was like to be around a normal human being; they don't tell many jokes here." He sat back, relaxing. "How are you?"

She felt her tiredness and hunger melt away. "I'm suddenly fine and suddenly very sorry I won't have you all to myself this afternoon. Still, Jerry Matthews won't be here for a while."

"How'd he talk you into it? When they said you requested permission for him to come along I was pleased, and a little surprised."

"Well, he found out I was trying to see you, and dogged me until in a weak moment I invited him. I kept seeing myself years ago and remembering what it was like to be so hungry to be in on things. Joseph," she said quietly after a moment, "how are you doing—inside?"

"Worse than outside, I think. More confused, more scared than before."

"Scared because you still haven't got your answer, or because you have?"

"You're a smart lady. I'm scared because I'm not sure. Do you mind if we don't talk about that right now?"

"No, of course not."

"What's been going on? I feel so cut off from the world. When did you get here?"

"Two nights ago. I came as soon as I heard."

"What's it like out there? I'm afraid to ask you, but I need to. How much—I mean, how's it being taken? Is anybody believing it?"

She looked surprised. "Haven't you seen the newspapers?"

"No. I wasn't ready for that."

"But you are now?"

"Uh-huh."

"OK," she nodded. "I'll tell you as much as I know. You're front page, everywhere except Communist countries. They're silent, of course. Everywhere else you're the lead story."

"But what are they saying; vhat do people think?"

"Well, a lot of people obviously believe it. Especially Catholics. They've declared holidays to rejoice and pray about the arrival of the Second Son of God. Some people are scared. They're afraid it's the Second Coming. Others believe it's some kind of a trick cooked up by the Catholic Church to bring the focus back on them."

He felt a surge of hope. "Then not everyone believes it?"

"Oh, no. Not many people are downright denying it. What have they got to deny yet? There's so little to go on. Some Jewish council said they were prepared to grant you prophet status, but Messiah—no way. The Protestant churches are playing it cool—they're saying wait and see, but just in case, remember Joseph Turner is not a Catholic and was, after all, baptized a Protestant' and so on. The political leaders back home and in most other Western countries are underplaying it as much as possible. They're afraid of some kind of panic, but the word's out that privately they're covering their asses."

"By doing what?"

"Oh, you know, consolidating their alliances with religious supporters, being publicly very visible yesterday at Thanksgiving church services, making frantic calls to their brokers to watch the market and sell if it starts to go, calling secret emergency meetings to prepare legislation to stop any business or public action that could get out of hand."

"What about ordinary people?"

"They're mainly hopeful, I think, but confused. The 'opinion-molders' for once, have been left with their mouths open and their pants down. They're afraid to say anything definite, so they're hedging like crazy."

"Jesus Christ. What a mess."

"Uh-huh."

Lunch arrived. His long silence while they ate reminded her of another lunch they had had together, not long ago.

"Joseph," she finally said. "I think you need to talk about it. What's happened to you since you've been here? Something has; the Joseph I knew in New York would have denied it and been out of here by now."

He sighed, nodding. "OK." Then he told her all of it—the kidnapping, the shooting, reading the documents, the conversation with Emil Rothstein, the terror of its possible authenticity.

"Holy shit!" she said when he had finished. "It's incredible, what they were willing to do, what they were willing to risk. I guess I shouldn't be surprised—God knows I've seen enough good men doing awful things—but I am surprised. What about right now, Joseph? What are you feeling, thinking?"

"Well, for the last twenty-four hours I've been going back and forth between thinking I've got to stay here and play this thing out, and deciding to walk out the front door."

"Metaphorically, I hope."

"Huh?"

"I don't think you can get out the front door."

He looked puzzled. "What do you mean?"

"You really don't know, do you? I think you better take a look at St. Peter's Square."

"Why?"

"I think you better see for yourself. Go on. I'll wait."

He shrugged, without understanding, but found Carlo and asked the young man to take him where he could see the Square.

When he returned later, he looked pale, shaken. "My God, Lou. There are hundreds of thousands of people out there."

"All over Rome. All waiting for you. They're still coming."

"Damn!" He slammed his fist down on the table. "I feel like a prisoner here! Maybe I should just go out there and deny it all, tell them it's a big mistake, get it over with."

"But you aren't sure it is, are you?"

"No . . . I'm not. But then what am I supposed to do? Live here in this, this museum? Put on a robe and start preaching to the masses?"

"Oh, it doesn't look like you'll have time for anything so mundane."

"What do you mean?"

She opened the briefcase and dug through some papers, then pulled out a file, opened it. "Well, your schedule says private audiences with heads of state begin next week, immediately following the coronation, and then—"

"Give me that! What the—where did you get this?"

It was her turn to be surprised. "You haven't seen it?"

He read the page headed: "Proposed schedule, prepared by the Commission for Service to the Second Son of God, for the first week in December:

8:00 P.M., Sunday—Formal coronation. (Refer to attached Coronation Commission report.)

9:00 A.M., Monday—Appearance and blessing, Piazza San Pietro.

9:20 A.M., Monday—Private audiences, heads of state.

12:30 P.M., Tuesday—Private audiences, princes of the Church.

3:15 P.M., Tuesday—Meeting of the Commission for Service.

He flipped through the pages numbering the days of his life, his rage growing.

"Where did you get this?" he asked again.

"From a source within the Commission. A friend of a friend of a friend of a friend. I've been here for two days. Do you think I just sit around?"

"Obviously not. What else have you got in there?"

"I did some checking into who really runs things around here. I was curious about their motives."

"Well, who really runs things around here?"

"The Pope."

"I'm afraid that's no scoop, Lou."

"Right. Neither are his motives. A boy from Genoa, perfectly sincere, an impeccable history. He's not entirely simple, of course—Marco Girolamo Vasari reached the Papacy through respect for not only his piety but also his business acumen. But he's a good man. I can't say as much for his apparent successor."

"I thought no one knew who that would be."

"Well, no one does, of course, but there's plenty of gossip, and lots of subtle politicking. The odds-makers give it to Belazzi. So I followed up on him, and he's a more interesting character. Ambitious from childhood, has never failed to get power when he wanted it. Uses it fully when he's got it."

"Emil said the Pope relies heavily on him for decisions, especially since his heart attack."

"Not the ones about you, from what I gather. There's some talk that Belazzi has doubts about you. He has great influence on the men who handle financial affairs for the Vatican, and there he's been busy. You've been an asset to the Church already—even more than they'd anticipated."

"What do you mean—an asset already?"

"Catholic Churches these days are full. So are the coffers. And stock in Church-controlled corporations has shot up incredibly."

"Church-controlled corporations?"

"Sure. The Vatican is into everything from public utilities to spaghetti, munitions to yarn, housing—hell, it owns the Watergate buildings in Washington. This Church is big business, an ecumenical corporation. It's got a lot of money, and a lot of power. And it's more, much more, since you're here.

"Within twenty-four hours of the press release," Louise went on, referring to a small notebook, "the Vatican's holdings in the U.S., Canada, and Europe increased by ten percent. They bought in the first panic, all very indirectly of course. Now they're holding on until *you* 'go public'—excuse the pun —and the market shoots for the sky."

"It's incredible. It's too much to think about. It's so hard to believe all of this has anything to do with me."

"Well, it does. Even more than you think. For instance, they've commissioned a three-hundred-thousand-dollar painting of you, planned for a new wing of the Vatican in your honor. The coronation ceremony's supposed to top anything given for any monarch or Pope in history. Of course, you're paying your own way. Look," she said, pulling a large envelope out of her bag and carefully dumping its contents on the table. Joseph's face registered his shock at what he saw: small cards with his picture on one side and a prayer to him on the other, commemorative stamps and coins; medals, all shapes and sizes, engraved with his likeness surmounted by a halo; the tiny white box stuffed with what looked like cotton.

"What on earth is this?"

"Mattress ticking from your bed, a relic."

"I've had a new mattress every day since I arrived."

"Enough to make relics for every church altar in the Western world. These, and the sacramentals—the medals and cards that go out to anyone—they've already produced hundreds of thousands of them, and they're just waiting for you to say 'yes' before they go out. There's plenty of money in them—in donations, of course. In fact, there are already a few available on the local black market, as you can see."

"That's disgusting!" Joseph slammed his fist on the table causing the coins to bounce. He picked up a gold one and shook his head.

"It's not just disgust you're feeling, Joseph. It's good, solid anger. It's rage. Let it be there. You've got a right to it."

"I've got to stop this, now. Last night I really tried to convince myself that even though I'm not sure and even though these people have different ways of doing things, I might be able to find a life here. They're so impressive, so overwhelming. I don't know how I let things like the kidnapping and the shooting go. It didn't matter. Their motives seemed good. But it's impossible!"

He had turned away from the door and stood looking hopelessly out at the rain. "You know, the way they treat me around here should have told me. They kneel and bow and try to do everything for me. I'm sick of looking at the tops of people's heads. I'm not a person to them. Except to Emil, and sometimes Carlo, I'm just an image, like the head on this coin."

"Holy Son," a man's voice came from behind him. He turned to see the guard bowing before him. "Mr. Gerald Matthews has arrived."

"Thank you. Show him in, please."

A moment later Jerry Matthews appeared on the porch. He held out his hand, then pulled it back and bowed his head. "Joseph, uh, I mean, Holy Son."

"Oh, dear," Louise murmured.

"Cut that out, Jerry. I'm just me," Joseph said, going to him and embracing him. "It's good to see you, really good.

Sit down. Having you two here is like returning to the world."

"I'm sorry I'm so late. The crowds. Boy, the people out there are really waiting for you," Jerry said intensely. "There's nothing more important to the world right now than what you've got to say. You've got the whole world ready to listen. As soon as you tell them, OK, here I am, and here's what you're supposed to do, they'll do it. You're going to have more power than anyone—all the power anyone could ever want." Jerry watched Joseph shake his head slowly. "What's the matter?"

"I don't want it, Jerry."

"But what else can you do? You've got it!"

"Oh, dear," Louise murmured again.

"Well, I'm going to do something about it. Look, I can't explain right now, Jerry. I've got something I have to do. Louise, I'm going to talk to them, and then I'm getting out. I may need help. Is there somewhere I can call you?"

"Sure My room at the Hilton."

"Good. Thanks."

"Hey, Joseph," Jerry said, reaching into his pocket. "I got this medal for my wife and I wonder if you would bless it for me—"

Joseph was already gone.

TWENTY-SEVEN

Marco Vasari felt his chest tighten with excitement when the call came from Emil Rothstein saying the Holy Son had requested a meeting—"as soon as possible, as private as possible." He restrained himself from asking the one question in his mind, knowing that Emil would have told him if he knew. "Please escort the Holy Son to the office; we will be there in ten minutes—only Cardinal Belazzi and myself."

He's just the Pope, Joseph told himself again as he stepped out of the elevator and followed Emil toward the office. And if he believes I am who he says I am, then he'll have to listen.

His determination to insist that they stop this Son of God business and let him out of here was not weakened by his nervousness, but he knew how much he feared the awesome power of these men and their willingness to do anything they considered necessary to achieve their single-minded vision. Nonetheless, he had given up trying to rehearse how he would tell them. He would let it come out however it came out.

He entered the office and endured the embarrassing bowings and greetings. They looked at each other in uncomfortable silence. Finally Pope Alexander spoke. "Holy Son, we pray that You have had time to come fully to an understanding of Your spiritual station, and that You are ready to accept our service and assume direction of Your Church."

"No, Your Holiness, that's not why I'm here. This," he said, gesturing around the room, "is not 'my Church.' Whatever it is that God—or whoever—has in mind for me, I can't do it here. I've come to tell you that I want to go home."

Pope Alexander blinked in astonishment. "You have come

to this decision so soon?" he asked. "But You've given Yourself so little time!"

"If you're right about who I am," Joseph replied, "I don't have much time."

Pope Alexander closed his eyes and lifted his head in prayer. Joseph watched the struggle in his face. If this was the Son of God speaking His will, the old man told himself, then his own duty was to accept it. But if this was the frightened human being speaking, his duty was to do all in his power to show Joseph Turner what he believed with all his heart was the road God had chosen. The old man opened his eyes. "Blessed Son," he said in a pain-filled voice, "have we somehow failed You?"

Joseph felt baffled by the question. They had "failed him" in so many ways—and from their point of view in none at all. "I know you've done only what you believe to be right," Joseph said. "It's just that your whole way of doing things isn't my way."

"May we ask for an example?"

"Well, this for instance," Joseph said, pulling the medal Louise had given him out of his shirt pocket.

Belazzi started. "Where did you get that?"

"It doesn't matter," Pope Alexander said, silencing him. "Holy Son, do You object to the likeness on the medal?"

Joseph sighed, aware more clearly than ever of how differently they saw things. How could he explain? "No," he began. "I object to your making these at all. And I object to your making them for sale. And these, too," he said, pulling out the cards and throwing them on the table.

"Holy Son, pardon me, but these things are for the people. The sacramental medals are sent out in answer to requests."

"Just requests? Or requests accompanied by money?"

"Well, ordinarily requests do come accompanied by donations."

"And just how much in 'donations' do you expect to receive?"

"We have no idea."

"And in sales on the cards?"

"We do not know."

"Well, it seems like a big waste of money to me—a waste of money people could use better for themselves. I don't want

to be a part of your trinket business. So I'd like you to stop
making and distributing these, and give back any money people have sent in to you that has anything to do with me. If
you can't give it back to them exactly, then give it to charity."

Pope Alexander thought a moment. "We will of course do
whatever You wish, Holy Son. But please do consider that
the people take great hope from what You call 'trinkets'—it
means a great deal to them to have a symbol of Your blessing. Also, in spite of appearances, our Church's wealth is
spread very thin, and we must count on special donations
such as these for certain plans that have been made in Your
honor."

"Like portraits and new buildings? I'm not interested in
things like that. And I don't want to encourage people to get
their hope from little symbols they pray to. I want them to
get their hope from themselves."

Pope Alexander listened, understanding what Joseph said
and feeling the widening distance between them. How was it
possible that this Man knew so little of the way of the human
spirit? Nevertheless, he had little choice now but to accept
His request. "We accept Your guidance in this matter, Holy
Son. The medals and cards will not be put into circulation,
and the plans made for monuments in Your honor will not be
put into effect without Your approval. Is this more satisfac-
tory to You?"

The Pope's quick agreement to his demands gave Joseph
an eerie sense of his own power among these men. Yet it
wasn't the specific things the Pope had agreed to that were
the problem. He tried again. "Your Holiness, I appreciate
your doing as I asked, but the basic differences between us
are still there. I understand that you're planning some kind
of coronation ceremony—"

Belazzi looked at him strangely, almost fearfully.

"Is something wrong?"

"May I ask, Holy Son, whether someone has informed you
of these things or whether you just knew them?"

Joseph smiled. "Someone told me. Don't worry, I'm not
reading minds. Anyway, even if I was certain of who I was,"
Joseph returned to the issue, "I couldn't take part in anything like that. I don't believe in kings or crowns. Besides, it
costs too much."

"But, Holy Son," Pope Alexander answered, "ceremonies of this kind are expected by the people. The world will want to honor You. It is a ritual, a confirmation, a—"

"I wouldn't take part in any 'ritual' that raised one human being over another. Especially when 'another' is footing the bill."

"But God has already elevated You above others!"

"Then anything you do can't make that much difference, can it?"

"Joseph, please try to understand. We have been in this—"

"Business?" Joseph heard his voice say.

"In this work much longer than You have. The Church requires ceremony and ritual to reach men's hearts. Those are simple people out there."

Joseph felt his anger rising. These men were so sure they knew more than ordinary people about what was right, what was good for people. "Your Church may need ceremonies and symbols and rituals," he said harshly, "but I don't. And I don't think those 'simple people' out there do either. Most of my friends are simple people, and some of them are Catholic," he said, thinking of Sammy and Rosa, and Mrs. Rodriguez and her children, so many others, "and sure, they get some comfort and some happiness and some security out of your Church, but they pay a lot for it—and not just money. They pay in fear, trying to live by all the rules you set up, fear and guilt. It's taken me some time to connect up all of you and all of this place with what I've seen in the Catholics who're my friends, but I remember now how much the Church runs their lives. Well, I'm not interested in running other people's lives. I've got enough problems and make enough mistakes trying to run my own."

Pope Alexander had watched and listened to him with increasing excitement, for whatever criticism Joseph was making of the Church, it was not nearly so important as the fact that the Holy Son was for the first time speaking from His heart about humanity. And God was giving him the opportunity to teach this young Man, to lead Him toward the knowledge of His own responsibility. "Holy Son," the Pope said, walking to the window overlooking St. Peter's Square, "look at the people who await Your guidance. They have come here because they know they are full of ignorance, full of evil, and that their Heavenly Father has given them the most precious gift of a Second Son to lead them toward righteousness. Those of us who have been given in a smaller way the duty of preparing their souls for life everlasting can in part understand and share Your sorrow at this burden upon You. But to see the faces of those children out there uplifted in hope brings home to all of us the inescapability of our duty."

Joseph had walked to the window and stood looking out at the mass of bodies, nearly a hundred thousand of them, packed into and overflowing the square as far as he could see. It took him a minute to register the fact once more that these people had come here for him; he felt it finally in the nausea of anxiety and fear that began in his stomach. They had all been led to believe that he could give them— what? Anything? Everything? What could they want that he could possibly give them? And when they found that he could not answer their needs—what then? The man beside him was telling him he was responsible for all those—had he said "faces"? "Your Holiness, I can't even make out a face from here, not one person's face."

"Yes, Holy Son. It is difficult to reach out to each individual soul when we have been given so many under our care."

"And so you stand here watching from a third-story window, and you take care of them with ceremonies and trinkets."

Pope Alexander did not answer.

"Don't you see? This just won't work. You want me to help you teach those people to kneel and to pray to beings 'higher' than they are and to pretend that faith and symbols are enough. Everything you do here, everything you stand for, is to prepare people for the happiness of their souls in the hereafter, when what they need is for someone to help them find happiness now, while they live."

It was Pope Alexander's turn to feel confused. While he was elated that the Holy Son was, almost in spite of Himself, taking hold of His spiritual authority, he was deeply troubled by the increasingly obvious chasm between them. It was much more than any theological difference. As far as he could tell, this Blessed Ironworker had no theology. It was an alienation of spirit and purpose and understanding of what God's work among men necessitated. He must speak carefully now, for so much depended on his own powers of explanation and persuasion.

"Holy Son, will You tell me how You believe we should be different?"

Joseph shook his head. "I don't really mean that you should be different. I only know about me. If I wanted to help people, I couldn't do it holed up here waving from a third-story window. I'd have to be with them just like I've always been with my friends in the streets. I'd have to be somewhere I could talk and be understood. I'd—" He broke off, startled by what he heard himself saying.

"Holy Son, I am deeply moved by Your devotion to Your people and by the simplicity of Your vision, a simplicity shared by the simple Carpenter we also serve. But I feel it my own duty to remind You, forgive me, that our world today is large and complicated. It is not possible to live publicly in a civilization as advanced as ours without organization and support. It has been my faith that God sent You to us in order that we may offer You the power, the influence, the shelter of the temporal Church. We can do much, practically, to ease Your way. Already You have millions of followers, and no doubt You have enemies. Take us as Your weapons and Your shield in Your battle for men's hearts."

Joseph turned away. Had this man seen his fear a few moments ago? "I don't need weapons," he said quietly. "I'm not fighting any battles. I don't want a shield. I don't see things the way you do. I want to go home. Today."

"If I may speak, Holy Son, Your Holiness?" Belazzi began, his cool formality carefully concealing his growing anxiety. "There are practical matters to consider. Today, it would be virtually impossible for you to get out of Rome. A few days, a few weeks perhaps, would provide time for matters to sort themselves out. Meanwhile we would have the opportunity to reach a mutually acceptable way of explaining our disagreement to the people."

"I have nothing to explain. You are the ones who have caused all these people to come here. Now I'm not a prisoner here, am I?"

"Of course not! It's only—"

"You got me in here. You can get me out."

"Holy Son," Pope Alexander intervened, trying again, "is there nothing we can offer to keep You with us?"

"Nothing."

The Pontiff looked at him sadly. He had used every means of persuasion available to him in these short moments, and the determination of the Holy Son to leave had only hardened. It must then be the will of God that He should leave for a while and return temporarily to the world. Perhaps He would learn how much He is in need of His Church. The same firm conviction that had led Vasari to believe Joseph would come quickly to acceptance led him now to acquiesce to Joseph's leaving.

When he spoke, it was with the determination of an unshakable faith. "I beg Your forgiveness, Holy Son, for whatever failure of mine has led You to this decision I do believe that You are in tragic error. But if this is Your will, so be it. God will bring You back to us in His time."

"You'll make the arrangements, then?"

"We'll make arrangements for You to leave privately. It would be easiest if it were early tomorrow morning. We'll have a car and the Vatican jet at Your disposal. Emil Rothstein will come to You with the details."

Joseph held the Pontiff's gaze. He felt his own hands shaking. "Goodbye, Your Holiness," he said softly, then turned quickly and left the room.

Belazzi burst out of his seat as soon as Joseph was gone. "Your Holiness! We must make some statement immediately! Once he leaves here we will have no way of interpreting what he might say to the people."

"Dominic, what He says is in God's hands."

Belazzi could contain his anger no longer. It poured out, not against his Pope, but against the self-blinded man in front of him. "Marco, have you grown so overconfident that you cannot see what you have done to the Church God has placed in your hands? His entire way of thinking is in direct opposition to every doctrine of our faith! Have you considered his entire way of living? He might return to cohabiting with that woman! I beg you to save our Church by the only means left to us: by issuing a public retraction and apology for the error—and by announcing your retirement."

"Dominic!" Pope Alexander cried, striking his cane on the

floor. "You are asking us to bear false witness against the Son of God! It's unthinkable. It should have been unspeakable! I know that there are many among the cardinals who will agree with you that I should retire. But so long as I live, I will not leave this office and watch you—or anyone else— sit on the Throne of Peter and deny Him!"

Belazzi threw up his hands in utter frustration. "And how will you explain his departure to the world to those people out there?"

"We will tell them the truth, Dominic. The Holy Son has gone to begin His Work in His homeland. We all pray for His blessing. Now, Dominic, go . . . please."

When the cardinal was gone, Pope Alexander walked to his chair and sat down feeling weaker and older now, and very much alone. He prayed for the wisdom and the strength he would need to hold all of them on the difficult road God had chosen. And he prayed that he should live long enough to see the Holy Son return.

TWENTY-EIGHT

FOR THE FIRST TIME in two days sunlight poured through the shifting clouds onto the Roman landscape. The rain had stopped. Accompanied by Carlo, Joseph returned to the porch of the private garden cottage, wanting to be outdoors in a world that felt real.

There was nothing to do but wait during the hours that remained to him here—wait and think. With heavy steps he walked down from the second-floor porch onto a pebble path weaving through the landscaped gardens, past ornate fountains, and into a clump of scrub oaks. Carlo let him go on alone into the trees, where he found a small white marble bench. It was the kind of place, he thought, where others go to talk to God—or where God might talk to them—if there were talking to be done. But he didn't know what to say, and he heard only the quiet sounds of evening.

He realized this was a kind of silence and serenity he was not likely to enjoy for a very long time. Beyond the walls of this retreat, a few buildings and streets away, the people-filled world waited. Nonetheless he felt stronger, surer this evening than he had felt for a long time, and he knew that his strength came from having once more taken control of the direction of his life.

Little was resolved; he felt no nearer to answering the question of whether he was in fact who they said he was, or to knowing how he would handle the hopes and expectations of all the people out there who believed it. The English-language newspapers brought by Carlo confirmed what everyone had told him and what he had experienced painfully with Maggie and ridiculously with Jerry Matthews: Son of God or not, he would reenter a world intent on watching him and listening to what he had to say.

What disturbed him most about the stories he read was the determined note of hope, even demand, in people's minds. IS WORLD PEACE ABOUT TO ARRIVE? one story was headlined. DOLLAR RISES ON WORLD MARKETS AS INVESTORS ANTICIPATE SOLUTION OF AMERICAN ECONOMIC CRISIS, another began. And others: EPISCOPAL BISHOPS MEET TO DRAW UP LIST OF ISSUES OF FAITH TO BE RESOLVED. CANCER VICTIMS IN MASSACHUSETTS GATHER FOR PILGRIMAGE TO ROME.

He did not even know just what it was in his power to do. Everything that had happened in the last few weeks had come from outside—even every "miracle" had just happened, like some accident. He had never really chosen to "make" any of them, to test the limits of the power he feared.

Well, maybe it was time to try something. Something simple. He looked around him. Then he saw it: a small brown sparrow resting on a lower branch of a leafless olive tree. Okay, why not? he thought. "Hey, bird? . . . hey, bird, come here," he whispered, self-consciously motioning with his hand. But the bird didn't move. Not so powerful, he thought, feeling foolish.

The real question, he knew, was the question Louise had asked him weeks ago, John had asked him on the phone: what did he *want* to do? He had been taken by surprise when he heard himself talking to Pope Alexander as if he knew what a person others looked to for help and spiritual guidance should be like—but he knew, though he had always thought of that as John's job, that he had long been that sort of person to his friends.

His friends . . . simple people, people who didn't have much, people who didn't expect much, people who didn't ask for much, people who struggled for just the basic things they needed to be happy, people who could be happy with just a little hope, people who didn't even know sometimes how much they suffered . . . If he really could make miracles, then he wanted to make miracles for them . . .

He heard a rustle and saw the shy face of Carlo Lambessi emerge through the trees. The thin young body moved hesitantly toward him. He looks more like the Son of God than I do, Joseph thought affectionately, and he acts more like it, too. He's not angry or bitter about what life has been like for him, but it must have been hard, very hard, sometimes. It's people like Carlo who—

The idea struck him suddenly—struck him as the most natural thing in the world.

"Carlo, come here," he called, motioning excitedly. "Sit here with me."

The young man sat down, watching Joseph's lips intently.

"It's OK—I want you here with me."

Carlo settled onto the bench and pulled out his pad. "Carlo do something for You?" he wrote.

"No, Carlo," Joseph said smiling. "Joseph do something for you?"

Carlo's brow furrowed in confusion.

"Carlo, I want to do something very special for you. Is there something you want—something no one else could give you but maybe I could?"

Carlo flushed with embarrassment, then turned back to his pad. "Before you go, Holy Son, You give Carlo forgiveness for sins? You give Carlo blessing?" Joseph watched as he wrote, but when he had written the last word he scratched over the writing, crumpled the paper and turned to a new sheet. "Holy Son, Carlo not worthy."

"Of course you're worthy! . . . Look, Carlo, I want to give you a gift. Because I care about you, because you've been my friend. I'm sad to leave you. Let me leave something with you. I don't know how to give forgiveness or blessings, but if you want them, you've got them. But I mean something more—something . . . real, something very important to you. Surely there must be something from me that you want. But I need you to have the courage to tell me."

Carlo looked into Joseph's eyes, seeming to be searching there for courage. He put his pen to the pad once more. "Truly, Holy Son, You have greatly honored me to treat me as a friend. There is nothing I want from You." He stopped writing, staring at his own words, then began again, writing the words smaller this time, as if in a whisper. "Only sometimes I wish"—he crossed it out—"I regret never to hear sound of Holy Joseph's voice."

Joseph swallowed hard. And he knew it was not for Carlo that he was afraid. "Carlo, would you like to hear?"

Carlo frowned, puzzled.

"Do you want to hear? Yes or no?"

He nodded and lowered his head.

Joseph put his hand under the man's chin and gently raised his head. "Do you believe that I could make you hear?"

Carlo's eyes widened as he wrote rapidly then held his pad up for Joseph to read: "You are the Son of God. You can do anything. But I am not worthy."

Joseph's voice was an intense whisper. "Carlo, follow me closely now. I do not know if I am the Son of God. But you *are* worthy. You deserve to hear. Hearing is beautiful. These birds," he pointed, "they make beautiful sounds. And the wind whistles through the trees. And the dead leaves crackle when you walk on them. There is the sound of water splashing in a fountain from over the hedge. Carlo, I want you to hear these things."

Carlo's face was filled with the wonder of Joseph's words; Joseph knew there was no way he could stop now. It's like the first time you walk out on a beam, he thought. You don't look down at the empty space. You just keep moving. "But I'm not exactly sure how to take the first step," he said aloud.

Carlo pointed to Joseph's hands, then put his own hands over his ears.

"No, not like that, Carlo. Because if this can be done, it doesn't take my hands. It's in you, Carlo, that's what I think."

He took Carlo's hands. "Let me show you. Let me teach you. Now look. In a moment, I'm going to get up and walk away. When you hear a sound, it will be me, calling your name. When you hear it, I want you to get up and come to me. Okay?"

Carlo nodded.

Joseph released Carlo's hands, stood and moved down the path. His back to Carlo, he called softly, "Carlo."

He strained to hear Carlo rise, but heard nothing. He felt the fear in his stomach. If he couldn't do this, then what had all that had happened meant? He raised his voice, "Carlo!"

He waited a long moment, then turned back. Carlo hadn't moved.

Joseph sighed, shaking his head, then walked back to

Carlo. "I'm sorry, Carlo," he said, "really sorry. I failed you. No, more than that. I tried to use you to prove something to myself about me. I—"

Carlo's eyes had widened and his mouth dropped open.

"Carlo? Did you hear that? Can you hear me?"

The man's mouth moved, and he began to nod his head up and down. Then he scraped his foot over the ground, staring at it, scraping back and forth, nodding all the while. When he looked back at Joseph, tears were streaming down his face, a face full of joy and pain. He pointed at Joseph's mouth.

"Carlo, you can hear!"

Then Carlo went to his knees and grabbed Joseph's hand. Joseph reached down and lifted him. "No, Carlo, stand up! This miracle was for you, Carlo! It's in you!"

Carlo shook his head, laughing and sobbing in strange sounds of joy, pointing at Joseph, then pointing to the sky.

And Joseph laughed too. "Okay, Carlo, okay. We did it." He felt tears in his own eyes and he lifted his head and looked around the sky. After a few moments, he put his arm around Carlo's shoulders and they headed toward the palace.

Just before they reached the porch, Joseph stopped.

"Carlo, will you do me a favor? I don't want them to know until I'm gone. Okay?"

Carlo nodded a puzzled assent and scribbled on his pad. "I will do anything You ask, my Lord."

Joseph took the pen and scratched out the last two words. "Then I ask you not to call me that."

Alone in his room again, Joseph flung himself onto the couch, lay back, and looked up, staring at the painted ceiling. For the first time since the fall, he felt free—free of confusion, free of fear, filled with excitement and wonder. "Okay," he said aloud, "what else am I supposed to know? There must be something I'm to do now. I'm asking. Are you going to tell me?"

He stared at the ceiling for a long time.

It didn't answer.

"You don't make this easy," he said. "But I guess you know what you're doing."

TWENTY-NINE

THE DOOR OPENED before Emil Rothstein had a chance to knock, and the young ironworker, looking fresher and stronger than he had ever seen him, smiled and stepped back for him to enter. It was an hour before dawn.

"Hello, Emil. Come in. I'm ready. Is everything set?"

"So far, so good. Were you able to reach your friends in New York?"

"Yes, finally. Sammy and Rosa agreed with you about my apartment—said it's the last place I should go if we're going to keep this quiet. They'll be coming over to the hotel. So will the Stantons."

"And Miss Dillion?"

Joseph shook his head. "I can't find her. No one seems to know where she is. John's trying."

"Perhaps she'll find you," Emil said gently.

"I hope so," Joseph answered.

"Joseph, before we go, may I talk with you for a moment?"

"Sure."

The older man stood tensely, hands at his sides, but his clear gray eyes looked direct, open. "Your decision to leave has confirmed a feeling I've had for some time, Joseph. I think I was in error to bring you here. Not that the prophecy was in error or that you do not fulfill it—not that. But somehow it was wrong to bring you into this world. It has been long since I've been in Rome myself. I had forgotten, almost, what it was like. Watching you with the others here has made me in some moments almost ashamed of my role in all of this. I'm sorry."

Joseph put a hand on his shoulder. "Thank you for telling me, Emil. I don't like what you did, but I know you were doing what you thought was right. It's funny, but I'm beginning to think something like this had to happen. Something had to make me stop running. You've helped me a lot through the last few days. You're the only one who's treated me like a human being. It's meant a great deal. I'm sorry to say goodbye."

Emil looked down a moment, then back into Joseph's eyes. "I do not wish to say goodbye. I wish to go with you."

"With me?"

"I've left the service of the Vatican. You will need help once you return to New York. Will you have me?"

Joseph smiled. His hand tightened on Emil's shoulder. "Sure—I'd love it. I don't know what I'll be doing, but why not!"

"Thank you, Joseph, thank you," Emil said, smiling back now. "Shall we go? It's a long way back."

It took two hours to crawl through the still-clogged predawn streets of Rome to the Leonardo da Vinci Airport outside the city. To avoid potential problems Emil had ordered an undistinguished Fiat for their trip. Louise and Jerry were already on board when they arrived. Within minutes, the unmarked 747 had lifted off the runway, climbed through the clouds blanketing the imperial city, and turned westward for the eight-hour journey home.

When they were airborne Joseph entered the rear cabin alone and looked out at the limitless blue sky and the white clouds below. Relief washed over him, seeped in slowly, and ran together with his anticipation at being on his way home. There would be hours, days, maybe even a week or two, of being in his city, being with his friends, just being himself again. He drew the curtains, sat back, and closed his eyes, letting himself be carried, letting himself drift.

By 7:00 A.M. the jet was screaming over the Atlantic an hour out of New York. The door to the cabin opened and Emil entered.

"What's up?" Joseph asked.

"Look out the window."

He pulled back the curtains and peered out. An F-16 jet fighter was positioned just off the 747's starboard wing.

"What in hell—?"

"The Air Force."

"Why—?"

"You haven't slipped in unnoticed. We've got a four-jet Air Force escort into Kennedy. They've just radioed a greeting from the President."

"Of the United States? That President?"

"Uh-huh."

"But how did they know?"

"Evidently the Vatican told them. They've been in close communication about you through the American Embassy since you arrived in Rome."

Joseph sighed. "I wonder who else they've told."

"Everyone, apparently. Kennedy says there are about fifty thousand waiting down there. Your official reception party includes Mayor Wyatt, Governor Magill, Vice President Ruddock, and several religious leaders."

"Shit!"

"My reaction exactly."

"It's started already, then. Guess we better make some plans."

"I'll get you some coffee. Join us when you're ready."

Joseph took another look at the Air Force jet. Not bad for an orphan kid from the Bronx, he thought.

"What do we do now, folks?" he said as he came through the cabin door. "All of you know more about this sort of thing than I do. Tell me what to do. What's going to happen?"

"We can't get any information on what they've planned," Louise answered, "except for the reception committee. It's a good guess the press will be swarming all over. They could even have microphones set up. Probably the first thing you should think about is whether or not you want to say anything."

"I don't. No statements to the press, no statements to the crowd."

"It might be less awkward if we ask the captain to radio that ahead."

"Good. What else?"

"The politicians."

"What are they going to want?"

"They're there to honor you as representatives of the

American people and, no doubt, to be seen with you. Magill is a presidential contender on the Republican ticket, and—"

"I've got it," Joseph grimaced. "Let's just get through it as fast as possible."

"There's going to be a lot of that, Joseph."

"Yeah. Anything else?"

"Not that I can think of."

"Then we might as well relax."

The seat-belt sign flashed. Joseph stared out the window before touchdown. He saw thousands of people packed together outside the front of the international terminal. The observation deck was crowded to overflowing. It's worse than St. Peter's, he thought, settling back into his seat. The big jet wheels touched down and the engines screamed into reverse.

Rothstein handed Joseph his coat as the plane taxied to the terminal gate. When the jet stopped and the doors were opened, a well-dressed man in his early forties came up the steps.

"Mr. Turner?" said the man, extending his credentials. "I'm David Otley, U.S. Secret Service. I've been instructed by the President to handle your security, sir. We have already cleared you and your party through Customs and we have a car waiting."

"Are you expecting trouble?"

"No, but when you get this many people together you never know for sure."

Rothstein stepped forward. "Mr. Turner wants to get out of the airport complex as quickly as possible. We'll be staying at the Waldorf. Shall we?"

The Secret Service agent nodded. "Yes, sir. But—uh—you know that the Vice President is here?"

"We're aware of that." Joseph motioned for them to disembark. As they headed to the door Louise reached out and took his hand, squeezing it reassuringly. Joseph drew a deep breath and followed the others out the door.

As he emerged through the doorway the airport crowd erupted with cheers and applause. Joseph stood on the top of the stairs, bracing himself against the cold winter air and scanning the faces in the crowd, in spite of himself, for a glimpse of her chestnut hair.

But he could make out no one, only a mass of bodies.

The New York Police crowd-control squad had its hands full holding back the onlookers. A wave of fear almost stopped him; he pushed it away and began to descend the steps. Suddenly gunshots rang out; he flinched, stopped, then looked down to see the U.S. Navy drill team firing off a nineteen-gun salute. His fear turned to embarrassment when the Marine Corps Band struck up "The Battle Hymn of the Republic." Joseph continued his descent toward the waiting reception line headed by Vice President Ruddock. "Might as well get this over with," he mumbled.

As he stepped to the freshly snowplowed asphalt, ten Secret Service agents moved in strategically around him.

When Joseph arrived in front of Carl Ruddock, the Vice President took Joseph's extended hand and genuflected. Joseph tugged gently to get Ruddock back to his feet. Once there, the Vice President announced loudly, "On behalf of the President of the United States and the American people, it is my honor to welcome you back home, Your Holiness."

"Thank you," Turner said. "Please just call me Joseph. His Holiness is still in Rome."

"Yes, sir, of course." Ruddock looked flustered as he half-bowed, then quickly introduced Governor Jeff Magill.

Magill smiled broadly and shook Joseph's hand. "Welcome home, Joseph. It is a great honor, a great honor."

The presidential hopeful turned to the balding man to his right. "This is Charles Wyatt, Mayor of your great city." Wyatt extended his hand to shake Joseph's. His eyes scanned the photographers to make sure they were still taking pictures. "If there is anything, anything my office can do for you, all you need is to call."

"Thank you," Joseph said, beginning to move past them.

"I'd like very much to drop by your hotel room, Joseph," the Governor said, "so that we might discuss your views on a few matters. You know, even though I'm not Catholic, I am a religious man and I'd hate to see your situation exploited."

"We appreciate your concern," Emil said, hastening Joseph forward. "We'll let you know when we can schedule an appointment."

Joseph moved quickly down the reception line, coolly but politely acknowledging the Chancellor of the Catholic

Archdiocese of New York, who introduced him in turn to the Presbyterian representative of the World Council of Churches and the rabbi representing the Reform Jewish community. When he had finished he turned to the head of the Secret Service team. "Mr. Otley, you said you had a car?"

"Yes, sir," Otley snapped out politely, waving the waiting limousine forward.

With Joseph, Emil, Louise, and Jerry securely inside, Otley climbed into the front seat and snapped up a walkie-talkie. "This is Guardian One to all units. The Messenger is secure. We are rolling. Respond."

While Joseph peered out the window, the car leaped forward. He didn't hear the other units call in to Otley or the motorcycle escorts turn on their sirens; his attention was riveted on the railing of the observation deck and the chestnut-haired woman who turned away from the motorcade and disappeared into the crowd.

They rode in silence into midtown Manhattan, weaving through honking cars whose startled drivers craned their necks toward the limousine. Joseph stared out the windows at the faces of curious pedestrians who stopped to watch them pass.

"A lot of cars have followed us from the airport, Mr. Turner," Otley said from the front seat. "You'll need to get into the hotel quickly."

The motorcade finally came to a stop under the porte-cochère of the Waldorf. Emil, aided by the Secret Service, hurried Joseph into the lobby.

The hotel manager met them with exaggerated deference. "Welcome to the Waldorf," he said, bowing low. "We are most honored to have you here, most honored. The Presidential Suite has been prepared for you."

Joseph looked reluctantly at Emil.

"Go ahead. We can't discuss it now," he said, indicating the crowd beginning to form around them.

Before they reached the elevator, a small high voice called out across the lobby. "Uncle Joseph!" He turned to see Amy Stanton waving excitedly, and beside her John, Bonnie, Sammy, and Rosa, all smiling. He broke from the men around him and reached his friends in a few steps.

"Don't move, any of you," said Joseph, holding up his hands, "I want to just look at all of you for a minute."

Amy broke from Bonnie's grasp and threw herself into Joseph's arms.

"I love you, Uncle Joseph."

"I love you too, sweetheart," said Joseph, hugging her tightly. He gently untangled himself from her small arms and moved to the others, hugging them one by one. Bonnie reached up to kiss him on the forehead, her eyes glistening with tears. John held him tight an extra few seconds, and Joseph felt the message of support in his arms. When he turned to Sammy and Rosa, they held back, their impulse to reach out to him checked by their nervousness and awe.

"Come here, you two!" he said, putting an arm around each and pulling them to him. "It's just me! I'm glad to see you!" His boyish enthusiasm melted their reserve. Rosa broke into happy tears and giggles and Sammy slapped him hard on the back. "I knew it. I knew you wouldn't change. Not our Joey!"

Otley's voice came from behind him. "We really must go, Mr. Turner. The lobby's beginning to fill with people coming to see you."

"Come on," Joseph said, leading his friends to the elevator.

Otley and his aides checked the rooms of the Presidential Suite and departed. With Emil, Louise, and Jerry taking care of arrangements with the hotel, answering the barrage of telephone calls and knocks on the door—most of them flower deliveries—the friends talked through the afternoon.

They brought each other up to date. Joseph listened intently as they answered his questions about the trouble his publicity had caused them. They told of prying reporters, desperate people begging them to deliver messages to him, curious people wandering around their neighborhood—no serious incidents, just intrusions into their privacy. These had been manageable so far. "But it got to Maggie fast," Bonnie said, and then, to his unspoken question, "No, we still haven't heard from her, Joey. I'm sorry."

He turned quickly to Sammy to ask about the progress on the building and listened a little wistfully as Sammy described the work, explaining how he had found a temporary partner —"just temporary though, he knew that, until we heard from you."

Rosa told him they'd been spending more time at church. "But we don't want to talk about us, Joey," she said. "We want to know about you."

He answered their questions as well as he could. Sammy and Rosa were shocked and puzzled that he did not know for sure whether he was "the Second Son of God." He reassured them that he no longer rejected the idea completely.

John drew from him the loneliness, confusion, and pain of his days in Rome, and they all listened solemnly as he told them of the events that had brought him out of that confusion to an acceptance of his special power. Sammy and Rosa crossed themselves repeatedly as he recounted the miracle of Carlo Lambessi. "But, John," he said, finishing at last, "it wasn't like I thought it might be. There were no voices telling me what to do, and I didn't even feel sure it could happen. I still feel uncertain about what's possible, and about where it comes from, but . . ."

"But now it doesn't seem to matter," John finished for him.

"No," Joseph said, smiling. "It doesn't."

They sat quietly for a few moments.

"You've changed, Joseph," Bonnie said, "in subtle but important ways. You're more serious, deeper somehow, and more—vulnerable."

Rosa nodded her agreement.

"I think you're right," he said thoughtfully. "I do feel different. I used to feel this way only when I was up on a building, like I could see for a long way, and very clear, very much inside myself, but connected to the world, connected to the building and the people around me. Alone, but not lonely . . . and knowing how much every movement counted. Not afraid, just very, very careful. I used to feel it only up top. I felt it last night, and it's still with me." He paused, remembering Carlo, then he pulled himself back to the present. "Well. Now you know everything. Will you excuse me for a minute?"

When Joseph had gone, Sammy called across the room to Emil, "Mr. Rothstein, can I ask you a question?"

"Of course," Emil said, joining them.

It was the one question they'd all avoided.

"In the newspapers," Sammy started solemnly, "they said the prophecy said Joseph has Divine protection until Good Friday. Me and Rosa, we've been worrying about what that means."

"So have we, Sammy," John added.

Emil nodded. "We don't know for sure what it means. If you're worried about whether it means he will die—there's no reason to think so, but we just can't know; he might. And we have to face the fact that we're not the only ones who've read or heard the prophecy. It's possible—no, it's likely that someone will try testing it."

"You're saying that someone will try to kill him," John said.

"No!" Sammy exclaimed.

"It just makes sense, Sammy," John said. "There are plenty of lunatics out there who'd do it just for the fame."

"We've got to be prepared for it," Emil agreed. "However we can, we all need to protect him, help him be careful."

"Help who be careful?" Joseph asked, coming back into the room. They all looked up at him silently, sadly.

He looked around. "Isn't anyone going to tell me what's going on?"

"We're talking about the prophecy, Joey," John said. "The last part of it."

"Oh. Well, let's worry about that when the time comes. Right now I'm more interested in tomorrow than I am in what's going to happen four months from now. Let's take it one day at a time. OK?"

"Joseph," Emil said, "there are some calls we need to talk over—some things you might want to take care of."

"OK. Sammy, Rosa, will I see you tomorrow?"

"Sure, whenever you want."

"How long will you guys be in town?" he asked John.

"For a few days, anyway. We're at the Warwick."

"How about if we meet for breakfast?"

"You better plan to come here," Emil said. "I'm afraid the crowds outside might make it difficult for Joseph to get out."

"Well, we'll think of something," Joseph said. "I'm not getting stuck here like I was stuck in Rome. We'll call you in the morning."

They embraced again warmly before they left. All were full of the consciousness that they had entered a new phase of their friendship, that the life Joseph had now to live would change all of them in ways they could not yet imagine.

THIRTY

BREAKFAST NEVER HAPPENED.

By Sunday morning the public return to New York had plunged Joseph into a turmoil of activity with little time to do more than cope with the problems descending upon him. When he had grasped the immensity of the tasks that lay before him, he telephoned his friends to delay their next meeting. He learned that the night before, the identity of his friends had spread quickly through the crowds outside and they had narrowly escaped being mobbed. This confirmed Joseph's decision that for the time being they should stay away from the hotel.

Although Emil had gone out late the first night to tell the hundreds gathered around the hotel that Joseph would make no appearance or public statement for at least a few days, and that he asked everyone to go home until then, it was late the next day before most of them had left. The city police force worked to disperse the rest, but during the next few days smaller groups crept back, some of them curiosity-seekers, some carrying placards demanding "A Blessing!" others waving angry signs damning "the false Prophet." Occasionally scuffles broke out on the sidewalk.

"What we need now is a good, heavy snowstorm," Louise had said, but the New York winter had unhelpfully turned mild, sending only a cold wind blowing over Manhattan. The snow that had covered the streets melted swiftly as temperatures climbed into the forties, and the flow of people to the hotel only increased.

The pleasure of the hotel at hosting the Son of God waned quickly once the initial excitement was over. The confused jumble of people continually wandering through and around the hotel severely hampered normal operations and, even with the Secret Service detachment, required the doubling of hotel security forces to keep inventive interlopers off the sixteenth floor.

Though the manger said nothing, Joseph was aware of the difficulties he was causing. He also felt trapped. His separation and insulation from people was worse than in Rome, but Emil and Louise had persuaded him that if he started out to talk to them, he wouldn't get past the elevator door. It wasn't the kind of "being with people" he had in mind. What he did have in mind was only beginning to come clear to him, and it had nothing to do with being stuck in this hotel room.

He needed a place to live, a private place, where he could come and go if not freely at least carefully without being mobbed. Sammy had volunteered to spend some time looking —"Frankie'll give me a few days off." He set out Tuesday morning with his list of impossible conditions: big, out of the way, close to subways and bus lines—and cheap.

There wasn't much money. Joseph had refused to accept the hotel's free hospitality for more than one night, and he also refused to live on the donations pouring in. They would pay their own living expenses. The few thousand dollars in his savings account wouldn't stretch far.

Joseph's hours were filled with trying to keep up with the problems inundating them by phone and by mail the first week. Though the hotel had agreed to hold all but "urgent" calls—or calls from a list of names they had been given—the phone rang incessantly. They picked it up to hear people with impressive political, religious, corporate, and social-organizational titles urging, requesting, pleading, demanding the Son of God's presence at their functions or endorsements of their causes, positions, and products. The President of the Ironworkers Union called to request his presence at the dedication of a building. The Chairman of the Board of Quality Tire, Inc., urged his endorsement of their new line of "fail-safe tires." The President of Citizens Against the Destruction of the Earth demanded that he lead their march against insecticide manufacturers. The head of the Interfaith Council pled for his appearance at their National Prayer Breakfast. The secretaries of state of numerous foreign governments called to "establish initial communications" and "arrange a visit with our Head of State." United States senators, congressmen, and state governors with large Catholic constituencies called "just to let him know we are available should he need anything and—oh, yes, would he be available to join me at . . ."

Many sent wires, telegrams, special-delivery letters. In a corner of the hotel room, mailbags piled up with the urgent pleas of sick and troubled and unhappy people who begged for prayers, blessings, healings, forgiveness, and money.

His friends saved him. Emil fielded most of the phone calls. Louise handled the press, weeding out the most important requests for Joseph's decision. Their answer to everyone was, "Don't call us, we'll call you," but certain issues were going to need immediate action. There was the call from the orphanage where Joseph had grown up pleading for help against an organization called "The Joseph Turner Memorial Society" which was attempting to buy the property and turn it into a shrine. Newspapers and magazines were full of stories detailing Joseph Turner's life and habits, most of them creatively elaborated with rumors. Some of them were troublesome, especially the reports of "miracles" he had performed throughout his life, and Louise was kept busy arranging press corrections of all but the fall from the building, the healing of the gunshot victim, the rescue of the children from the fire, and Carlo Lambessi. The Vatican had released the news of Carlo on Sunday night.

With the exception of fabricated reports of miracles, Joseph had told Louise to ignore anything that had only to do with him, unless she wanted to issue simple denials. She was cautioned to keep track of anything that might be hurtful to any of his friends. Already the story of Mrs. Rodriguez's jailed husband had shown up in two or three papers and Louise had told them to lay off. In particular, Joseph had asked her to look for any rumors about Margaret Dillon and to do everything possible to keep Maggie out of the news. They had been lucky.

The first of the advertising exploiting Joseph's associations had appeared in print and on television. One of the boys from the Boys' Club appeared in an advertisement for basketballs "just like the one we used when we played with Joseph Tuner." Ironworker dolls—"that can climb ten-foot scaffolds and fall without a scratch"—were to be on the mar-

ket within the month. Worldwide Insurance, Inc., advertised
their group plan as "the same plan that protects Joseph
Turner with the Ironworkers Union." The Fund for the Poor
began their Christmas campaign by reprinting a donation
card Joseph Turner had signed two years before.

Jerry announced that he had taken a leave of absence
from his job to help out. He relieved the others at the phone
and culled through newspapers when they were too exhausted
to work longer.

John sent Bonnie and Amy back to Provincetown and on
Monday night rejoined Joseph at the Waldorf. He handled
matters relating to religious groups, but also answered the
phones and processed mail. Joseph found himself turning to
John so often for advice that by Wednesday John had agreed
to stay on, leaving the Provincetown retreat in the hands of a
long-time friend and associate. He planned for Bonnie and
Amy to join him as soon as things were under control.

The five worked in shifts, napping a few hours here and
there, waking to find the phones still ringing and the bags
of mail piled higher.

John, Emil, and Joseph combed through the growing lists
of problems. Emil worked on petitions for several Superior
Court injunctions against advertisers and restraining orders
against the harassment of Joseph's friends. The three
drew up tentative schedules of meetings with political figures,
religious groups, social organizations, and ordinary people,
only to find that they hadn't even begun to meet the demand and that the calendar was filled for the next eleven
months. They tried again—laboring over it, shuffling and
reshuffling. The scheduled meetings got shorter. The lists of
unfulfilled requests got longer. The demands kept pouring
in.

By Thursday night the pace and stress were intolerable,
and Joseph, who had slept less than any of them, called a
halt.

"OK, folks," he said, pushing aside the papers in front
of him and flipping his pen down on the desk, "we're declaring a cease-fire. We need a breather. I can't even think
anymore. We're taking the phone off the hook and putting
a "Do Not Disturb" sign on the door. Jerry, you get home to

your wife. Louise, you haven't been back to your place since we got here. All of us need to get some real sleep. We—"

The phone rang again. He jumped a little inside. Maggie? It was the first thought that had come to him with every call; four days of ringing telephones hadn't changed that. He pushed the thought aside.

"Want me to get one last one?" Louise asked.

"I don't care," he said, getting up. "I'm going to bed." It rang again.

"I'll get it," Jerry said, as Joseph left the room. Jerry lifted the receiver. "Mr. Turner's suite . . . Who? . . . Yes, sir, just a moment please." Jerry looked nervous as he cupped his hand over the mouthpiece. "My God, it's the President! He wants Joseph. What do I tell him?"

"Tell him he's asleep and to call back in the morning," Louise said, coming back into the room.

Jerry started. "You've got to be kidding. This is the President of the United States!"

"I don't care who it is," Emil said with irritation. "He needs his sleep. And right now, it's our job to protect him."

"OK, OK." Matthews cleared his throat and put the receiver to his ear. "Hello, Mr. President. No, no, this isn't Joseph. He's asleep right now. No, sir, I can't. I won't. I will not wake him up. Matthews, M-A-T-T-H-E-W-S, Jerry Matthews. Yes, I understand that your people have called twice this week already." Jerry threw up his hand. "Look, he'll get to you as soon as he can, Mr. President. Yeah. God love you, too." Jerry hung up the phone and smiled from ear to ear. "I don't believe it," he said, pleased with himself. "I think I'm building character. Do you realize that I just told the President of the United States to—"

"Yeah," Louise said, "you sure did. You told the President of the U.S. to go fuck himself. Someone should have said it long ago. Come on, now. Let's get the watchdogs to see us home."

Joseph was up early the next morning. John found him sitting at the desk, staring at the schedules. "Any luck?" he asked.

Joseph reached for the calendar pages, picked them up,

crumpled them, and tossed them one by one into the waste-basket. "This isn't the way to do it, John. The whole idea is a mess. It won't work."

John chuckled, shaking his head. "I knew a good night's sleep would do you good. What now?"

"Now I'm going to do it my way. I had an idea this morning, but I need to think it through a little longer before we talk about it. Did Sammy call in last night?"

"Yes, still nothing suitable."

"It's OK. Next time he calls in, I've got to talk to him. It's important. I remembered a place this morning—a place I went to with Frankie Corollo once—and I want Sammy to check it out as soon as he can. If it's available, it'll be perfect."

THIRTY-ONE

JOSEPH HAD REMEMBERED a converted loft over a warehouse near lower Fifth Avenue north of Greenwich Village. Frankie Corollo's brother had lived there; Joseph and Frankie had stopped by for a few minutes one evening just a month ago. The next day Frankie had mentioned that his brother was planning to move to California at the end of the month.

"It's perfect, Joey," Sammy said excitedly after taking a look. "It's partitioned off into several rooms, a little kitchen, and a bathroom. The warehouse downstairs is almost always deserted; they make pickups and deliveries once a week. At night businesses around there close up and there aren't many people around on that block until seven in the morning. There's even a rear entrance."

"Sure does sound perfect. What's the catch?"

"It's not cheap. I think you can swing it. It's only a hundred a month more than you said. And Frankie's brother is moving this week. There are other people interested, but I talked the landlord into giving me fifteen minutes to call you."

"Take it," Joseph said unhesitatingly.

They moved in the next week. Rosa cleaned and Sammy found enough used furniture to set them up with working tables, chairs, and beds for six people. Emil worked through a contact at the phone company to get phones installed immediately and arranged a post office box for their mail. Joseph, Emil, and John moved out of the Waldorf in the middle of the night, telling no one except Otley, who protestingly arranged to move them out. He created a diversion in the street in front of the hotel and took them through the service

237

elevators to the basement, where they left through the delivery entrance.

"You're not going to be able to keep this quiet for long," Otley grumbled when they arrived at the loft. "We'll be as inconspicuous as possible, but sooner or later someone's going to attract attention. And when it does leak, this isn't going to be any place for you to be. You're smack in the middle of Manhattan in an indefensible structure."

"I'm sure you'll handle it all just fine," Joseph said, grinning mischievously at him.

Early the next morning Louise, Jerry, Sammy, and Rosa joined them at Joseph's request to discuss his new plan. They gathered around the table where Rosa served breakfast while they talked.

"I'm going out," Joseph announced.

They all looked at him quizzically. "Out where?" Emil asked.

"To the streets of New York. To the people."

The faces around him filled with concern. "But where? To what people? And how, without being stopped?"

He pulled several carefully folded letters out of his shirt pocket, spread them open on the table. "I've kept out a few letters that meant the most to me, from people who really need help, the kind of help I want to give. This one, for instance—from a kid in Harlem." He read it to them.

My ma drinks, we ain't got much to eat, it's getting bad. My friends is on horse but I don't wants to sell, they say you was a poor kid, how'd you make it?
                         Claude.

And this one—

I'm writing you about my wife. She's scared. I'm old. The doctor says I could go any day. We got no friends and our sons both died in the war. When I go she's got no one to take care of her. We sit every day in the park and she just gets scareder of being left alone. I don't know what to tell her. She's in a lot of pain from her arthritis but the fear's worse. I know you got a lot of people with worse problems to take care of. But I don't know who else to ask what to do. We got so little time left together, and its all ruined this way. Maybe you could just send her a note? Something to hang on to?

Yours truly, Albert Kochinsky.

"Something to hang on to," he repeated looking up. "It's people like this I want to talk to, at least to start. They can't come to me, so I'm going to them."

"But what are you going to do?" John asked, his exasperation showing. "Just show up? Just appear on their doorstep as if by magic?"

"Exactly."

"But how?"

Joseph turned to Sammy. "Sam. I have a big favor to ask you. I'm gonna need you. If I could talk Frankie into it, would you stay with me for a while?"

"Sure, Joey. Anything."

"Good. Then here's what I want to do. Tomorrow morning I want you to pick me up at six, take me down to the Tompkins Square Park. You know, where the old people sit around? Then you go to this address—" He handed Sammy a torn piece of envelope. "—and tell these people a friend is waiting for them in the park down the street. Then go here—" He handed him another address. "—and find Claude and ask him what school he goes to and tell him to meet me in the schoolyard at noon. Otley can check out both places in advance, have men there if he wants to. When I'm finished, if everything goes OK, we'll try another one or two, then drive around until it's late enough, then back here. Nothing big for a while, nothing like people call miracles, I just want to talk to people, see what they need, see what I can do."

They sat stunned.

"Otley'll die," Louise said finally.

"Joseph, you can't!" Jerry said. "It's too dangerous!"

"Dangerous to who, Jerry? To me? I don't think so. I have a strong feeling about it. Anyway, I have to try it."

Nothing they said could change his mind, so at 6:00 the

next morning Sammy brought his Chevy to the rear entrance
of the warehouse. Joseph, huddled in a heavy wool jacket
and scarf and a cap pulled down over his eyes, waited inside
while Otley and two of his men came out the door, scanned
the street, and between passing cars opened the rear door
of the Chevy for Joseph to get in. Fifteen minutes later the
car pulled to the curb near Tompkins Square Park and Joseph emerged alone onto the grass. With Otley and the two
others following at a discreet distance, Joseph walked to a
bench beneath some trees and sat for the next half-hour
watching the park come to life with joggers and people walking their dogs. He savored the freedom of being out once
again in the world and unnoticed, his excitement warming
his cold body from inside.

Soon a bent old man in worn baggy pants and an old
woman, clinging to his arm, entered the park and looked
around hesitantly. Joseph stood up and motioned to them.
"Mr. and Mrs. Kochinsky? Over here." They held back suspiciously until he said, "It's OK—look, there are people all
around." They cautiously approached the bench.

"Please sit down," he said, sitting again and patting the
bench beside him. "I'm Joseph Turner."

Their eyes widened as they sank slowly onto the bench
and bent forward to see his face more clearly, then looked
at each other in astonishment, then back to him. "You!
But—" the old man started.

"We don't have much time, and I want to help you if I
can. Mrs. Kochinsky, your husband wrote to me that you're
in pain, and that you're afraid."

She nodded, clutching her husband's arm tighter.

"What would make you less afraid?"

She cleared her throat. "I—I guess knowing someone will
always be there. But they won't." Her face was lined hard,
bitter.

"You don't have any friends?"

She shook her head.

"Any neighbors to help you out?"

"No. They're all too busy. They don't know what it's like,"
she said. The bitterness was in her voice now. "It's not fair.
They leave you all alone. Nobody knows what it's like."

He reached into his pocket and pulled out several letters,

handing them to her. "These are letters from people just like you, Mrs. Kochinsky, people who are old and already alone. This one," he said pointing to the one on top, "is from a lady who lives just two blocks from here. Her husband died a few months ago and her kids live in Arizona. She's afraid, too."

She took the letters and looked through them for several minutes. Her face softened as she read. "I didn't think," she said looking up, "I didn't think there was so many other people like me. Except I've still got Albert." She looked at her husband. "Maybe we could help them, Albert."

"I think you could," Joseph said.

"You think maybe there are even more people like these around here?"

"There must be," Joseph said. "And not even all old people. But many people who are alone and scared."

She shook her head slowly. "I guess I've been all closed up into myself. I guess maybe I could look around, find them, maybe we all could help each other out."

"There are a lot of people out there who need you, Mrs. Kochinsky."

"You make me see things clearer," she said, dropping her husband's arm now. "If I'm trying to help out all of these people, I'm gonna be too busy to be afraid. I'll still miss Albert awful," she said, looking at her husband lovingly, "but he won't need to be worrying about me."

They talked for another hour, answering Joseph's questions about their sons through tears and smiles, growing younger as he led them into the past.

Finally Joseph stood. "You two take it from here?"

"Sure," Mr. Kochinsky said gratefully. "You done a lot for us this morning. I don't know how to say thank you."

"You just did," Joseph said, smiling. He turned away and started toward the Chevy, which had reappeared at the curb a few minutes before. When he was halfway there he turned back. "Mrs. Kochinsky, you didn't ask me to help you with your pain."

"You did," she smiled. "It really isn't bad. Just enough to keep me reminded to go slow with these old bones."

He smiled back at her, then joined Sammy in the running car. He waved to the old couple as they pulled into traffic.

"On to Harlem," he said happily, answering Sammy's silent question. "And don't worry about Otley; he'll catch up."

His meeting with Claude in the schoolyard was more difficult. He had no easy answers for a boy too young to escape the brutality and ugliness of the ghetto world around him. He talked with him about taking care of himself the best he could, told him how to get work here and there, gave him a few names, encouraged him to find help at the Boys' Club. But he knew these weren't enough of an answer, wouldn't be more than a bandage on the deep wounds inside. So he began to talk about the world that waited for him outside, a world where even poor kids like them could make it in struggles where the odds weren't all against them. He talked of his own pain, his own loneliness as a child, and of how finding something to work and wait for had made that pain bearable.

The young boy listened, eyes and ears wide open, drinking in his words greedily. But Joseph could see the bewilderment and pain still in his face, and he had to reach deeper, draw out whatever strength lay deep inside this boy. "Claude," he said softly, "tell me what you hope for. Tell me what you dream about."

He watched the young face fill with embarrassment and suspicion. "How you know I gots any dreams, mister? Can you see inside my head?"

Joseph smiled. "Not really. We all have dreams, but some people bury their dreams when they get scared."

"Like me."

"I don't think so, Claude. Because you're here. You reached out for help. That takes a lot of strength, a lot of hope."

The boy shook his head. "My ma says dreams is silly, dreams is kid stuff."

"Your ma is wrong, Claude. She's mistaken. She's confused."

"You have dreams?"

"I sure do."

He watched the boy struggle inside, then saw the suspicion leave his face.

"Will you tell me, Claude?"

They poured out of him then, hesitantly at first, then faster —dreams of leaving the ghetto, of traveling the country—"I saw pictures of California on TV"—dreams of swimming in the ocean—"gettin me one of them surfboards"—dreams of owning a hot-dog stand on the beach—"just sittin' there in the sun"—dreams of having a dog to play with—"one of them big red ones"—dreams of girls—"real pretty ones, like is in *Playboy*"—dreams of houses—"with lots of grass"— dreams of sunshine and comfort and room to run and some-one to kiss. "But I guess these is only dreams," he said, watching Joseph carefully.

"Don't make fun of yourself, Claude. Don't make fun of your dreams. They'll keep you alive."

The boy fought back tears. "You is something, mister. No one's ever listened to me like you, but they're hard to hold on to by myself."

"You've kept them this long, haven't you?"

"I guess I have, yeah."

"Well?"

"So I guess I can keep 'em."

"I know you can. And you know what'll make it easier? Telling other kids and asking them to tell you their dreams too."

"I don't know."

"Will you try it?"

"I'll try it."

"And when things get really tough, Claude, you can call me." He wrote on a scrap of paper and handed it to the boy. "And if I'm not there, you ask for Sammy Sweet. He likes dreams too."

When the bell rang, the young boy stuck out his hand; Joseph shook it, holding it hard for an extra moment. Then Claude walked away, carrying his scrap of paper like a pre-cious gift. "I'll make it, man," he shouted as he disappeared into the building.

Yeah, Joseph said to himself, you'll make it.

"It works!" Joseph shouted ecstatically as he bounded through the loft door that evening. "It works!" He grabbed up a startled Louise Ryan, swung her around, laughed as the others breathed heavy sighs of relief.

"Lucky," Otley mumbled to Emil as he came through the door after him. "We were lucky."

That night he talked excitedly to his friends of what he had learned. "They need so little, really—just someone to help them see beyond the small worlds they live in, someone to care a little bit, someone to say, 'Hey, look, there's a world out there and you can do it, you can do something in it.' And they listened, really listened, just as if I was just another person talking to them."

They smiled with him.

The second evening Joseph returned looking less happy, more drained, more tired.

"What is it, Joey?" John asked him when Louise and Jerry and Sammy had left and Emil had returned to his makeshift office to finish up for the night. Joseph looked up from the day's stack of mail and clippings. "I guess I'm just tired. No, that's not all. I saw seven people today, John, seven people. There are so many. Maybe this isn't the way to do it."

"But it's your way."

He sighed. "I don't know. I don't know how much good I'm really doing. Sometimes I can tell I've hit something in someone. Other times I don't even know what to say. This afternoon I was listening to a woman who'd just lost her whole family—her husband, her kids, her brother—in an accident. She looked so desolate, and you know what I felt? Three years old again, and right there with her in all that hopelessness. Well, I finally said to her, 'Ellen, tell me what you want me to say to you,' and she said, 'Tell me I can live or die but I have to choose, I can't sit here in the middle anymore,' and I just repeated it back to her, and her face broke and she cried and that was all she needed. She knew, John; a lot of them know already what they need, but they think they need me to tell them what they already know, like it's not real unless it comes from outside. And then there are the others, the ones who don't know. Either way, I can't always tell whether I've done any good that's going to last past tomorrow. I keep thinking that if I ever did get through all the people who want to see me, the ones I'd already seen would already be in line again. And there would still be millions of people who need help who wouldn't even ask. Still, I'm learning a lot, John, and as long as our luck holds out . . ."

His luck held out for three days. On the fourth, he met with a young man in the Village, who had written Joseph that he was near giving up, near suicide. Their meeting was interrupted by a middle-aged woman who recognized him as the two walked along the waterfront below Wall Street. She had run up to him, screaming, then stopped suddenly and backed off as he said calmly, "Please, be quiet, ma'am; it's OK, but we need to be easy about this." It was too late; other people began to gather and Otley moved to him and guided him quickly to the waiting car. Joseph just had time to touch the young man on the shoulder before he left— "OK?"

"OK."

By the next day the newspapers had the story and somehow had traced two or three other people Joseph had met that week. SON OF GOD MYSTERIOUSLY APPEARS IN WASHINGTON SQUARE, one headline ran. JOSEPH TURNER IN SECRET MEETINGS OF HOPE, another read. Against the advice of his friends he went out for two more days, but reporters and determined Messiah-seekers haunted the parks now, haunted the playgrounds, the waterfront walks. By the end of the week the search for him had grown almost to a hysteria, and Otley warned him that another trip out would end inevitably in someone following them back to the loft.

He stopped then, handing his remaining pile of letters and calls over to Emil. "We'll see if we can do something," he said, but in the next days Joseph withdrew to his "office," withdrew to the mail, his discouragement settling heavily around him. The others tried to shake him out of it but failed and watched helplessly as his discouragement solidified into depression.

"You're angry, Joseph," John said to him late at night several days later. "Why don't you show it? You're angry that the world won't let you do this your way. Why don't you tell them?"

"You're right, John. But—"

"Joey, it's time to get out there and talk. You have things you want to say. You've got hundreds of thousands of people who want to listen. What's stopping you? Getting up in front of a crowd of people isn't going to make you a Bridger, isn't going to make you a Pope. You'll still be you. They'll see that, they'll hear that. Look, we've got a whole pile of invitations, a box full of offers. Why not take one? You could try Shea. Why not try?"

Shea Stadium had been offered by the Mayor's office for Joseph to "deliver a Christmas message" on December 20. The newspaper stories had brought a second wave of people into the city hoping to see the Son of God, and Mayor Wyatt had been calling every day since, pleading for Joseph to speak to the "pilgrims." The network television exposure would be a boon for New York tourism and would be a political boost for Wyatt, who wanted to make the most of it.

Though Joseph at first rejected the idea, after his conversation with John it began to seem more and more the only possible solution to the problems besieging them.

There was the money, the staggering amount of money. Almost three million dollars had arrived in the mail.

"I know you don't want to deal with this, Joseph," Emil had said, "but I need to know what you want to do with the money. There's cash in almost every letter that arrives."

"OK, Emil. Have you kept track of it all?"

"Yes, just like you asked."

"Here's what we're going to do. We take ten percent of whatever comes in. That'll give us more than enough to keep everyone here going while they're not working and to help out people we run into who are really desperate. The rest goes back, with a note that says, 'Thanks, but we don't need all of it. You can decide better than we can who you want to help.' I'll be damned if I'm going to be the administrator of some charitable fund. People can take responsibility for that on their own."

"But, Joseph," Emil objected, "it's going to take a lot of work to get all this money back. We could spend four hours a day just doing that if the mail gets any heavier."

"Tell Louise to get out a statement to the press that we don't want any more money."

The statement went out, but the flow of money continued.

The exploitation of Joseph Turner, spurred by the Christmas production boom, had outrun Emil Rothstein's capacity to keep up with it. Joseph T-shirts were coming off the line as fast as the machines could run. There were plastic statues for car dashboards, pendants with his picture, toys, paint-by-the-number kits, and a new box game entitled "Blessed Be the Son." A copy of a film called "Joseph and the Miracle of the Fire," could be purchased through a wholly-owned subsidiary of ABC for fifteen dollars. All the ingenuity of American commercialism turned its energy to packaging Joseph Turner for the masses, and the sheer volume of it, coupled with the clogged courts, stifled Emil's attempts to get it under control.

John had been under heavy pressure from religious denominations that wanted some sanction from Joseph Turner to reassure their parishioners. Though John had issued statements declaring that Joseph was most definitely not Catholic and would remain strictly nonaligned with any particular faith, religious leaders continued to press for "a statement of religious principles from Joseph Turner." Many complained that the money that had formerly flowed into their Sunday-morning collection plates was being siphoned off "into Joseph Turner's organization."

The politicians grew adamant in their demands for meetings. The pictures of Joseph with Mayor Wyatt, Governor Magill, and Vice President Ruddock had raised cries of "unfair political practices" from representatives of the opposition party. With every day that passed without some word of Joseph Turner's political preferences, the campaigns of the candidates grew increasingly difficult to organize. Like the religious leaders, the politicians were alarmed by the interest and money being drained from their organizations by the peoples' new fascination with Joseph Turner. Large contributors to the campaigns now held back their pledges until they learned which direction Joseph Turner was heading.

President Dewey Harper had not called again. Emil had called the White House to "delay any meeting until after the holidays." He was told that the President was much too busy himself to consider a meeting. But the next day Emil received another call from a staffer advising them that life could be difficult for anyone—"and that means Anyone"—who turned down Dewey Harper a second time.

Joseph sensed the concern behind Emil's calm, even though Emil had told Joseph only the gist of his conversations. If for no other reason than to relieve his friends from the stress of coping with such pressures, a public appearance and statement from him seemed necessary.

It was a particularly gray afternoon when he went to Emil with his decision. "Set it up," he said simply, relieved at least to have it done.

Emil saw the weight and conflict of the decision in the circles under Joseph's eyes, the tightness in his mouth. He was a man, Emil thought, still torn by the life thrust upon him. "Joseph, is there anything at all that would make all this easier for you?" he asked.

The answer came out before Joseph had a chance to stop it. "Maggie."

Emil's heavy eyebrows raised. "You want me to find her for you?"

"You think you could?"

"I think so."

"Find her, Emil."

"I'll put someone on it right away."

THIRTY-TWO

ON DECEMBER 17, news broadcasts carried the announcement of Joseph Turner's forthcoming personal appearance in Shea Stadium. A station in Fort Lauderdale extended its late-night news program for a special report on the preparations for the event. Maggie Dillion sat watching, fighting the desire to pick up the phone and call him, plead with him, scream at him not to go through with it. She told herself she had no right to make such a call.

At midnight she switched off the set and walked outside into her secluded backyard, into the balmy air of the Florida night. A sliver of moon glowed above her. She walked around the pool, her arms wrapped tightly around her, her eyes following the shimmer of light in the still, blue-green water.

She wanted to cry, but there were no tears left. Why was it so hard to stay away? She had told herself again and again that she could only hurt him by going back. But the voice inside her that called to him, that wanted him, would not be silent.

She turned and walked back inside quickly, went to the telephone, began to dial—and hung up.

The night before he was to speak at Shea Stadium, Joseph sat alone in his small bedroom. He tried to force his mind to think of what he would say, but the act of planning his words in advance felt unnatural and even unecessary. His mind wandered to the sounds coming from the other rooms —the low murmuring of his friends' voices as they worked and talked over last-minute arrangements, the occasional noises of chairs scraping the floor, footsteps, the whistle of the teakettle. He heard the telephone ring and felt the familiar rush of adrenalin in his chest, the catch in his breath. The feeling had grown stronger since he'd asked Emil to find Maggie. For the last three days he had not been able to push away the hope that the news of his public appearance would somehow move her to call.

Tonight there was also another reason to listen for the telephone: Jerry Matthews's wife had gone into labor early in the afternoon and Jerry would be calling from the hospital to let them know when the baby came. What a wonderful Christmas present, Joseph thought. It made him feel wistful, feel envious even of the little family, of the kind of private, warm, loving Christmas they would have together.

He had hardly realized Christmas was coming until Rosa arrived yesterday with a tree and insisted they all stop work for an hour to help her decorate it. He watched them all happily hanging foil icicles and colored balls on the branches, felt grateful that his "family" of friends had grown since last year.

Rosa had volunteered to do some shopping for him, and he finished his notes to her about what to buy for friends in his old neighborhood and the kids at the Boys' Club and the orphanage. He made a special note to pick up a card for Claude Robinson, and wrote the note to go with it—"There's one bus ticket to California waiting for you when you're ready." He thought about the other people he had met in the last month, of others who had written or called him, hoping that what he said tomorrow would make this Christmas more than a day of tinsel in their lives.

It was quiet in the loft now. He turned off the light, undressed, got into bed, told himself he needed to sleep. His mind filled with images of tomorrow night, crowds of people swarming around him, reaching toward him, closing in. Anxiety rose in his stomach and his eyes refused to stay closed.

After three in the morning Joseph gave up trying to sleep. What you need is a walk, he said to himself. He got up, dressed in the dark, and walked to the window, peering down at the sidewalk below. It appeared deserted, but he knew there was a Secret Service agent, possibly two, in the van parked across the street. Others would be watching the front entrance and alleyways, and by now Otley would have come in the living room for the night; security had been tightened since the publicity on his "outings." Feeling trapped and restless, he stepped quietly out of his room to listen. The gentle snoring that drifted through the thin partitions dividing up the loft told him Emil and John were asleep. He didn't want to wake them; he didn't want arguments, and anyway, there was no reason to cause them needless worry.

He moved down the hallway until he could see into the living room. Otley had fallen asleep on the sofa, but he slept lightly. Joseph was careful not to disturb him as he walked to the stairwell door, unlocked it, cracked it open, then closed it. Even if he found a way out through the warehouse, he couldn't be certain of getting past the agent. He didn't want to be stopped and he didn't want to be followed. If this was the last night he was to have any sort of private life, he would spend it privately.

He sighed and turned back to the living room, where his eyes fell on Otley's walkie-talkie, placed next to him on the coffee table. Joseph moved silently, cautiously, to the table, lifted the instrument, and returned to his room. He went to the bed and mounded blankets with the pillow in the middle. Feeling like a boy of ten again getting ready to sneak out of the orphanage, he stood back and approved his work. Then he turned his attention to the walkie-talkie. It looks simple enough, he thought, praying they hadn't changed the code names he had heard so frequently in the past two weeks. He formulated what he hoped was an official-sounding message, then mentally rehearsed it. After a few anxious moments he pressed the transmit button, brought the instrument up to his lips and, lowering his voice to imitate Otley's, snapped out softly, "This is Guardian One to all units. We have an intruder to the perimeter on the roof. I'll remain with the Messenger. All units move in."

Releasing the button and switching the walkie-talkie off, he looked out the window and grinned as he watched two men scramble from the van, guns drawn. When they had raced up the steps onto the fire escape, he grabbed his coat and hurried back into the living room. Otley had not moved. After replacing the instrument in front of the sleeping officer, Joseph again unlatched the door, then stepped out of the loft. Inside the stairwell he paused, feeling his heart race wildly. As noiselessly as possible he took the flights of stairs downward three and four at a time. He bypassed the ware-house floor and headed for the basement. By the time he reached the street-loading elevator only precious moments remained. By now the officers on the roof would have deter-mined that there was no intruder. "Faster!" he urged the load-ing lift carrying him inch by inch to the street. The heavy steel door opened above him and the cold night air rushed in. At street level the elevator clunked to a halt. The ex-hilaration of stepping out onto the icy asphalt nearly sent him running down the middle of the street. He ordered him-self to take it easy. He was almost free. No sense in ruining it now. He kept close to the buildings in the shadows until he had put enough buildings between him and Otley's agents so he couldn't be seen from their rooftop vantage point.

Then he broke into a run. The strain on his muscles slowed him and he grumbled at himself for letting his body get so out of shape. Then he chuckled, happy to feel his body so undeniably human.

On Fourteenth Street he passed still-open bars, and as their patrons entered and left, he pulled his overcoat collar closer around his face. No one even looked in his direction. He loved their indifference to his presence, loved feeling so invisible. It gave him more nerve and he decided to push his luck farther; when a cab pulled up from behind him he decided suddenly to take it. He held his head down getting in.

"Where to, mister?" the cabby said.

He hadn't known what he wanted until he said it. "Home," he heard his voice say.

"What?"

"The Bronx—433 Devon Street."

He huddled in his coat, his face turned out the window, looking at the bare branches of trees outlined in small white Christmas lights. The city was festooned for the holidays, elaborately decorated to entice Christmas shoppers. He had always loved the beauty of it, but tonight he felt angered by the expensive display; it was like a mask over the unhappi-ness of the lives of so many people who lived on these streets, on streets everywhere. And when Christmas was over and the lights and the colors came down, the inner emptiness would be laid bare again, would feel even barer because the promise of the decorations would have proved false.

He had been lost in these thoughts, but as they crossed the river into the Bronx and drove toward Southern Boulevard he noticed that the cabdriver was looking more frequently into his rear-view mirror, beginning to stare at him a little too long for comfort. "You can let me out here," he said when they neared the familiar bus stop across the street from the platform of the elevated subway. He paid the driver and got out quickly, before the question in the man's face formed itself in words.

The cab pulled off and he turned, looking at the now-deserted bus stop and remembering the faces of the tired, blurry-eyed workers who would be here only a few hours from now. He missed being here, missed his work; no, he missed the familiar security of the life he had etched out for himself. He would never ride that bus again, never again work iron. The certainty of it saddened him, but he also knew that he had moved beyond it. Tomorrow some of those people would be in Shea Stadium, and they would be there because they too believed he was different. He started down Southern Boulevard ready to enjoy the walk home.

About a block away from the bus stop he heard a car moving slowly behind him. From over his shoulder he could see a beige Plymouth with three men inside. He walked faster, trying to convince himself it was nothing, but when he reached an alley he darted into it. He heard the car accelerate and make a sliding turn behind him. He began to run and within three strides was running full out, running from a racing motor and the clamor of crashing garbage cans sideswiped by the careening car. In seconds he was out of the alley and across the street, barely missed by a newspaper-delivery truck whose braking slowed the honking Plymouth. They're not kidding, he thought, his mind filling with images of the kidnapping, shootings, Emil's warnings to him. Enemies. He struggled for breath in the frozen night air and pushed his body forward. It was just another block, just one more block. He would be home. If he could make it, somebody would help him.

As he turned onto the four hundred block of Devon Street he chanced another look over his shoulder at the car, now closing fast. Then he felt the side of his face and his chest hit into something hard. He lost his footing and fell. Arms and legs and a big body sprawled near him on the icy sidewalk. "Hold him!" a voice shouted from behind as he scrambled up and ran again. He heard running footsteps behind him, but now he saw the front steps another fifty yards ahead. As he reached them the beige car shot past and slid on the ice to a stop in front of the brownstone. All three men jumped out and headed toward him. Joseph stopped, turning between them and the two men behind him, readying his body to fight.

"FBI, Mr. Turner," said one of the men, holding out his identification. "Please don't run. Relax, please. We didn't mean to alarm you."

"What?" shouted Joseph, his anger mixed with relief.

"One second, please," said the brown-suited man, turning to one of his colleagues. "Harry, call it in," he ordered.

"Would you tell me what the hell's going on?" Joseph demanded.

"You're a very important . . . uh, man, Mr. Turner. The Secret Service thought you'd been kidnapped."

Joseph smiled wryly. "They're a little late for that."

"Sir?"

"Nothing, nothing."

"Will you accompany us back now?"

"No, I won't. I came here because I wanted to be alone, I wanted to see my old place." He looked up at the brownstone. "I'm here, and I'm going in."

The five men looked at each other nervously. "I see, of course. Well, when you're ready to leave, we'd appreciate it if you'd allow us to drive you back."

Joseph nodded and walked up the icy steps. One of the agents began to follow but was stopped by his superior, who simply shook his head.

Inside, the entry hall was silent, indefinably eerie even for the early hour of the morning. Something felt different, hollow, he thought. A feeling of foreboding came over him as he stared up the familiar worn stairs at unfamiliar signs tacked up on the paint-flaking walls: "Keep Out"; "Private Property—Trespassers Will Be Prosecuted."

When he reached his door he fished in his pocket for his

key, then realized he didn't have it. Quietly he went to the glass-enclosed fire-extinguisher cabinet on the wall and opened it; the spare was still there. He returned to his door and put the key into the lock; it didn't fit. He tried again, but the door wouldn't open.

"Hold it right there, or I'll bash your head in," a grave voice warned from behind him.

Joseph stood perfectly still. "It's just me, Abe. Joseph. Joseph Turner."

"Yeah, and I'm St. Benedict. Turn around. Real slow."

Joseph did as he asked and the burly super moved in closer, baseball bat ready to swing.

"Holy Mother—it *is* You!" Abe lowered the bat and took two steps backward, cowering and blabbering. "Please don't do nothing to me. I tried, Your Worship, I really tried. I even . . ."

"Abe, Abe, take it easy. Everything's OK. I just can't get my key to work. Would you open the door for me?"

"I changed the locks—made 'em double. I tried. I really tried." Abe fumbled for his keys and moved cautiously to the door, but he was shaking too much to get the key in the lock.

"Here, let me," Joseph said, reaching out and taking the key from the frightened man, who recoiled from Joseph's touch.

Joseph unlocked the door, opened it, stepped inside, and flipped on the light switch. "Oh, my God," he gasped. He stood in the doorway, stunned, his eyes moving across the room slowly, disbelieving. Little remained of the place he'd called home. Patches of wallpaper were torn from the walls and the threadbare carpet was in shreds. All of his books, pictures, personal effects, were gone, even his bedding.

He stumbled into the room. One drawer in the dresser was missing. He opened the others. Every one of them empty. He walked around tearing open cabinets, kitchen cabinets, bathroom cabinets. Every shelf was bare. Someone had even tried to pull the sink from the wall. The boards on the windows barely concealed the broken glass.

He turned to face the frightened man standing behind him. "What happened, Abe?"

"Souvenir hunters, scavengers. I never saw nothing like it. Ever since the Church made the announcement."

Joseph felt something under his foot in the torn carpet. He bent down and picked up a scrap of metal. It was his broken watch. He stared at it, clutching it tightly. The hands still said 9:23. He put the watch in his pocket.

"You comin' back here?" Abe asked, his voice shaking.

"No, I'm not, Abe. I'm sorry about all this. It must have been real hard on you."

Abe's eyes widened. "You ain't mad at me?"

"No, Abe. Not at you. How're the others here?"

Abe sniffed and ran the back of his thumbs across his teary eyes. "Not so good. The people coming around here wouldn't leave them alone. Then after the cops finally showed up to keep everyone away, the owners raised the rent a lot on account the building's so famous. Rodriguez is already gone. I heard she had to move into a smaller place, had to break up her family. Some of the kids are staying with her cousin. Old lady Wilkerson, Hacketts, Mendez, most of the others, going to have to move. All except Cochran. He died, overdosed. Heard he was makin' money sellin' stories about you."

Joseph slumped against the wall.

Abe looked down, then after a moment looked up, his fear turned to awe. "They says you's the Son of God, Joseph. Is you? I always knew you was different, but I never . . ."

"Abe," Joseph cut him off, "I want you to do something for me. Talk with the people here. Tell them if they want to stay I'll work it out for them. Find Mrs. Rodriguez and bring her back. Tell them I said everything is going to be OK. Will you do that?"

"Sure I will, but how?"

"Sammy Sweet will come by later and take care of it. Come on now, walk me down." Abe nodded and left the room. Joseph took a last sad look around, shook his head, and snapped off the light.

Joseph rode silently in the back seat of the Plymouth into Manhattan. It was almost six when he arrived at the loft. He walked in slowly.

His friends looked tense as they sat together around the table. Louise jumped up first. "Dammit, Joseph, anything could have happened!" she shouted at him angrily.

"Joey, we was so worried!" Sammy said.

"Why, Joseph?" Emil asked, his anger showing through his stony-eyed calm.

He shrugged, shaking his head. "I'm sorry. I needed to be alone. I just had to go home one more time."

"Well, I hope to hell it was worth it," Louise said, storming out.

"It must have been very important to you, Joey," John said gently.

Joseph stood motionless for a few seconds looking out the window at the soft flakes of snow drifting by. They were both right. It hadn't been worth it. But yes, it was important. He ran his hands through his brown hair. "Is there more coffee?"

Rosa brought him a cup. Her eyes were red-rimmed and puffy.

"Sorry, Rosa," Joseph said as he took the cup.

"The FBI told Otley what you would find, Joey," John said. "You need to talk about it?"

He shook his head.

"Well, then, let's all forget it and get to work," Emil said. "You need to get some sleep. We've got ten hours before you leave for Shea. The truck will be here to pick up the mailbags in an hour."

Joseph turned toward his room. Then he remembered. "You hear from Jerry?"

"A son," Sammy said, smiling now. "Joseph Turner Matthews."

THIRTY-THREE

MORE THAN FIFTY THOUSAND people were packed into Shea Stadium; the networks estimated the TV audience at nearly one hundred and fifty million. They all watched restlessly as the limousine, flanked by Otley and his men, emerged from the bullpen area and stopped beside the large temporary stage erected in the middle of the playing field. Many of the crowd grew rigid in their seats, anxiety growing as they realized how little they knew of what this man, this announced Son of God, might say or do. Their conversation dropped to calls of "He's here!" and admonitions of "Shhh-h!" as the figure dressed in jeans, flannel shirt, and fleece-lined jacket got out of the car and mounted the stairs to the platform.

At the top of the stairs Joseph stopped and looked around, feeling inexplicably calm. His eyes scanned the mass of oddly quiet bodies, passed over the banners draped over the railings of tiered stadium: "Blessed Be the Second Son of God!" "Joseph Saves!" and one, in a corner far above left field, "God Punishes Imposters!"

He turned, started for the microphones, then stopped again. Behind the stage, rising twenty feet into the air above him, was a gold-rimmed white cross. "Emil," he said to Rothstein, who had come up beside him, "tell them to get that thing out of here." Then he walked to a chair in the center of the stage, sat down, and waited for the next twenty minutes while the stadium crew scurried to lower and carry off the cross. The crowd's silence was broken by shocked and questioning whispers.

When the cross had been removed and the crowd was again silent, he motioned to Emil. Three men carried huge bags of mail onto the stage. Joseph rose and walked to the microphones. A sudden feeling of precariousness, as if he were about to step off into empty space, made him step back and close his eyes for a moment, wishing he were more sure of how to speak to this crowd of people, so many of them eager to believe he could save them. He breathed deeply, opened his eyes, and stepped forward again, willing to trust that he would find a way to reach them.

"I can't speak with you individually," he began slowly as the cameras moved in closer, "but I don't know any other way to do this than just as if we were having a conversation, face to face. You all know who I am. My name is Joseph Turner. Until a few weeks ago, I was an ordinary man with a simple life. I worked as an ironworker, a connector, to be exact. My job was to help place the iron and steel beams that make up the skeleton of new buildings. Some things you all know about have happened to change all that. I'm not working with iron and steel anymore. But maybe, in some ways, I'm still a connector and still helping people build."

The crowd, relaxed by the informality and gentleness of his voice, leaned forward expectantly.

"The kind of building I'm doing now is a lot harder," he continued, pausing to let the booming of his voice over the loudspeakers catch up with him. "It's helping people build better lives. It's harder because . . . well, for instance, a lot of you have been coming to me, writing to me, calling me, thinking or hoping I can do it all—that I can do it for you. The fact is, I can't."

He was getting the hang of it now. The words were coming easier. The people were really listening, and he was feeling stronger, more assured.

"Many of you have come here today because you believe or hope that I'm the new Messiah. You've been told about the prophecy, and some people are even calling me the Second Son of God. To be honest, I don't know if I believe it myself. I haven't had any visions, any talks with a . . . with God."

The crowd rustled uncomfortably.

"For a while that worried me, but it doesn't matter to me anymore. What matters to me, and I hope what matters to you, is that I do know I've been given a special power, a special mission, a special chance to do good in the world. I can tell you honestly that I didn't want it and that I fought against it, but I've accepted it. And I want to make it worth what it's cost me." He stopped for a moment, wondering if she was hearing him. The crowd waited.

"I said a minute ago that I can't do the work I'm doing now by myself. You've heard that I can do miracles, and it's true that some pretty miraculous things have happened. But no matter what it looks like, I'm not a God. I still have to eat and sleep. I still have human feelings. I'm still just a man, and I can't do all that needs doing alone.

"These," he said, gesturing to the mailbags, "are letters that arrived this morning in just two hours. They've come like this every day for the last four weeks. Most of them are letters asking for help, pleas from some of you and from your families, friends, and neighbors.

"You've got to see that as much as I'd like to help every one of you, even if I did a miracle a minute, it's not humanly possible for me to do it—not in the time they say I have left." He saw some nods in the crowd and continued faster now, encouraged by their understanding.

"So many people have so many problems. They tell me they're lonely, they're sad, they're sick, they're poor. But the worst part is that they think they're helpless—helpless to do anything about these things. And so when they look for solutions, for ways to change what's wrong with their lives— what's wrong with the world—they look far away from themselves. They look everywhere except to the power that's inside them and around them.

"They look to where everyone else tells them the power is. They feel helpless and they say, 'The real power's with the government and the politicians.' They feel helpless and they say, 'The real power's with big business'—or 'with the labor unions.' They feel helpless and they say, 'The real power's with the churches' or 'with some supernatural power.' They feel helpless, and when someone comes along and is called the new Messiah, they say, 'The real power's with him.' "

He heard murmurs of agreement from the crowd now.

"So what happens? These people, they—no, these people *you* believe have so much power turn around and agree with you. They say, 'Yeah, you are powerless, you are helpless. We know best how to run your lives.' The businesses say, 'We'll tell you if and when you can work.' The government says, 'We'll tell you how much of your money you can keep, and we'll decide where to spend the rest.' The churches say, 'We'll tell you what's right, what's wrong, who to love, who to hate. We'll tell you whether you're good or you're bad. We'll tell you how to live and how to die, and we'll tell you whether you get to go to heaven or hell!'"

He was excited now and he felt the crowd excited with him.

"And so you try to do what they say. And the problems turn out to be still there. Then they say it's because you've got to give them *more* power. And when you do, you feel even *more* helpless. And you get sad, and frustrated, and angry. And because the big powers seem so far out of reach, you turn your sadness and frustration and anger against your neighbors, your friends, your families, yourselves. And it seems like there's no one to turn to.

"So now, when this person comes along you think might be the new Messiah, you turn to him. You turn to him and you say, 'He'll perform the miracle that will save us.'" He paused. The crowd was electrified.

"What I've come here to tell you today is that he—I—can't. But more important, you don't need me to! The real power you need is not out here, out there. It's in *you!*

"Your own letters tell me that most of what you need to make your lives better—to make you happy—doesn't depend on any special powers. And I've seen that myself in the last few weeks. Since I got back from Rome, I haven't done one single miracle. I've talked to a lot of people who thought a miracle from me was their last hope. But after we talked, they began to see that the real *miracle* was having hope and belief in themselves, that they could make miracles for themselves.

"You can do that too."

He felt their questioning now, their beginning to doubt, and he hurried on.

"But to do it, you have to be willing to give up something. You have to be willing to give up the idea that you're helpless. You have to give up the idea that you need someone, some politician or businessman or labor leader or minister or rabbi or priest, or me, to tell you how to live your life.

"You don't. *You* know what you want, what you need,

what you think, what you feel, what matters to *you*. There's a lot of power in that."

He looked around and saw the heads nodding once again.

"The second thing you have to do to make miracles happen is to see that you're not alone. Turn around, right now, to the person sitting next to you, and look—really look—into that person's eyes. That person, just like you, has a lot of fears, a lot of hopes, a lot of dreams for a happier life—and a lot of power."

He paused, watching the crowd hesitate, then begin to move. He felt their hesitancy, their shyness, and then, as they turned back to him, their warmth.

"Every one of you has the power to give yourself—and that person beside you—something very precious: the understanding that life is hard sometimes, the gift of trust in asking for help when you need it, the gift of seeing what help they need and, when you can, giving it. The gift of being on their side and having them be on yours.

"I said a while ago that I couldn't help every one of you. But *you* can help each other. I can't reach every one of you. But *you* can reach each other.

"When you discover you're not alone, and that the power you need to make your life happy is inside you and all around you, you won't be giving it away anymore. You'll begin to take it back, to see that the building of your life is yours to do.

"There are times when we need to hire other people to help us build. The businesses you buy from, the labor leaders and politicians you elect, the churches you support—they are your hired help. You pay them in money, and you pay them in votes.

"But in the building of your life, *you're* the owner, *you're* the contractor. All the power those big organizations have, they get from *you*.

"Now on a building, no one gets paid until the work is inspected and approved. The way to take back your own power is not to pay the people who work for you until you've inspected and approved their work. Don't give them your money or your votes until you're sure you're getting what you want, what you've contracted for.

"The people you've hired to work for you know how much

power is yours. They know how to work on getting more of it from you. A lot of them—politicians, social groups, churches, businesses—have been coming to me lately to try to get me to convince you to support them, vote for them, buy from them.

"As they see it, I'm just one more way to get to you. They're trying to sell you things by putting my picture or my name on them. All the Joseph Turner pictures with politicians—all the Joseph Turner products—they're just using me to get your votes and your money. Even the churches are doing it. They put up a cross here today, and I asked for it to be taken down because I'm not part of any particular religion.

"I won't be part of anyone's attempt to tell you what to buy, who to vote for, what faith to choose. And if anyone tries to tell you different, they're lying. It's got to be up to you to make your *own* choices about how your life is built. It's up to you to see when someone you've hired is doing good work or shoddy work, or to see when they're making empty promises. It's up to you to hire them or fire them yourself."

He felt the crowd's power growing, felt them taking hold of it.

"And it's up to you not to depend on them for things they really can't give you. The letters you've sent me tell me that the things you really need aren't things politicians or social groups or churches or businesses can do. The problem is—well, it's like what sometimes happens at Christmas. We think what people need at Christmas are presents. And it feels good to give them. But all of us have given or received gifts on some advertiser's promise of happiness and then found that the gift was useless. When a child is hungry for food or for love, a toy that will break in a week won't fill up the empty places in his stomach or his heart. When someone we care about is hurting from our neglect, a present won't make up for the words we don't say, the time we don't give, the guilt we feel.

"Maybe this Christmas you'll want to give things to each other, and to yourselves, that will be more meaningful, more real. At least I hope you don't buy something just because it has Joseph Turner's picture on it."

He stopped to listen to their answering murmurs of assent.

"There are just one or two more things I want to say. Many of you have sent me money. In the next few weeks you will be getting most of it back. I'm grateful that you've wanted to help me do my work. But I don't want you to give away to me—any more than to the big institutions in your life—the power you have to help each other. People around you, much closer to home, need it more than I do. Because I can't know who they are as well as you can, and because I will not always be here, you need to learn to help them on your own.

"There's one more thing; it's very personal. Last night, I went back to my old apartment and found it ripped to shreds. There's nothing there anymore, because people wanted pieces of my life, souvenirs, as if those things would somehow make their lives better. They won't.

"It made me angry, and it hurt me very much to see what people had done. But it made me even angrier to hear how my friends and neighbors where I used to live were hurt by curious and greedy people who made their lives unlivable. Please, leave my friends in peace; please don't hurt them anymore."

He paused; the crowd had grown solemn.

"I've talked today more than I expected to. And I've asked you for a lot. I know some of the building I've asked you to do seems difficult. But I know that it's the only kind of building that will last.

"I'll be here to build with you. I don't know how much time I've got. I don't know how much I can do. But if we're all working, if we're all using the power we've got inside, the special power that's been given to me can be used to help when nothing else can."

He stopped and the crowd hesitated, not knowing whether he was finished. He was thinking that he wanted to thank them somehow, for being here, for listening. Then suddenly there came a bold, deep voice from the upper deck. "Show us your power!"

Another voice: "Yes, give us a miracle!"

He looked up in confusion. "What I've been trying to tell

you today is that the real power, the real miracle, is in you. It's in every one of you."

"A healing!" came another loud and boisterous voice off to his right.

He was bewildered. He was so certain they had heard him, had understood, yet these voices . . .

"If you're the Messiah, show us! Prove it!" came another voice.

"I'm not here to prove anything," Joseph said.

"He can't!"

"Blasphemer, he can too!"

Near the sign over left field he saw people jumping up, arms flying. The fight stirred the crowd, and small scuffles broke out in other areas of the stadium. Then he saw a young man leap from the right-field wall. "Touch me!" he screamed. The police quickly corralled him but not before others scrambled over the wall onto the field. The police struggled to hold them back, but two broke through their line.

"Wait, please!" Joseph said into the microphones, but they had gone dead.

Otley leapt onto the stage and guided Joseph firmly down the stairs and into the limousine. Within seconds Emil and John were beside him. The door closed, and the car was moving.

On the field the crowd was out of control, converging on the platform as the black Cadillac raced across the outfield to the bullpen exit. Some among the throng of believers reached the passing car and touched it as it left the stadium.

"Emil, I thought they heard what I said, I thought—"

"They did, Joseph, it was only a very few of them down there, only several hundred out of all of them. And most of them were just overly enthusiastic to get near you. This sort of thing just happens."

"You reached them, Joey," John said. "You really have begun your work. You reached them."

Two hours later at the loft, Joseph saw on WCBS news that twenty-nine people had been injured at Shea Stadium and taken to Bellevue for treatment.

"I'm responsible for this, Emil," Joseph said, "and I'm going to take care of it."

Over his friends' objections, Joseph called in Otley and insisted on going to Bellevue.

THIRTY-FOUR

WITH LOUISE, ROTHSTEIN, and two Secret Service agents, Joseph reached Bellevue late that night. The pleasant atmosphere of Bellevue's main reception area was a startling contrast to Joseph's memories of his recent hospital entrance into the chaos of the Emergency Room.

When he approached the reception desk, the busy receptionist did not look up from her work. Joseph's request to see the people who had been injured at Shea Stadium was met with curt hospital formality. He would have to have the names of the people he wanted to see and, besides that, hospital visiting hours were over.

"Can you tell me at least if any of them are still here?"

"Six or seven, I think. But I still can't let you go in there."

Louise stepped up beside Joseph. "Excuse me, Miss Walker, I'm with the *Times*. Do you know who this man is?"

The receptionist looked up. "Oh!" she said. "It's you! Oh, dear, Mr. Turner, I'm not authorized to make exceptions in the rules, but let me call my superior—"

"That may not be necessary," Joseph said to the flustered young woman. "Is Dr. Weisman on duty?"

She flipped through the duty cards and nodded. "Yes, sir, he is. Would you like me to have him paged for you? I'll tell him it's extremely important!"

A short time after the announcement on the public address system, James Weisman strode through the double doors. His face broke into a broad smile when he spotted them. "Joseph Turner! What are you doing here?"

"Hello, Dr. Weisman. I'm here to see the people injured at Shea Stadium today. These are my friends, Louise Ryan and Emil Rothstein."

"Mr. Rothstein and I have met before," Weisman said, shaking hands with both of them.

Joseph saw Emil flush slightly at the reminder of his investigation, but now was no time for explanations. "Can you admit me to see the patients?" he asked Weisman.

"Glad to," Weisman said, picking up the phone. When he finished his call he handed Miss Walker a list of names, and while she called Admissions for the rooms, he turned back to Joseph, shaking his head in wonder. "That was Dr. Bartell in Emergency. He's the grumpiest, hardest-nosed resident on the staff, but he actually sounded human. Said all but seven people were treated and released. Emergency's still in shock over the other twenty-two. They were the calmest, most cooperative bunch of casualties ever to come through the doors. Bartell hopes you'll stop in Emergency and work your miracles on the regulars."

Joseph seemed to be considering the idea. Rothstein whispered, "If you go in there, you'll never make it to the others. We've got to keep it quiet and move fast."

Joseph nodded and sighed, wondering how often he would have to deal with similar choices. Being able to help meant he had to make choices about *whom* to help and whom to turn away from. He knew the "regulars" of Bellevue Emergency—automobile, shooting, knifing victims, battered children, kids beaten up in street fights. Many were poor people struggling for survival, many strung out on drugs, and many uncared for and underfed. They wouldn't get the special attention he'd received. So many people needed so much. He shook himself out of it. First he had to take care of those he'd come here to see.

As soon as Weisman had the room numbers, he escorted the group to a fourth-floor ward. One of the injured, a middle-aged woman who had suffered broken ribs and a dislocated hip, slept in a bed beside the wall. Joseph went immediately to her bedside and touched her gently on the forehead. "Mrs. Sweeny." Her eyelids fluttered open to reveal soft brown eyes that immediately welled up with tears. "I knew—I knew that you would come," she said, wiping her eyes with a corner of the sheet. "I'm sorry. I'm just so happy to see you."

"And I'm sorry to have caused you so much pain," Joseph said, taking her hand and squeezing it gently.

"It's not so bad. And it really was worth it to see you."

"Would you like to go home now?"

Tears flowed down her cheeks. "Yes, there's so much I want to do now. My husband, my family—I left them four months ago. I ran away. What you said about seeing, and helping ourselves and helping each other . . . I want to go back and try." Her face tightened in an effort to control her tears.

"Shhh-hh," Joseph whispered. "Quiet now. Be still."

When her breathing had become deeper, more relaxed, Joseph spoke again. "Don't be afraid of your tears. They heal a lot of pain inside. And I want you to know that you also have the power to heal your body. It's in you to give yourself everything you need and want. When you're ready, you can get up and walk out of here."

Her eyes held his for a long moment, widening in astonishment and happiness. "The pain in my hip, my ribs. It's all gone!"

"I understand this hospital has a shortage of beds." Joseph nodded. "Are you ready to give this one up?"

"Oh, yes, but—"

"I believe you can, now."

She accepted it, nodded. "I think I'm going to need help to get out of this get-up."

"Dr. Weisman, will you?"

"Well, I—" He looked questioningly from one to another, then stepped up to the bed. "I guess it wouldn't hurt to take a look." He pulled the drape around the bed. "Gentlemen, if you don't mind . . ."

Rothstein paced nervously through the ten minutes it took Dr. Weisman to remove bandages and check the patient. When he pulled back the curtain, Mrs. Sweeny was sitting on top of the bed. The bandages lay beside her. "I'm healed. I'm well."

"You could put us out of business," Dr. Weisman said to Joseph in his dry, good-humored manner. "It looks like we can go see patient number two; she's just down the hall."

Rothstein took Joseph's arm and started to guide him out of the room.

"Joseph," Mrs. Sweeny called, "could I talk to you privately for a moment?" Joseph went to her and she took his hand. "Will you forgive me for my sins?"

Joseph studied her intently, saw her sincerity. "Do you?" he said.

She thought for a moment, "Yes."

"That's all that's needed."

She pulled his hand close to her lips and kissed it tenderly.

"I have to go now."

She nodded and he left.

He went to the others, one by one, relieving their pain, healing their bodies, listening to them tell him of the impact he'd had on their lives. Two were instigators of the disruption. He calmed their fears and when he had finished, they watched him leave with awe-filled eyes. By the time they reached the fifth victim, the entire hospital was buzzing with the news of their arrival, and nurses and interns, as curious as the patients, were hard pressed to control ambulatory patients wandering the halls and checking rooms for him.

The last Shea victim was on the ninth floor, being prepared for surgery. When a weary Joseph and his entourage stepped from the elevator, they were greeted by a very angry young doctor and a distinguished-looking man in a well-cut business suit.

"Dr. Weisman!" the young doctor exclaimed. "What in hell is going on here? What gives you the right to interfere with my patients?"

"Just a moment, Dr. Perez," the blue-suited man said, putting his hand on the doctor's arm and turning to Joseph. "Mr. Turner? My name is George Crutchfield. I am the administrator of this hospital. Dr. Perez and a few others are upset that Dr. Weisman has been taking you to patients who are not under his care. We have certain procedures—hospital protocol, you might say—and your visit here tonight has been quite disrupting."

"I understand, Mr. Crutchfield, and I do apologize. We've tried to keep this as quiet as possible. As a matter of fact, there's just one more patient I must see. Then I'll be happy to leave."

"You *don't* understand, Mr. Turner. You and your friends will have to leave now."

"George," Dr. Weisman intervened, "the patient we're about to visit is *my* patient and I want Mr. Turner to see him."

"And I'm telling you that I don't want miracle-workers, or healers, or—or—"

"The Son of God," finished Rothstein.

"Whatever," Crutchfield sputtered. "You're not going to continue doing whatever you're doing in *my* hospital! There are patients roaming all over the place, sick people getting up and leaving like there's nothing wrong with them. What are *you* doing?" he said, glaring at Louise.

She smiled sweetly. "Just taking notes."

"I'll be happy to leave, Mr. Crutchfield," Joseph said, "as soon as I've finished what I've come here to do."

Weisman turned to Joseph. "He's just down the hall. Let's go."

Perez and Crutchfield, their mouths open in astonishment, watched the group walk away. "Weisman!" Crutchfield called after him. "I'll have you brought before the board for this!"

"Hold it," Joseph said, stopping midstride and turning to Dr. Weisman. "I can't have you losing your job on my account."

"Joseph, he doesn't have that kind of authority over me. It's not the first time we have been at odds with each other, and I've been thinking for a long time about leaving here. This seems like an opportune time."

"Where will you go?"

"With you. I suspect you're going to be seeing a lot of sick people who can't or won't come to a hospital. If they don't need a miracle, I'll be there to help. And if they do need a miracle, it might help you to know what kind. Now come on. We've got a patient waiting."

He escorted them to Peter Hansen, a youthful, long-haired man lying on a gurney pushed up against the corridor wall. He had a compound fracture of the left leg. He appeared to be in great pain. James Weisman bent over him and said, "Peter, I'm sorry you've had to wait so long. There's someone here who wants to see you."

The youth's head turned and he saw Joseph. "You came. You came," he murmured.

Joseph moved in closer. "What was that, Peter?"

"I didn't know for sure whether you'd come," he said. "I came to New York just to see you. I'm a minister from California. A month ago I left my church to find you. I thought I might learn from you, work with you, but today—" he gasped, grimacing with pain.

"Let's talk about that later," Joseph said. "First we've got to do something about this leg."

"No, please, let me finish. I loved what I heard you say today, but when the fighting broke out and you left I thought you'd abandoned us. I'm sorry to have lost faith. Can I still go with you, be with you?"

"He's a pretty smart kid," whispered Weisman. "He's been working with young people, doing fine work, from what I can gather."

"What is this, a conspiracy?" Joseph asked, smiling.

"Not exactly," said the doctor, winking at Peter. "It's just that he's the one who gave *me* the idea."

Joseph looked at Louise and Rothstein and shrugged his shoulders. "Looks like our family's just grown by two. Now, let's take care of this," he said, laying his hand on Peter's leg, "before we have the whole hospital down around our ears."

He talked softly, privately, to Peter, whose face began to relax and soften. In a few minutes the young man sat up on the gurney and put his arms around Joseph.

"You are who they say," he said. "Blessed be the Lord."

Joseph turned to Weisman. "Why didn't Peter have a room?"

"Not enough beds," the doctor said simply.

"Seven isn't going to help a lot. Maybe—" He looked thoughtfully down the corridor at the numbered doors.

"Mr. Turner," a voice said from behind him. He turned to see Crutchfield and two uncomfortable security guards. "I must insist that you leave now. If you force us—"

"Listen, Crutchfield, you've got patients here you can't help."

Emil stepped up next to him. "Joseph, this is only one hospital. What are you going to do? Heal everyone here?

Everyone in all of them? Mr. Crutchfield does have the law on his side. And you are exhausted. Perhaps we could talk tomorrow, agree on some compromise."

"But there are people dying, Emil! And I'm not in the other hospitals. I'm here!"

Crutchfield cleared his throat. "Mr. Turner, your associate sounds like a reasonable man. Perhaps we could reach a compromise right now. How would it be if we allowed you to see the terminal patients here? I must say I doubt that anyone can do anything for most of them, but if you'd like to try I'd have no objection—on the condition that you leave directly following those visits and give us your word not to cause such disruptions in the future."

"Fine," Joseph answered. "Let's go."

THIRTY-FIVE

PRESIDENT DEWEY HARPER was mad. Here he was, stuck at his desk on Christmas Eve while the White House Christmas party was in full bloom downstairs, with God knows how many important campaign contributors waiting to have their picture taken with him. He had three more "Urgent" memos to read before he went down—all of them on this Joseph Turner business.

If his damn staff had been keeping him posted, this whole thing wouldn't have gotten out of hand so fast. In only two days his problems with Joseph Turner had escalated to unmanageable proportions. Since Turner had made his public speech and performed his "Bellevue miracles," many of Harper's wealthiest and most influential business and political supporters had been pounding on his door demanding that he do something about Turner's public influence. Manufacturers and retailers had been hit hard by a drastic fall in Christmas sales, and millions of dollars of their special "Joseph Turner merchandise" had been returned or left unsold. The party's public-opinion surveyors had learned that people were spending their money this year on "private charity." Even more disturbing was the news that Joseph Turner had remained far more interesting to the public than any politician, including himself; despite denials, it was impossible for Dewey Harper to believe that this man had no political ambitions. Many of Harper's friends in both parties had spoken to him in the last two days to let him know that Joseph Turner was making all of them very, very nervous.

And now this report from Intelligence, which made the whole business even more serious. For weeks the Irish, Libyan, and South African governments had been making noises about "delaying" Harper's upcoming State visits. Only two

274

hours ago State had informed him that the reason was that all three were trying to arrange a visit from Joseph Turner instead. The fact that Turner's people had turned them down for the time being only made matters worse—it was an embarrassment that this American was refusing overtures from important foreign governments, and it put the President of the United States in the position of a second choice. There were issues that urgently needed discussion, but he could not possibly enter such sensitive negotiations with the knowledge that his own power and importance was rated second to that of some religious fanatic.

Well, something had to be done about this man, and soon; evidently it was all up to him. He put down the last four memos of suggestions from his staffers—none of them worth considering. Time for a little flesh-pressing and holiday cheer, he thought as he got up and headed downstairs for the party.

Cassie Harper joined her husband for the formal entrance, squeezing his arm affectionately as she smiled broadly up at him. "What's Paul Bridger doing here?" he mumbled to her through his smile at the crowd.

"To give you a Christmas present, sweetheart," she whispered toward his ear.

"Oh, yes? Is he taking you away from me?"

"Not yet," she answered matter-of-factly. "He has a solution to your problem about Joseph Turner." She guided him toward the fireplace where the White House photographer stood talking with Paul Bridger and a group of campaign contributers waiting patiently to have their picture taken with the President.

"Mr. President, could I have you and Mrs. Harper right here in front?" the photographer said, arranging the group.

"Certainly. Merry Christmas, everyone," Harper said, smiling and shaking hands with the guests.

Paul Bridger had moved in next to Harper, and when the pictures were over, Harper turned to him.

"Paul, how's the show going?"

"Fine, Mr. President."

"I catch it every morning I can."

Cassie whispered in her husband's ear, "It's 'Coffee Break with God.' "

"And I love the title, Paul," Harper continued. " 'Coffee Break with God.' Catchy, real catchy."

"Oh, no, Mr. President," said Bridger, visibly hurt. It's 'The Morning Miracle Hour.' "

Harper looked nonplussed toward Cassie, who smiled sweetly back at him.

"Sorry, Paul, I've just been busy lately," Harper said. "Forgive me, my friend," he said, resting a hand on Bridger's shoulder and moving him away from the group. "Say, Cassie tells me you have a suggestion about a little difficulty we've been having."

"Well, actually, it's an idea that came to me a couple of weeks ago when Cassie mentioned that you'd been having some trouble making contact with Joseph Turner—"

Harper shot an angry glance at his wife. She shrugged.

"—And I thought I'd mention it to you, because it could do us both some good to have Turner a little more, uh, under control."

"Go on."

"Well, Mr. President, it seems to me that what you need is something that Turner wants. As you undoubtedly realize, the greatest difficulty facing all of us who strive to help large numbers of people in a spiritual way is the limitation on our own time and resources. Now if the government had a plan that would appeal to Joseph Turner, a plan to give aid to large numbers of the weak and the poor and the sick and the old, you might offer him such a plan in exchange for his endorsement of your Administration's efforts . . . or whatever else is needed."

Harper smiled genuinely for the first time that day. "Why, Paul, what a fine suggestion! Tell me," he said, his smile disappearing suddenly, "what do you get out of it?"

"Nothing but your good will, Mr. President," Bridger said smoothly, "though there is the small matter of the networks' offers to Turner—I wonder if the FCC might want to take some time considering whether another religious program would truly be in the interests of the American people."

"I see. You realize of course that we do not control network programming, Paul."

"Of course."

"But perhaps the FCC should look into the matter—for an extended period of time. Thank you for your suggestion," Harper said, turning away. "I will remember where it came from."

THIRTY-SIX

THE MEETING BETWEEN Joseph Turner and President Dewey Harper took place in New York's Central Park at 6:00 on a snowy mid-January morning.

Joseph sat in a Plymouth with Sammy and Otley at the North end of the Central Park Reservoir, watching the Marine Corps helicopter coming in through the thick maze of menacing gray clouds for its landing. Joseph had agreed to the meeting partly at the urging of his friends, who were genuinely concerned about the increased hostility to Joseph among those in power since the new wave of public enthusiasm after the Shea Stadium address and the incidents at Bellevue. But he had also come because he felt a responsibility to explore an offer of help President Harper's aide had told him would be coming.

As the helicopter touched down, its huge jet-propelled rotors churned up the snow into a small blizzard. Otley motioned to Joseph as the chopper steps were set out and two Secret Service agents descended to the ground. Joseph pulled the collar of his coat close around his neck, got out of the car, and made his way to the helicopter steps.

"Mr. Turner, we need to pat you down—standard procedure," said a tall lanky Secret Service agent at the foot of the stairs.

"Okay," replied Joseph, holding his arms up.

Otley frowned, shaking his head. "Drake, he's the Son of God, for crying out loud!"

"Procedure, Otley, procedure," remarked the agent, moving in on Joseph, who allowed the frisk without comment.

"Your Worship, I'm terribly sorry for the inconvenience," Harper said, descending the steps.

"It's okay, and 'Joseph' will do," Joseph said, extending his hand to the President.

"Dewey, Joseph," Harper said, shaking the ironworker's hand enthusiastically. "Why don't we walk while we talk?" Behind Harper, Otley motioned for the other agents to fan out.

"Whatever," said Joseph, following the President's lead.

"So, tell me, Joseph," Harper asked, taking him by the arm and heading onto the snow-laden path around the reservoir, "how are you?"

"I'm fine, Mr. President. And very busy, as I'm sure you are. If it's all right with you, can we get to the point of our meeting?"

Harper looked nonplussed. "From my point of view, Joseph, a little friendly conversation *is* the point of our meeting. I hope we're going to become good friends, Joe, because a good friend is someone you can trust."

Joseph did not answer.

"So now that that's established," Harper said, "let me tell you why I asked you to meet with me today. I'm a great admirer of your work, Joseph. All of us in Washington are very moved by what you are doing for the people. You might say you've shown us the way. Put us back on the right track. And in line with that, I've formulated a plan that will reach out to hundreds of thousands of people in this country—the poor, the helpless, the weak, the sick, the old. It'll reach out to them with the help they need and that one person can't possibly give them all."

"That's been bothering me a lot—how little one person can do."

"I'm sure it has, as it does all of us who give our lives to public service. But we in government have the advantage of being able to design and carry out huge programs. This one I'm telling you about, which incidentally will be named in your honor, provides over a billion dollars in aid."

Joseph thought about what a billion dollars could do for many of the people who had written to him. He knew that what most of these people needed had nothing to do with money, especially government money, more government programs that raised their hopes then dashed them when most of the money went into bureaucrats' pockets, and the programs were dropped. He knew that what he had said in Shea Stadium was true—that relying on gigantic institutions for help meant giving your own power away. But a billion dollars—that was more than any program he'd ever heard of. And what Harper said was true. He couldn't reach everyone. He didn't even want to spend all his time and energy on problems money could solve, and there were people who really needed it. He listened as Harper spelled out some of the details of his plan—help in rent, in food, in clothes, in social programs. It sounded attractive. "I've got to tell you, Mr. President, that this plan of yours sounds awfully good."

"I'm glad you like it."

"When will you be putting it into action?"

"Well, Joseph, that's why I wanted to talk with you today. Whether we can do it at all depends on you."

"Meaning what?"

"The only way we can be assured of getting such a program through is having our own people in Congress, and in the Administration, too, of course. It's going to be a tough election, and your support would mean a lot. Your active support would mean even more."

Joseph bent down, picked up a handful of snow, and packed it into a ball. The icy cold felt good in his hands; it seemed to cool the anger boiling up inside him. "Is that all?" he asked.

"I'm glad you understand how these arrangements are made," Harper said. "I like your sophistication. As a matter of fact, there is one more small request I've been asked to make of you. That speech of yours in Shea Stadium—the part about the people looking to themselves rather than to their public servants for help and guidance—a lot of people seem to be taking that as a suggestion that they turn their interest away from politics. And the parts about our other American institutions—your criticisms of business, for instance, and established religious institutions—I'm sure you didn't really mean for people to stop spending their money that way, but it's confused a lot of people. We think it would be to everyone's advantage if you didn't say anything else like that."

Joseph threw his snowball at a tree, hitting the trunk

squarely. The Secret Service agent closest to the tree flinched. "Sorry," Joseph yelled, holding up his hands.

"Am I making myself clear to you, Joseph?"

"Oh, very clear. You want me to lay off. You want me to stop causing trouble."

"Well, yes. You've begun to do some things, quite unintentionally, I'm sure, that are upsetting a lot of important people. Maybe you've just overstepped your religious responsibilities. You know, there's always been a clear separation of Church and State in this great country of ours, and it's worked well so far. We'd like that to continue."

"I thought the separation of Church and State meant that the government wouldn't interfere with religion."

"Right. But surely you understand—and I'm talking to you straight now—that the kinds of things you've been saying and doing, and the public following you're building, affects much more than religion. And certain plans you've made are clearly out of bounds. A lot of people in Washington have been suggesting that if you're going to come into their neighborhood, they're going to have to come into yours."

"What plans?"

"Well. we hear you might go to Ireland. That's really not a religious matter, is it? It's a sensitive political matter; it's being handled by experienced people, and shouldn't be interfered with by someone who doesn't fully understand all that's at stake. Except in areas where you're invited to work with us, we're only asking you to stay out of our territory in exchange for noninterference from us."

Joseph stopped on the path and turned to Harper. "Asking or demanding?"

"Right now I'm asking. But if you continue to cause problems in economic and political matters, I can't promise that's the way it will always be. That's why I'm offering you the chance to join us in a project that will benefit the whole country. It will give us a way to work together."

"On your terms? Under your control?"

Harper shrugged. "I'm afraid that's the way it has to be."

Joseph began walking down the pathway again, feeling the enormity of the pressure that Harper was smoothly putting on him. That the President of the United States would come to him like this showed how afraid the people in power were of his own influence on ordinary people. What Harper was asking him to do was to sell out and buy a political program with the betrayal of his own conscience. He turned back, stopping. "No."

Harper's face tightened. "No, what?"

"No, I'm not going to join you. No, I'm not going to stop saying what I believe needs to be said. No, I'm not going to sell out."

Harper looked at him hard, his eyes openly menacing. "That attitude could be very expensive for you."

"Maybe. But not as expensive as what you have in mind."

"I don't mean just about the program, Turner. There's the matter of your security detachment, for instance. There are other means at our disposal, and we'll use them if we have to."

"I don't like your threats, Harper."

"This is the way the game is played. You've got thirty seconds to think it over."

Joseph looked at him disgustedly, turned, and walked away back down the path.

"Otley!" Harper shouted. The agent hurried to the President.

"Yes, sir. Shall I drive them back?"

"Not if you want your pension. Turner and his friend are going to walk." Otley nodded and raced off to the Plymouth where Joseph sat. "Screw around with me, will you, you goddamned evangelist," Harper mumbled under his breath.

At the car, Otley searched for the right words to explain. "Uh, Mr. Turner, the President has instructed me not to drive you back. I'm really sorry."

"That's okay, I understand. Come on," he said to Sammy. "I think this is where we're supposed to put one foot in front of the other."

As the Marine Corps helicopter lifted off and winged its way toward Washington, Dewey Harper called his Secretary of State.

"We're in trouble, Curt. He isn't going for it. I want you to make some calls to our most important backers. Stonewall those you think you can, and confide in those you can't."

"What do I tell them?" Curtis Winslow asked.

"That I can't control him. That I'm only human and he's the Son of God, for Chrissake. The usual bullshit."

"Consider it done."

"And he's not to get a passport to leave the country. Period."

"Sure . . . Want some good news?"

"Who wouldn't?" Harper answered.

"We've got someone inside his organization."

"What? Who does?"

"The Agency, actually. It was an accident—a stroke of luck."

"I want someone to brief me this afternoon. And I want that operative under my direction."

"I've already taken care of it."

"You always come through, Curt. Thanks." He hung up the phone. "Well, son-of-a-bitch," he laughed. "Son-of-a-bitch!"

When Joseph returned to the loft, Emil was waiting for him. "I've found her, Joseph," he said.

Joseph's breath caught. "Where is she?"

"She's in Florida, and—" Emil stopped.

"And?"

"And she said to tell you she's getting married."

A stab of pain pierced Joseph's chest. He closed his eyes. When he opened them again he looked deeply hurt, but calm. "I don't believe it, Emil."

"You want me to find out for sure? You want me to send someone down there?"

"No, leave her alone. If this is the way she wants to keep me away from her, I'll do what she wants."

"You know, Joseph," Emil said gently, "it might be her way of keeping herself away from you."

THIRTY-SEVEN

IN THE WEEKS following the meeting with the President and the news about Maggie, Joseph plunged into his work with new determination. He traveled throughout America, speaking to huge groups that gathered in Chicago, in Atlanta, in New Orleans, in Los Angeles, in Seattle, in Denver, in Detroit, to be inspired by the words of the man they called Messiah. He went to smaller cities and country towns, encouraging people in their struggles, healing people in sickness and pain, teaching people to ask for and give each other help. Where Joseph could not go, John or Peter or James or Sammy would go for him, leaving with those who reached out to them new strength and new hope.

At first the rejection of Harper's demands seemed to have few damaging consequences. With Otley gone, Sammy recruited unemployed ironworkers from the union to act as bodyguards for Joseph and his friends. In the beginning they were little needed; Emil had devised a workable system for Joseph to arrive at his various visits with little advance notice. The people he met waited patiently and greeted him warmly.

It was in the third week after the meeting that the trouble started. Joseph would arrive at a meeting place to be met not only by the people he went to see, but also by small, well-organized groups of hecklers. The possibility that advance warning of his visits was somehow being leaked seemed compelling—and bafflingly impossible. His friends asked Joseph to curtail his activities until they understood what was happening; he refused. When the *News* appeared with a front-page story announcing the location of the Manhattan loft, complete with pictures, Emil begged him to arrange some kind of internal security. Again, Joseph refused. "Every day I'm telling people to trust themselves, to trust each other, to trust the goodness and power within them to overcome any problem they face. I'm not going to betray that myself," he said.

Joseph and his friends continued their work. They were met with increasing enthusiasm from ordinary people—and increasing animosity from many, though by no means all, of the powerful. Permits for meeting places were increasingly difficult to get. Disruptions by hecklers grew, and were stopped not by the public authorities but instead by the people who had come to see or hear or touch Joseph Turner. Though the disruptions clearly were coordinated by someone behind the scenes, Joseph and his friends had neither time nor resources to expend on trying to discover their instigators.

Joseph did have one new indentifiable souce of opposition. Shortly after news arrived from Rome that Pope Alexander had died, the announcement came that Dominic Belazzi had succeeded him as Pope Leo XIV; within another week groups of Catholic protesters, too loudly proclaiming their independence from the Church, had begun showing up to demand that Joseph Turner "preach the Christian gospel." Joseph ignored them as he ignored the others.

What was important, he told his friends, were the results of their work. Self-help groups sprouted up in local neighborhoods across the country. The news began to fill with stories of people who joined together to fight for what they wanted—and won. Sometimes they were small victories—a family saved from losing an overtaxed home, a local park made clean and safe for its children. Sometimes the victories were larger—a neighborhood saved from the ravages of a crime wave, a town saved from the ravages of early spring floods, a city saved from the ravages of corrupt politicians. Everywhere ordinary people were actively challenging the power of big institutions. To the dismay of the labor unions, wildcat strikes were becoming increasingly common; to the irritation of big business, small investors and boycotting consumers were banding together to press for changes in corporate policies.

Joseph prodded, encouraged, applauded the people's efforts, and reached out to those who could not help themselves.

He was near exhaustion. He was often torn by the inability to reach everyone in need. But he was, like the people, riding high on the wave of confidence and good news sweeping the country.

The wave broke in the early morning of March 4 near Pueblo, Colorado.

It was no ordinary freight train that pulled its forty tank cars that morning through the frozen countryside of northern New Mexico and headed northeast through the edge of the Sangre de Cristo Mountains into Colorado. The train's engineer had been specially chosen for this run, selected for his competence, his long experience with similar cargo, and his absolute confidence in his superiors' provisions for safety.

As he moved his train over the carefully cleared rails on this early morning, the engineer did not know about a letter sent directly to President Dewey Harper a month before by Bob Pincus, Scientific Field Director for the Department of Energy, who protested the movement of nuclear waste materials in tank cars with cooling systems that were not only possibly, but likely, subject to design-system malfunctions. He did not know that Pincus had sent twenty-one such warning letters during the preceding eighteen months of his tenure.

So the engineer experienced a split second of bewildered surprise that morning before the white flash of exploding light disintegrated his body, his train, the rails, the land for miles and miles around him—and a huge mushroom-shaped cloud rose twenty thousand feet over the great plains of southeastern Colorado.

President Harper was lunching with several congressmen in the White House when the news reached him. Within forty minutes, Air Force One was carrying the Chief Executive, the Secretary of the Interior, and the Secretary of the Department of Energy toward Colorado Springs. Flushed with anger, Harper railed from across his desk in the forward cabin at Albert Zehrt, head of the DOE, who shifted nervously in his chair. "Al, I'm holding you personally responsible! Now you tell me how the hell something like this could happen!"

"Me?" Zehrt exclaimed. "Mr. President, it was your 'executive decision' to store the waste at Fort Carson! As far as I was concerned it could've stayed at Los Alamos. In fact, I've got a memo that says—"

"Gentlemen, please, this is not the time," Secretary Rockwell interrupted. "We're in the middle of the worst horror this country has ever seen. Al, can you give us any idea how or why the waste exploded?"

"Has to be a design-system malfunction. My guess is the cooling system. It had to be the cooling system. The strontium ninety overheated and . . ."

"That's good, Zehrt," Harper said sarcastically. "This whole abominable event is just an unfortunate design-system malfunction. Give that to the press. Now, who installed the goddamned cooling system?"

"The Army," Rockwell replied.

"Then that's who you should hang," Zehrt said, scratching at the nervous rash on his forehead. "If anyone screwed up, they did."

The plane's intelligence teletype began rattling out paper. A Presidential aide tore off the printout, handed it to Harper, then retreated to safety. While he read, the President shook his head several times, then raised his eyes to the two that sat across from him. "It's even worse than we thought. Preliminary intelligence rates the strength of the explosion at over ten times that of the bombs on Hiroshima and Nagasaki."

"Jesus," Rockwell whispered.

"Twenty square miles of Colorado is gone. *Twenty square miles!*"

George Larkman, the President's White House head of staff, entered the cabin. "Mr. President, we've got to check over the press release. They're already screaming about being excluded from the restricted area."

"It's for their own safety." Harper nodded.

"I've cleared the boards with the networks for an emergency broadcast statement."

"Fine. Give me five minutes, and we'll get to the release."

"Dewey?"

"What?"

"We've gotten information that Turner's on his way to Pueblo."

"Great. Just great," Harper mumbled. "I need Joseph Turner right now like Nixon needed more tapes!"

"But he may not make it before we do. He's been down in Mississippi with the hurricane victims in Pascagoula and all the lines were down. He's just gotten word. And he'll have a hell of a time getting to a plane that can bring him out."

"Well, for once God is on our side," Harper said. "But we're gonna help out. You get to whoever's running things down there and tell them that 'no unauthorized personnel in the restricted area' includes Turner. I don't want him within fifty miles of the place."

"You shouldn't be either," Zehrt said. "The risk of fall-out—"

"The risk of losing the election is what I'm looking at. I won't stand a chance in hell if I don't go in there and show my personal concern. Believe me, we're not staying any longer than is necessary, and of course we're taking all possible precautions."

Bumper-to-bumper cars, pickups, and campers filled with people fled westward up Highway 50 from La Junta toward Pueblo. James Weisman, at the wheel of a rented car carrying Peter Hansen and John Stanton, looked into the terrified faces as he drove hastily in the opposite direction toward the blast site. It was the same terror he had seen on the faces of the people in Pueblo when the plane had landed an hour ago. He pushed the accelerator harder. Nearer La Junta, the traffic moving west grew thicker as the private vehicles were joined by military convoys of huge trucks and jeeps which had begun evacuating the towns nearest the blast site —Timpas, Ayer, Delhi, Thatcher, Higbee, Ninaview, Ville-green. Weisman negotiated around some trucks blocking the highway into La Junta.

He turned onto a side street to the American Legion Hall on Santa Fe Avenue, which was now the combined U.S. Forces Command Post. They hurried out of the car into the three-story building. Inside, men ran from one ringing telephone to the next. Some shouted orders while others huddled over maps spread out on tables. When the three identified themselves, they were taken to Brigadier General Gilbert "Gunny" Nicholson, a craggy-faced, gruff man who minced no words. "Where's Turner?"

"He's on his way, but he won't be here for several hours. We want to go ahead and see what we can do. Can you tell us what's happened?"

"I can't tell you much. I've had a preliminary briefing from the DOE people and it looks awful. South of here between Pinos Canyon and a little place called Higbee there ain't nothing left. I mean nothing, for miles around. The problem now is the fallout."

"What about the people who live there?" John asked.

"*Lived*, Mr. Stanton. There ain't enough left of the dead to bury the lot in a teacup, and anyone who survived the blast will be dead soon. We had recon satellites shoot the whole area. Looks like the moon."

"How many people have been overexposed to radiation?" Weisman asked.

"We don't know yet, but the guesstimate so far is around six hundred."

"Does anyone know what caused it?"

"Some problem with the cooling system in one of the tank cars. It's officially been called a design malfunction.

" 'Design malfunction'—I'm sure that will be comforting to the victims," Peter said tensely.

"Yeah," Nicholson agreed.

"How close can we get?" Weisman asked. "We'd like to be there."

"You should know that I've received orders directly from Air Force One not to let Turner or anyone connected with him in there, Doctor. But since I was busy, I never saw you. I'll be busy when Turner arrives too. You get going. Go as far as Thatcher, but if the wind shifts in that direction you hightail it back here. Fair enough?"

"What's in Thatcher?"

"DOE's working out of there. They've set up a temporary decontamination center."

"Thank you, General," Weisman said, shaking his hand.

"I'll call Bob Pincus—he's in charge out there—advise him you should arrive in about an hour. You'll like Pincus."

"Why's that?"

"Cause he's pissed as hell. He won't give you any bullshit political crap. Know what I mean?"

The trip down Route 350 to Thatcher took about an hour. While they rode, they watched the sky turn deep red, then almost black, then back to red again. "It'll be like this for days," Peter said. "A thermonuclear explosion plays hell with the atmosphere." Winds seemed to blow from all directions at once. Huge clouds of smoke, dust, snow, and debris were clearly visible to the east as they pulled into the government-occupied ranching town of Thatcher. Most of the buildings had fallen or burned to the ground from the blast. Military police directed them around the extensive damage southward to an open, almost flat field outside town. There they saw the beginnings of a makeshift tent city rising under the darkened sky.

When Weisman found Bob Pincus, a huge, lanky, sad-eyed man in his midthirties, he was giving last-minute instructions to two six-man disaster teams outside the command post tent. The men were dressed in full protective gear—oxygen tanks, white suits, protective gloves and shoes. Weisman listened intently to his rapid, urgent orders. "Keep your geigers on at all times. No one takes his headgear off! The area's hot as hell. Stay out of any area reading over a hundred and eighty rems. You can't help the dead. Just get the living back here as soon as possible and maybe we can save some. The wash area and the hospital will be set up by the time you get back. Get going! We're running out of light."

"I've been praying he'd come," Pincus said when Weisman had introduced himself and the others and explained that Joseph was on his way.

"What can we do?" John asked.

"Wait. Wait till we get some of the survivors in. They'll be overdosed. We won't be able to do much except watch them die. But when Joseph Turner gets here . . ."

"Isn't there something we can do now?" Peter asked. "What about helping to set up the place?"

"If you'd like, grab a hammer and start knocking in stakes. Raising crew'd be glad for the help."

"Bob, before you go, tell us straight how safe we are here," John said.

"Very—unless the winds change. And there's no reason to think they will. The hot zone starts about three miles east."

It took three more hours for the decontamination center and hospital to be raised and outfitted. By 9:00 P.M. Pincus was pacing the well-lit compound. It was another hour before the five disaster trucks came across the snow-covered field from the east. When they approached Thatcher Camp, Pincus bullhorned a message that a wide berth be given the victims; their skin and clothing were dangerously radioactive. Everyone in the camp watched from fifty feet back as two hundred grotesque figures were led or carried from the vehicles into the gray-white artificial light. Many were vomiting. Some were naked, others only partially clothed in blast-shredded garments. Many had been burned so badly that they no longer had hair. Their skin hung loosely from their faces, necks, and limbs. Their faces were expressionless; almost all looked straight ahead through burned and lacerated eyes. To avoid more excruciating pain, many held their arms out as if carrying some invisible burden. Others carried the pitiful burdens of small children burned raw and wide-eyed with shock.

It was a gruesome review of the living dead. Tears streamed down the onlookers' faces as the victims were formed into lines and directed into the huge tent.

"God help us!" John moaned as he watched the naked, flash-burned body of a young boy carried by on a stretcher. "Can't we do anything for them now?"

"Some will get morphine inside before the decontamination wash," Weisman answered, "but it may not do much for them. We'll have to wait until decontamination is finished . . . You OK, Peter?"

The young man was hunched over, sobbing. Weisman put an arm around him.

Peter lifted his head to the starless dark red haze. "Why?" he cried angrily. "Why?"

"Joseph will be here soon, Peter," John said comfortingly. "We've got to get ourselves ready to help."

From inside the tent, screams of pain from the first being

washed and decontaminated filled the night. Many outside pressed their hands over their ears to shut out the hideous cries.

"Listen!" Peter screamed at a man beside him, pulling the man's hands down. "You have to listen, so you can tell the world outside what this was like!"

"Come on, Peter," Weisman said, drawing him away. "Let's go to the hospital and get ready."

Joseph, accompanied by Sammy, Emil, Louise, and Jerry, reached Thatcher Camp before midnight. He was briefed immediately by Bob Pincus. On his way to the hospital he heard running footsteps behind him and then felt a strong hand on his arm. "Secret Service, Mr. Turner. The President would like to see you."

"I don't have time," Joseph said, trying to pull away.

"You'll take time, Mr. Turner."

Dewey Harper and his entourage of aides and Secret Service had entered the perimeter of Thatcher Camp followed by a van carrying several members of the White House Press Corps. When Joseph was brought to him, the President and Zehrt were already before the cameras, announcing to the world their sorrow over the great tragedy, their commitment to massive aid for the people affected, and their assurance that dramatic steps had already been taken to prevent a recurrence.

"Well, thank God," he said loudly as he saw Joseph approach. The cameras moved out to get both of them. "We're glad, very glad, you're here. We tried to reach you immediately but couldn't get through."

"Will you tell this man of yours to let go of my arm so I can get to the people who need me?" Joseph interrupted.

"Get those cameras off," Harper said aside to Larkman. But Bob Pincus was suddenly in front of him. "Mr. President, I sent you my twenty-first letter just last month warning you that this was going to happen. That train—"

"Turn off those cameras!" Harper ordered.

"No," Joseph shouted at the newsmen. "Leave them on." The cameras clicked off.

"The government has no right to transport dangerous materials in secret."

"Mr. Pincus," Harper said recovering himself, "I don't recall ever having received your letters."

"Well, they were sent. They said—"

"I'll look into the matter." Harper cut him off.

"You do that," Joseph said angrily. "But, excuse me, please. I'm going to the hospital."

Harper motioned to the agent to let Joseph go, and Turner sprinted across the yard toward the huge green tent.

"It's possibly very dangerous for you here, Mr. President," Zehrt said loudly. "I advise you to leave immediately and not expose yourself to further risk." Within minutes Harper and his staff were driven away to safety from Thatcher Camp.

When Louise saw the press whisked away without ever getting near the victims, she turned angrily to Jerry. "Where's your camera? Somebody has got to get this on film."

"Louise! We're on restricted property. Everything's classified. They specifically said no press."

"I don't give a damn what they said. Where's your camera?"

"It's in the trunk of the car, but we left in such a hurry I forgot to bring film."

She rushed off to find Pincus and within half an hour he had gotten a message through for her to a former associate she'd spotted hanging around the general's office in Pueblo. Within two hours three cans of mini-cam film were in her hands, snuck past the military guards with a boxload of medical supplies, personally marked and sealed by the cooperative General Nicholson.

Joseph entered the hospital tent and immediately began working feverishly with the moaning victims to take away their pain and heal their wounds. The doctors watched in awe as burns melted into new skin and hair grew again where it had been. The healed blessed him but he heard no words as he moved quickly from cot to cot, hurrying against time to reach the dying before it was too late. His body ached with exhaustion but he paid no attention to his own pain or to his horror at the ghastly visions before him.

Throughout the night the disaster teams brought new victims into the decontamination center. The clothes they wore, the water that cleaned their oozing burns and lacerated bodies, were saved for burial in leaden crypts sunk two hundred feet into the ground. By the next evening nearly seven hundred victims had been brought into the hospital. Blood, IVs, and cots were running short. Joseph's companions sat with the new arrivals waiting for him to reach them, listened to the tales of horror from those who could speak, and comforted the grief of those who had lost loved ones in the silent flash of white light.

"Somebody's going to pay for this," Louise said bitterly to John when they met once between cots. "You better get to that woman over there. She's crying for a priest and they're all busy."

James Weisman worked with the other doctors doing what he could to keep the waiting victims alive. On the afternoon of the second day he was working at the far west end of the hospital tent when an Army physician approached and whispered into his ear. "Dr. Weisman, there's something over on the other side you need to see."

"In a minute," Weisman said, not looking up from his suturing.

The doctor waited until he had finished, handed him a clean towel as he stood. "What is it?"

The doctor pointed to the other side of the tent, where Joseph had first begun his healings. "Come with me, please. It's the patients we've kept under observation."

Weisman was led to the cot of a young woman whose body appeared to be perfectly healed, but as he neared he saw that her muscles were completely slack. She was not breathing. Her hair and her bedsheets were wet with sweat. Weisman turned quickly to look at the other patients around her. Nearly all had begun to sweat, a few were vomiting, and a few were delirious. "Radiation poisoning." Weisman felt a chill sweep through his body. He heard himself say slowly, "The burns and cuts heal, but the poisoning doesn't." He shook his head, staring at the terribly sick people around him, searching his mind for some explanation. Maybe there was something more Joseph needed to know in order to heal them completely. He looked quickly around the room, saw Joseph sitting several aisles away beside a badly burned man and a young child, and hurried over to him. "Joseph, I must talk with you, now."

Joseph nodded. "I'll be right back," he said softly to the man staring up at him. He moved with Weisman to the side of the tent. "What is it, Jim?"

Weisman swallowed hard. "Joseph, it's not working."

"What?"

"The people you've healed. The burns and lacerations are healing, but they're still poisoned. They're dying, Joseph. One of them is already gone."

Joseph stared at him, uncomprehending. "But why—how? Oh, Jim," he said as understanding reached him. "I don't know what else to do!"

He could not help them. All of his words, all of his touching, all of his praying made no difference. One by one their fevers shot up and their nausea increased. They lapsed into delirium. Curtained dividers were drawn between the victims Joseph had already seen and those he had not yet touched, but the screams of those behind the curtains could not be shut out, and as word spread, panic seized the others. "He can't heal us! Oh, God, he can't heal us! We're gonna die, we're gonna die awful!"

He tried to comfort them. "Be still now, let me take away your pain, let me heal the wounds." Many turned away from him.

He returned to the man holding the child. The little girl in his arms was dead, and the man was badly in shock; he was sitting up, cradling her, rocking back and forth, kissing the blackened forehead. "You mama's coming, baby. They're gonna find her. They're gonna bring her to you."

"You need to rest, now," Joseph said to him gently. "Would you like me to take her for you? Want me to watch over her until her mother comes?"

The man looked at him out of sunken, lost eyes. He sighed heavily, nodded. "You hold her close, now. You don't let her be afraid. She likes horses and climbing trees. She don't care about dolls. You find her a tree. Promise me."

Joseph reached his arms out for the little limp body, pulled it close to him. "I promise. You sleep now," he said to the father as the man sank on the cot. He stayed until he saw the man's eyes close. Then he looked for Weisman, and took the child to him. "Will you lay her somewhere safe for me until I can get around to the others? It'll be just another two or three hours."

Weisman looked at him sadly. "She's dead, Joseph."

"I know she's dead," Joseph said, his voice hard. "Will you just do what I asked?"

"Sure."

He worked until evening with those who would have him, moved through the hospital surrounded by angry faces, bitter voices. When he had seen the last victim he found the child again, wrapped a blanket around her, picked her up gently, went out of the tent into the darkened red-gray night.

"Mr. Turner! Mr. Turner!" some of the rescue workers outside called to him from behind the ropes cordoning off the hospital area. "Is it true the people aren't healing?" "How many have died, Mr. Turner?" "Are they all gonna die, Mr. Turner?"

He walked past them without speaking, without turning toward them. He stared straight ahead, feeling nothing but the weight of the burden in his arms and the strain of exhaustion in his legs. The rest of him was numb. To the west he made out a small hill, still covered with snow. The military officers, the AEC teams, the doctors and nurses and orderlies standing around the decontamination center yard stepped back and watched him as he moved through them and out the gate. Emil Rothstein saw a small group following him. He walked quickly to them and put an arm out in front of them. "Leave him alone now," he ordered quietly, his eyes fixed on the figure walking westward toward the hill.

Joseph walked for a mile, and when he reached the bottom of the hill he headed up through snow-covered rocks to the single small tree near the top. At the foot of the tree he sank to his knees. He looked down at the child in his arms. "I've found you a tree," he whispered. "I've found you a tree to climb. It's not a very big tree, but it's the best I could do. . . . Oh, no," he moaned. "I didn't want you to die, little girl. I don't even know your name. I didn't even ask your daddy your name! Wake up, little girl! Dammit, wake up!" He shook her. His frustration turned to rage as his vision filled with the mutilated bodies he couldn't save. The rage flooded him and he threw his head back, looking up at the bloody sky. "Damn you!" he began to scream. "Damn you!" His screams dissolved into wordless roars, violent, guttural cries of a tormented animal, of a man crazed by the horror he had witnessed. He screamed until his throat was too dry for sound, until his breathing heaved.

Finally he stopped, his fury spent, his body shaking uncontrollably. He rocked back and forth, clutching the child close to him, trying to warm her cold body with his own. He reached with one hand to smooth back a strand of blond hair. Its softness brought tears to his eyes and then, as if he had tapped a wellspring of all the tears he had not shed for the last twenty-four hours, all the tears he had not shed for the last months, they streamed down his face, flowed out of some bottomless depth inside himself, washed onto the child in his arms. He pulled her closer and pressed her face into his sobbing chest.

A moment later he thought he felt warmth against his neck. He drew her away. The little body was still, but as he reached out to place a shaking finger beneath her nostrils a small, pulsating warmth bathed his skin. He clutched her again, unable to believe what he had felt. His eyes closed tight.

A warm wind, quite unlike the sharp, cold wind surrounding him moments before, began to envelop his body. "Still," he heard a voice inside say. "Be still, and listen." It was a soft familiar voice, not unlike his own. "This child has been reborn as a sign to you. She has been reborn through your own tears."

Joseph sucked in his breath. A chill of terror crept over him. I really am losing my mind, he thought.

"She was sent to you to reach into your heart," the voice continued, "to help you find the source of your power in your own sorrow, your own caring."

The terror left him slowly as he heard the words.

"The tragedy you have witnessed was a senseless tragedy, born out of deception and error. Your own tears are not enough to wash it away. All, all must feel the pain. All must shed tears of grief. All must share the darkness.

"But their tears will also be tears of regeneration, which will seal a new covenant.

"Except for this child, who shall return to the world in joy, all who have died will remain at peace. No more need die. You must make known to all eyes and to all ears this pain and this horror. You must obtain from all mouths and from all hearts a promise that such a tragedy will never be allowed to happen again.

"Go now. When the promise has been made, you will be led by light, to bring those who suffer to the place where darkness began."

The voice ceased.

He sat for a long time until the cold wind returned to freeze the melted snow around him to ice.

Then he stood, his own pain soothed, cradling the child, who was breathing freely now, and looked down over the long flat land below, as if he could see far into the distance. He took a step and began his walk downward, his long walk back into the world.

At the camp gate a woman stood waiting beside John Stanton. "You have my child," she said, her face full of agony.

"They brought her in an hour ago. She was away when the blast hit," John said.

Joseph held out the child to her. The little girl opened her eyes. "Mommy?"

"Ohhh," the woman moaned, her eyes filling with tears. "They told me you were dead!" She took the child from him.

"They made a mistake. Your child is alive," Joseph said to her.

He looked openly into John's awe-filled face. "Tell Jim no one is to know. Then come with me. I need you now. I need you very much."

THIRTY-EIGHT

ON THE THIRD DAY following the explosion, press from all over the world had joined those already gathered in Pueblo in response to the news that a live, all-network press conference had been called by Joseph Turner.

Before he appeared, Bob Pincus and Louise Ryan gave the world its first official account of the tragedy. Government agents watched helplessly as Pincus, in his last act in his post with the DOE, detailed how common such movements of nuclear waste materials through populated areas had become, how likely they were to result in accidents, and how much destruction such accidents could cause. The full meaning of his figures did not reach them until Louise turned on her film of the scene inside the hospital tent, and the world saw the burned faces with empty eyesockets, fluid from melted eyes crusted on raw, bloody cheeks, pus-covered wounds that had once been mouths, swollen, discolored, putrid limbs, and living bodies that looked like skinned and swollen carcasses. The world heard the shrieks of agony, the screams of terror, of roars of unendurable pain. The world felt the torment of poisoned bodies racked with vomiting and driven by fever to delirium. The world learned the relief of watching a human body cease its tortuous writhing and become a corpse.

"DON'T TURN AWAY." Joseph's voice came from the back of the darkened room. "SEE THIS. HEAR THIS. ALL OF IT." The men and women in the room sat rigidly in their seats, knowing that this was an order to be obeyed. Those who had hid their faces in their hands and had doubled over with nausea, fastened their eyes again on the screen. "THOSE ARE HUMAN BEINGS. WHAT THEY'VE SUF-FERED, ARE STILL SUFFERING, MUST NOT HAVE BEEN ENDURED FOR NOTHING. LOOK INTO THE

EYES OF ONE OF THEM. THAT COULD HAVE BEEN
—STILL COULD BE—YOUR HUSBAND, YOUR WIFE,
YOUR MOTHER, YOUR FATHER, YOUR FRIEND,
YOUR CHILD, YOU. THIS IS HELL BEFORE YOU.
AND IT WILL NOT END WITHOUT WITNESSES!"

The camera moved over every one of the seven hundred
and fourteen victims. Then the film stopped and the lights
went on. The people watched Joseph Turner, his clothes di-
sheveled, his body held rigid against his exhaustion, his eyes
rimmed with heavy circles, walk to the front of the room.
He turned and spoke to the sickened, sweating men and
women in front of him and behind television sets around the
world.

"What you have just seen is the truth—the truth that some
have tried to keep from you, just as they kept from you the
truth of the terrible risks they expose you to every day. The
sickness of the people you've seen will not stop, the dying
will not stop, until all of us make it known that we share
this agony, that we cry for this pain, that we mourn for these
deaths, and that we *will not let it happen* ever again. We
know who is responsible for this horror. Those of you in
other countries must understand that many of your leaders
are risking the same for you. Every one of us must take back
into our own hands the destiny of human beings on this
earth.

"You've heard that I can perform miracles. You've heard
that I haven't been able to perform the miracle of healing
the poison inside these victims. But a way has been shown
to me. I know now that I can't do it alone. Only you can
make it possible.

"I need your strength. I need a sign from you that you've
seen, that you've heard, that you mourn, that you have from
this moment made a new commitment to the value of human life.

"I ask you to show me this by the simple act of spending
a night without lights. I ask you to join with me tonight and
live it, as these victims will live it, in darkness.

"One hundred and sixty-seven people have died here. I
need you to help me save the rest."

The men and women in the room stared at him, stunned
by his words, drained by the vision he had forced them to

see. He waited. Finally a young woman near the front spoke, her voice shaking. "We would all like to believe that there is still hope. But are you aware that Pope Leo has just announced that his predecessor's proclamation of your divinity was in error—that the Church now denies your claims to be the Son of God?"

"I've never made that claim," Joseph answered her. "All of you know the things I've done. What you believe is up to you. But if anything I've ever said, if anything I've ever done, means anything to you, I ask you to be with me now —for those people's sake."

"They listened, Joseph. Lights are out all over the country."

John had found him resting against a post at the north perimeter of the camp, looking at the few stars that had made their way through the darkened sky. "And there's something else—Jim said to tell you that they've stopped dying. The people in there are not getting better, but they're holding their own."

Joseph closed his eyes, then opened them slowly. "John, I'm so tired. I keep trying to think of what it meant—'by light.' What light?—when?"

John put an arm around him. "Something will tell you, Joey. Something will guide you."

Joseph leaned closer to him. "You're right. It said that. It's just so hard just to wait. Are you OK?"

"I think so. I'm holding up pretty well."

"You always did."

"It's OK to be afraid, Joey," John said. "You've been afraid before. It's never made any difference."

"But it's different this time. I'm not afraid for me, anymore. I'm afraid for them."

"They're not dying anymore, Joey. You've already given them that."

Through the silence of the red-black night, they sat together, feeling the closeness, the warmth they had shared many years ago, when they were still two small boys alone in the world at night and wondering, very hopefully, what life would hold for them in the years ahead.

Two hours before sunrise Joseph suddenly put a hand on John's arm. "Johnny!" he whispered intensely. "Did you see that?"

"See what?" John turned to look eastward.

"There's a second one!"

"My God, Joey," John said as they watched a third star shoot low across the sky and join two others that seemed to hover together near the horizon.

"John! That's it! That's where the darkness began! That's where I have to take them!"

"But that's . . ."

"It's back into the blast site."

Bob Pincus, a volunteer now but still in charge by common consent, stared at Joseph open-mouthed when Joseph told him what they had to do. Then he turned to his team leaders. "OK, boys, suit up. Get those people on trucks. We're going back in." The men scrambled in all directions.

"Thank you," Joseph said.

"You can pick up a suit over there."

"No, I won't need it."

"Joseph, it's hot, very hot. I don't know how far in you're going, but—"

"Neither do I."

"Those poor people have already been overexposed, but you need a suit."

"Please," Joseph said impatiently. "Get them ready."

An hour later the procession of trucks bearing the victims headed into the blast site. They rode for more than an hour under the still-darkened sky toward the three stars, through mile after mile of scarred, reddish land. Around them, charred and naked trees stood like sentinels over the dead. Whole herds of cattle slumbered in ashes, and human bodies were scattered about the waste.

Joseph's eyes searched the distance. Suddenly he pointed. "There!" he said to his driver.

The driver leaned forward over the wheel, then turned the truck slightly southward toward a knoll bathed in light where the three stars seemed to have lowered over the land.

In another mile Joseph saw near the knoll the long rails

of train tracks running toward a place at the top where they broke in all directions.

When the trucks finally stopped he jumped out. "Quickly, quickly now. Move them up there," he said, going to the back of his truck and lifting out the first stretcher.

A suited team leader from the truck behind approached him, carrying a loudly clicking geiger counter. "I have to get my men out of here, now! It couldn't be a hotter area," he said, pointing to the machine. "It's off the dial. The suits won't protect them!"

Joseph bent down and looked through the protective face plate directly into the man's eyes. "You'll be OK. I need you to help me get these people out."

"I've got a wife and family!" the man begged.

"I don't have time to argue with you. If you want out, then take your men and get back wherever you feel safe, and wait for us."

The man turned away and walked toward the other trucks. The few victims able to walk joined Joseph lifting out stretchers, but they moved painfully and slowly.

"I'll take this one," Joseph heard a voice say behind him. "Sammy!"

He turned and saw all of them coming toward him from a truck that had been in the rear—Sammy, John, Louise, Jerry, Emil, Peter, James. None wore suits. Then the AEC team leader was beside him again. "The men want to stay."

They worked together until the knoll beside the tracks looked like a strange battlefield, littered with stretchers. Moans of sickness and fear rose from all around. When the last stretcher had been let down, Joseph walked to the center of the crowd.

The moans seemed louder now in the eerie silence.

"I'm cold!" a little boy cried.

"Be still now," Joseph said. "We are not alone here. Be still, and wait."

They waited breathlessly, looking at each other and up at the three strange stars in the sky. Some moved their lips in desperate prayers. Then someone on the edge called out, "It's getting warmer!" And they looked at each other fearfully as the warm wind came, bringing with it clouds from nowhere into the cloudless sky. The clouds clustered above them, hiding the stars.

"The light's gone!" someone screamed.

"We're going to die!" another cried out.

"Don't be afraid," Joseph said.

"Wait—it's rain—it's raining!" someone whispered, as drops of water fell. The rain came faster. It was warm, healing water, pouring over them, washing them as Joseph's tears had washed the child, washing away their sickness and their pain.

One by one the victims rose, walked, reached out to each other, and reached out to Joseph and to his friends, crying with relief and joy.

"He did it!" Sammy shouted gleefully.

"Let's go home," Joseph said, tears and rain streaming down his face as he hugged the people pushing in around him. "They're waiting for us back there. Let's go home."

PART III

THIRTY-NINE

"So THAT'S IT," George Larkman said to Dewey Harper as they glumly reviewed the situation on the day after the miracle of Thatcher Camp. Our insiders at Gallup give you nineteen percent—most of them loyal Catholics."

"It's an improvement on Harris," Vice President Ruddock volunteered.

"You're a comfort, Carl," Harper said dourly.

Ruddock squirmed uncomfortably in his seat. "I was thinking that, well, it just may be time for us to turn around —you know, let the people know we're behind Turner. There's not a politician in the country going to be elected this year without the support of Turner's people. Hundreds of the locals are facing recalls already—even judges—for things they've said, or not said, about him. The union rank and file are doing the same thing to their officers. Even the churches—this morning's papers are full of stories about pro-Turner factions getting together to fire their ministers and put in pro-Turner people."

"Anything else, Carl?"

"Well, I just think that since the pro-Turner people are taking over, we'd better let them know we're on their side."

"Be grateful you live in a civilized country," Secretary of State Curt Winslow said to him. "Turner factions in every tiddlywink country on the planet are pressuring their governments to get Turner to tell them how to run things. And did you see that little item on the second page of the *Post* this morning—about some Arab tribe in North Africa converting to Turner and going on a crusade to convert their neighbors —at gunpoint?"

"Don't scare Carl," Harper said to him. "Anyway, we've got more important things to talk about. Turner's not a person anymore—he's a goddamned cause. A few more strikes, a few more boycotts, a few more investor revolts, and this country's economy is gonna be hurt bad."

"All the reports we've got say the dislocations will only be temporary," Larkman objected.

"Not temporary enough. If he keeps it up, the market's not going to recover before November—or before some of our more generous contributors lose a bundle. And you can damn well bet they'll take their losses out of their campaign contributions."

"If your popularity rating doesn't improve, we aren't going to have to worry about our campaign budget," Ruddock said, "and that brings us back to my suggestion."

"It won't work, Carl. There's just not much Turner's people want that we can support. So we have only one other option—discredit him, fast."

"The prophecy said he only has another month. Why don't we just sit back and wait?"

"Because we don't have a month. The damage he's already done might be too much. We've got to change the people's attitude toward him."

"So what are we going to do?" Ruddock moaned despondently.

"We're working on it, Carl, we're working on it. The IRS is still digging, and we've got some other things going—the indictment against Sweet should be out from Justice in a few days; the AMA is reviewing Weisman's participation in the questionable medical practice at Thatcher; and the ABA is onto Rothstein for his part in encouraging various illegal activities."

"That's not much. It's not enough to blow Turner. Especially when everyone's convinced he performed that fucking miracle."

"Well, our fine Surgeon General has been working on that. He's finishing up a long statement explaining just how that so-called miracle was pulled off."

"But even if that can be explained," Ruddock said, "what about everything else he's done? Right now he's working with the people in Pueblo making sure the victims all get resettled. The people in this country don't care about anything at the moment but him—they're looking to him for everything. We might as well not exist."

"Jesus, doesn't that guy ever sleep?" Harper hit the arm of his chair in exasperation.

"Maybe he'll die of exhaustion," Winslow offered.

"Don't hold your breath," Larkman said.

"Well, sooner or later he's going to get tired," Ruddock said. "Sooner or later he's going to disappoint someone. You saw how fast people turned against him when they thought he couldn't heal those victims. And now, with all the things people are asking him for, he's going to blow it sooner or later. I mean, they really think he can do anything—the newspapers from here to Bangkok are full of appeals to him. And I'd hate to see his mail. It's just not humanly possible to give all of them everything they want."

"I wouldn't count on people's disappointment," Winslow told him. "They may have turned against him fast, but they sure turned back in a hurry as soon as he got on the tube for five minutes. Anyway, it's possible that the whole thing will be taken care of for us." He turned to Harper questioningly. "Shall I tell them?" he asked Harper.

Harper nodded. "Go ahead."

"The CIA's picked up some very reliable intelligence that the leaders of certain communist nations are privately very upset at the idea that some American is running around with some kind of power over the effects of nuclear explosions. At the moment they're trying to decide whether they want to bring him in for tests—or just assassinate him."

"Assassinate him!" Ruddock exclaimed. "That'd make him a martyr!"

"At this point we might do better with a dead martyr than a live Messiah," Harper grumbled. "What are you smiling about, Larkman?"

George Larkman sat in the corner, looking smug. He had been thoroughly enjoying the knowledge that he was sitting on the one piece of information that the men around him would give their eyeteeth for—the one piece of information that could blow this whole Joseph Turner business right out of the water. He let Harper wait.

"I'm thinking about what I'm going to do with my raise, boss," he answered finally. "Think I'll take Jeannie to Morocco this year—she's always wanted to go to Morocco."

Harper smiled. "Now, gentlemen," he said, not taking his eyes off Larkman, "what do you suppose George has got in that little bald head of his that's gonna be worth a vacation in Morocco?"

The others looked at Larkman blankly.

"How would you like it, Dewey," Larkman said with the familiarity he used only when he knew he had aces in the hole, "how would you like it if it turned out that this new Messiah of ours wasn't the pure little all-American boy he looks like?"

"For instance?"

"Well, suppose he'd had a nice little fling with a nice little whore?"

"That would be worth a trip to Morocco."

Ruddock's mouth dropped open. "I don't believe it," he said.

Harper's smile broadened. "Now, Carl," he said, "George wouldn't make something like that up, would you, George? Where'd you get it?"

"At a small meeting of some of our most prestigious labor and business leaders, who have been drawn together at last over their mutual problems with Joseph Turner."

"They gave it to you?"

"Let's just say they're willing to do anything to stop Joseph Turner now."

"Aren't we all," Dewey Harper said, sitting back and looking pointedly at the men around him. "Aren't we all."

On the evening of March 18—at Castel Gandolfo, the Papal summer residence several miles outside Rome, Pope Leo XIV sat across from the ministers of the Sacred Congregation of the Faith he had called to meet secretly with him. Their faces, like his own, were set with resolution. He knew that the instructions he was about to give them would be met with neither pleasure nor opposition—nor surprise. They were as well aware as he was of the damage Joseph Turner had caused Holy Mother Church, and they had themselves been responsible for the secret meetings with those among the leadership of other faiths who assented that Turner should no longer be left free to do his evil work.

The fathers had met formally three days ago to condemn Joseph Turner as Satan's own issue. And one of them had already been instructed to make provisions for the action he was about to initiate.

Belazzi was well aware, nonetheless, that in the hundreds of years since the Inquisition, the Holy Office had done little to preserve the sanctity of the Faith, other than to issue condemnations; what was required of these men now was an act none of them had ever dreamed, until one month ago, that they might be called upon to perform. It was imperative, then, that he should avoid any sign of hesitation, any opening for question. His statement must be simply a formal declaration of what must now be done.

"My brothers," Belazzi began, wrapping his fingers around the gold crucifix chained around his neck, "we have called you together because the hour has come when we must consecrate ourselves to our holy duty to save Holy Mother Church. We have lost great numbers of our children —the numbers of those who have strayed grow daily. The dissension among those who remain rends the cloth of our faith"—even, he thought but did not say, to the extent of demanding that he himself leave the Throne of Peter. "We are locked in a desperate struggle with a man who claims to come from God but whom you yourselves have come to know as Satan's own wizard, capable of deceiving even the Blessed Pope Alexander himself.

"We have been charged by God," he continued, watching the tension grow in the shallow breathing of those around him as he approached his charge to them, "to stop the spread of this serpent's poison. We have been left with no alternative."

The faces before him did not change; only Gio Cardinal Fumboli, the youngest among them, moved his hand to touch his own crucifix. But that was the only movement in the room save for the almost imperceptible nodding of heads, as each cardinal in turn acknowledged the Pontiff's decision.

"Cardinal Mendetti," Belazzi said, "we instructed you to begin preparations for this eventuality should it become necessary. Is all in readiness?"

Giulio Cardinal Mendetti nodded solemnly, a small sigh

of relief issuing from him now that the words had finally been spoken. "It is, Holy Father."

"Then we charge you to see that it is done. Blessed be the Father, Son, and Holy Ghost. Amen."

FORTY

"MAGGIE?"

"Who is this?"

"It's Tom—Tom O'Malley."

"How did you get my number?"

"I have friends in high places."

She chuckled. "You mean you bribed some poor fool at the phone company. You always did know how to get what you want."

"Right now I want to see you. I'm in town."

"I'm not in the business anymore, Thomas."

"That's not what I had in mind. I just want to talk. Can I buy you a drink?"

"I mean it, Tom."

"So do I."

"OK, why not," she said after a moment. "I'll meet you in forty-five minutes at Caruso's. You know where that is?"

"See you there."

An hour later she sat across from the distinguished-looking man in his early fifties, watching him run his finger around the rim of the glass. "You still do that when you're nervous."

He smiled. "You're the only one who's ever noticed."

"So what's up? You didn't call me here for small talk. You need another loan? Your company on the rocks again?"

"As a matter of fact it is, but I'm not here to ask you for money. I'm here to offer you some."

She started to get up. "I told you—"

"Sit down, Maggie. I believe you. I've been asked to talk to you for someone else."

"What about?" she ask, puzzled.

"About your relationship with Joseph Turner."

She laughed. "You're kidding. You mean the man they're calling the New Messiah? Come on."

"It's worth a great deal of money to you now, Maggie. And I know how you like to live."

"This is ridiculous! Who on earth gave you the idea that I have some relationship with that man?"

"Had."

"Whatever."

"He's causing a great many important people a great deal of trouble right now. And they're willing to pay handsomely for a public statement from you about your connection with him. They asked me to show you this," he said, handing her several typewritten pages. "They're willing to publish it without anything from you, of course, but then you just might deny it, and anyway, the public would be much more interested in your personal account than in some second-hand story told by witnesses. There's much more available to you than the initial payment. They'll arrange a publishing contract, talk-show appearances, all of it."

She read quickly through the pages in front of her, holding herself very still, trying to think past the screams inside her head. She was reading an incredibly detailed account of her own history, including her months with Joseph.

"My friends assume that the reason you haven't come forward before is that Turner's people have made it worth it to you not to. But believe me, we're prepared to offer whatever it takes."

"It will take a lot," she said coolly, putting the papers down. "Mind if I hang on to this?"

"Of course not. It's your copy. I have another one here for you to sign."

"Exactly how much are your friends prepared to pay?"

"Two hundred thousand in cash—for starters."

"Not bad," she smiled at him. "Well, now, my friend, you've certainly surprised me. That would of course more than pay for what you still owe. But how do I know they've got it? I want to know who it is, Tom."

"And you know I can't tell you. You'll get the first big chunk when we get your signature. Is that enough assurance?"

"I guess it will have to be. When do your friends need an answer?"

"If you mean you want time to see about a competing bid, don't bother. They'll beat whatever offer you get."

"We'll see."

"They haven't got much time to wait, Maggie. They want some sort of answer from you within forty-eight hours. If they don't hear from you, they'll have to go ahead without you."

She put the papers in her purse and took out her keys. "Oh, don't worry, Tom. I'm sure I'll be back to you before then."

Emil Rothstein stared at the dead receiver in his hand, half wishing that John had been here to take Maggie's call. He debated trying to reach a few contacts who might be able to find out who was behind the offer. She'd been included in his own investigation, and he'd heard recent rumors of pressure on Belazzi to vacate the throne, so he immediately suspected Rome. But when he questioned her about O'Malley, she said that even though he was Catholic, it was pretty farfetched; his political and business connections were closer to home.

I can't discount any of them, Emil thought as he put the receiver back in the cradle. And even if I knew, I couldn't stop it from happening. Too many people have access to the information. Too many people have reason to try to discredit him. The thought made him angry. No matter how much good Joseph had done, no matter how many people he'd helped, there would be those just waiting for a reason to turn against him and a reason not to believe.

Well, Emil said to himself as he got up from the motel-room desk and headed out to find Joseph, if the whole thing blows up now, maybe it will at least force him to slow down a little, get some rest.

In the days after the miracle at Thatcher Camp, Joseph was swamped with pleas for help. Though his friends had tried to persuade him that many of the requests were things they could take care of for him or that people could take care of themselves, he did not listen. He tried to help them all, working nonstop, working out of his motel room in

Pueblo with the people affected by the explosion and making quick trips to other parts of the country whenever he could get away.

All of them begged him to slow down, begged him to let them do a little more of the work and let other people solve more of their problems themselves. He refused. His teachings hadn't been clear enough, he said, and now a lot of people were using his name to justify many actions he not only didn't approve, but knew wouldn't succeed.

"I have to teach them that they have to work peacefully together and that I'm not just one more cause to fight over. I've got to keep trying to help them see that the power they have in themselves is enough to make their lives happy. Using it peacefully is the best way to get others interested in doing the same."

Louise had once tried to tell him that he couldn't expect to change people that fast, and that they needed time.

"I may not have much time," Joseph had said.

"Then give a little of it to yourself," Louise had answered. "Leave them for a while. It doesn't have to be for long. Leave them so they'll have no choice but to look to themselves. Give them a chance to show themselves and you that all you've done for them has meant something."

"I won't do it, Lou. I can't abandon them now. Besides, where would I go? What would I do? This is my life now, this is the work I do, and the job's not finished. It doesn't exactly feel terrific knowing I may not have much time, but it sure keeps me from wasting any of it."

And Emil remembered, too, the conversation he had had with Joseph only yesterday . . . "There's only one thing in the world that means almost as much to me as this—one thing that I'd leave it for, for a while. And that's a door that's been closed to me."

I wonder if it's closed tighter now, Emil thought as he lifted his hand to knock on Joseph's door—or if it's just been opened a crack.

"Those bastards!" Joseph shouted when Emil told him what Maggie had said. "Those lousy bastards!"

"We knew they'd find out sometime, Joseph."

"I guess so," he acknowledged. "But I didn't think they

were desperate enough to go after Maggie—to get her involved like this. I expected to see it in some crummy scandal sheet. Whoever's behind this wants to drag her across front page, prime-time news. Does she have any idea who it is?"

By the time Emil had finished telling him everything he knew, including Maggie's intention to "go somewhere where they'll never find me," Joseph had made a decision.

"Emil, I've got to talk to her. I don't care what they do to me, but I'm not going to let them get to her. Besides, I want to see her."

"Here's her number." Emil handed him a small slip of paper and left the room.

"Hello?"

Joseph caught his breath at the sound of her voice. "Maggie, I need to talk to you." There was a long silence on the other end. "Maggie . . ."

"I'm here. No, Joseph. No. It won't help. Please just leave me alone. All I wanted to do was warn you. I'm leaving tomorrow."

"For God's sake, Maggie, this is no time for games. Don't run away now!"

"I've got to."

"No, you don't. You can come here. We can face it together."

Her voice was angry. "What for, Joey? So the world can hurl garbage at both of us while we stand there bravely and take it? What for?"

"I want to see you."

"You want me to help you prove something to the world?"

"Not to prove anything. We have nothing to apologize for, nothing to defend. Partly to teach them something. But that's not all."

"Joey, you have changed. I guess you had to. Well, listen, I'm not interested in teaching them anything. They took away from me the most precious thing in my life. They own you now. I tried to disappear to protect you. I'd even begun to think it had worked. It took away a lot of the pain of losing you. Now I can't protect you anymore, but I don't have to sit here and watch the most important moments of my life be used to destroy you. I don't have to, and I won't."

"Maggie, this isn't going to destroy me. But you're right. I can't use us to teach the world a lesson."

"Then let me go!"

They were the first words he'd heard from her that told him he had some chance. "Maggie, you didn't let me finish a minute ago. Don't you see, there's no reason for us to be apart any longer. They're going to know anyway. You said you couldn't protect me anymore. I never wanted you to try. I wanted you with me, again. That's why I asked Emil to find you. When he told me you were getting married, I knew what that meant. You didn't want any part of my life now. But—"

"I almost did get married. I couldn't."

"I didn't think you would. Maggie, just yesterday I told Emil that there was only one thing in the world that could make me leave all this for a while. I *will* leave it for a while, to be with you. I'm exhausted, baby. Everyone's been telling me to get away. Now I have something to get away to. And I'd know you were safe. Don't go, Maggie. I don't know what's going to happen in the next month. Don't let us end like this!"

He waited through her long silence. His heart pounded. "How long?"

He closed his eyes. "Ten days, no, two weeks."

"And we'll really be alone. No work, no people taking you away from me?"

"My friends here can take care of everything for a couple of weeks. No one even needs to know where we are."

"No one?"

"Well, I'll have to tell someone just in case there's a real emergency. I'll tell John. That's all."

"OK," she said after another silence. "I'm going to my uncle's cabin in the Sierras. I used to go there when I was a child. It's twenty miles from anything. No telephones and no roads; you have to fly in. I've arranged for my uncle to take me. He has a plane and I can trust him. You want to meet me there the day after tomorrow?"

He thought for a moment. "Could you come here instead? Pick me up at an airport outside town?"

"Sure. I'll call you later with the details."

"I'll see you soon, then, my love."

She felt the words painfully, as if they reopened an old wound. "Soon, Joseph," she answered, hanging up the phone.

That evening Joseph met with John to tell him his plans.

"I'm glad you're going," John said when he was finished. "You need it; you need it badly. I won't get in touch with you unless there's a real emergency. In fact, I'd just as soon forget you ever told me where you'll be."

"Will you talk to Emil and have him tell the others I'm going? I have a lot of things to finish before I leave."

"I don't like it," Emil said when John phoned him. "It's too risky for him to go off alone like that. The threats against him have been picking up ever since Thatcher. Now this thing with Maggie. Whoever approached her was serious, and I'm worried about what they might try next."

"But he needs to get away, Emil. Believe me, where he's going he'll be safe."

"And you're the only one who'll know?"

"That's the way he wants it."

Emil thought for a moment. "I agree, that's best. I'm still concerned about those leaks in New York. The others don't even need to know you—wait a minute, John." He thought he had heard someone outside the door, and he put the phone down. He opened the door, put his head out. Louise Ryan was walking away from him down the hall. "You need something, Lou?" he called.

She turned and waved. "No, I'll talk to you later. I'm late for an appointment."

Emil watched her turn the corner, then returned to the phone.

"Anything wrong?" John asked.

"No, I'm just being cautious. I thought I heard someone at the door, but it was just Louise passing by. Anyway, as I was saying, the others don't need to be told you know where he is. Now I better get to work on everybody's schedules so Joseph can see that everything's under control before he goes."

"See you in the morning, then. Good night."

Two days later, in the early morning, a red and white
Cessna landed at a small airstrip outside Pueblo. Joseph
stood with John near the runway, watching the plane taxi to
them. When it came to a stop, the right door opened and
Maggie stepped down. "Hello, Joey," she said softly.

He walked to her slowly and stood before her. She stepped
closer and put her arms around him. He reached around her
small body to bring her hard against him.

"We better go," she whispered.

John waved them off, then got into the car to head back to
town. He and Sammy would stay in Pueblo to finish the last
of the resettlement problems there. The others would divide
up Joseph's work. Emil, Louise, and Jerry would return to
New York the next day to reestablish what they had come to
call "headquarters" at the loft.

Their first business would be to handle the two releases
Joseph had prepared for the press. The first, to be released
immediately, was an announcement that he was going away
to an undisclosed location for a rest, and that he would return before Good Friday and would speak at a sunrise service in Central Park on Easter. The second, to be released
only if the information about his life with Maggie appeared,
was a simple statement:

> I want people to know that my relationship with Mar-
> garet Dillon has been, and still is, the most important
> of my life. I have lived with her because I loved her. I
> still do. I ask that you leave this precious part of my life
> in peace.

The flight to the cabin in California took nearly all day.
Joseph and Maggie used it to try to bridge the distance between them. In the beginning, they made polite conversation,
asking harmless questions that helped to break the ice. But
after they covered the events of the last four months, there
were long deep silences as they looked down on the snow-
covered peaks below, both of them wondering if they were
doing the right thing.

They were silent as Leon Dillon circled a small valley and
skillfully brought the ski-equipped plane down onto Grassy
Lake's frozen surface.

They hauled their supplies to the log cabin Leon had built more than thirty years earlier. Then Joseph and Maggie stood on the bank watching as the Cessna lifted off the ice, tipped its wing to them, and disappeared over the crest of a mountain.

Long after the plane had disappeared, they avoided looking at each other, feeling more shy and awkward now in the intensity of being alone. Maggie turned suddenly and started for the cabin. "Come on, I'll race you!" she yelled. When they had run inside she looked at the piled supplies. "Whew!" she said. "Think I'll get all this stuff put away."

"I'll help."

"No, let me do it. You build a fire."

When the fire was blazing, he stretched out on the bearskin rug in front of it and watched her move around the cabin. He began to relax, aware for the first time in weeks just how much he needed to rest—and just how lonely he had been for her. He looked at her arms, her breasts, her belly, her legs, taking her in with his eyes. He gave himself permission again to want hungrily and selfishly.

She felt his eyes. He saw it in the way she moved, but she avoided looking back at him and said nothing. When he saw that her work was finished and that she was simply puttering around, finding unnecessary things to do, he called to her from across the room. "Maggie, come here."

"In a minute," she said. "As soon as I get these cups dried."

"Now."

She put down her towel and sat beside him. She stared into the fire.

"Maggie, look at me. You haven't looked at me yet."

She looked down, then back into the fire. "This is crazy," she said impatiently. "Our lives are so different now. I'm sitting here beside a man the world calls the Messiah."

He reached up with his hand and turned her face toward him. "That's not who came here to be with you."

Her eyes filled with tears. "Don't you understand?" she said fighting them back. "I wanted to see you, but I didn't want to care so much! I've been through all that pain before. I was almost getting over it, and now . . ." Her words trailed off as the tears spilled over and her body sank down.

He sat up and took her into his arms. "Let me hold you now, baby," he said, rocking her and feeling his own eyes fill with tears. "You've been alone a long time with the pain. I'm so sorry, my love. You held me like this once. Let me hold you now."

FORTY-ONE

JAY NIGHTINGALE ran his hand through his gray-brown hair and took another sip of his heavily laced chicory coffee. He turned away from the jazz quartet strolling through the Commander's Palace Restaurant to look at the tourists snapping pictures of the indoor floral gardens. He was taking his time, enjoying his Thursday ritual of a jazz brunch. If last night's call from the husky-voiced man had been someone's idea of a practical joke, he would know soon enough.

At two o'clock Nightingale pushed his solid six-foot frame out of the chair and walked out into the almost unbearable humidity of the New Orleans afternoon. It was a ten-minute drive to his shotgun-style cottage in the Quarter. He parked his Corvette and walked up the steps to his front door, then entered his elegantly furnished living room. His dark eyes scoured the room for any sign of a visitor. Nothing. He walked into the cherrywood-paneled den, where he was surrounded by the framed photo journal of his nineteen years as a soldier of fortune fighting in Africa, South America, Vietnam, and the Middle East. His eyes swept the bookcase and tables, then rested on a small plaid suitcase beside the leather couch. He lifted the unfamiliar case carefully to the burl coffee table, took a deep breath, held it, and ran his fingers around the edges looking for any sign of a trip wire or tamper switch. When he had inspected the case thoroughly he slowly pulled the center clasp down and gently raised the lid. His lips pursed as he ran his fingers through the cash. Half a million dollars, the first half of the payment. Whoever they were, they meant business.

Nightingale waited patiently for the second phone call. At four o'clock he answered the ring and listened once again to the husky voice giving him instructions. "There's only one person who knows where Turner is—John Stanton. He'll be in Spokane Saturday night, the twenty-second, speaking at the Opera House. We have reason to believe that you're not the only one looking for Turner. But we're paying you, Nightingale, to find him first." The phone clicked off.

By 9:00 P.M. Nightingale had contacted and secured the services of two former associates. He trusted Turnbow and Veck, and their experience as Snatch and A Team leaders with the Phoenix Operation in Vietnam had made them proficient kidnappers and killers. More important, he knew they trusted him. That would make his job easier when their time came. The voice on the phone was paying for a no-loose-ends operation, and Nightingale always delivered what was paid for. He had thought for a while that morning about one possible hitch in this particular job. Turner might somehow really be the magician people said he was. But Jay Nightingale was not a man to be stopped by magic, and he had dismissed his slight concern with the thought that it could make his job even more interesting.

By eight the next morning Nightingale was on board a flight headed for Spokane. Veck, coming in from Houston, and Turnbow, coming from Los Angeles, would be waiting for him at the airport. He decided there was no sense telling them his ultimate target. There was no point in taking a chance on their getting cold feet at the prospect of getting rid of the man most people believed was the Second Son of God.

FORTY-TWO

"WHERE ARE YOU GOING?" Maggie called from the kitchen. "I'm not through with you yet."

They had lain in bed together all morning, talking and making love, as they had for so many of their hours during the last week. But it had been difficult to get Joseph to be still for any length of time. He had grown accustomed to being busy. Now that they were up, his restlessness seemed again to have seized him.

"I'm going out to see if I can perform a little miracle—get the lake thawed for a swim."

She came out of the kitchen and stood frowning at him. "Oh, no you don't!" she said threateningly. "No miracles. Anyway, even if you did get it thawed, we'd freeze to death in the cold."

"You don't think I can warm it up?"

"I don't care if you can make it boil. No miracles—you promised."

"Now wait a minute," he objected, coming to put his arms around her. "I promised no unnecessary miracles. What if we're out walking and find a hunter who's shot himself in the leg?"

"You'll bandage it."

"What if it's really bleeding badly?"

"Then I'll bandage it."

"Well, what if we can't stop the bleeding?"

"Then we'll take him to a doctor."

Joseph cocked his head to the side in a challenge. "How close is the nearest doctor?"

"Hmmm . . . no, we can't take him to the doctor. OK, you can heal any hunters we come upon who've shot themselves in the leg."

"Thank you."

"But it'll never happen," she said, leaning back and shaking her hair away from her sparkling blue eyes. "It's not hunting season, dummy!"

"A smart one, huh!" he laughed, picking her up and dumping her onto the couch.

"Smart enough to know you're not going out there to unfreeze the lake. Let's see . . . aha! We're nearly out of wood. You're going out to decimate the forest."

"Right you are," he said, bending down to kiss her. "And I'll need lots of coffee. So get busy."

When he had gone she got up and went back into the kitchen to put the coffee on. In a few minutes the clop-clop sounds of his axe against the tree were hammering in rhythm with the plunking of the percolator. She leaned over the sink and looked out the window to see him, a man in the snow, naked from the waist up, already covered with sweat, driving a double-bladed woodman's axe deep into the dead trunk of a seventy-foot pine. She smiled, partly in enjoyment of his body and partly in an almost maternal feeling of happiness for the man in the snow. He'd worked hard outdoors a lot since they'd been here, recovering his physical strength and taking the time alone to think through what he had accomplished, what he still wanted to do. She had watched the weight of seriousness and worry lift off him day by day. Life here was simple. There was nothing to existence but walking, working, eating, playing, talking, and loving, in this little valley isolated from the outside world by mountains laced with giant pines. She wished they could live here always . . .

She turned back to the stove abruptly. The one and only source of pain for them here was the knowledge that it might be their last time together. He had told her of his strong sense that this phase of his life would, as the prophecy had foretold, end after Good Friday, and that he wanted nothing more than to return to her then. But she knew, though it was never mentioned between them, that the nature of this "ending" was ambiguous.

The sound of sizzling made her jerk up her head and grab for the boiling-over pot. "Damn!" she said.

"Damn what?" He had come in behind her; she had been so lost in thought she had not heard his chopping stop.

"I just ruined the coffee again."

"Hey, is something wrong, sweetheart? You look sad."

She smiled. "No, nothing's wrong, Joey," she said, snuggling into his arms and reaching her head up to his neck. "Nothing another week with you won't fix."

From Sammy's vantage point backstage at the Opera House, he saw the tears of joy in many faces in the audience, tears called up by John's words as he spoke about Joseph and his hopes for the better world the people had begun to create. Until this trip he'd never been very close to John and felt uneasy in the presence of a man so much more educated than himself. Often he felt jealous of John's closeness with Joey, but in the last eight days he'd developed a strong affection for this gentle, unpretentious, spiritual man. He listened intently as John talked informally with the people, answering their questions and listening to their fears, encouraging their hopes.

After John had led them in a closing prayer and the last of the few who had stayed to talk with him had left, Sammy walked out to meet him. "Those was some beautiful words you said out there tonight," he said, slapping John on the back with awkward affection.

"Thanks, Sammy."

"I'll get the car and bring it around back," Sammy said, turning toward the stage door.

"Fine. I'll say goodbye to the woman who made the arrangements here for us."

John was looking toward the back of the auditorium for his hostess when two men in dark suits and overcoats approached him. "Mr. Stanton?"

John smiled. "Yes?"

The two men flashed their FBI identification. "Mitchell, Special Agent, FBI," said the older man. "This is Agent Parks."

"Yes?" John said in bewilderment. "Is something wrong?"

"Please don't be alarmed. We'd like you to come with us. Our office here has been notified by Washington that there's been some trouble with your wife and daughter."

"Are they OK?" John asked anxiously.

"Yes, sir. But we need you to come with us immediately. We have a car waiting outside. This way, please."

"Why, yes, yes, of course," John said, following them to the stage door.

Outside a light blue Chrysler waited at the base of the stairs.

"Wait a minute. My friend has gone to get our car—" John started.

"We'll see that he's notified," the younger man said, opening the rear passenger door.

"No, just a minute," John said, beginning to feel suspicious.

Just then Sammy pulled up behind. "John, what's going on?" he shouted as he jumped out of his car.

"In the car, please," the senior of the two men ordered.

Sammy came around to the side of the Chrysler. "FBI. Everything's all right," the older man said.

"Oh, yeah?" Sammy said, looking at the car. "Since when did you guys get whitewalls?" He finished the sentence with a haymaker to the left side of the man's head, knocking him back into the car. The younger man turned on Sammy with a flurry of karate chops. Within seconds Sammy lay on the ground in a disquieting stillness.

"Veck, you drive." Turnbow pushed John into the back seat and got in beside him. Veck jumped in front and the Chrysler, tires screaming, raced out of the parking lot.

Within a few minutes the three of them had reached the spot where Jay Nightingale waited with a switch car, and within another minute the black four-wheel-drive Cherokee was carrying a terrified John Stanton toward the Idaho border.

"Was there any trouble?" Nightingale asked from the back seat.

"Naah. One of his buddies tried to jump us but I took care of him," Veck said, grinning proudly. "He was dead before he hit the ground."

Turnbow gingerly touched his swollen jaw. "Jeez, that dude hit like a prizefighter."

"For fifty grand you shoulda let him break it," Nightingale said.

John stared at the 9mm automatic Nightingale pointed in his face. "What do you want with me?" he asked.

Nightingale ignored him. "Just follow the signs to Coeur d'Alene," he said to Veck.

"Jesus, Jay, this snow's coming down so fuckin' fast I can hardly see the signs."

"If you've taken me for ransom," John said, "you've made a mistake. I—"

"Shut up, preacher!" Nightingale ordered, "or I'll split your skull with this." He shook the Browning ominously from side to side. "And you can sleep till we get there."

"You don't really think you can get away—"

He felt the blow of the weapon above his left eye. His sight fogged with pain, then went black with unconsciousness.

Less than two hours after the call from the Spokane police, Emil and Rosa were on board a late flight out of New York. By the time they reached Spokane, Sammy would be out of surgery. His condition was serious. He had a badly broken nose, a concussion, and a couple of cracked ribs, but he would be OK. He was lucky, the doctor said; another quarter inch and the nose cartilage would have been driven into the frontal lobe of his brain.

Rosa was quiet now, lying back in the seat with her eyes closed, her lips moving in silent prayer. Emil held her hand, wishing he could do more to comfort her and knowing there was nothing he could say. At least he had protected her from further worry. He had not told her that Sammy had been with John that night and that John was missing. The police had found their rented car near Sammy, and had told Emil they would continue looking for Stanton. Emil tried to tell himself that John probably got busy working with someone who had come to hear him that night, that the police would find him at the hotel, and that he'd be at the hospital waiting when they arrived. But the knowledge that John was the only one who knew where Joseph was nagged at him. Emil Rothstein never found "coincidence" a likely explanation for anything.

At the hospital Emil and Rosa waded through a crowd of reporters. "No comment. Let Mrs. Sweet through, please. No, no comment," Emil told them.

Sammy was in recovery but had not yet regained consciousness. When Rosa had gone to him, Emil took the waiting police investigator aside; they had not been able to locate John Stanton.

At 3:15 A.M. Rosa came out of the room, looking concerned. "He's awake and he wants to talk to you. He told me not to worry but I know it's something bad."

Emil hurried quickly into the room. He stood close to Sammy's bed, leaning down to the pale, bruised, bandaged, half-drugged ironworker.

"Sammy, it's Emil. I'm so sorry."

Sammy opened his eyes and moved his lips painfully. "They took John. I tried to stop them."

"Who, Sammy? Who took him?"

"They said they was FBI, but I knew they wasn't. Blue . . . Imperial. '76, I think. Dummies had whitewalls. You gotta . . . find him."

"We will, Sammy. We will," Emil said softly as Sammy's eyes closed.

Snow had accumulated heavily on the highway between Couer d'Alene and Sandpoint, making the going slow even for the jeep. It was after midnight when Veck finally turned off and headed for the isolated house three miles from the highway on the edge of Pend Oreille Lake. John was awake but fuzzy-headed when they drove over a pine-studded knoll and came to a stop at the side of a battened-down house. The car's headlights bathed a deer in light as it swam away toward the other side of the cove. "Damn," Turnbow said, "wish I had my rifle."

"Get your mind back on your work," Nightingale said, opening the back door and removing a toolbox. "Help him." He pointed to Stanton, then went to the cabin door, unlocked it, and shouldered it open. Veck and Turnbow half-carried, half-dragged Stanton inside.

"Fuck, it's cold in here," Veck said, watching his breath fog out of his mouth.

"Build a fire, Tony," Nightingale ordered.

"What about the smoke?"

"Nobody around for miles. It's all right. Dave, you keep your eyes on our friend here. Put him in the bedroom. Let him rest for a while. He'll need it. I'm getting something to eat. Then I'll get set up."

A chill ran through Dave Turnbow's body at Nightingale's words; he'd seen Nightingale "set up" once before. John was walked into the bedroom and set on the bed. He lay back, praying silently for whatever strength he would need.

A short time later, Nightingale called from the pine-paneled living room. "Bring him in here."

John watched through glazed eyes as Turnbow took him by the arm and half-jerked him from the bed onto his feet.

"Make it easy on yourself," Turnbow whispered through gritted teeth. "Tell Jay whatever he wants to know."

John wrenched his arm from Turnbow's grasp and shakily walked into the living room. It was warmer now; the flames in the stone fireplace crackled and sputtered into the dry pine logs.

"Sit down," Nightingale said, pointing at the chair opposite him at the dining table. As he sat his eyes fell on the tools spread out on a clean white towel—a pair of pliers, a small can of turpentine, a paintbrush, and a wood-burning tool, already plugged into an extension cord. "I don't know what you want," John said, "but I can't help you."

Nightingale answered with a saccharine edge to his voice. "Yes, you can, John. You don't mind if I call you John, do you? Good," he said, not waiting for an answer. "I'm sure we'll get along just fine, aren't you?"

John pressed his lips together and moved nervously on the chair.

"John, let's talk man to man. I'm a lot older than you are. And while you preached the Good Word to your congregation, I was beheading Gooks in 'Nam. While you were having a family—you've got a little girl, right?"

"You leave her out of this," John said angrily. "You do whatever you want to me, but you leave her alone!"

"Yeah, well, while you were raising your daughter I was learning to interrogate prisoners in Africa. John, I haven't had an easy life. And because of all of it I'm a no-bullshit kind of guy. Right, Veck?" Nightingale's eyes drifted toward the kitchen, where Veck was listening to the radio and cramming a peanut-butter sandwich into his mouth.

"Right, Jay," Veck replied between chews.

"They're my good friends, good old boys. Always been able to count on them when I needed to—" Nightingale started casually.

John cut him off. "What do you want from me? What, damn it!"

"You in some kind of hurry, John? OK. You've got a little piece of information I've got to have. You know where Turner is," he said, pointing his index finger at John, "and you're gonna tell me. I promise you that. Without a doubt, you'll tell me."

John's eyes widened in disbelief. How did this monster know he knew where Joey was? It was impossible.

"You look confused, John. Talk to me."

"I don't know where Joey is. Don't you read the papers? Listen to the news? He didn't tell any of us where he was going."

"Really."

"Yeah, that's right."

Nightingale called into the kitchen. "Hey, you two! Get in here."

When the two men appeared, Nightingale reached into the open toolbox, extracted five heavy leather straps, and tossed them to Veck.

"Strap him up. Is the coffee ready?"

Veck nodded, and Nightingale headed for the kitchen.

"Wait a minute!" John yelled.

"You can yell all you want. There's no one for miles," Veck said, grabbing Stanton from behind. He held the struggling minister while Turnbow buckled straps, tying his arms, legs, and neck to the chair.

When Nightingale came back, he looked at Veck and Turnbow and said nothing. John's eyes fell on the Army pistol belt around his waist. On one side hung the holstered automatic; on the other, a sheathed Special Forces knife. Nightingale shrugged, then removed both and set them on the table.

"You know what kind of gun that is, John? Of course you don't. It's a 9mm Browning High Power, with 160-grain hollow points. They really do the job. Make a little hole going in, and big hole coming out. Now, why don't you tell me where God's Gift is?"

John was silent.

"John, John, John," said the man shaking his head. "You remind me of a story my granddaddy used to tell me. He was a farmer. He bought this mule . . . stubborn old lop-eared thing. Used to say that in order to train that mule he had to get its attention first. So he carried around a length of two-by-four that he'd hit that sucker between the eyes with. You know, after a while that mule did tricks like a puppy dog. I guess I've just got to do something to get your undivided attention."

Nightingale picked up the Browning and fired three thundering shots. One took the top half of Veck's skull off. The other two split Turnbow open from sternum to waist. Both fell dead on the floor.

"Better than a two-by-four," Nightingale said, putting the automatic back on the table and smacking his lips together. "Now, those two boys were friends of mine, but they made a little mistake. The radio says your friend in Spokane isn't so dead after all."

"Thank God," John said, closing his eyes.

"Now like I said, those were friends of mine, and you aren't. For friends I make it quick. But you, I'll work on you till you tell me what I want to hear or till the stink gets too bad. Now where's Turner?" Nightingale stood and unsheathed the knife.

Stanton closed his eyes and prayed loudly. "Father in Heaven, help me! Give me your strength."

Nightingale placed the blade's edge at the crown of John's scalp.

"Sweet Lord, accept me . . ."

His words were cut short when Jay pressed the blade a quarter inch into his scalp and tore the razor edge forward, ripping a four-inch strip of hair and scalp off all the way to his eyebrows. A blood-curdling scream born in John's lower abdomen exploded from his lips and he passed out. His head hung limp at the neck as Nightingale watched the raw scalp turn from a pinkish white to a crimson red.

"I can't let you bleed to death," he said as he dipped the brush in the turpentine and began painting the bloody head. Though unconscious, John recoiled violently, and the chair toppled over backward.

"Jesus," Nightingale muttered as he labored to get the

chair upright. After a few minutes the bleeding stopped. He checked Stanton's pulse; it was still strong. Then he broke an amyl nitrite under Stanton's nose. The fumes made him jerk his head back as far as the leather neck strap would allow. Tears streamed down his blood-dripped cheeks.

"Hope you won't make me do something like that again."

John heard Nightingale's voice but he couldn't open his eyes.

"I won't do anything to your ears or mouth. You've got to be able to hear me and speak, right? Right. But I'll do almost anything else I have to, to find out where Turner is."

"He's my friend. I love him," John said, wincing in pain. "I'm not telling you . . . anything."

"I know he's your friend, and I think it's admirable of you to try to protect him. But it's useless. Believe me. Look, I love my mama, I'd kiss her feet. But if someone was going to do to me what I'll do to you, I'd spill her guts right here on the floor. Trust me, John. I wouldn't lie to you."

John struggled to open his eyes. He struggled to think through the pain. Maybe he could give Nightingale some plausible story. "What will you do if I tell you?" he asked through heavy breaths.

"I'll let you go, of course," Nightingale said.

"I mean to Joey."

"We just want him out of the way for a while."

"No, and you're not going to kill me, because then you'll never know. You'll have to keep me alive."

"I can make you wish you weren't, Johnny boy. I think you'd better tell me now."

Johnny boy . . . Miss Vickerman used to call him that when he lived in the boys' home. Funny, he thought, that I should be called Johnny boy at the beginning and end of my life. His eyes began to close slowly. He fought to keep his head up but it dropped.

Nightingale knocked his face up with the gun butt. "Don't fall asleep on me."

The second wave of pain made it harder to breathe. Bonnie . . . Bonnie . . . he said over and over to himself, you take care of our little girl. He struggled to bring their faces in front of him, to look into her eyes, to hold on.

"Shit!" Nightingale exclaimed as he picked up the wood-burning tool, stuck it into Stanton's left nostril, and pushed the sliding button to on. The beveled tip heated and John began to moan. Soon the moans turned to screams. Nightingale turned his head as the flesh burned from the inside out. He turned back when the screams stopped, looked to make sure Stanton was still breathing. The tool had eaten the flesh away like a vulture. But there was no blood; it had been cauterized by the thousand-plus-degree heat.

Nightingale switched off the instrument and sat across from Stanton once more. "You got guts, kid. I admire that. You're stupid, but you got balls. You aren't gonna be so easy as granddaddy's mule."

On March 23, Emil sat wearily in the office of Pete Copal, Special Agent in Charge of the Seattle office of the FBI, who had flown in to conduct the kidnapping inquiry. Several hours earlier, Emil had given Sammy's statement to the police, then telephoned Bonnie. She had wanted to fly to Spokane immediately, but Emil persuaded her that she should stay in Provincetown on the chance that the kidnappers might contact her with a ransom demand.

"I'm so frightened, Emil, and I feel so helpless here!" she had cried.

"Do you have anyone there with you?"

"Oh—yes. The Sorrels—the friends who took over the retreat here—they're living in a cottage on the property."

"Well, I want you to go get them now. You shouldn't be alone. Then come back to the phone. The police will want to talk with you. Will you do that?"

"Yes, sure I will, Emil," she said through her tears.

"I'll be in touch with you if we hear anything at all."

He then telephoned the others, telling them to do everything possible to assure their own safety and asking them to stay available to talk with the police, or to come to Spokane if they were needed.

His own interview with the police detective had been short. "What can you tell us?" the detective had asked.

"What do you want to know?"

"A motive."

"I can think of two—both involving Joseph Turner. It's well known that Stanton is his best friend. If someone wanted to bring him out of his retreat, they might use John to do it. And there's something else. As far as the world is concerned, no one knows where Joseph Turner is. But the truth is, John Stanton does know."

The detective's eyebrows raised. "That's very interesting, Mr. Rothstein. And who else knows that Stanton has that information?"

"Only I do."

"And I am to understand that you know of no way we can reach Mr. Turner himself?"

"Yes. I don't."

"That's very inconvenient. Is it reasonable to assume that when he hears about his friends, he'll return on his own?"

"I don't know. I don't even know if he's any place where he'll hear."

"You don't know much, do you, Mr. Rothstein?"

"I'm afraid not."

"OK. We'll be back in touch. Meanwhile, we'll be talking with Mr. Stanton's other associates."

"Here's a list you can start with," Emil said, handing it to him. "And I have a question of my own. Sammy said the men who took John said they were FBI. That's impersonating a Federal officer, a Federal offense."

"Very good, Mr. Rothstein. We've already been in touch with them. They're coming into the case. I'm sure they'll be in touch with you."

"Will you tell me what else has been done?"

"We've got an all-points out on the car, and our artists are at the hospital now waiting to talk with Mr. Sweet so they can do composites on the kidnappers. Anything else?"

"No, thank you."

"That will be all, then, for now."

Before leaving the police station he telephoned the hospital again to check on Sammy's condition, and Sammy talked to the officers. Rosa had gone to the Davenport Hotel. He had just started out to go there himself to get some sleep when an officer stopped him. "Mr. Rothstein? The FBI would like to talk with you. Here's the address."

Now Emil sat wearily in the office of Pete Copal, Special Agent in Charge of the Seattle office of the FBI. He watched the agent, who was on the telephone. Copal had just informed him that the President himself had intervened in the investigation, "giving us a special charge to put every available man on the job, seeing as how Stanton is one of Joseph Turner's closest associates." Harper's involvement had made Emil immediately suspicious, but he had decided he had little choice except to trust them.

"They've found the car," Copal said, looking up and putting his hand over the mouthpiece.

"Where?"

"In a parking lot at Gonzaga University. Just a few miles east of where they took Stanton. Notify Idaho and Montana," he said into the phone, "just in case they headed in that direction." He hung up and leaned over the desk toward Emil. "Now, Mr. Rothstein, do I understand correctly from the police that you believe Stanton's abduction is related to Joseph Turner's recent withdrawal from public life?"

"I don't know what else to think."

"And you've stated that Stanton is the only one who knows Turner's whereabouts?"

"Yes," Emil said with exasperation. "But I've already told the police all this."

Copal ignored his objection. "And you also stated that you are the only person who knows that Stanton knows?"

"Correct."

"Mr. Rothstein," Copal said, tapping his pen on his desk pad, "I find that a little hard to believe. Mr. Turner is an important man, and—"

"Try harder."

"What?"

"I said 'try harder.' It's the truth."

Copal sat back in his chair. "In that case, Mr. Rothstein, you must realize that this may place some suspicion on you."

Emil smiled, surprised. "I must be more tired than I thought. That's the one possibility that didn't occur to me."

"Well, you'll understand if we ask you to stick around."

"Of course. I'm not going anywhere. If I change my plans, you'll be the first to know."

FORTY-THREE

JOSEPH HEARD THE WHINE of the plane as it dipped over the jagged High Sierras and swooped down over Grassy Lake. It was an hour after sunrise. The brass bed creaked as he got up, and Maggie awoke to find him standing naked looking up out the window which overlooked the lake.

"What is it, baby? she asked softly.

"Your uncle's plane," he answered, frowning with concern.

"But he's four days early! We've got four more days here!"

Joseph started to dress. The plane touched down as he got his last sock and boot on. He grabbed his jacket and raced out the front door. Jumping down the front steps, he ran through the snow toward the lake.

As the red-and-white Cessna taxied near the edge of the thick ice, Joseph's concern deepened. Dillon's face was tense. As soon as the feathered engine was cut, Joseph dashed to the door. It opened and Dillon stepped down. "What is it, Leon? What brought you back so early?"

"There's some trouble. It's your friend from Massachusetts, John Stanton. He's been kidnapped." Leon handed him a newspaper. "It's all over the news. I just heard last night. I didn't know what else to do. Who to call."

Joseph's eyes raced over the story. "I'm glad you came for me. We'll be ready to leave in ten minutes. Come on." He headed in full stride toward the cabin. "Leon," he said as they reached the steps, "I've got to get to Spokane."

"I can have you in San Francisco in two and a half hours. United's got a flight to Spokane at ten-twenty. I booked you and Maggie."

"Thanks. Maggie!" Joseph yelled. "We've got to get out of here," he said as she came out of the bedroom. "John's been kidnapped."

Her hand came up to her mouth. "Oh, no!"

At 12:30 Nightingale heard the radio report that Joseph had been recognized at the airport in Spokane. "Shit," he said disgustedly.

John did not hear him. He was slumped over in the chair unconscious. He looked like a carved piece of bloody meat.

Nightingale switched off the radio, pulled the Browning 9mm from its holster, walked behind John, and placed the muzzle a few inches from the back of the minister's head. "I don't need you anymore, Johnny boy," he said.

Outside, about a hundred yards away, a big buck whitetail foraged on the bark of a tree. At the sound of the shot the heavily racked deer froze, then leapt to the right and galloped through the snowy forest.

Jay Nightingale took his toolbox, got into the Cherokee, and headed toward the main highway, looking in the rearview mirror to see the flames that were already shooting out the roof. The house would be engulfed in no time. He kicked in the four-wheel drive and accelerated.

His target was now out in the open.

Joseph had phoned the Spokane police before his flight left from San Francisco, and the inspector had alerted Copal to Turner's arrival. Joseph and Maggie were met at the Spokane airport by two FBI agents, who drove them to the Federal Building on Riverside Drive. The agents drove around to the back entrance to the building, avoiding the large crowd of irate citizens pacing back and forth in front of the gray four-story. Many of them had heard John speak two nights before, and as the car passed, Joseph and Maggie saw that several carried placards demanding that the Bureau find John Stanton.

When the two of them were ushered through the squad room and into Pete Copal's glass-enclosed office, a haggard Emil Rothstein, seated just inside the door, jumped to his feet and embraced them. "I don't know whether to be glad you came back or not," he said. "I don't know where you're safe anymore."

"Don't worry about me, Emil. I'll be OK. I had to come

back." He turned to the man across the desk. "I'm Turner. This is Maggie Dillon. Can you fill me in?"

Copal extended his hand. "Pete Copal. I'm afraid there's not much we can tell you. We've had no ransom notes, no calls, nothing. We've got a few leads, but so far we're drawing blanks. We're doing everything we can, Mr. Turner."

"I'm sure you are. Would you mind going over what's happened?"

Copal recounted the events as they understood them from Sammy—as well as Emil's theories of a motive.

"That's how I see it," Joseph agreed sadly. "If I hadn't told John, he'd never be in this mess."

"We don't know that for sure," Maggie said. "And anyway, Leon also knew."

"Leon?" Copal asked.

"My uncle, Leon Dillon. He flew us in and out."

"He wouldn't have told anyone," Joseph said, shaking his head.

"We'll have to check it out anyway."

"Mr. Copal, is there any other information I might be able to give you?" Joseph asked.

"Nothing right now. We've talked to Stanton's family, his friends, and your associates. I'll have a man stop by your hotel this afternoon for a few questions."

"We've got a suite at the Davenport," Emil explained. "Security's set up. Three agents at the room, two agents on the roof, and a detachment of police outside."

"Thanks," Joseph nodded. "We'd like to go to the hospital and see Sammy first. How's he doing?"

"He was pretty badly hurt, but he's doing OK. Right now the pain isn't bothering him as much as guilt. He feels like it's his fault."

"Better not go there, Mr. Turner," Copal said. "Until we're sure what this is about, we'd like you to be especially cautious. Why don't you go to the hotel? If we learn anything at all, we'll call you there."

"I agree," Emil added. "Sammy's OK. He's already on the phone recruiting local ironworkers for your protection. Jim and Peter flew in this morning, and they're with him. So is Rosa. He'll probably be out of the hospital later this afternoon. You can see him then."

"All right," Joseph assented. "Thank you, Mr. Copal," he said as they stepped out of the agent's office.

"How are Bonnie and Amy?" Joseph asked Emil as they walked toward the elevator.

"Not so good. They've got friends with them and the FBI sent a man from Boston."

"I want to be with her," Maggie said.

Joseph shook his head. "No, you could be in danger now too. Wait—Emil, did the story about us come out?"

"It came out—'from an unidentified source'—and fizzled. Most people accepted your statement. The little bit of anger it caused has been doused completely by the news about John and Sammy."

Joseph squeezed Maggie's hand.

"I'm glad you were right," she said, squeezing back. "Now, I'm getting a cab to the airport. I don't think I'm in danger. If we're right about why they took John, they've got what they wanted. You're back. And Bonnie needs me."

"I agree," Emil said. "Jim could go with her. It might not be a bad idea to have him with Bonnie anyway, just in case."

Joseph pulled Maggie close. "You be careful. Give them both my love—and tell Bonnie I'm sorry."

Jay Nightingale stood on the mahogany-banistered balcony surrounding the lobby of the Davenport Hotel. He looked down at the crowded room below him. They wouldn't bring Turner through the lobby. What he needed was a way to get up to the top floor near the Presidential Suite. But security was tight.

An aged blue-uniformed security guard approached him. "Excuse me, sir, but the balcony is closed for the day."

"Certainly," Nightingale replied. "You've got a hell of a job on your hands here."

"Yes, sir," the guard beamed proudly, motioning Nightingale to the stairwell. "We've had presidents and heads of state stay with us at the Davenport, but no one as important as Joseph Turner."

"He's important to all of us," Nightingale nodded, "in our own way."

Joseph and Emil waited through the afternoon in the lavish suite of the Davenport. Joseph had finished his questioning with the FBI. Shortly after they had gone, Sammy arrived from the hospital.

"I'm sorry, Joey!" he cried with anguish when the door opened. "I'm sorry!"

"It's not your fault, Sam. You did everything you could. Come in here," Joseph said, leading him gently to the couch. "I'm sorry you got hurt, that I wasn't here to help you. Will you let me help you now?"

Sammy drew back. "No, Joey, I'm fine, really. I don't need no healing. I'm patching up myself."

"He says he wants to hurt, Joey," Rosa said, "says as long as John might be hurting somewhere, he's got to hurt, too."

"But there's no need, Sammy!" Joseph objected. "John wouldn't want that. This is stupid."

"No," Sweet said with determination. "No. Now you leave me be."

Joseph was not able to persuade him, and after a few more minutes catching up, hearing once more the story of John's abduction and sharing their sadness and tears, Sammy and Rosa went to their own room.

When he and Emil were finally alone, Joseph had time to feel his own pain, anger, and bewilderment. "I know I've made some enemies out there," he said, pacing the room, "but I didn't really believe anyone would go this far. Who would do this, Emil?"

"Plenty of people," Emil answered. "The businesses affected by the boycotts, the labor unions affected by the wildcat strikes, the White House. Harper's chances of reelection have dwindled almost to nothing. A lot of other politicians are in the same boat. Even Rome—"

"Come on, Emil."

"Belazzi is capable of it, Joseph, especially if he's convinced himself that you're evil incarnate, which he probably has."

"But kidnapping? Attempted murder?"

"Even Vasari was capable of risking that when the stakes were high enough. And now, for Belazzi, they're even higher."

"Well, whoever it was," Joseph said, clenching his fist in anger, "I wish they'd gotten to me first." He stopped at the window to look down at the crowd in the snow below. "What do they want from me now?" he asked loudly. "Can't they understand that I'm worried sick, that I have human feelings, that right now I just don't have much to give?"

Emil got up from the couch and moved beside him. "Didn't you see the signs they were carrying when we drove by?" he asked gently.

"I didn't pay any attention."

"I did. I saw one that said, 'Dear Joseph, We Wait With You,' and another that said, 'We Love Him Too.' There's even a 'Get Well, Sammy.' They're not asking for anything, Joseph. They're giving—to John, to Sammy, and to you."

Joseph turned, his eyes filled with tears. "I'm sorry. I guess I just needed someone to be angry at."

Emil looked directly at him. "Try me."

"You?" Joseph asked, puzzled. "Why?"

"Because I was the only one who knew John knew. Copal's already suspicious. Aren't you?"

"Of course not," Joseph said seriously, putting his hand on Emil's shoulder. "It's insane. You're my friend—you're the last person I'd suspect."

"If it were the other way around, Joseph, I wouldn't be so generous. I've grown to be a very suspicious man. I even suspected Sammy for a while. I'm ashamed of that now. I still suspect the others—Louise, Jerry, Peter, Jim. I can't get those leaks in New York out of my mind."

"You're tired, Emil," Joseph said, putting an arm around him. "You're distraught. The fact is, none of them knew. And none of them had a motive. Look at how much of themselves they've given in the last months!"

"You're right," Emil said. "I am tired, and I'm feeling guilty. It was my responsibility to assure everyone's safety. And in my old age I failed, terribly."

"We're all blaming ourselves, Emil—you, me, Sammy. But what's done is done, and it might have happened no matter what we did. You get some rest, now. I'll call you if—"

The telephone rang and Joseph picked it up. "Turner."

"This is Copal, Mr. Turner. We may have something. I just heard from our Resident Agent in Sandpoint, Idaho. They've found three bodies in a burned-out house on Pend Oreille Lake, not far east of here. All three have been shot.

The fire's definitely arson. I'm having the bodies brought here so we can have the teeth checked against Stanton's dental records. Our Boston office has the records on the way."

Joseph felt sick. "How soon will you know?"

"We should have something by six-thirty at the latest. I don't want to worry you needlessly, but I told you I'd keep you informed."

"Thank you."

"I hope they don't check, Mr. Turner."

"You fucked up, Nightingale."

The husky voice on the telephone startled him. If they knew he was at the Davenport, they sure had been watching him closely.

"I got him out where I can get him, didn't I? I mean that wasn't exactly the plan, but it'll do."

"We're taking you off the primary target."

"What!"

"Only for a while. Now that he's back, we don't want to risk it. We may get only one chance. And just in case that prophecy had something to it, we want the odds in our favor."

Nightingale's anger flared. "What am I supposed to do for a week and a half—sit around and pick my nose?"

"Stay cool, Nightingale. We may have another little problem coming up. You get your ass on a plane to New York—you've got a room at the Warwick. We'll be talking with you there."

Copal had not called by 7:00. Peter, Sammy, and Rosa had joined Joseph and Emil in the suite. Peter appeared drained with exhaustion and worry. The deep circles under his eyes told Joseph that, like the others, he hadn't been getting much sleep. They waited anxiously for Copal's call.

It came at 7:45.

"I'm afraid I've got bad news, Mr. Turner. We've got positive identification on one of the bodies. They're doing the autopsy now."

"Oh, God, no . . ." Joseph moaned.

"The coroner says it looks like Mr. Stanton was tortured. I'm sorry."

"So it was me they were after."

"It looks that way."

"I'll—I'll call his wife."

"We called the agent at the house just before we called you."

"I asked you to let me tell her if this happened!" Joseph yelled into the phone.

"We forgot. I'm sorry, Mr. Turner. I—"

Joseph slammed the phone down and bent over, feeling his knees go weak and his body begin to shake.

The others stared at him, rigid with horror and grief.

"John's dead," he choked out. "I've got to call Bonnie."

Sammy stood up, then he broke, sinking to his knees, crying. "Oh, no. Oh, no, if I just hadn't left him."

"I know, Sammy, I know," Joseph said, going to him and putting his arms around him. "Come on now. Come on, I have to talk to Bonnie."

An unfamiliar voice answered the phone in Provincetown. "Let me talk to Bonnie—to Mrs. Stanton."

"Who is it, please?"

"Joseph Turner."

"Oh yes, Mr. Turner, this is Bill Sorrel. Dr. Weisman just sedated her. He says she'll be asleep for a good twelve hours."

"How is she taking it? Does Amy know?"

"She's taking it awfully hard, Mr. Turner. Of course. My wife and Miss Dillon are with Amy now."

"Tell Maggie—tell Miss Dillon I called. That we're coming back. We'll get there as soon as we can. I'm going to get the FBI to release the . . . body . . . to us. I'm bringing John home."

Late that night, Joseph, Emil, Sammy, and three iron-workers stood in the cold winter darkness near the taxiway, their eyes fixed on a bronze casket being carried by a conveyor belt into the belly of their plane. Joseph stood rigid, staring dry-eyed at the casket. He had shed no tears. When the door closed behind it, Peter and Emil guided Joseph silently to the steps and boarded the flight to Boston.

"We've reserved the first-class cabin for you, Mr. Turner," the flight attendant said to him. He looked at her blankly.

"Here," she said gently, pointing to the seat at the window.

He sat down and then, as if finally giving in to the pain, he slumped over and his body heaved with sobs. Peter sat down beside him. "He'll be OK," he said to the stewardess. "He'll be OK, now."

FORTY-FOUR

LOUISE RYAN RODE huddled in her coat in the nearly empty subway car. She had been in the *Times* newsroom when the news came over the wire. She had gone there often in the last two days, and half an hour ago she had heard the teletype bells signaling an important story and then the voice calling her—"Louise . . . you're going to want to see this." She had stood over the machine watching the purple capital letters spelling out the description of the discovery and identification of John's body. They punched it out coldly, brutally. When the machine stopped, she ripped off the copy and, speaking to no one, her face expressionless, her movements trancelike, picked up her coat and left.

At Penn Station she got off the subway and walked quickly in the cold the few blocks to her apartment. She did not respond to the security guard's sympathetic greeting: "Good evening, Miss Ryan. Any word yet about your friend?" She walked past him to the elevator, and he watched the lights flashing as she rode to her floor.

The old guard's puzzlement increased when, four minutes later, he saw her car emerge from the ramp of the basement garage and pull out, tires squealing, as it sped onto the street.

"Is she awake?"

"Yes, but she doesn't want to see you."

Joseph had arrived at the Cape early in the morning and Maggie met him at the door. He held her close to him another moment, then leaned back. Her eyes, like his own, were dulled with grief. "What's she thinking?"

"She's not thinking. She's just in terrible pain. She said— she said that right now she hates you, and she needs some time."

"And Amy?"

"Sleeping."

He sighed. "Will you come for a walk with me?"

"Sure, love. But not too far from the house. We've still got to be careful."

Emil Rothstein was unable to reach Louise Ryan before he left Spokane. He missed her at the *Times* and got no answer at the loft or her apartment. He had continued to try to get through to her after his arrival in Provincetown, and when he failed, he decided that she must be en route. By afternoon she still had not been heard from. Jerry Matthews called from New York to let them know he would not arrive until tomorrow afternoon. Sherry was frightened and he was taking her and the baby to her parents in Harrisburg. He would stay there with her for a while, but would of course arrive in time for the funeral. He asked to speak with Louise and seemed concerned that she was not there. He, too, had been unable to reach her in New York and had concluded she must already be in Provincetown.

Emil said nothing to Jerry of his own concerns, nor did he mention them to Joseph. It was possible Louise would show up before the funeral tomorrow, and he did not want to intrude on Joseph's sorrow with still another problem.

But Emil Rothstein had become increasingly worried. It was possible that whoever had killed John might, for some unimaginable motive, wish to harm others close to Joseph Turner. There was something even more troublesome: Emil had remembered that during his phone conversation with John about Joseph's leaving, Louise passed by his room. He believed that the possibility she overheard something was slight. The possibility she would betray Joseph was even slighter. So he wanted to talk with her himself before giving the information to the FBI, especially since his suspicions about the White House's involvement in the investigation remained strong. If Louise did not contact them by tomorrow night, he would have no alternative but to tell Joseph and to go to the authorities.

The news of the public reaction to John Stanton's murder filled the front pages of the evening papers and occupied much of the evening news broadcasts on March 25. Significant public figures issued statements of shock and condolence. Ordinary people who had come to love Joseph Turner and his friends turned their sorrow to anger against those who had regarded him as an enemy, convinced that the murder of John Stanton was the work of someone determined to harm Turner himself. Angry crowds gathered at the churches of ministers and priests who had preached against him, at the headquarters of business and labor unions that had issued public statements against him, and at 1600 Pennsylvania Avenue.

A wake was held that night in the white chapel at the edge of the Stanton retreat. The Provincetown police had their hands full containing the growing crowds that stood in line to pass before the closed casket. It was nearly 11:00 when the officers closed the gates to the compound and turned the mourners away. Joseph watched from Amy's bedroom window as the chapel door was closed.

He looked across the room at Amy. She was finally asleep. Two hours ago Bonnie had sent Jim to say Amy was asking to see him, and he had been with her since then. His heart ached for this frightened, bewildered little girl. He left her room quietly and went to the living room where his friends sat together. "I need to be with John for a while," he said.

"Do you want me to come with you?" Maggie offered.

"No. Thank you, but I need to be with him alone."

A few minutes later he opened the door to the candle-lit chapel. The casket lay before the altar, crowded by many flowers. Slowly he approached the bronze coffin and reached out to touch it. His hand shook as he moved it over the blanket of red roses covering the casket. "Oh, Johnny. I'm so sorry. Why couldn't it have been any other way? I don't understand. I was given the power to help so many people I don't even know. And it killed the man I love most, killed my . . . brother." He sank to his knees. "Please!" he cried. "Tell me how to bring him back. You let me bring back that little girl. Please! take me, but bring Johnny back!"

"No, Joseph."

The words came softly from behind him. He spun around.

"He's gone," Bonnie whispered. "He died for what he believed in—you. And he's at peace now."

He looked up at her. His eyes were full of sorrow and guilt. She reached her hands out to him. "Please hold me."

He took her hands and stood, bringing her to him. They held each other for a long time in silence, sharing their agony and their love for the man they had lost.

The funeral had been scheduled for 2:00 on March 26. Jerry Matthews arrived shortly after noon, as the others were preparing to leave for the cemetery. His clothes were rumpled, his shoulders sagged, his youthful face was drawn. "Come in—you've had some calls," Bill Sorrel said when Jerry introduced himself at the door. Sorrel walked to the table by the phone, picked up a list and handed it to him. "This one said it's urgent." He pointed to a number. "Called a few times, but then they're all 'urgent.' She didn't leave a name."

"I've got to see Joseph," Jerry said tensely. "It'll have to wait until after the funeral."

"He's in the den."

Jerry found him with Maggie and Bonnie. He was startled by the change in Joseph's appearance. He expected the grief, the somber mood, but not that Joseph would have been so aged by suffering. "Mrs. Stanton," Jerry said when he and Joseph had embraced. "I'm sorry, really sorry. We all loved him."

"Thank you, Jerry."

He didn't know what else to say, and he turned awkwardly back to Joseph. "I got here as soon as I could. The radio said the networks are carrying it live. You need any help with the press? I can go over now if you want."

"I think it's taken care of, Jerry. Why don't you stay and come with us?"

"OK, thanks. I don't feel much like working anyway. Are you going to be speaking?"

Joseph shook his head. "No. This is John's time. I'm not going to help them turn it into some kind of show."

Jim Weisman stuck his head in the door. "It's time. The FBI people are ready with the cars."

Peter delivered the eulogy on the hillside overlooking the Atlantic.

When he finished, and everyone but Bonnie and Amy had filed past the casket, the cameras followed Joseph as he stood and went to John for the last time. Full of pain, he leaned down, pressed his lips to the cold bronze. "I can't say goodbye," he whispered. "I promise I'll take care of Bonnie and Amy. I love you, Johnny."

He felt a small hand slip into his own. He turned, knelt, took Amy's other hand, and looked into her tiny saddened eyes. Her chin quivered as she fought to hold back her tears.

"It's all right to cry, darling, it's good to cry. Let the tears go."

"I don't want to," she said bitterly as they came, "I'm so mad. Mommy said God took Daddy away, but God wouldn't do that. The television said it was some men. Who were they, Uncle Joseph?"

He pulled her to him, laying her head on his shoulder. "I don't know, sweetheart. I can't promise we'll find out, but I promise we'll try. You say goodbye to your Daddy now."

FORTY-FIVE

"JERRY—IT'S YOUR WIFE."

They had returned from the burial five minutes before, and they were still together in Bonnie's living room when Mrs. Sorrel interrupted with the call.

"Excuse me," he said, walking across the room to the phone. "Hello, sweetheart," he said in a soft, mournful voice. "Is everything OK?"

"Keep acting like it's Sherry," Louise Ryan's voice came back. "No, everything is not OK. I need to see you now. It's very important. You can tell the others there's some emergency with the baby."

"Uh, I'm not sure I understand."

"You will."

"But."

"Now, Jerry."

"Well, all right, honey."

"I'm on the Jersey shore, south of Atlantic City, at Townsends Inlet. A beach house—1232 Coast Highway."

"I've got it."

"And Jerry, you should know that there's a letter with my editor in New York. If anything should happen to me here, he'll have some very interesting information."

"I understand. I'll be there as soon as I can." He hung up and turned to the others in the room.

"Something wrong, Jerry?" Joseph asked when he saw that the young man's face had paled.

"I have to leave. The baby's sick. I don't think it's serious, but Sherry's upset and wants me there."

"Of course. Keep in touch. Let us know how he's doing. She knows she can call me here if she needs to?"

"Sure," Jerry said, going to the door. "Thanks."

"Drive carefully," Emil said. "The roads are really iced. Take care of yourself."

"I will."

The telephone in Room 313 of the Warwick Hotel rang twice before Jay Nightingale turned down the television and answered it.

"You enjoy the funeral, Nightingale?" the husky voice said.

"Not particularly. But I didn't have anything better to do."

"You do now. The parasite bug in the house paid off. Go to 1232 Coast Highway, Townsends Inlet, New Jersey. You know where it is?"

"I'll get a map."

"Fine. I'll expect to see it on the news—soon."

Jay Nightingale knelt behind the icy pitched roof of the deserted beach house adjacent to 1232. The lights inside the peeling wood structure revealed Matthews and Ryan through the thin drapes of the living-room window. Nightingale clutched his high-powered rifle tighter and crawled a few feet closer on the roof. He lay down in the snow, placed the weapon across the pitch, and sighted through the infrared scope. The figures were obviously engaged in an argument, both of them gesturing wildly. The woman paced around the small room. Nightingale reached into his coat pocket and extracted a clip of handmade mercury-tipped magnum rounds, each of which would explode like a miniature grenade. He gingerly pushed the magazine into the receiver, then brought the stock into his shoulder and sighted. Damn it all! Where did they go? He swung the scope toward the kitchen window. One silhouette. But which one? He'd have to wait. He focused again on the living room.

The minutes passed slowly. His pants were already soaked and his legs were getting cold. "Come on, you guys, come on. Have a heart. I'm freezing to death." A few minutes later they came back into plain view. He aimed carefully and squeezed off the first round.

Louise was just sitting down when the bullet struck Jerry behind his right ear and his head exploded in a million fragments of blood, bone, and brain. His headless body stood for a second, then collapsed.

Louise screamed, throwing herself to the floor as a second explosion blew off the back of her chair. "Jesus! . . . God!" She crawled to the wall next to the shattered window and eased her hand up to the light switch, clicking it off.

Nightingale slid down the roof and dropped to the porch of the deserted house. Slowly he made his way around to the beach, chambered another round, and quietly made his way up the steps of Louise's cottage. He edged in next to the door and tried the knob. It was free, unlatched. As he threw it open and crouched into a firing position he heard the whine of a starting engine coming from the rear of the house.

"Come on! Come on!" Louise urged the car as she heard something crash into the steel garbage can at the side of the house. Suddenly the engine ignited, and she slammed the shift into drive. The car fishtailed onto the Coast Highway.

Nightingale reached the road just in time to see the gray Firebird pull out of range. He raced for his black LTD.

Louise was traveling at eighty when she went through Sea Isle City. She saw the headlights of her pursuer about a mile behind her. She reached for her brown leather purse in the bucket seat next to hers, opened it, fumbled for the tape recorder, and switched it off. "Just five more miles," she said aloud as she saw the sign for the toll bridge. There are police there. The image of Jerry's mutilated body kept flashing into her vision and she fought to keep it out. You have to get there, she said to herself over and over. You can deal with it later. *You have to get there.*

As the LTD screamed through Whale Beach, Nightingale overaccelerated. The Ford's rear end slid sideways and suddenly he was spinning around out of control down the middle of the highway. When the LTD finally came to a stop, it rested sideways in the oncoming lane. Nightingale frantically tried to restart the dead engine, but it failed to catch in time. He watched helplessly as the Firebird's tail lights disappeared into the winter darkness. He slammed the heel of his fist into the steering wheel.

Emil Rothstein answered the phone in Provincetown. "Louise! Where are you? We just found your telegram saying you were all right. It got buried yesterday in the flood of condolence messages, and—"

"I'm not all right," she said urgently. "Get Joseph— *please.*"

When he was on the line her voice came shakily. She was using the last of her strength to keep clear.

"Jerry's dead."

"Oh, Louise. Dear God, when is all this going to end?"

"I can't talk this way. Your line may be tapped. I've got to see you, and I can't come there. I'm at the *Times.* I'll wait here until you're back. Tell Sammy to get every man he's got to the loft. When you're safe there send a car to pick me up."

"OK," he said looking at his watch. "We'll leave now."

He heard her sigh of relief. "Be careful, Joseph. And don't trust your official protection."

"The FBI?"

"Nobody! Please, Joseph, just come. Hurry."

When the car carrying Louise Ryan neared the back entrance of the loft building, she saw the line of ironworkers already standing shoulder to shoulder on the sidewalk outside the warehouse. "And we've got them up on the roof, too," said one of the men who had ridden with Emil to get her. On the way she told Emil that the dried blood on her dress was Jerry's, and that she had been able to extract promises from the people who had seen her at the *Times* to say —or print—nothing until they heard from her.

Joseph had left Maggie, Rosa, Jim, and Peter in Provincetown with Bonnie and Amy, under the protection of local police and—without explanation to the police or to the FBI —several hurriedly recruited ironworkers from Boston. When Louise and Emil entered the loft, Joseph and Sammy were waiting. "I'm glad you're OK," he said, hugging her. Her body sagged in his arms, then she pulled herself up. "I think you might want to hear what I have to say alone."

He guided her into a back room and closed the door.

"Here," she said taking the tape and recorder out of her purse.

"What is it?"

"A conversation with Jerry, just before he died."

She put the tape in and pushed the playback button.

"*I don't know what you're talking about,*" Jerry's nervous voice said.

"*You're the only one I mentioned it to, Jerry.*"

"*Well, Emil knew, too. So did you, for that matter.*"

"*But Emil told the police he knew.*"

"*To throw them off. Don't you see?*"

"*Bullshit, Jerry. It wasn't Emil.*"

"*Well, what about you, then? I know you're in love with him. You've been in love with him since the beginning. And when you found out that Maggie came back to him, well, that blew your chances for good.*"

"*So I got his best friend killed to make him fall in love with me?*"

"*Well, maybe you didn't know they'd go that far!*" Jerry's voice grew louder. "*Maybe you just wanted Joseph back. Maybe they convinced you they just wanted to know where he was in case there was some kind of emergency!*" The voice was desperate now. "*Maybe they said it was for his own protection! Maybe they said they'd hurt Joseph!*"

"*Is that what happened, Jerry?*" Louise's voice shouted over his. "*You told them for his own protection?*"

"*Yes!*" Jerry broke, his words coming between sobs. "*Yes, but God, Louise, believe me. I didn't ever think they'd do anything like that. I didn't!*"

"*And in New York, Jerry, you let them know where he'd be, you told them about the loft?*"

"*I was scared for him! I was scared for all of us! It was my job, it was——*"

"*It was what?!*" Louise's voice screamed.

Jerry was blubbering now. "*It was my job. Passing along information. At the network, too. You don't think they'd have hired me and kept me on in New York after all these fuckups if there hadn't been some pressure somewhere, do you? Well, there was. I was a plant. They recruited me in Philly, and then helped me get on in New York. And it was just an accident for them that I ended up with Joseph, just chance.*"

"*You little shit.*"

"*I didn't tell them anything for a long time, Lou, I*

*didn't, but they kept putting the screws on, tighter, and
finally when they threatened Sherry and the baby—"*

"Why the hell didn't you tell Joseph?"

"Because I was too scared. And I really didn't think
they'd hurt anybody."

There was a long pause. *"Who, Jerry? Who's 'they'?
Who the fuck do you work—"*

There was an explosion. Louise's scream. Another
shot.

Louise reached over and switched off the recorder. "So it
was Jerry, Joseph," she said, her voice drained of expression. "It was Jerry all along."

He was sitting leaning over, his head in his hands. He
lifted his head. "But who was behind him? Who's responsible
for his death and John's?"

"What he said about being a plant—about 'for his own
protection'—sounds to me like some kind of intelligence operation. It could be CIA or FBI. But we can't be sure. It
could still be the White House, business, the unions—any of
them. Anyway," she said despondently, "whoever's behind
it, I'm responsible for John's death. I told Jerry that John
knew where you were."

He started. "You? How could you know that?"

"I overheard Emil on the phone one day. It didn't seem
like anything then, and later Jerry and I were talking about
your leaving and he said, 'But what if there's some kind of
emergency?' and I said, not really thinking about it, 'Well,
John knows.' It seemed so unimportant I even forgot I'd said
it until just before the news came that John was dead. And
then I was going home to call you and let you know, but
when I reached my apartment it had been ransacked and I
was terrified. I just panicked. I didn't know if I'd been wrong
about Jerry and someone was really after all of us, or if
Jerry had told someone he'd gotten the information from me
and they were afraid I'd figure it out. I didn't know what to
think."

"What did you do?"

"I drove around for a long time, trying to figure out where
I could be safe. I decided to go to a beach house in Jersey
I'd rented once before. I got it in the morning, and when I

finally calmed down. I decided I'd have to confront Jerry first
—get some evidence if there was any—but I couldn't reach
him. I figured he couldn't do anything to hurt you in Provincetown. Everyone knew where you were anyway. But I
didn't want you to worry about me, so I sent the telegram.
I put in calls to him in Provincetown but he never called
back, so when I saw him at the funeral on TV I waited until
I thought you must all be back at the house and then called
him, saying I was his wife—"

"So that wasn't Sherry, then. It was you."

"Yes."

He reached out and put his hand on hers. "You've been
through a lot, Lou."

Tears filled her eyes. "I feel so responsible, so guilty, so
ashamed. I've killed the man you loved most in the world,
Joseph. I've hurt you more than anyone ever has, and I did
—do—love you more than . . ."

"I know, Lou. I've known. I'm sorry. I'm sorry you told
Jerry, but you had no way to know, and what matters now
is that you've gotten us information that will give us a way
to protect ourselves. You risked your life to get it. We know
it's up to us now. We can't trust anyone else. I'm grateful
you found that out."

She looked up at him strangely, disbelieving. "You don't
hate me for all this?"

"No, no," he squeezed her hand. "You're very dear to me,
and nothing has happened to change that. Come on, now.
You need to sleep. I'm going to talk to the others and see
what we need to do."

"The police—the FBI—they'll probably be here soon."

"Fuck them."

FORTY-SIX

On the morning of March 27, the friends at the loft awaited a telephone call from Harrisburg, where Jerry had told them he had taken Sherry and the baby. "We can't afford to wait much longer," Emil said. "If Jerry's body is found, Louise will be under suspicion immediately, and the police will be here in no time. We have to decide what we're going to do with this tape."

Joseph looked troubled. "I can't understand why Sherry hasn't called. Surely she's tried to reach Jerry in Provincetown, and Maggie was going to tell her to call here immediately. I've got to be the one to tell her about Jerry—not the police."

"Are you going to tell her all of it?"

"I don't know what else to do. The FBI needs to know the two murders are connected, and they're sure to tell her even if we don't. What bothers me more is making it public. It's going to make all this even harder for her."

"But it's the truth, Joseph," Emil said, "and making it public is a way to protect ourselves if the FBI's involved. It could also be the only sure way to protect Louise from the killer. If we let it be known that she's not the only one who has the information, he'll know that killing her won't do him any good."

Joseph shook his head. "Jerry's killer would have to figure that if Louise knew anything she'd have already told someone. So she's not in any more danger that way."

"I still can't figure out why someone bothered to tear up my apartment. If they wanted me dead, why not just wait there for me and do it?"

"Whoever did that may not have wanted you dead. They may have wanted you scared," Emil answered. "You aren't

359

the only one who's had problems lately. Several of us have been getting threatening letters, warning us to stop working with Joseph. Jerry had a telephone threat. That's why he took Sherry and the baby away. What happened at your apartment might have been the same kind of thing."

"Makes sense."

"What about the police?" Joseph asked. "Do we need the tape to prove Louise didn't kill Jerry herself?"

"No, the physical evidence will corroborate her story," Emil answered.

Joseph sat quietly, thinking. He hated the idea of hurting Sherry and the baby further by making public Jerry's betrayal. But it was the truth, and if he tried to cover it up, wasn't he doing exactly what he had been telling people was wrong?

It was Sherry who helped him decide. When he finally reached her just after two and told her of Jerry's death, she became hysterical—and her single, agonizing question was *Why?*

"It's so senseless! Just another senseless killing! Joseph, why? Why did they do it? For what?"

He told her, helping her to understand that Jerry had acted out of fear for the safety of all of them, especially for her and her son. "But no one else needs to know," he said. "We can probably get the FBI to keep it quiet."

"You have to release the tape," she said when she was calmer. "You must. It's the truth—it's everything you stand for. And it will make sense of all this horror."

He was deeply concerned for her, afraid that people angry at Jerry's betrayal might harass or even try to harm her or the baby. She assured him that she and the baby would stay with her parents and keep their whereabouts from the press as long as possible. She would notify him or Emil Rothstein should there be any trouble.

"Please, Joseph, release the tape," she said. "We'll be all right."

When he had hung up the phone he turned to the others. "OK," he said. "We make it public. Louise, give us the name of someone at the *Times* we can trust. We'll make a copy and Sammy's men can take it over. They can print a transcript in the evening edition. Emil, we may as well call the police."

At two-thirty-three the Atlantic City police received a call from Emil Rothstein reporting Jerry Matthews's murder and giving them the information he had. Because the case was connected with the Stanton murder, the police informed the FBI, who immediately opened a concurrent investigation.

Within an hour of Emil's call, three agents from the New York City office of the FBI arrived at the loft. They questioned Louise and listened to the tape. At its conclusion, Agent in Charge Jack O'Hallaghan, a tall red-faced Irish Catholic, seemed shaken. "We'll need the tape, of course," he said. "Who else has heard it?"

"Just us, so far," Joseph said.

"Good. It would probably be best if no one else had the information for the time being."

"You've got about an hour."

"What?"

"I've already filed my story," Louise said. "You'll see it in the *Times*."

O'Hallaghan's eyes widened just a little.

"And of course we've made copies of the tape," Emil added. "I hope you understand."

O'Hallaghan nodded uncomfortably. "I do. If I were in your shoes I'd have done the same thing, under the circumstances. Mr. Turner, I want you to know that I see how this must look to you—that someone in the intelligence community might have been involved."

"It's occurred to us," Joseph said dryly.

"I've been with the Bureau for almost twenty years," O'Hallaghan said, "and I can't believe anyone there would do anything of this kind."

"Come on, O'Hallaghan," Louise said. "But don't worry—you haven't been singled out. There are plenty of others on our list."

"Miss Ryan," O'Hallaghan answered, his voice sincere, "if anyone in the Bureau is involved in any way, they'll be caught and dealt with accordingly."

"Can I print that?"

O'Hallaghan gave up and turned back to Joseph. "I'll be

in touch. You should all be careful. I saw outside that you've already taken precautions for your protection. We also have men in the area."

"That's comforting," Louise said.

O'Hallaghan ignored her.

"Before you go," Joseph said, "can you tell me if you've made any progress on John Stanton?"

"No, we haven't. I checked just before I left."

"Nothing at all?" Emil asked.

"I'm afraid not. If any of you come up with anything else, you'll let us know, of course. There's no sense in our duplicating our efforts. Maybe the Matthews case will give us a break. We'll keep you informed."

Louise watched him walk to the door. "We won't hold our breath," she said.

Public response to the news that Jerry Matthews had been an informant for some organization was worse than Joseph had anticipated. People had been angry at John's death, but they took the tape as confirmation of their suspicions, and now anger boiled over into violence. Demonstrations, vandalism, and bombings at the offices of those identified as Joseph's enemies spread across the country. Instead of returning to the work he had left before going to the mountains, Joseph found himself spending the week before Good Friday —the week he and his friends all thought of, but never referred to, as the "last" week— trying to stem the tide of public outrage, taking time out only to attend Jerry's private funeral. By April 2nd, two days before Good Friday, the violence had diminished in response to his pleas.

Then rumors began that the scheduled Easter sunrise service in Central Park had been canceled, rumors emanating from sources Joseph and his friends were not able to discover. When the rumors appeared in the press, the public's anger was rekindled against those thought responsible for the cancellation. Joseph had to issue statement after statement reassuring them that he would be there.

As Easter approached without any suspects in the Stanton and Matthews murders having been found, Joseph's friends grew increasingly frightened for him. Their fear was magnified when Emil learned from an anonymous phone call that the FBI had information on a possible suspect they believed to be in New York.

The Bureau would neither confirm nor deny the information.

By the day before Good Friday, everyone had returned to New York to be with Joseph, even Bonnie and Amy, who came, Bonnie said, to be where John would have been. They gathered in the loft that night. Hesitantly at first, and then more urgently, they asked him to reconsider his public appearance, to delay until whoever was behind the murders of John and Jerry had been discovered and the killer or killers had been apprehended. He refused, determined to keep his promise to the people and not to allow the deaths of his friends to have been in vain. They had died, he said, because his enemies wanted his work to end. There was a chance that after tomorrow it would end anyway. But he would not have it end like this.

On Friday afternoon, at the edge of the crowd watching the stage and television camera towers being erected in Central Park's Sheep Meadow, Jay Nightingale stood reconsidering. It would be an extremely difficult hit to make. The location was much too far from any building, and he sure as hell couldn't get himself stuck up a tree. But if he had to go into the crowd to get close enough, he'd never get out.

He called his contact number and left a message for a return call. He wasn't looking forward to it. The last time they'd talked was after the newspapers published that transcript and he'd had to listen to their crap about the Ryan woman's getting away. He'd told them if they'd sent him down sooner he could've gotten her before Matthews even arrived. As it was, they were just damn lucky Nightgale got him before he could name names.

When the return call came he explained why the park wouldn't work.

"You go into the crowd," the voice said. "We'll have men there to get you out."

"You think I'm stupid enough to trust that?"

"You better be, Nightingale. If you don't go into that crowd and hit Turner on Sunday morning, you won't live until Sunday night. You do, you have half a chance."

Nightingale searched for an alternative. Turner was holed up in his loft. The goons were all around it. Surrounding buildings were also out. He spotted several men obviously using them as vantage points, no doubt for Turner's protection. He could try to split, but he knew he was being watched. And anyway, his pride said that somehow, on Sunday morning, a possibility would occur to him. He settled for the park.

In the loft, activity in preparation for the Sunday appearance had been hectic since early evening. Representatives from the networks requested a meeting to review their plans for media coverage and Joseph agreed, eager to assist them in seeing that his message reach as many people as possible. Emil sat on the meeting, concerned to learn exactly who would be up in those camera towers on Sunday morning. They would make Joseph a clear target, and he wanted Sammy's men informed of the identities of authorized personnel. The NBC representative was particualrly cooperative. He had taken pains to assure them that an investigation was underway of just who had arranged for Jerry Matthews's hiring.

"We're more interested now in making sure your security is tight for Sunday," Emil said.

"Of course, Mr. Rothstein. We'll choose our people carefully and send over photos for you tomorrow."

A contingent from the Mayor's office and the Police Department had also requested a meeting to discuss security problems, but it was 9:30 that night before Joseph, Emil, and Sammy could see them. The FBI had wanted to join the meeting but Joseph had refused, knowing that the police would inform them anyway and wanting as little to do with them as possible.

"Well, the main thing is to keep Joseph safe," Sammy said. "And we got over two thousand men out there to do that."

"Oh, Jesus," the Assistant Police Chief said under his breath. "Mr. Sweet, how can I put this? We really appreciate the help, but those men are untrained. They're not professionals and—"

"At this point we can use all the help we can get," the Mayor's assistant interrupted.

"Yeah!" Sammy said, pleased for the support. "And with a bunch of us up there around the stage, and the rest going through the crowd, nobody's even getting close to Joseph."

They talked for nearly two hours, arranging the details of security at the park. After the officials had gone, Emil called in the others to fill them in. They were engrossed in their plans when the sound of a small crash of tinkling glass came from a back room.

"What's that?" Sammy asked, his head snapping around in the direction of the sound.

"It's probably Amy," Bonnie called from the kitchen.

"I'm already up. I'll check," Maggie called back.

"I better go with you," Joseph said. He was up and past her down the hallway before any of the others had a chance to stop him. "It's OK," they heard him call.

He had come into the bathroom to find Amy standing at the sink over a broken glass. "I was getting a drink of water," she said out of teary eyes, "and it slipped, and—"

Her finger was bleeding. Joseph knelt beside her and reached for her hand reflexively, automatically, accustomed now to using his power of healing. But when he had closed his hands over hers and opened them again, the cut was still there. He tried again. There was no difference.

"Joseph." Maggie was standing beside him. "Look," she said, holding out her arm and pointing to her watch as he turned to her. "It's twelve-twenty."

He stood up slowly. ". . . after Good Friday," he said softly, his eyes wide. "Could that be all the prophecy meant?"

Maggie went to Amy and held her finger under the running water. "She's OK. Just a little cut. Jim can look at it."

"Will you kiss it, Uncle Joseph? That'll make it all better."

"Sure, sweetheart," he said, bending down to kiss her extended hand.

"What's up?" Bonnie had come into the hall behind them.

"Amy just cut her finger a little."

"But you two look so strange." Bonnie looked back and forth at them questioningly.

"It didn't work," Joseph said.

"What didn't? Oh—" Bonnie said as it dawned on her. "But then—"

"It's OK. My heart's still beating. Come on, you two," he said, guiding them out. "Get Amy back to bed and I'll tell the others. At least now we know what the prophecy meant. I'll send Jim in. Looks like he's going to have to go back into business around here."

FORTY-SEVEN

HIS FRIENDS TOOK the news hard. Though they had always been concerned for him, some of them not even fully trusting the idea that he could not be mortally harmed, all knew now that he was once again fully vulnerable. They made a last attempt to convince him to cancel his appearance, but failed. As the hours of Saturday passed, the mood in the loft grew increasingly solemn.

They sat quietly around the table together at dinner that night.

"Hey, everybody," Joseph finally said. "Will you all stop acting like doomsday's arrived? This is driving me nuts! Isn't anybody happy that I'm still around? You're all behaving as if this is the Last Supper."

"Well, look at us," Peter answered. "You've got James, Peter—"

'But Louise and Emil?" Louise objected wryly.

"I don't think I want to talk about this," Maggie said.

"The Last Supper should have been Thursday, anyway," Rosa added. "What an ignorant group of people."

"See, what did I tell you?" Joseph said.

They were still frightened, but the teasing had broken the dark mood, and they spent the last hours of the evening talking warmly together of all they had shared in the last months and of how much they missed the two men who were no longer with them.

They went to bed early to get plenty of sleep for the next day, but Joseph and Maggie lay awake holding each other far into the night. He had spoken to no one of what he intended to say tomorrow. He wanted to tell her first, and he was finding it more and more difficult as the minutes passed.

"Sweetheart," he said finally, "I've got to tell you that John's and Jerry's deaths have changed things for me."

"I know," she said gently. "For me, too."

"But we haven't really talked about it since Spokane. I told you when we were at the cabin that I really felt Easter would be the last of it. I thought somehow it would all end after that, and we could be together, finally."

She held him tighter. "I *know*," she said more intensely. "And now you don't want it to be over."

'I just don't see how it can be. I can't heal people anymore, but there's so much more to do, always. Whoever killed John and Jerry would like nothing better than for me to quit, and my work's not close to being finished. And it's my life, now."

"You aren't paying attention to what I'm trying to tell you," she said. "I understand, Joey."

"I want you to understand all of it—how desperately I want you, need you with me in my life, in whatever I do—"

"I'll be here."

"—because you're the one person on this earth who— what did you say?" He pulled back to look at her.

"I said, I'll be here."

"You will?"

"It's changed for me, too. I'd never been with these people before, never seen you with them, with the people out there. And it's lovely to see, Joseph. They've been lovely to me, too, most of them, even when they knew. And the days in Provincetown with Peter and Jim—we talked a lot about what life was like for you. I really think I can do it now. I know I can."

He kissed her, hard, long, pulling her warm body next to his and loving her through the night.

Central Park was filled with people waiting in the predawn darkness, most of them seated and huddled together against the early morning chill.

"Come join us!" said a cheerful young black man sitting with three friends around an open fire about a hundred yards from the stage.

The man in brown pants and a heavy tan parka stepped through the crowd.

"Thanks," Jay Nightingale said as the young man handed him a plastic cushion and a cup of coffee.

"This is gonna be a wonderful day. Weatherman said we're going to get a real sunrise."

"I'm sure it is," Nightingale said, sipping the coffee. "Looking forward to it."

"You guys keep your eyes on those monitors," O'Hallaghan said to the four agents with him as he pointed to the news trucks. "We've got a hundred and twenty men out there, but they can't check a million faces. And if you spot him, you contact me. No one else. Now get going."

As darkness lightened into dawn, the din of the crowd grew louder with their growing excitement. Then from the west side it started—"Jo-seph—Jo-seph" the chant came, and as the other voices joined, it grew to a roar, reverberating through the budding tree branches and off the walls of the buildings surrounding the park. "Jo-seph!—Jo-seph!—Joseph!"

The chant broke into thunderous applause when the police motorcycles, red and blue lights flashing, appeared, leading the motorcade to the front of the stage. The people were on their feet, craning their heads to see the man emerging from the center car. Jay Nightingale walked through the crowd, moving closer to the front.

The ironworkers surrounding the stage were dressed in suits and hard hats. Joseph stopped before he mounted the steps. "Hi, Frankie," he said, smiling.

"We've got you covered, Joey," Frankie Corollo said, shaking Joseph's hand enthusiastically and then turning to watch him walk up onto the platform.

Joseph walked directly to the microphones and stood looking out at the sea of faces that stared back. A few near the front were faces he knew, including a little girl from Colorado sitting on her father's shoulders.

As the gold light of the sun began to color the sky to the east, the crowd quieted, the television cameras came on, and the satellite hookup beamed the picture around the world.

Joseph turned to the friends who now stood around him on

the stage. "Thank you for being with me," he said, his voice filled with the warmth of his happiness. "Thank you for being my friends."

He turned back to the crowd. "And thank you for being with me on this morning. I feel blessed, today more than ever, with the joy of sharing so much with so many of you. And I feel that joy even through the sadness of our loss, our great loss, of two men.

"One of them, Jerry Mattthews, was a friend who had long lived in tremendous fear, and who died before he could know that his torment was something we could understand. The other was a man I loved beyond any words I can say to you. He died in agony out of loyalty to his love for us, and for our work.

"Many of you are angry for these deaths. I share your anger. I share your hatred of those responsible. But anger and hatred will not bring them back, and revenge will not lessen the pain their families and friends feel. I ask you to share our sorrow and to build from our loss, to stop the cycle of hatred and fear and violence, to stop it here, today, not to give up your demands for justice and for truth, but to make them in peace, to teach others by your own example that fear and hatred can be conquered by gentleness, by honesty, by caring, and by love for the human life we share . . ."

"See anything yet?" The agent in the CBS truck had his eyes glued to the two monitors sweeping the crowd.

"Nope," his partner said. "Just a lot of serious faces."

"Don't blink."

"Nope."

". . . and so today I feel especially close to all of you, because I know whatever power I now have is no different than your own—no greater and no less.

"Many of you are disappointed that I did not reach you, and I am sorry for the pain that remains. I could not reach everyone, but I have learned that there is much we can do, many miracles we can perform together, without any supernatural power. You have taught me that I have much to give beyond that, and I will keep giving what is left to me . . ."

"There! Tell your man on two to hold the camera!" O'Hallaghan whispered sharply.

"Hold on that, two!" the ABC director yelled into the headset as the agent snapped on his walkie-talkie, his eyes fixed on the screen.

"Sector Three-A, our suspect is wearing brown slacks and a tan ski parka." There was no response to O'Hallaghan's traffic, and he repeated it. Again nothing.

"Shit!" he shouted as he burst out of the remote truck in a run, fighting the thought that Louise Ryan had been right.

Nightingale had moved close enough to the stage now. His mouth was dry, his muscles tense. At fifteen yards Joseph Turner was a dead man. The ultimate hit, and best of all, he was going to get out to relish it. He had noted that the crowd around him contained no locals or Feds, no pros at all, just a bunch of ironworkers looking the wrong way, captivated by his target. The husky-voiced man had done his part. The fix was in.

". . . my life will be different now in another way. I want, I need to have a private life, too, with the woman I love . . ."

O'Hallaghan was thirty yards away, fighting through the crowd. His eyes were fixed on the back of the tan parka.

". . . And that is possible now because this work is no longer only mine, because you've reached out to help each other, have joined together to carry it on." Joseph stopped, seeing a young man in the second row take the hands of the people on either side of him. "That's beautiful," Joseph said. "Everyone, reach out to the person next to you. Hold hands . . ."

Nightingale reached inside his parka and curled his fingers comfortably around the butt of his automatic. From that moment his reflexes took over and he no longer needed to think. The gun was coming out, and then—suddenly—it wasn't.

For a second Nightingale couldn't figure it out. He froze. Something was stopping his hand. Someone had taken his arm. He snapped his head to the side in the same moment that the woman on his right turned to smile at him and then he felt his left hand grasped too and he looked around to see people on every side of him holding hands.

He next felt the barrel of a gun pressing into his right rack of ribs. "That's just fine," O'Hallaghan said, "you just keep right on holding hands. We wouldn't want to disturb these nice people around here, now, would we?"

". . . so I will be with you, even now. I am full of joy that we have come so far, and that we will continue together what we have begun."

When Joseph had finished he looked into the calm, peaceful, open faces before him, feeling their love and letting them see his own. Then someone began to hum softly, a peaceful, joyful song, and other voices joined in. He nodded in acknowledgment and turned to his friends, whose eyes held happy tears. They embraced him one by one. "I'm so grateful to be your friend," Emil said.

"Thanks, Joey," Bonnie whispered.

"Come here, Sam," Joseph said, putting an arm around him. "You see, it went OK. Thanks for everything."

When he had hugged the others he took Maggie's hand and the two walked across the stage and down the steps to the waiting cars.

"All set, Mr. Turner," the Assistant Police Chief said.

Maggie started into the center car, then felt Joseph's hand holding her back. She turned to look at him. He was looking at her strangely, as if he saw her from very far away.

"Wait," he said.

"Is something wrong, Joey?"

"Not wrong. Just, strange. Maggie, I have to go back alone."

She felt his eyes holding hers. A great serenity flooded her body. She reached up to kiss him. "All right. Whatever it is. It's all right."

"I love you, Maggie."

"I know."

Joseph walked from her to the lead car. "I want to drive back by myself."

The driver looked confusedly toward his superior. The Assistant Police Chief shrugged. "OK, I guess."

Joseph got in behind the wheel. The motorcycle escorts fired up their motors, hit their red lights and sirens, and pulled away. He followed them out of the park and onto the streets of his city.

His city. His world. His life. He felt so free, so much freer than he had felt ever before. So sure now of what his life meant to him. So full of all the possibilities before him. Before him and Maggie.

The motorcade picked up speed through the empty streets, and Joseph pushed down the accelerator, enjoying the feeling of movement, of being once more fully in control.

In the second car several hundred feet back in the motorcade, Sammy sat in the front seat watching the motorcycle escort turn east on Fiftieth, followed by Joseph's car. As the construction site across from St. Patrick's Cathedral came into view, Sammy smiled a little in wonder. "That's where it all started, you know," he said to Emil and Jim in the back seat. "Right there, that's where he landed that morning when he fell. Hey!"

The brake lights on the car in front of them lit up suddenly and the car lurched to a stop. Sammy's driver hit his brakes hard to keep from ramming into the rear.

"What's going on?" Sammy shouted as he caught himself from flying into the dashboard. He heard the screech of the tires of the car behind him. Ahead, the motorcycle escort, which had continued down the street, suddenly turned and circled back.

In a moment he had his door open. He ran full out toward Joseph's car, followed by Maggie, Emil, and the others from the car behind.

At Joseph's car Sammy reached a hand to pull the door open, then froze. It was locked. All the doors were locked. The others gathered around him and stared through the windows of the car.

The car was empty.

Maggie's eyes were full of tears. "He knew . . . somehow he knew. . . . Look," she said, pointing inside.

On the driver's seat was a small piece of crumpled metal. Sammy bent down to get a closer look through the glass.

"It's the watch," Louise said in a shocked whisper. "The one he broke in the fall." She looked at her own watch and began to sob. "Oh my God—the time. Do you see?"

Sammy backed slowly away from the car.

The crumpled watch read the same as his own: 9:23.

IN HOLLYWOOD, WHERE DREAMS DIE QUICKLY, ONE LOVE LASTS FOREVER...

"I love you," she said. "I've loved you since the sun first rose. . . . My love has no shame, no pride. It is only what it is, always has been and always will be."

The words are spoken by Brooke Ashley, a beautiful forties film star, in the last movie she ever made. She died in a tragic fire in 1947.

A young screenwriter in a theater in Los Angeles today hears those words, sees her face, and is moved to tears. Later he discovers that he wrote those words, long ago; that he has been born again—as she has.

What will she look like? Who could she be? He begins to look for her in every woman he sees . . .

Always

A Romantic Thriller
by
TREVOR MELDAL-JOHNSEN

AVON

41897
$2.50